THIRST TRAPP
Farms

Also by Christina Hill

ii

Love at First Flight
Love has a Name (#1)
To Love Again (#2)
Love Finds a Way (#3

THIRST TRAPP Farms

CHRISTINA HILL

ISBN: 979-8-9857199-9-4

Edited by: imPRESS Millennial Books

Cover Design: Christina Hill

Illustrations by: Dylan Ehman

Cover Photo: Canva

To the ones who do the thing scared.

"The secret to doing anything is believing that you can do it. Anything that you believe you can do strong enough, you can do. Anything. As long as you believe."-Bob Ross

One

Wyatt

"Anytime you learn, you gain."-Bob Ross

Wyatt! Where are ya, boy? Are you going to make me come in there and find ya?"

"I'll be right out, Granny! Don't come in here, it's slippery," I say, looking down at the piles of crap lining the stall like a second skin. Leaning the shovel against the wall, I exit as she reaches the end of the row in the horse barn. "Granny."

She places her hands on her frail hips, the ones she likes to remind us are still originals. "Did you forget about me?"

I stare blankly, pulling off my gloves. "Uh, no?"

"You were gonna take me to the feed store, so I could pick up more grain for the horses," she explains. "We need a few extra salt licks for the cows, too."

She's pinning me with that hard stare of hers that's as hot as a branding iron on flesh.

"Granny, I told you over breakfast I'd go pick everything up."

She crosses her arms and shakes her head. "I don't remember agreeing to that."

She's right; she didn't agree. But she also didn't outright say *no*, either, which I considered an improvement from the ready-made answer she likes to give me: *I got it.*

Granny has spent most of her life here at Trapp Farms in Big Timber, Montana selling cuts of meat and alfalfa. Yet, despite having our farmhand and token pretty boy, Ronny, she can't keep up with all the work this place requires. Between the cattle, horses, chickens, three barns, one house, four cabins, and one-hundred and fifty acres, it's too much even for someone with two good hips.

"You don't need to do it all on your own now that I'm here." I toss my gloves on a stack of hay and bracket my hips with my hands, giving off vibes that I can do this work, even if I only half believe it. "I just need to finish cleaning out this stall, and then I'll go."

She huffs. "I'm eighty-one-years young and have been doing this work all my life."

"And you've done a fine job, Granny." There's no way I'll tell her otherwise. "Since I'm sticking around at least for the rest of the summer, you might as well use me and these…" I kiss my biceps, and she rolls her eyes as I continue. "You've come with me every other time to pick up feed. Why don't I try it this time to see if I remember what to do?"

She squints up at me. "I guess I could call Esther to come have some pie with me. Wouldn't want it to go to waste."

I nod in agreement, though there is zero percent chance her home-made pie would ever go to waste. "I'm sure Esther would love that."

Esther is Ronny's mom and our closest neighbor. She's my mom's age but has been a good friend to Granny, especially after my Gramps died of cancer a year ago. She brought meals and pie—it's a love language—helped around the house, and organized the folks around town to take shifts working the farm to keep everything running smoothly. I owe her more than pie, but that's the only currency I've got right now and Granny's paying.

"Alright. I'll call her. But don't forget to tell Bob I said hello, or he'll think I up and died. Can't have him thinking I won't show up for Bunko and whoop his ass."

I smile down at her. "I'll stop by the house before I leave to say bye."

She nods and slowly turns to retrace her steps on the floor of dirt and hay then swivels even slower back to face me. "You might shave before you go. That thing is looking mighty shaggy." She rubs her cheeks and chin to reference my beard she's never been a fan of. "At least trim it so we can see your mouth."

Shaking my head, a laugh escapes as I rub the thick hair on my chin. "I like my beard."

"Your wife doesn't."

"Good thing I don't have a wife," I say and stick my tongue out at her.

She does the same thing then says, "It might just be the reason you don't."

This beard has been the only thing keeping me warm at night since dumping my ex. I started growing it right after I left San Francisco and a job that sucked my soul dry for half a decade. It's my emotional support beard now, and no matter what happens, the beard stays.

I pick up my gloves and slip them back on so I can finish the job, like a live-action pooper-scooper. It's the least glamorous part of the job. Actually, there are plenty of those.

"You know," Granny starts. Pausing outside the stall, I face her. That gleam in her eyes is saying enough without her having to open her mouth. "Vicky's granddaughter is coming to visit soon. Maybe you'd want—"

"No more granddaughters," I say then trudge back into the stall. I quit them cold turkey the second I stepped onto this farm two months ago and realized Granny had a list of numbers for me in her phone book.

She isn't ready to give up that easily. "Wyatt, you're gonna have to move on sometime. Might as well be now."

"Or never," I murmur. It's not like I'm anti-relationship, but more like anti-letting my Granny set me up.

"At least get her number."

I grab the shovel a little harder. "And what? Use it to wipe my—"

"Don't you finish that sentence, boy," she says with a raised finger.

That finger tells me how serious she is.

I go back to mucking. Push, lift, sling. Push, lift, sling. Farm work is repetitive, and I think that's what I like most about it. As a teenage boy during the summer months, I was forced to do the grunt work around the farm. Waking up early, flinging hay, gathering eggs, and milking the cows were torture to the younger me. The only thing I had to show for it was a mean farmer's tan and the skill of identifying different kinds of animal shit. Neither helped with the ladies.

"I'll get her number for ya," Granny says, waving a hand as she walks out, indicating the conversation is over.

I yell after her. "I'm not calling her."

"You'll want to shave that beard before your date," she calls back.

I grunt loudly, so she knows how I really feel.

That woman is a firecracker. I don't know how my dad survived his childhood. I thought relearning how to muck stalls, milk cows, and fix fences was going to be the hardest part about moving back to Trapp Farms as a thirty-year-old man. Turns out, it's getting told off by my Granny and trying to convince her I don't need a woman. Tell that to the speed dating night at the local bar she signed me up for without me knowing. I thought I was picking up dinner for us, not picking up Winnie, a girl who likes moonlit dinners and long walks on the beach—good luck with that in Montana. It's worth mentioning her brother terrifies me. He looked like a full grown man with a beard and a shotgun when we were in high school together. He's only gotten taller, and that didn't seem to bother anyone but me.

Women aside, I'm terrified of disappointing Granny, because it's not just her that I'd be letting down if my plans for the farm don't work. It's the legacy my Gramps left. It's a lot of pressure. More than lighting a match and watching my own life crumble into ruin. For all her grumbling, she needs the help, even if it's hard for her to admit.

I use the back of my forearm to wipe the sweat from my brow. There's a lot of that happening this early in June: sweat. Morning, noon, and night. A scorching hot summer in Montana is the one thing that hasn't changed since I was young. It'll only get warmer, which reminds me, I need to get a few fans for the cabins. The first guests are coming in a week, and even though we don't have the budget to get AC units, I want everything to run as smoothly as Granny's well-oiled hips.

With extra cabins sitting vacant, I figured we might as well fill them with city folk ready to do some nature bathing and marvel over birds, maybe a barn cat or two. It's all part of the rebrand I've been working on, trying to draw in folks who aren't used to this lifestyle. After my life imploded, I needed a project and Trapp Farms was it. Or, should I say, *Thirst* Trapp Farms. I haven't told Granny about all the other ideas I've got typed up in my business plan. It was hard enough for her to agree to having strangers stay on her property, so I'll have to ease her into the cow-hugging and name change later. If she wasn't so desperate to keep the farm out of the bank's hands, she wouldn't have even considered my proposal.

Trapp Farms has been the same since I was a kid, and it needs to move forward with the times. Even the rickety wooden sign swinging from the archway as you enter the farm is looking drab. Gramps probably should have used something stronger than zip ties to secure it—his solution to every problem. He used them for broken doors, bird feeders, tractor fixes, and even holding up his pants that were always too big. I still smile every time I find one. The new sign with the new name is sitting in the back of the truck, and I've just been waiting for the right time to hang it. Preferably when I believe Granny won't run me off with a shotgun, or worse, threaten me with more granddaughters.

Leaning the shovel against the stall, I use the pitchfork to toss new hay over the ground to prevent slipping. Then, I fill the water trough and feed bin, getting it ready for Axel. He's my best friend who happens to have four legs and makes me pick up his shit. I don't mind, though. He's gotten me through a lot and been my most faithful friend besides Ronny.

I fetch Axel from the horse pasture, leading him by the bridle until we reach the clean stall. "Time for a rest, bud."

He whinnies his thanks, ignoring me for his favorite snack and the welcome shade.

"Yeah, yeah. You're welcome," I say, then finish putting away my tools and gloves, and close up the barn to head for the house.

Pulling out my phone from my back pocket, I navigate to my email and wince right before the messages load. I never know what I'll find in there. Another notice? Another offer to buy the farm? Another email from my ex-girlfriend after I blocked her number? It's usually some mix of all three. But today, it's good news. I get an official acceptance for the massage therapist position I listed on social media a few weeks back. That's another thing I'll have to tell Granny about soon.

Avery Ellis her email signature reads. She'll be the first person that'll come live and work on the farm for the summer in order to start a spa complete with massages, facials, and whatever else happens involving cucumbers and mud. I may not know, but Avery, licensed massage therapist, does.

I advertised massages in the listing on Experiences R Us, a website dedicated to giving people immersive experiences in a different way of life, because I wanted people to come. Nothing says vacation like a spa. I'd started researching online how Ronny or I could get a certification in massage if we couldn't find anyone. Thank God that's off the table. Rubbing oil between my palms and laying them flat on a stranger's back is just about the most unappealing thing I've thought up. If I had to choose between feeling up a stranger or mucking Axel's stall, I would shovel crap every time.

I pause and face the wrap-around porch of my grandparent's 1920s farmhouse. It's outdated in more ways than one, but Granny won't let me renovate the *charm* out of it. One of the hinges on the screen door is currently being held to the frame by a zip tie, and the windows like to rattle every time we have a thunderstorm. But it's home.

Clicking on the number Avery has listed by her name, I listen as it rings. We've stuck to communicating via email, but now that she's accepted the job, I think it warrants a call.

"Hello?" a soft voice says on the other end.

"Hi, Avery? It's Wyatt Trapp."

She clears her throat. "Mr. Trapp, hi."

I try not to gag when she calls me this. I'm not my dad. "You can call me Wyatt, remember?"

"Okay...Wyatt."

I rub the back of my neck, feeling the dirt and grit beneath the collar of my t-shirt. "I just saw your email accepting my offer."

"Yup. That was me and not at all my friend who sent that email."

"Right," I say, lengthening the word.

I turn around and face the long dirt road leading into the farm where the cabins sit nestled beneath the shaded arbor of trees. I'm more confident at this moment than I've been all month. Maybe things are looking up.

"I'll send you the last few documents to sign, and then you'll officially be a Thirst Trapp Farms employee."

"*Thirst* Trapp Farms?" she questions.

I rest a hand on my hip. "Uh, yeah. We're in the middle of a rebrand, trying to draw in a younger demographic." There's a pause on her end of the line, and I check to see that we're still connected. We are. "So, can you be here in a few weeks, toward the end of June? I'd like to show you around the farm and get you acquainted with the space you'll be working in before the guests arrive."

"I...uh, wow. Really? Are you sure? I don't really have a lot of experience. I mean, I've worked in a spa for the past three years, so I've seen how things are done." She stops talking, and I'm about to interject when she presses on with the conviction of a Sunday preacher. "Not that I'm saying it would be easy, because I've seen how things are run. I'm a hard worker, though, and I could figure it out. But maybe I'm not what you're looking for right now?"

Picking up a stick on the ground, I start swiping at the dirt caked on the bottom of my boots. I'm not sure if she's agreeing to take the job or trying to convince me not to give it to her.

"Look, Avery. Your resumé seems solid." Ronny read it and told me so. "You're exactly what we're looking for." At this point, all we need is a human being with a beating heart and magic hands.

"Okay. Um, well, I'll need to tie things off here, but I could be there in a few weeks."

I sigh in relief. "Great. I'm looking forward to meeting you. I'll send you those docs to sign soon. If you have questions, let me know. Otherwise, I'll see you in a few weeks."

She releases a shaky exhale. "Alright, I'll see you then."

Two

Avery

"Don't forget to tell these special people in your life just how special they are to you."-Bob Ross

Three Weeks Later

Trapp Farms in Big Timber, Montana is a straight-up postcard. The tree-lined gravel drive, acres of land leading in every direction to foothills where the rocky terrain begins to climb upward over mountaintops. Horses and cattle dot the brown and green fields. The barns look like they've posed for plenty of photos over the years, with the backdrop of nature sticking up like bunny ears behind them.

Beatrice, my periwinkle blue sedan that requires words of affirmation to get her to rev her engine, is tired after the almost five-hundred-mile journey from Bismarck, North Dakota. Lord knows I've already put her through enough during the winters there, and I had to bribe her with an oil change just to make it here. Then, she spent the whole drive threatening me that she'd take a permanent break in car heaven while I bit my nails with worry, like I had no need for them anymore.

Goodbye nails. It was nice knowing you.

I still wonder if I'm making a huge mistake as her tires crunch along the narrow drive, and I pull in front of an old farmhouse that has a slight lean to it. The wind whips through my open window as well as the many outbuildings, trees, and crops, pushing the porch swing back and forth. The smell of manure hangs heavy in the air, and though I've never chewed on grass, the taste of it is already in my mouth with every breath I take. The entire scene pictured through Beatrice's dusty windshield looks as if it were plucked from a wild west movie. In every direction are steep cliffs and deeper valleys. A big sky with clouds shaped like fish, a banana, and Leonardo DiCaprio. Maybe I'm only seeing Leo since I listened to the Titanic soundtrack almost the entire eight-hour drive here. It really puts me in my feels.

Tilly, my best friend and roommate, told me about this gig when a friend of hers saw it on social media. Wyatt of Trapp Farms is hosting a few short-term stays throughout the summer and wants to offer spa services to guests. Massages, facials, maybe an eyebrow wax here or there. I happen to have a license stating I know how to do one of those things: massages. But, I'm sure I can figure the other ones out. I have to. Eventually, if this two-month trial proves successful, I can hire other people who specialize in those areas.

Now that I'm here, I should call Tilly, so she can talk me off the ledge for the seventeenth time since leaving. Lowering the seat all the way back so I won't be seen, I click her contact and wait to hear her familiar voice that always puts me at ease.

"What's up, bitch?" she answers breathlessly.

That's not helping.

"Dear Diary, you'll be glad to know I decided to drive to Alaska instead. I'll be sure to take a picture with a narwhal and scrapbook my whole adventure," I say.

The sound of a motor turns off. "First off, narwhals are made-up mythical creatures from storybooks. They aren't real..." They definitely are, but I'll let this one slide. "Second, you're already there, so nice try."

I cross my arm over my chest and stare at the odd-looking stain on the ceiling of my car. It could be Leo if I turn my head...never mind. "How do you know I'm here?"

The bangles she likes to wear on both arms clink and clank as she moves around. "I set up location tracking on your phone."

Too many follow-up questions race through my mind, making me dizzy. I palm my forehead and take a deep breath with the next gust of wind that whips through my car window. I don't do things like move to a farm for a short-term gig. I had a great, stable job back home. Responsibilities and people that depended on me, like Matilda, who needed someone to pick up her fungal cream from the pharmacy—I was that someone! Or, my neighbor, Cynthia, who has a rambunctious dog that I'd take on walks a few times a week, even though he liked to hump my leg. I still can't fathom the hole I'm leaving at bingo every other week at the senior center.

"Am I making a mistake?" I ask.

The soft but steady clank of the refrigerator fills Tilly's side of the line—we should really get that noise checked out. "It's the curse, isn't it?" she questions. "Avery, you can't let a fake curse keep you from living your life and chasing your dreams."

I starfish my hand between the back of my head and the headrest. "Why not?"

She doesn't even have to reply for me to know how ridiculous I sound. The problem is, I'm stuck.

It started when our family lost my younger brother, Justice, right after I went to massage school. My dream was put on hold since grief threw eggs at our lives and then added toilet paper to the mess. After he died, I finally finished the program locally, then got a job in my hometown. But I hadn't gone far, preferring to live within a twenty-minute drive of my parents' home in case they decided they wanted a relationship with their daughter again.

My brother's death was the birth of what I call Avery's Curse.

A year later, the family cat died when I saved enough money to move out. Then, after graduating from massage school, my grandpa decided he was tired of grandma's cooking and threw up a peace sign on his way out. And when Tilly, who is also my hairdresser, cut my hair, I knew I was playing with fire, or at least signing a death certificate. She found our goldfish floating on the top of his aquarium later that day.

Goldfish aren't supposed to float upside down.

Avery's Curse can be broken down in two easy-to-understand rules. First, anytime I make a monumental change in my life, someone bites the dust. No, not like tripping over their own feet. More like tombstones and eulogies. Second, see rule number one.

The curse likes to remind me what happened to Justice and tells me to sit and most importantly stay. This is why I quit change, like a bad habit that could wipe out the world's population. I wasn't always afraid of change like I am now. As a kid, life was good. Family trips and weekend strolls through the farmers' market. Hikes on Saturdays and church on Sundays. But for the last three years, I've been working in the same spa I interned at, listening to the same music—50 cent, obviously—living in the same house, same room, same bed since moving out of my childhood home and into a duplex with Tilly, my opposite. And had it not been Tilly's bizarre idea we get a goldfish, we wouldn't have been performing his funeral days after bringing him home.

Hell, I haven't even changed my coffee order at the small drive-thru near our place just in case the curse decides it needs to strike in unlikely places. I don't even like caramel lattes anymore, but every time I look into the innocent eyes of the barista, I still order it, knowing she could be next.

Tilly chugs something then burps loudly. "This is a dream opportunity! You've wanted to own a spa since you were in high school and here you are, doing it. What if this spa becomes a success and ends up being featured on social media or blogs? What if you meet amazing people? What if this becomes the most pivotal experience you've ever had in your entire life?"

Sure, moving to this farm instead of a beachfront bungalow with crashing waves as the soundtrack is different from the life I envisioned but *semantics*. I'd be swapping out the sea glass color scheme and the chatter of seagulls for chickens and humble country-folk who wear flannel and cowboy boots. And I'd finally be able to learn how to ride a horse.

Then again, I'd probably ride it straight into an early grave.

Maybe I should just get a tattoo instead.

But I have to admit, her perspective sounds a lot more appealing right now. Despite the middle finger she likes to throw up to the world, this is why she's my best friend. We immediately hit it off in middle school, because she is nothing like me. She's a fun-seeking optimist, and I'm well...not.

"You need to take the advice on your shirt," she says.

"How do you know which—"

"I just know, okay?" she cuts in. "Now, what does it say?"

I tuck my chin to my chest, the llama on the front reminding me right away. "You are Llamazing," I say out loud.

"Exactly."

I tilt my head. "I don't get how—"

Tilly stops me with a serious tone. "You can do this, even if it's scary, because you are llamazing."

"I'm llamazing."

"You're llamazing."

I close my eyes briefly and try to envision a world where I reach for what I really want. A world where fear doesn't hold me back. I can't do this, but I need to. Out of all the changes I could choose, this is the one I want the most.

It's been five years since my mom has truly smiled, five years since my dad held a conversation with me, and five years since I let myself think about the vision board I created for my senior project detailing the spa I'd own one day.

Twinkle lights and lavender, hot rocks and yoga classes. There'd be couples' massages with champagne and an onsite chef that would make food so good, it would be sourced straight from heaven.

But then my heart died, or as my therapist reminds me; it was sad. I quit massage school, canceled my plans, and burned that vision board, like it would take away that dream. It didn't. And now, I'm rubbing my forehead and letting a llama be the confidence I need.

I exhale slowly. "Okay."

"Okay," Tilly repeats. "And don't forget to celebrate with the bottle of champagne I put in your suitcase."

"You did what?"

"Champagne. Suitcase. Celebrate. I have to go, though. I just needed to stop home real quick before my hot date tonight," she explains in a sing-song tone. "Literally, since we're going to a hot yoga class together."

"Keenan?"

"No."

"Anthony?"

"Hell, no."

"Then, who?"

Her bangles scream loud, but good thing Tilly's voice is louder. "Bill. His crow pose did it for me, so when he asked me out, I said *duh*. I'll let you know how it goes."

This is the difference between us. She is carefree—and a little careless—in almost everything she does. She's the kind of person who walks everywhere, even at night. As a hairdresser, there are days she comes home with different colored hair, or no hair at all—bald was a good look on her. And she does things like speed dating and bungee jumping. Once she did both at the same time.

A motor starts up again on her end. "I rented one of those electric scooters, and it's impossible to talk and steer, so I really have to go. But I love you forever. Don't forget to celebrate tonight! Byyyyye!"

I shake my head at the terrifying thought that Tilly has tried talking and scootering. At the same time.

"Bye," I say to the dead line.

Pulling the lever on the side of the seat, I sit upright and stare out at the farmhouse again. Celebrating is the last thing I should do. I need to call everyone I know and tell them to stay away from heavy machinery and sharp objects for the next two months. Then, I'll do my best not to step on a crack and break my mother's back.

Three

Avery

"It's life. It's interesting. It's fun."-Bob Ross

Getting out of my car and shutting the door, I squint to look up at the house. It's white, or at least it was white when it was first painted by the early settlers a century ago. The Little House on the Prairie vibes are strong with this one. The years of grit are starting to show, but the beauty of the place is in the details. The shutters framing the windows, flower boxes full of annual blooms, and the covered porch are ready for Joanna Gaines to go crazy with.

I rock back on my heels, darting my eyes from one end of the farm to the other. A water barrel sits at the edge of the house ready to catch any rain that decides to fall. A promise the hot weather will have to break at least for the summer. Tractors sit unmoving by the barn, and a mower straddles the line between the grass and gravel in front of the house. I emailed Wyatt to let him know I'd be here today, but there's no one around. It's quiet if I don't count the cows lowing in the back pasture, the cluck of chickens nearby, and the wind chime going absolutely bonkers on the porch.

I decide to knock on the door, though I'm not sure who to expect on the other side, or if this is even the right one to knock on. There are other cabins and barns on the property, too, spread out a good distance from each other and separated by burn piles along the drive in. But only this one looks like it's seen enough life and death over the years based on the creak of the steps and the bang of the screen door that doesn't latch properly.

It's a little eerie.

Balling my fist, I knock twice and wait. A bird sings from somewhere above me, and a brush of wind rushes through, lifting the threads of my jean shorts and tickling my legs. I slap at my upper thighs where the phantom bugs crawl up my legs, ready to eat me alive. Turns out they aren't real but try telling that to my brain now on high alert. I rush to knock on the door again, peering behind me and in every direction my head will turn.

Despite exchanging a few emails and a brief phone call to tell me that I got this job, I know nothing about Wyatt. His wife and six children could open this door, and I'd have no clue they even existed. Or, maybe Jason Voorhies himself lives here in the off-season when he isn't terrorizing teenagers who always run the wrong direction. I tap my foot and try to remember every bad decision ever made in a horror film that I shouldn't make: don't lose my phone, don't pretend like nothing is there, steer clear of the kitchen where the knives live, and my God, avoid doors that shouldn't be opened.

This place looks serene, but it could also be a good setting to create nightmares.

It could be haunted.

There might be ghosts.

Is Wyatt a ghost?

I need to stop freaking myself out. I wasn't hired by a ghost.

Striding to the edge of the porch again, I shield my eyes and peer back out the way I came. Should I try one of the other buildings or barns? No, Freddy Krueger will probably be in one of those. Maybe Wyatt is out in the fields or doing what someone does with the animals? Feed, water, change their diapers? No, wait. That's a baby.

He told me I'd have a room to myself, but now that I'm here, I have no clue which one, or if I'll live to see it. My heart rate picks up, like a stampede of horses.

"You're fine, Avery," I mutter under my breath. "You're...llamazing."

Turning back to the door, I pull open the screen and notice the front door is ajar. My brain tells me Chucky is waiting just inside, but my hand is pushing it open, like I have no fear of haunted dolls that carry knives. I hate horror movies but teenage Avery watched all of them. Now, I'm living one.

The door squeaks in protest, and I pause. Maybe I should just wait for Wyatt. But waiting for him means waiting in the heat outside. I'm already sweating through my t-shirt and the twenty-degree temperature difference inside the dark entryway is whispering to me: *come inside, my precious.*

I'll just go in, cool off, grab a glass of water, and then look for Wyatt. No closets will be opened, and I'll steer clear of looking under any beds.

I step across the threshold and let the screen slap back into place, startling me in the process. I raise a hand to my chest and coach myself down. "It's just the door. Relax."

Three steps into the small entry, and I startle again, jumping back and bumping into the door as I'm greeted by a large moose head mounted on the wall above me. Did Jason do this? No, this looks like the work of a rifle and a hunter wearing neon orange. Are moose color blind? The head is huge and serves as a giant warning to whoever enters. I swallow and walk underneath it, never letting my eyes leave its glass one. It's the window to the soul that's no longer there.

The next room I enter is a small formal living room with a couple of wingback chairs, a sofa with a floral pattern covering it, and a couple of side tables. An ancient piano stands in the corner of the room, and the walls are lined with so many family photos, I'm not sure what color the walls are. I think they're family photos, but I resist the urge to step closer to confirm. The last thing I want is to get trapped in a small room with a retractable wall that will lock me in like the movie Saw 57.

I step on one floorboard, and it squeaks. The next creaks. The one after that croaks.

What am I doing? I should just leave.

It's not that hot outside.

But I don't. I'm fully committed at this point.

Passing by a formal dining room, the kitchen, and the bending stairwell, I find another living space. This one is darker than the front piano room, seeing as the curtains are drawn and the light is muted. As my eyes adjust, I notice a body slumped over in a rocking chair and I gasp, covering my mouth.

Oh no.

I freeze.

Then, I panic.

Did I...did I do this?

Did Avery's Curse do this?

I'm sweating actual bullets now, despite the cool temperature and one of them must have landed in this poor woman.

Moving closer to the chair, I notice the white, frayed curls are attached to a slim-bodied, old woman. I can't see if her chest is rising and falling as it should. The room is too dark, and I can't tell. I have to help her.

I did this.

Avery's Curse did this.

There's no time to think of that now. I quickly kneel in front of the woman, watching her chest and trying to hear her breathing. *Come on, please don't be dead.* It lifts and falls slightly, letting me know her lungs are still doing something. I search for her hand, which is tucked between her leg and the armrest of the chair. Wasting time isn't an option, so I grip her wrist and search for the spot that will tell me she's not dead.

Please be alive.

My fingers are shaking while looking for her pulse. I curse my curse and scold myself for coming. "I should have stayed home," I say to the dead body. "I knew this would happen. No one believed me. Tilly thought it was fake. It wasn't. I knew it wasn't."

But then I find a strong pulse, and the old woman rises from the dead.

I scream.

She screams.

I stop screaming.

She continues screaming.

She finally stops, but then grabs the glass of water beside her chair and throws it in my face. "What in the devil's name are you doing?" she yells.

I leap up and back, trying to breathe through the water dripping down my face, neck, and chest. "Oh my God! I'm...I'm...I thought you were...but you're not...I was worried that..." I clutch my wet chest. "You're alive."

"Of course I'm alive. Haven't you seen an old lady napping before?"

A nap. She was just napping.

She sits up in her chair, no longer slumped over like a rag doll. "You thought I was dead?"

I swipe water droplets from my eyes. "What? No, no. That's crazy. I was just..." I wave my hand, but I've got nothing. Every one of my actions communicated that I was seconds away from performing CPR. I don't know CPR, but I would have figured it out. I've watched enough TV.

She exhales. "If you think I'll kick the bucket while my grandson is trying to modernize the farm, you've got another thing coming. I'd be no good as a ghost, haunting him every time he had a crazy idea."

My heartbeat is still erratic. "And your grandson...is his name, Wyatt?"

"You guessed right," she says with a pointed stare and curt nod. "He's probably out there right now putting tutus on my cows in order to livestream the whole thing."

All I can do is stare and tilt my head to the side, as if what just came out of her mouth has a different explanation than what she said.

"Don't act so surprised. I know what livestreaming is," she says, pointing at me. "And sorry about the water."

"Thanks." I tug at my wet shirt so it isn't suctioned to my breasts. "So, uh, Wyatt. Is he here? I was trying to find him and when I noticed the door was open, I came in here to look. I'm so sorry I disturbed your...nap." Not your death.

"You aren't that ex of his now are ya?"

My brows dive together. "No."

"I don't have my glasses on." She waves a dismissive hand. "Never mind. I needed to get up anyway. If Wyatt knew I was sleeping, he'd get all smug-like."

Scooting to the end of her chair, she braces herself on the armrests and stands on shaky legs. I'd consider reaching out to help if I weren't positive she was the type to swat my hand away.

"So, who are you?" she asks, looking up at me.

I'm taken aback. "Me?"

"Yes, you. The woman who is standing in my house, thinking I just rose from the dead."

"I'm Avery." I laugh nervously and scan the rest of the room with my ghost-ray vision. "Wyatt didn't tell you I was coming?"

"I'm not his keeper." She heads for what looks like the kitchen at the back of the house. "Now, what are you doing here?"

I follow after her, hoping there won't be any other bodies in there to resuscitate. "I'm a massage therapist, and he hired me to start a spa for the guests."

She peers over her shoulder before opening a cabinet. "Mhm. That sounds like Wyatt."

I fidget with the hem of my shirt. "Does he work with someone or have a wife I could check in with while he's working with the...cows and tutus?"

Pulling two glasses down and setting them on the counter, the old woman cackles loudly. "A wife? Dear, Wyatt doesn't have a wife. Far from it." She cranks the faucet on and fills a glass. "He's got a beard."

I'm not sure how to respond to that, so I don't, and just accept the full glass of water she hands me that I'm not thirsty for and chug it like I live in a sorority. "So, what's your name?"

She thinks about it while filling her glass, then says, "Granny."

A drip of water escapes out of the corner of my mouth, and I wipe it away. "Is that what I should call you?"

She studies me then sets her glass down. "Of course that's what you should call me," she says, as if there's no other potential option.

The start of a smile pulls at her lips, and I relax my shoulders. I'm more on edge than I thought I was since my pep-talk with Tilly. As long as the girl from the Ring doesn't crawl out of my TV and no one dies, I'll be fine.

"I don't know everything that Wyatt has planned for the farm. I gave up trying to keep up weeks ago, but that boy follows a schedule like clockwork. He may not know what day it is, but he knows the time. It's three in the afternoon, so you'll find him over at the creek taking his break." Granny walks to the sink and points out the wide window. "Go past the chicken coop, around the red barn, and head straight until you reach a small creek. You'll see him."

I place the glass in the sink. "Thanks. I'll go check in with him."

She nods once. "You do that."

I start back to where I entered but stop and turn to face her. "And I'm really, really sorry for waking you up."

She smiles and points at me. "I'll forgive ya if you don't tell Wyatt I was sleeping."

"Deal."

"Oh, and Avery?"

I meet her eyes. "Yeah?"

"You'll want to change that shirt before you go."

I look down, though I don't need confirmation. And there's the outline of my black bra.

I sigh as my shoulders droop. I'm still llamazing, even if I have to change.

Four

Wyatt

"Use absolutely no pressure. Just like an angel's wing." -Bob Ross

Using my arm as a pillow, I'm flat on the blanket I lugged up here and breathing in the thick smell of grass and English Lilac that spell out early July in Montana. Summer is here again for another year as it pinky-promised. The relentless winter likes to trick us all into thinking we'll be stuck in a snow globe forever. But the warmth always comes back, full and fresh as it ever was.

Taking breaks here at my favorite spot on the whole farm after doing all the morning chores is like a big reset on my day. Cow dung on my boots? Don't care. Blood on my sleeve from butchering chickens? Can't touch me. Constant calls and texts? Well, that isn't happening even when I do have a couple bars of service. Out here, I'm safe from it all. The rolling hills interspersed with Ponderosa Pines that remind me of freckles dotting a smooth shoulder provide a barrier I didn't know I needed after leaving San Francisco.

At first, I was as restless as a chicken being chased by a horny rooster. But as the days spun into weeks and morphed into months, I'm breathing easier now. Eventually, I'll roll up the blanket and trudge back to the barn to continue working on the never-ending honey-do list, minus the honey.

It isn't easy to find a *honey* in Big Timber where I know every person by name and the rest are tourists who are usually here for pit stops and a cold beer. When Ronny and I put on our nice boots and head into town, we find ourselves down at the Thirsty Hippo Bar and Grill. It's more of a bar with a grill they don't like to use. These nights I might notice a rare species called a *single woman*, but she'll usually go for Pretty Boy Ronny. He's got the naturally tanned skin and cowboy hat thing going for him. Ladies eat that shit up, apparently.

The tall grass rustles around me as another breeze whips through the valley, sifting invisible fingers through my hair. It leaves faster than it came, but the sound of moving grass continues. The ground vibrates with movement, and I keep my eyes closed, listening. It's the hottest part of the day, the sun high in the sky, so I know it isn't an animal. Most have already found shade beneath a tree or near one of the outbuildings. I'm the only one out here.

But as a shadow passes over me, blocking nature's lightbulb, I realize I'm not.

I blink rapidly, letting my eyes adjust and noticing straw-colored wisps of hair caught in a new breeze that rolls through. I squint up at the shapely figure that stands at my side, looming over me and completely still.

Rubbing my eyes, I blink again.

"Wyatt?"

I don't answer, because I'm convinced she's an angel. The sun's rays are bouncing off her head, making it hard to see her face and casting her in a glow that would make any influencer with a ring light jealous. I squint up, looking for wings. There aren't any. No halo, either.

But what I do find is Jesus, in all His glory, sprawled across her shirt and sitting on top of a dinosaur with one hand raised, like he's lassoing the sky.

I have to be dreaming.

"I'm Avery," the woman says.

I'm not dreaming.

"Avery?" I repeat, scrambling to my feet with as much grace as a cow trying to stand.

She clears her throat and darts her eyes up to the sky. "Yes, Avery."

Confused, I look up, too, in case there's an eagle I missed. But there's nothing. Just endless blue and shapely clouds.

I drop my chin and study her. "*Spa* Avery?"

She trains her eyes on the stream now, avoiding my gaze completely. "That's me."

I rest a hand on my hip. "What day is it? I thought you'd be here tomorrow."

She shifts on her feet and glances at my face before looking away again. "It's Sunday."

Her clear blue eyes are sharp and soft at the same time, making me forget the question I'd asked her and the answer she'd given. She's so delicate with her ivory skin and slim fingers. I'm not sure what I was expecting. An ogre? Another eighty-year-old granny ready to scold me for my life choices while offering me her granddaughter on a silver platter? I have no clue except it wasn't *her*.

I scrub a hand down my face, combing through my beard to make sure there isn't a piece of timothy hay stuck in it. "Sorry, I must be off by a day." Granny likes to say I feel the time instead of actually knowing it.

"It's okay." She points to the farmhouse as she studies the earth below and asks, "Where should I put my stuff?"

Why isn't she looking at me? If it's not hay in my beard, is there dirt on my face? It wouldn't surprise me. I'm usually covered in a layer of it by the end of the day. Food in my teeth? I haven't eaten since breakfast. Is my zipper down? I use my hands to cover the front of my jeans just in case. I chalk it up to nerves since I can't come up with a clear reason why she's already avoiding me, like I have cooties.

"Right, yeah. Let me show you." I look around to make sure I've got everything and see my shirt lying discarded on the blanket. My bare chest explains so much. Looks like I do have cooties after all.

I bend and snag my shirt, throwing it over my head and shoving my arms in. The only problem is, I'm pushing my head through the arm hole and my arm where my head should be. I struggle for what feels like minutes and finally pull it off and start again, combing a hand through my mess of hair once I get it right. My horse, Axel, could do a better job of getting dressed.

"Shall we?" I gesture toward the path, like the whole shirt thing never happened.

The coy smile on her pretty lips peeks through her curtain of hair.

I point out a few of the different areas on the farm on our walk back, promising her a full tour tomorrow after she gets settled in. She listens and asks questions here and there, but mostly, she seems to be taking it all in. Bending to pluck a wildflower from the ground, running her hand along the outside of the barn, and inhaling the smell of freshly cut grass I took a weed eater to earlier today.

We're almost to the chicken coop and walking by a row of fruit trees when Avery calls out from behind me. "Wyatt!"

I turn to see how far ahead I've gotten and lock eyes with Avery's foot smashed into a big cow pie and the wide "O" shape of her mouth. Her white sneakers never stood a chance out here. She would've been better off walking barefoot.

I jog back to her. "You alright?"

"Yes, but my foot isn't," she says with a pinched expression. "I wasn't expecting to go traipsing through the fields, otherwise I would've worn my boots."

At least she has boots. That's a step in the right direction since there's never a shortage of shit underfoot. I offer her my hand, and she takes it with the power of a great white shark's jaw. Her hand might look small and bony in my large work-worn one, but it's strong and thoroughly moisturized. Massage hands, I dub them.

A few apricots fall near us with a thud as a distant chainsaw starts up somewhere else on the farm. I'm used to these noises, but Avery startles and leaps forward, yanking her foot out of the dung and ramming into my chest with the impact of a full-grown rhino knocking me off my feet. I trip over my own boots, a stick, more shit—I don't really know—and fall back on the ground with her chest smashed against mine. I grunt in pain. Her massage hands are curled around my midsection, and she's panting, like a thirsty animal in the desert.

I lift my head from the grass, thanking the good Lord I didn't land in another pile of crap. "What just happened?"

"It was just…" Relaxing her hold on my torso, she tries to find a place to plant her hands. My pecs are a viable option, but she makes a last-minute shift and puts them on the ground instead. She's staring down at me now, her hair a privacy wall around us. She closes her eyes briefly. "The chainsaw…do you always have chainsaws going out here?"

I try to ignore my immediate bodily reaction to having her laid flush on top of me and focus on the words she just said. My brows furrow. "Uh, most of the time, yeah."

Ronny's probably cutting up more tree limbs to add to the burn piles. The way she reacted was intense, but the sight of her above me is better than any fantasy I could have come up with on my own.

She pushes herself off of me, adding pressure to all the right (but also wrong) places. My hands instinctively find her waist to help as her eyes rove over the front of my jeans and widen. She straightens her clothes when upright and says, "Sorry about that. It won't happen again."

"Don't worry about it." I get off my ass and do my best to distract her from the tent we just pitched in my pants. "You might try wiping your shoe on the grass a little."

She tries her best to wipe her shoe, but the cling power this pile seems to possess is strong. Struggling to remove it all, she eventually gets them mostly clean and continues toward the front drive.

I turn and follow her, cupping my hands around my mouth to yell, "Watch out for snakes." I can't help myself.

She jumps sideways and looks warily at the ground as if there really is a snake. "Where?"

I hold back a laugh. "Sorry, no snake. But keep your eyes open."

It wasn't a total lie. There are snakes, but she'd hear the rattle before getting too close.

She doesn't respond but continues on, keeping her gaze glued to the ground around her.

We reach her car and she pops the trunk, which looks more like banging the top of it twice, apologizing, and speaking in a hushed tone she didn't think I could hear. *You are a brave warrior, Beatrice*, she says before it decides to open for her.

I grab her suitcases and a couple grocery bags, starting off down the gravel drive toward the cabin, which is half a football field away, while she slings a backpack over one shoulder. "I put you in the largest cabin, so you'd have space for yourself and the spa. It has two bedrooms and one bathroom, built by my Gramps about twenty years ago for family members to visit." The bags are heavy enough to strain my arm muscles, and I hope, if she's looking, she'll notice those before the grimace on my face. "I did some updates but not as many as the other cabins. It's still cozy, though."

She doesn't answer, and when I look behind me, she's ten paces back, struggling under the awkward size of a duffle that she's holding, like a small lamb. We don't have lambs on the farm, but she'd be a pro at carrying one if we did.

I pause and let her catch up. "Can I help?"

"I got it," she says, rolling her lips inward to disguise her effort.

Reaching the steps leading to the door, I set the bags down to open it. "It doesn't have AC, but there's a fan and all the windows have screens." Gramps didn't see the need for air conditioning since it cools off enough at night. "Welcome to your new home." I push it open and the hinges creak. "I'll get some grease for that."

Avery nods and follows me inside. "Does your family still come to visit?"

"Yes and no," I say to her back as she passes me to look around. I pick up the bags and trail her inside. "They all live in the area and we see each other often, but no one tends to stay the night much anymore. There's enough room in the farmhouse for that, so I decided to turn these into rentals."

"It's a good idea," she says, smiling over her shoulder before disappearing into the kitchen.

My blood is on fire from that one smile and maybe the chainsaw mishap. God, it's been too long since I've been around a beautiful woman. I don't know what to do with my hands or...other body parts.

Avery returns to the living room just as I put her second bag in the bedroom. My body feels huge in this space, or maybe that's just because Avery is so small. I could pick her up and throw her over my shoulder with one hand if I wanted, and I dunno, maybe I want to.

Focus, Wyatt.

I scratch at my beard. "So, usually, I'll be cooking meals for the guests, and you can either take your meals in here or at the farmhouse with us. Tonight, dinner's at six in the main house. That's where my Granny and I live in case you need anything. If you're not too tired, you're welcome to come on by. No pressure, though. It's family dinner night, so everyone will be here."

She sets her purse on the kitchen counter. "Everyone?"

I unsnap my hat from my belt loop and settle it on my head. "My folks, Ronny, Granny, and my sister and her family. Although, I'll warn you now that my sister and her husband bring their two kids, and they like board games."

Her mouth curves into a smile, and my heart beats faster. "It's a good thing I like board games. I won't go easy on them."

"I wouldn't expect you to."

My smile drops and my gaze heats up as it lingers on her. If she notices, she doesn't say anything. Just consider me a caveman seeing a woman for the first time. I need to get it together. This is a two-month trial where she helps me out, and I help Granny before figuring out my next career move.

She shakes her head. "Does the door have a lock?"

I look back over my shoulder at the navy blue door. "Yeah, it does. Want me to test it?"

"Please."

I've never locked any of the doors, but I do what she asks, backing up toward it and twisting the top lock, then the one on the handle and try to open it. It doesn't budge. "Looks like it works. Keys are hanging right here for when you leave."

She sighs and rubs her forehead. "Okay, good."

"Alright, well, I gotta go do a few more things before dinner. Let me know if you need anything."

She nods and bites her plump bottom lip I've etched into my mind already. "I will. Thanks again. I'm looking forward to this opportunity. I—" Her voice drops off. "I really need this."

She locks eyes with me, finally letting me study their bright blue hue. What I don't say is how much I need her, too. Losing anything else, including this farm, isn't an option.

Waving goodbye, I back out of the cabin and head toward the farmhouse to check on Granny. Everyone is going to take one look at Avery and think I rigged this whole thing. The woman is the brand of beauty that causes you to forget your own name. I obviously didn't choose her for her looks but try telling that to the people who basically host their own version of *The Bachelor* on a regular basis. Last week, my sister took sly pictures of me while I was repairing a few shingles on the barn roof. Except she wasn't so sly. I caught her red-handed, or at least with her finger on the red record button. She was fixin' to create an online dating profile for me. Granny actually beat her to it. She can't even set her own thermostat but knows how to navigate Google like a boss. It's a mystery.

I'll need to set them straight before dinner tonight. No setups or awkward comments. Plus, Ronny will be there, and ladies tend to go for someone like him anyway. Avery is an employee, and it needs to stay that way, even if the forecast for keeping these boundaries is cloudy with a chance of *yeah right*.

I bound up the porch steps and walk through the front door. "Granny, I'm back."

"In here!" she yells from the kitchen.

I'm no more than one foot onto the terracotta-colored tile floor when Granny's next words ambush me and make me second-guess not doing more of a deep dive into Avery's application. It'll be the last time I let Ronny vet potential employees. If I had only searched for a picture of her online, I'm sure it would've said a thousand words in only one: nope. If Granny could navigate Google, I could, too. The last thing I need is a beautiful woman to distract me.

She crosses her arms over her chest. "I met your wife."

Five

Avery

"I like to beat the bush."-Bob Ross

Abs. So. Many. Abs.

Are those all from shucking hay? Or, is it mucking? Hucking? I don't even know what you do with hay, but he clearly does. This farm apparently comes complete with a scantily clad farmer who likes to sunbathe by streams of water and smile like he's on an episode of *Farmer Wants a Wife*. I can, in fact, confirm he would make the perfect bachelor for that show. His body was slick, toned, and tan when I found him lying in the grass. Did he oil up before I got there? Was that whole thing about forgetting what day it was just a bit? It doesn't matter that I wasn't one of the contestants on his one-man show; I was still an innocent bystander whose eyeballs got caught in the crossfire.

None of it matters. The abs, the t-shirt, jeans, work boots, and beard I'd like to make a nest in (not really) don't mean a thing. He's my boss now, which means I am the most professional person on this planet.

But it would help if the vision of his body wasn't seared into the back of my eyelids, giving me a strip tease every time I close my eyes. It's like he was stuck in slow motion every time I looked at him. He nearly had me on my knees, begging for regular speed again. With an hour until dinner where I'll meet his family and act like a totally normal person who isn't attracted to her new boss whatsoever, I shoot my diary (aka Tilly) a long text.

Then, scurrying around the bedroom, I finish hanging and folding my clothes, organizing my books on the small shelf, and putting a few of the groceries I picked up into the cupboards. The time ticks down to forty-five minutes until dinner, which makes me forty-five minutes late to help with the prep. I should've just unpacked my things later and focused on making a good impression and getting there sooner. Exceptionally early is always better than fashionably late. Granny was on the brink of death earlier. The least I could do is help with dinner.

Slipping on a pair of sandals, snatching a sweater to tie around my waist, and grabbing the keys, I head for the door and lock it behind me. If Granny or Wyatt don't want to lock their door and wind up with an ax murderer strolling through it, then that's their choice. I'd prefer to sleep with the knowledge there isn't someone hiding in my closet, though.

The sky outside is painted with pink and blue streaks, creating a purple hue as the sun's shadow dips below the mountains. I'll probably have to use my cell phone flashlight to find my cabin after dinner. Or, I could ask Wyatt to whip off his shirt again and use the glow of his freshly tanned skin to light my way—the way. Probably not.

Okay, definitely not.

I head up the steps and knock on the door. The last time I was here, I thought I'd need to call 911. Not like much has changed since I never know when Avery's Curse will strike and I'll be attending a funeral. I shuffle on my feet, sliding my knees back and forth against one another while I wait for someone to answer. I'm coaching myself not to get too comfortable and let my guard down. Death could be lurking around every corner.

So could half-nude farmers.

No one comes to answer the door to save me from flashbacks of shirtless Wyatt that could easily send me into an early grave. I knock again. No answer. Where is everyone? Peering around, my eyes start to play tricks that aren't funny. I'm no longer looking at a lone tractor. It's an alligator with teeth the size of me. The rain barrel morphs into a torture chamber, and I swear the echoes of a chainsaw are ringing in my ears.

I swat at my ear. Okay, or it's just bugs, but either way, I'm done standing out here on my own for the second time today. I push the front door open and come face to snout with the looming moose head.

I clutch the phantom pearls I must have forgotten to wear for such an occasion as this then point at the taxidermied animal. "You need to stop doing that."

He only stares down at me like I'm his prey, and he's about to devour me. Too bad for him since I know he doesn't have a stomach.

I slip off my shoes and take a steadying breath, looking out the corner of my eye only to find the creepy animal with no stomach, but maybe some teeth, still looking at me. It doesn't matter which direction I shift, his glass eyes follow me.

I throw my hands in the air. "Fine. Keep staring," I huff, then get an idea. If I give him a name, maybe he won't seem so terrifying. I rest my hands on my hips and think. "Moose...Moo...Moosifer." I nod once. "That's it, *Moosifer.*"

A cross between a mounted moose head and the devil. *Perfect.*

Realizing it's still only Moosifer and me in the entryway, I cross my arms and call out, "Hello?"

No one answers.

I tentatively walk beneath the furry beast and toward the kitchen at the back of the house. The space is empty, and I question whether the rapture has happened and everyone has just disappeared, or the more rational line of thinking, which assumes no one is here, yet. Someone is bound to show up soon, though, right? I'll just wait.

Moving to the counter, I begin washing the few dishes that line the basin of the large farmhouse sink. I can keep my hands busy at least. It's what I do. It's what I've always done: stress clean. I'm also not above a panic bathroom scrub or an anxiety-ridden bedroom reorganization. Although, that may be slightly overdoing it in a stranger's home. I'm used to constantly doing and being idle has always been difficult.

I learned quickly that if I took care of others, they didn't have to worry about taking care of me. I've really made my therapist work for that one-hundred and fifty dollars per session. But that little nugget of truth was worth it. I should definitely send her some thank-you flowers.

I haven't been the only one suffering. My parents were devastated. They lost a son, and even though they still had me, they didn't have him. So, I cleaned. I folded laundry, mowed the lawn, and started cooking meals that were barely close to edible. Eventually, I figured out how to read a thing called a "recipe" and checked out several cookbooks from the library. I wasn't—and am still not—a chef, by any means, but we all survived, and I know I had a small part in that.

The kitchen in this farmhouse isn't modern by today's standards, but some pieces have been updated such as the new wide basin sink, a tall, matte black faucet, and modern handles on the upper and lower cabinets. It's quaint and sweet in a way that doesn't look like it's trying too hard.

I work in silence, the steady stream of water and the scratch of the sponge on the plate are the only noises I hear until they aren't. Heavy footfalls pound on the stairs, and I'm expecting an elephant to fall through the ceiling at any moment.

Unless elephants are tan with chiseled abs and chest hair that make you want to curl up in it, then I'm sorely mistaken.

"Granny, did you wash my shirts again—"

I whip around and throw up a hand in greeting, like I'm an alien from another planet. "Hi."

I widen my eyes and take in the sights like I did with the view of the farm earlier. My God this man is ripped. His low slung jeans and wet hair are doing nothing to help the situation sweeping low in my stomach.

"Um, hi," he says, running a hand through his wet hair. "You're early."

We stare at each other for so long until I realize my hand is still raised. I lower it but question where I should set it. My hip? The counter? His bare chest?

The sound of rushing water has me saying, "Oh shit," and spinning to shut off the faucet. Swallowing, I give myself three-point-five seconds before turning back around to act like a human and not an extraterrestrial being. *One. Two. Three. Point five. Spin.* "I came to help with dinner, and then...the...I..." I point behind me with a finger that could rival ETs, trying to find the words, but all of them have gotten lost in the dark curly hair forging a trail below his belly button. I snap my head back up to meet his eyes. "No one was here, so I did the dishes."

Explanation done. I'd give myself an A+ on the recovery and a triple F- on playing it cool.

"I was, uh, looking for a shirt," he says, waving a hand down the front of him.

Like I need another reminder he isn't wearing one.

I can smell him as he passes through the kitchen and heads for a room I assume is the laundry area off the small eat-in dining space. Sandalwood and vanilla. I know this only because I own no less than fifty-two candles with this exact scent. There is one in my cabin beside my bed right now.

This is not good.

My voice is breathy when I say, "No problem." But there is a problem. Six of them to be exact and packed on his stomach.

It's seconds before he's walking back into the kitchen, t-shirt on and looking hotter than the griddle that I cooked my chocolate chip pancakes on this morning. Sweeter, too, but I'm not about to bite him to confirm this.

"Not sure where Granny went off to, but I should probably get started on dinner. I hope you like spaghetti and meatballs," he says, moving to the pantry beside the fridge.

It's the only food Tilly has successfully learned how to make without setting the stove on fire. Somehow she's perfected that skill with almost every other meal.

I take a tentative step toward him. "What can I do to help?"

"I'll get the meat started if you make the noodles. There's a big pot in that cabinet," he says, pointing to the opposite side of the kitchen. "Here they are." He hands me a few bags of noodles that would take Tilly and me five years to finish. "We have a big family," he adds with a shrug.

I smile up at him and set the noodles down so I can get the pot. Filling it up from the sink, I feel every movement that Wyatt makes since he has to brush up against me to go anywhere in this cramped space. He moves around effortlessly, despite the fact I'm channeling a slippery banana peel from Mario Kart set on tripping him up at every turn.

Grabbing a bowl, a jar of seasoning, and the remaining items from the fridge, he sets it all on the counter and gets to work. I've been on this farm a handful of hours and already I'm living the most domestic life ever. I can't say I'm upset about it. I've dreamed up moments like these over the years. Cooking dinner with my husband, kids playing outside until the sun goes down, and large family gatherings. All of it centered on family and all of it ripped away by one careless drunk driver. I haven't thought about these things in a while. Not since my own family ceased to exist.

Wyatt finishes shaping the meatballs as I slip the noodles into the boiling water. "Thanks for helping," he says, heating up a pan of oil while leaning a shoulder against the fridge and crossing his hulk arms.

"Of course. I don't mind." I peel my eyes away as gracefully as pulling a sticker off paper. "When is everyone else arriving?"

He looks at his watch, which is really just a tan line. "Soon."

Unless the dark hairs, occasional freckles, and veins on the back of his hands can tell time, I'm not confident in his answer since there's no watch there. He seems too distracted to notice.

He pushes off the fridge and lowers the meatballs into the pan as the front door opens and Granny's voice rings out. "I'm back. Forgot the pies at Esther's, and then we got talking. I swear I'd lose my hip if it weren't attached." She shuffles through to the kitchen and smiles at us. "Well, isn't this a pleasant sight?"

Wyatt is facing the stove, adding the last meatball to the pan before facing Granny. "How was Esther's for the second time today?"

She shrugs and sets a soft-sided bag on the counter. "Same as it always is," Granny says. "Talked about Merv's new heifer he's planning to mate, and Helen's new pie recipe at the bakery that smells suspiciously similar to Esther's blue-ribbon apple one."

He nods. "Pie is pie, Gran."

"You heathen." She playfully swats him. "Don't you dare say that in my house."

Cinnamon immediately accosts my nostrils, and I inhale deeply, like it's crack and I'm an addict (I'm not). At least not for crack. Pie is a whole other story. I lean in closer and try to absorb it through all of my senses.

She pulls out one apple and one strawberry rhubarb pie out of the bag, and my mouth waters. "No touching until after dinner." She points at Wyatt. "I'm talking to you."

He throws both hands up in surrender then catches me picking up a stray piece of crust that fell off the side and needed a home...in my belly. "It's Avery you have to worry about," he says with a laugh.

My mouth drops open, and I feign shock. "Me?"

He winks at me and seals my fate. I'm dead. Is he...flirting with me? Does he know I'm probably the most un-flirty flirt ever? Turning back to the stove, Wyatt checks the meatballs, and I'm speechless. All of my words have evaporated with the steam coming from the pot. I shake it off and remember my job: noodles. When in doubt, or stress, or a major life crisis, focus on the noodles. It's what I always say. As of five seconds ago.

Standing side by side at the stove, I stir the noodles, and Wyatt tends to his meat—wait, no. Meatballs. Oh no, that sounds even dirtier. Now I can't stop thinking about...

Loud voices filter through the front door and steal our attention.

Wyatt looks at me. "The rest of the family is here. You ready?"

"Should I be worried?"

He pauses, considering. "Probably."

Six

Avery

"Every day is a good day when you paint."-Bob Ross

Wyatt sets the tongs down and exits the kitchen. I'm alone with my thoughts but not for long as a rambunctious young boy of about ten years old runs into the kitchen. Almost ramming into me, he pulls up short and puts his hands on his hips. "Who are you?"

I stare down, grateful I'm at least taller than him. That isn't always the case with kids I meet. The joys of being old enough to sit at the adult table but never quite tall enough. "I'm Avery."

A young girl, shorter than the boy and with two braids running to her hip, bumps into his back, and he shrugs her off. She sees the pies almost immediately, as if she's really a bloodhound disguised as a kid.

"Pie!" she screams in delight.

I startle at the sound. And I thought I liked pie.

Granny enters the kitchen from the living room. "No pie until after dinner you two."

They both groan and beg her to change her mind, but she doesn't budge. She offers them a carrot instead, and they turn up their noses, like she just offered them dirt. Granny just throws up her hands and continues to move about the kitchen.

"Are you Uncle Wyatt's girlfriend?" the little girl asks.

I pause before answering. I don't know why; it's not like this is a difficult question. This isn't a multiple choice quiz or the SATs that will determine my future. It's a question with only one answer.

But before I can respond, Wyatt steps into the increasingly tight area. "She is," he says quickly with a sly, flirty smile, but when he sees I'm having a heart attack he adds, "not. She's my employee."

I nod. Exactly. Employee. "Yup. Wyatt is my boss."

A brown-haired woman with a pixie cut pushes past Wyatt and extends her hand eagerly. "Hi! I'm Stace, and this is my husband, Bryan." She waves a vague hand in his general direction behind her. "We're so glad you're here! You already met Jack and Annie, our kids." Her smile is wide, eyes beaming, like I'm Superwoman coming to save the whole city from disaster.

I try to match her smile, but I'm not sure that's possible. "Hi, I'm Avery."

Stace shakes my hand, and Bryan does the same. I'm the focus of everyone's attention as we squeeze into the kitchen made for one that can sometimes accommodate two and likely the width of Wyatt's wingspan.

Wyatt tilts his head and stares straight at Stace, trying to catch her hazel eyes that look just like his. "Where's Mom and Dad?"

Stace keeps one eye on me while talking to her brother, as if I'll turn into fairy dust and vanish into thin air. "They had to go to some meeting with their finance person in Bozeman." She waves him off and puts all of her weighty attention back on me. Yay. "When did you get here, Avery?"

Before she can reply, Wyatt slaps his hands together. "Dinner's ready. Let's eat!"

Saved by the intensely loud clap, I exhale and start passing out plates. I'm not usually this awkward with introductions, but I can't seem to harness any chill. There are so many people all smashed in close together and caring about each other's lives. It's foreign and weird. The nerves coursing through me are a fuse lit by Avery's Curse and obliterated by Wyatt's...everything. Maybe I'll discover a weird trait that will be a huge turnoff and will help me survive this close proximity summer.

Once I drain the noodles and toss them in the sauce, everyone loads up their plates, and we sit around the formal dining table near the front of the house. We are packed hip to knee on the long benches, but I think that would be the case, even if I wasn't here.

The screen door opens and slams shut. I jump and my fork clatters on the plate. All eyes are on me before being directed to the tall glass of handsome that just walked into the kitchen.

He pulls off his cowboy hat and rests it over his heart. "Sorry I'm late."

My mouth actually falls open, and I stare as if he is more delicious than a slice of pie. Where Wyatt is rough around the edges with his beard and dark hair, this man is just dark. His skin is dark, made darker by the sun, with dark brown eyes and dark hair. He's clean-shaven, but with side burns that could rival any other cowboy's.

"I'm Ronny," the man says as he approaches the table with an extended hand.

I smile back—at least I think I'm smiling and not drooling—and shake his hand. "Avery. Nice to meet you."

Ronny sets his hat on the counter and takes the seat beside me. "So, you'll be here for the summer?"

I straighten my silverware. "That's the plan."

"Enough jibber-jabber," Granny pipes in. "Let's pray and eat. Then, you can all question the poor girl. Ronny, would ya?"

Ronny nods and bows his head along with everyone else. "God, thanks for the food, family, and new friends. Amen."

Everyone around the table murmurs "amen" at different volumes while lifting their heads and searching for which serving dish to start in on first.

Stace, with her intense gaze pipes up from across the table. "You're a massage therapist?"

I unfold my napkin and place it in my lap, acting as if it will hide me. "Yeah, I've worked at a spa in Bismarck for several years."

"And you do facials and pedicures then, too?"

About that. I've worked in a spa for several years, so I know what services are offered, but I'm only certified in massage. I'm barely qualified to be starting a spa. I'm running off my hopes, dreams, and the fumes of my essential oils. "Yes, I'll be offering those, too."

Stace hands each of her kids a piece of bread without looking, even though they're already eating a slice. "What made you choose to work here?"

I don't miss the glance she shoots Wyatt or the glare he gives her, though I pretend to. Her husband, Bryan, doesn't seem to notice since he's shoveling food in his mouth fast and furious.

"I was looking for a change," I say, glancing up in case the sky falls on us. "I've always wanted to own a spa, so I figured this would be a great experience."

"That it will," Granny adds between bites. "Nothing says relaxation like cows in tutus."

"Tutus?" Wyatt asks, twisting his fork in his spaghetti.

Granny waves him off and continues eating.

Stace leans her elbows on the table, ignoring her food to ask me more questions. "Do you have family in Bismarck?"

I push a meatball around my plate. "I do. They don't live far."

Ask me the last time I've seen them, and I'll make something up, though, since I have no clue when that was. Probably a holiday where we all sat around, pretending like we were a family that does family things. Nothing has been the same since my brother died. Most of the time, it feels like they live on Mars and have forgotten about their earthling daughter.

"Well, I'm sure you'll really enjoy your time here. I know for a fact it means a lot to Wyatt," Stace says, avoiding the warning look her brother shoots her. "He needs a woman's voice in his life."

My eye starts twitching as I try to keep it from bulging out of its socket. She can't mean what I think she means. But if she meant it that way then that means...well, that means more than I want it to mean after just meeting Wyatt hours ago. WHAT DOES IT MEAN?

"You got that right," Granny adds with a sharp nod.

Wyatt shakes his head. "Granny, really? Don't encourage her."

She stares at him while chewing. I don't think she blinks once. He stares back. I stare at the wall, my glass, and the hanging light fixture made of antlers, acting like things don't feel as tense as they really do.

Ronny clears his throat. "Did Wyatt take you on a tour of the farm, yet?"

"Not yet, but I'm excited to see it tomorrow," I say, then take a bite of my spaghetti.

"You know, I could take you," Ronny says.

Wyatt looks up from his plate and stares Ronny down. "I'll take her."

Everyone at the table peers at Wyatt, as if he just stabbed a knife into the table, like a viking declaring war. Forks hover in the air, conversations stop, and the air in the room gets sucked out.

Ronny stares back, chews then swallows. "I know how busy you are. I don't mind."

Wyatt peers around the room, like he's just made a grave mistake. His gaze lands on me, and I smile to soften the mood and maybe to ensure no one gets murdered by his menacing glare. He smiles back, then glares at Ronny across from him. "I'd rather be the one to show her," he finally says. "It's our family farm."

"And I'm basically family."

Stace tips her head. "Ronny has a point."

Wyatt clears his throat. "I have...plans."

This was clearly the wrong thing to say since Granny nearly chokes on her water, and Stace has to pat her back until she's breathing air instead of liquid. Bryan just asks for someone to pass the meatballs, unaware of the volleyball match going on at the table. Bump, set, spike. The ball's on Ronny's side.

Ronny leans farther into his elbows resting on the table. "What kind of plans?"

"Plans."

"Uncle Wyatt, will you tell me what plans?" Annie pipes in.

Wyatt sighs heavily, peering around at everyone staring at him before plucking the metaphorical knife from the table and holding it in front of Ronny. "I'll do the tour."

There's no way my gulp isn't audible.

I half-expect Ronny to respond by suggesting a duel out back until someone draws blood. But since we're on a farm, maybe mud-wrestling is the custom here.

"We could all go," I say, breaking into the conversation. The mounting tension was becoming too much. They were either going to point at me to decide, or I was going to say something.

Ronny tips his chin up. "It's alright. Wyatt has plans." His smirk is both playful and devilish when he meets Wyatt's glare. "You're the boss."

I bite my bottom lip to hide the smile pushing through. I can't say I'm not pleased with the outcome.

Everyone around the table begins to breathe again. Ronny and Wyatt start talking about the work they need to get done, like there was nothing happening between them just now. Does this happen often? They seem like...friends, not unhinged warriors with battle axes hidden inside their large fur coats.

I stare down at my lap. I need to keep focused on why I'm here. I'm not here for Wyatt. I'm here for me. I want to further my dreams, even if it kills. Though, hopefully it won't.

Seven

Wyatt

"That's where the crows will sit. But we'll have to put an elevator to put them up there because they can't fly, but they don't know that, so they still try."-Bob Ross

I t's Monday, and I only know this because Avery came on Sunday. She also raised a lot of questions at family dinner...on Sunday. And it happened to be a Sunday when I took a blood oath with myself to keep it in my pants. Down to the very minute Avery stood hovering over me with her light hair and invisible halo.

I'm fresh out of a breakup and never thought I'd be looking at anyone like this for a while, despite my family meddling in things they have no business worrying about since I got back. Stace would have asked Avery her dowry price if I hadn't faked a cough and accidentally spilled Avery's water cup in the process to which she exclaimed, *not again*. The diversion went better than expected, though I don't think Avery would agree since she left with a shirt more soaked than in a wet t-shirt contest. I was hours into meeting her and already had to renew my oath after my gaze slipped.

Attraction is one thing, but as her boss, I need to keep us on the straight and narrow. I could be living in Timbuktu after these two months are over. Starting something I can't see through isn't my thing.

Padding down the stairs in my socks, I fill my thermos with hot coffee to prepare for the tour I promised Avery. I stayed up late again reviewing every part of my business plan and making sure the guest experience this weekend would be the best one they've ever had. Maybe that's a lot of pressure, but I've always done better carrying a boulder on my back instead of a feather.

Hovering the coffee spout over the mug beside mine, I pause. Does Avery like coffee? Granny sure doesn't. Says it tastes like worm poop, which is really just dirt. Should I bring Avery a mug? I carried in a bag of groceries for her yesterday but didn't snoop to see if there was any coffee. The only thing I saw was a box of tampons. Okay, so maybe I did look.

What the hell? I'll pour her one, and if she doesn't drink coffee or already has some, then I'll know for next time. Next time? Who am I? She can make her own damn coffee. The cabin has a working machine with a timer and everything.

But today, I'll bring her some, because I'm a nice boss who wants happy employees.

Two thermoses in hand, I slip on my work boots and Carhartt jacket and head in the direction of Avery's cabin. The mornings are cool, even in early July, but I know the beanie and jacket I chose won't last long.

It's a short walk down the gravel drive since Avery's cabin is the closest. I'm raising a fist, pounding a complicated beat on the door that sounds an awful lot like the Happy Birthday song, and I immediately regret it. "What am I, five?" I say under my breath.

Shaking my head, I listen to every sound inside the cabin that I can gather in my ears like a squirrel preparing for winter. Her steps are light, but I hear them coming from the back bedroom. The cabin was built over a decade ago, but with the real hardwood floors Gramps salvaged, the creaking creates an orchestra of sound.

She opens the door, and the force flutters her hair off her shoulders, exposing the curves, dips, and freckles of temptation.

"Good morning," she says, like her shoulders aren't bare and beautiful in that cropped tank.

"Morning. You look ready for a tour," I manage to stutter through my gaping mouth.

My eyes dip to her chest. Not because...well, not entirely...oh, for fucks sake. There's a goose on her shirt! But this goose isn't alone. It's accompanied by the words *Silly Goose.*

I tear my eyes from the featherbrained bird on her shirt and hand her the thermos. "It's coffee. I wasn't sure if you liked it, or if you made any already, so I poured you some. No pressure, though."

Oh God, stop rambling.

She takes the thermos and grips it with both hands, clutching it to her chest. "Thanks, I love coffee. And I'm ready for the tour. I made sure to wear my boots today." She looks down and twists her foot to show off her appropriate footwear, despite her inappropriate shoulders.

It's the accidental wet t-shirt contest all over again. But worse. She pulled out all the stops with a damn goose.

I drop my gaze to her boots and slowly trail back up her lean figure to her eyes. She's wearing those blasted cut-off shorts of seduction, too.

"You're perfect," I say far too quickly.

Her smile fades. "What?"

I shake my head. "I mean, your outfit, it's perfect." I clear my throat and step back, allowing her to walk down the steps first. "I know you won't be doing farm work, but I wanted to show you the place and share my vision."

She nods and takes a sip of coffee. "Sounds great. Where do we start?"

"Chickens." I smile broadly. I can't help it. There's a goose on her shirt and yeah, maybe it's making me feel silly.

"Lead the way." She sweeps a hand in front of her.

I start walking down the drive, kicking up rocks as I go. "Have you ever gathered eggs before?"

"Unless the grocery store counts then no."

I laugh. "You don't have to wade through chicken shit in the grocery store."

"Very true. But I do have to wade through the options for which to buy—cage free, pasture-raised, organic, free-range—how am I supposed to choose?"

We walk around the farmhouse to the back where the chicken coop is. "For reference, these ladies—and a couple gents—are organic and pasture-raised. They get to roam free, and we only feed them organic scraps and grain. If you ask me, they're the best damn eggs you'll ever taste."

"The best damn eggs, huh?" she repeats. "I assume I'll get to try some eventually?"

"Of course. I'll make you breakfast." I pause when I reach the coop gate. "For you, the guests...and Granny," I correct, "because she loves eggs. Eats 'em every day."

Her smile is buoyant. "I'd like that."

I ignore how pretty her lips look turned up like that and set our mugs on a small, wooden bench outside the coop before opening the gate for her. She ducks beneath the trellis with peas climbing the outside of it, and I slip in after. I built the trellis a few weeks ago as an extra layer around the only entrance that raccoons like to sometimes take advantage of. I swore I'd make one of those mangy bandits into a hat like Davy Crockett the next time one tried to get in. Granny likes her chickens, and I like using my knife.

These are dual purpose chickens, I like to say, so some are laying hens where we sell the eggs and others are broilers raised solely for eating. They are each tagged to tell the difference, and it's one of the ways the farm makes money along with harvesting alfalfa and raising beef. Gramps had done it for years, but inflation isn't making it easy now. He always said, *meat will never go out of style if you raise and kill 'em right.*

The hens are eagerly flitting about the pen, ready to be released to peck and explore the farm. "Are you ladies ready to roam?" I open the hatch on the coop that stretches from one side of the pen to the other, and it's a cloud of feathers and dust as they rush through the obstacle course of our legs. There's a lot less bobbing and weaving and more banging into us than anything else.

"Oh my gosh!" Avery squeals in delight. "There are so many of them!"

I walk farther into the coop, holding the swinging door open for her to follow. My smile is too big, and I'm hoping my lady-killer beard covers the majority of it. "There's a couple of baskets hanging there." I point to the side of the coop. "Let's gather some eggs and give the people what they want."

She grabs a basket. "Where are the eggs?"

I lift another side of the small shed structure that Gramps and I rebuilt the summer I turned fourteen and use a small latch to hold it open, giving us access inside without having to go in it. Waving a hand in front of the open-boxed shelves with straw in them, I act like a magician performing a trick. Did I just bow?

She claps for me. "Impressive."

"It's easier to gather the eggs from out here, but there's a door on the side in order to clean things out when needed. It's a tight fit for me, but you're the right size." I bite my tongue to keep from blurting that I've checked her out in more detail than a full body scanner at the airport. "Your height. You're a good height and wouldn't have to hunch over like me."

Saved it.

She rests her hands on her hips. "Is it big enough for two people?"

My mouth falls open. Is she...did she just...are we...? "Uh, what do you mean?"

She points at the coop. "I was just wondering if we both have to get in there and clean it."

I shake my head and try to recover, since I was absolutely not thinking about us doing other things besides cleaning in there. "No, no. I cleaned it yesterday. We're good. Plus, you're not expected to do any of the farm chores."

"Okay. I'm happy to help, though. If you need anything, and I'm not busy, just let me know. I want as much of an immersive farm experience as you plan on offering the guests," she says, tucking her hair behind her ear and smiling at me.

That smile. I have two more months of this to look forward to. I've dated beautiful women. Caroline—my recent ex—was a smoke-show.

Unfortunately, that's about it. Where Avery seems kind and flexible, Caroline is edgy and rigid. But Avery seems as down to earth as she is easy on the eyes and for those reasons, I can't let that distract me.

I start plucking eggs from the hen boxes and setting them in the basket I grabbed.

Avery follows my lead. "I'm short like my mom, but once I put my brother, Justice, in a headlock when he called me a chicken nugget." She gasps and covers her mouth with her hand. "Sorry, I shouldn't say that kind of stuff here. It'll probably hurt their feelings. Sorry, Hennifer, just close your little chicken ears," she says to the brown chicken at her feet then turns to look at me. "Where are their ears anyway?"

I pause after setting another egg in the basket, glancing between Avery and the chicken that has only ever been called *the one that will die*. "Did you...uh, did you just call that chicken *Hennifer*?"

"Yes."

Oh, no. "I wouldn't do that if I were you."

"Do what?"

I peer around the yard outside the pen. "Name the chickens."

She juts out her hip and shakes her head with an innocent gaze. "What do you mean?"

I keep adding eggs to the basket like I'm not about to crush her heart. "Some of these chickens might just be chicken nuggets one day."

She stares off for a moment before saying, "I don't get it."

"Well..." I open and close my mouth. "One day we'll have to unalive about half of these chickens."

For some reason, the word "unalive" sounds a lot nicer than kill, slaughter, or chop up.

Her eyes widen, and she looks down at the brown chicken, like it's the farm's mascot. "Not Hennifer. You don't butcher all of them, right?"

The worry lines on her forehead make me want to run a no-kill campaign against myself. I'm second guessing our whole chicken operation. "We'll keep Hennifer."

She starts gathering eggs again then points at an all-white mother hen. "And Princess Lay-a?"

The chicken is sticking its head through the fence and trying to peck the ground outside the pen. It's giving me very few reasons to want to spare her life, too.

I shake my head and look at her. "How many chickens have you named already? We've been here for less than five minutes."

She adjusts the basket slung over her forearm. "Just a few."

"A few?"

"Yeah. That one over there," she points at a chicken with a mix of dark and light feathers, "is Dora the egg-splorer."

I roll my lips inward and bite them to keep from laughing out loud.

"And this chicken," she points to a hen still sitting in one of the boxes with yellowish coloring, "is Hilary Fluff."

My attempts at holding back a laugh are futile. The smile on my face grows so wide that I can't hold back my laughter. *Hilary Fluff!* "Those are good," I say, slapping my knee.

She beams and puffs out her chest a little more. "Thank you. I'm a big believer in naming animals. They need a sense of belonging, too."

I can tell she hasn't been around a farm much. Animals die. Sure, they're slaughtered, but they also die for other reasons. Hennifer could get picked off by a hungry predator, and Lord knows there are plenty of those in Montana. For Avery's sake, I hope that doesn't happen. Attachments to the animals are easy to come by and harder to handle. You're with them every day until you aren't. There's a natural order to things.

"Have you ever had any animals?" I ask her.

"Only one."

She doesn't elaborate, but I want to know what's making her frown. "What happened?"

"I killed him."

I keep picking up the eggs and placing them in my basket in a calm manner as she confirms exactly why I should have read her resumé. She's an animal serial killer, obviously.

Her laugh is clipped. "My goldfish, I mean."

"Oh. Right." I reach for her basket before she can murder my prized eggs and start walking back to the gate, tipping my head for her to follow. "I'm sorry to hear that. I'm pretty used to death out here, but you never forget the first time it happens."

The mood shifts and instead of laughing about chicken names, the conversation has turned morbid.

"When was your first time?" she asks, opening the chain link gate for me to exit. "Was it hard? The death, I mean. What kind of animal was it?"

I swallow and bow to exit the coop. "Our Lab. He was the farm dog here. Old and gray as can be by the time I was eight. My Gramps had him since he was a pup, and maybe seeing how torn up he was made it harder." We walk toward the farmhouse, and I point to the nearest barn where we keep the horses. "Found him over there along the side of the barn."

She rests a hand on my forearm, and it's as soft as I remember. "I'm sorry."

Her words are few and simple, but they're enough to cover me completely. It was so long ago, and I haven't thought about it in a while. I clear my throat, my eyes darting to anywhere but hers. Lifting the basket, I say, "We'll drop these off inside with Granny. She gets grumpy without her eggs and toast." I attempt a smile to lighten the mood.

She drops her hands, and the corners of her mouth curls up, too. "Okay."

I can't tell which would be worse: a grumpy Granny or never seeing one of Avery's smiles again.

Eight

Avery

We've been touring and working on the farm all morning, and I've spent an equal amount of time trying not to stare for too long. I'm overly conscious of the extra seconds I spend watching Wyatt stroke his beard or climb pretty much anything. The ladder leading to the second story in the barn where his jeans clung to his hips for dear life. The roof of the chicken coop that required his strong, calloused hands to hold tightly to, or the tree with the small kitten stuck in it that he had to rescue. Okay, that last one didn't really happen, but I can picture it with little effort. All of it will do it for me, apparently.

The way he shoveled the horse barn had me hot and sweaty and not because it's a sweltering day in this unrelenting summer heat. Every minuscule muscle in his forearms flexed and released in repetitive motions that had me gripping the stall door for support. It's dramatic and so unfair, which Tilly agreed when I whined to her via text.

And if that wasn't enough to remind me of how long it's been since I've seen a man perform manual labor, he drove a tractor—a *freaking* tractor—with the ease and precision of someone who's been doing it their entire life. And you know what? That makes it even sexier. Take my dollar bills and do with them as you please, because that show was worthy of an encore.

Granny packed us lunch and told him to take me to "The Tree" for a picnic lunch. Slay me already, will ya. Now we're sitting side-by-side in some sort of utility golf cart with wheels as tall as my hip that he called, *The Cougar.*

I'm not sure what's so special about this tree since the land is dotted with them. Most are higher up over the hills rather than the cavernous valley where the farmhouse is, but it all feels like the mountains to me since we're at such a high elevation.

I grip the side of The Cougar that's got to be going close to freeway speeds. I'm bouncing and jostling so much, I'll need to ice my boobs later.

Wyatt yells over the engine, "Almost there. You alright?"

I'm gripping the side handle and back of the seat tighter, as if this were a speedboat ready to flip upside down while biting my bottom lip and nodding instead of speaking. I should have asked for a life jacket. I'm sure the view is amazing, but I wouldn't know since I closed my eyes when we started ascending the hill miles and minutes ago.

I open my eyes as he slows the vehicle, and my weak stomach thanks him for it. As promised, when we crest the next hill, a huge tree stands looming over the lower plains. She's the mother of all trees and looks like she's outlived every breathing thing in this valley with her thick, sprawling branches. The green leaves covering her arms aren't leaves at all, but pine needles that huddle together in clusters.

We park behind it and hop out, though my legs are doing less hopping and more wobbling. Should I ask for a barf bag? It feels wrong to desecrate this place with my vomit. Before I can ask, my eyes are drawn up toward the sun shining through the gaps of her branches. Her presence is all-consuming among the few other trees on this ridge, with enough edges and points but plenty of width to give shade.

Standing straighter, I walk on my spaghetti noodle legs and pray I'll make it to the blanket Wyatt is laying out. "What kind of tree is this?" I ask through my raspy, unused voice.

"Ponderosa Pine," he says, shifting the blanket so it's partially in the shade. "State tree of Montana."

Looking up, I feel small. The view is the best I've seen, which is saying something since every view I see of Trapp Farms is better than the last. Cows spread across the back pasture while the horses swish their tails and chomp on grass nearest the house and the crops. All of their noises are quieter up here, but it's not silent. They're just...slower paced. A melody of wind pushes through the tall grass, creating whistling sounds in my ears. The flapping of wings can be heard above us, and pine cones fall at the base of the tree.

I inhale deeply and close my eyes, letting the sun caress my arms in its warmth. At this moment, I feel safe. Like the height of the tree, the magnitude of the rolling hills, and depth of the valley remind me of how much life there is, and for once, I'm not thinking about death.

I mean, other than just now.

"Are you hungry?" Wyatt asks, already sitting on the blanket and opening up the basket of food.

I sit beside him, greedy for the patch of sun near the edge of the blanket. "This is the most beautiful place I've ever been."

It's also the only place I've been outside the "Roughrider" state.

He follows my gaze. "I think so, too. The ocean was great, but this is home."

He hands me a sandwich, but I decline. I'm not hungry after the Extreme Scream ride I just endured. I'd rather talk and find out more about the farm anyway. "Have you always lived in Big Timber?"

"No, I moved to Billings after college and on to San Francisco after that."

"How long has your family owned the farm?" I ask.

"Since Granny and Gramps bought it sixty-two years ago," he says, opening the sandwich wrapper. "They were in their twenties with no farming experience. The farmhouse was the only structure on the acres of land, but they bought it with a vision in mind."

The story is so painfully sweet, it needs its own movie, or at least a spotlight on the Magnolia Network.

"So, they built everything else?" I try to hide the shock in my voice.

The only thing I've ever tried to build was a birdhouse when I was eight. I nailed scraps of wood together, painted it, and named it Bluebird Bungalow, but I was missing one important feature to make it habitable: an entrance.

"Yup. Gramps liked working with his hands."

I glance over at his fists gripping either side of his sandwich and wonder if this is the kind of work that creates those kinds of hands.

"What did you do for work in San Francisco?"

He pauses, sandwich suspended on the way to his mouth. "I worked for a tech company then started my own consulting firm."

"Oh yeah?"

He nods and catches me staring. "You sure you don't want any?"

I go back to studying the landscape instead of the bits of red in his beard. "Positive." I'm not hungry for food, just strong hands. "How long have you been back here?"

He swallows after his bite. "Three months."

I squint at him. "Seriously?"

He nods. "Yeah, I didn't have to move back." There's something distant about the way he says this. "But I did it to help Granny out with the farm."

His posture changes. It's more rigid than it was before and serves as enough of a warning not to press. At least for now.

"You and your Granny seem pretty close."

He nods. "We are. I spent every summer on the farm when I was growing up and came here a couple times a week during the school year, so when she mentioned needing more help around the farm I was...well, I was in a position to say yes, so I did."

He takes another bite, and I'm back to searching for his jaw beneath the scruff. "How did your grandpa die?" I ask, then quickly realize that this is a highly personal question. It's not that I'm overly comfortable talking about death, but after dealing with enough of it, my mouth knows no boundaries. "Sorry, that was really personal. You don't have to answer."

He stares out over the sprawling pastureland below us, the sun bouncing off his chocolate brown hair. "It's fine. It's good to talk about him. At least that's what my mom says."

I follow his line of sight. "Moms know these kinds of things," I say with a pang in my chest. This is probably what other moms would say but not mine who stopped talking about my brother the day after his funeral.

"They really do." He smiles to himself and then brushes dirt from his jeans. "Gramps had pancreatic cancer. It was a slow crawl to death until it wasn't. He was the rock we built our family on and losing him felt like losing a part of myself, too. It felt that way for everyone, but Granny the most. I know she misses him."

I swallow. Death is never easy. More or less time doesn't seem to lessen the pain. "I'm really sorry you lost him." I pause and gather my thoughts that scatter like the seed we fed the chickens. "I don't know you or your family well, but it seems like you're trying to do right by him with the farm."

He crosses his legs at the ankles and studies his lap. "Not sure how good I'm doing. Granny isn't all that excited about my ideas for the farm. But she needs the help, and she's letting me try. We don't really have a ton of options."

I pull my legs in and cross them as I bump his shoulder with mine. "What are some of your ideas?"

He swings his gaze to meet mine. "You really want to know?"

"I'm here to start a spa on a farm. That's one of your ideas. So, what are the others?" I press him.

He exhales, sets his sandwich off to the side, and straightens. "You can't laugh. Some of them aren't...typical."

I laugh then quickly cover my mouth with my hand. "I won't laugh...again."

He extends a pinky in my direction. "Promise me."

I hook my pinky with his, something I haven't done since I was a kid. Touching him like this is simple and small, but it feels like more. It feels like his finger is wrapping around my whole body. And based on the size of his hands, I don't think his finger would have a problem with that. "These have to be good if you're making me pinky promise," I say a little breathlessly.

I stare into his warm, hazel eyes, which teeter on the edge of green most days, until he drops my pinky like he just realized he'd been holding more. He looks away and gives a sharp nod that's accompanied by a laugh. "That was as good as a nondisclosure form."

I lift my chin. "Spill."

"Alright." He clears his throat. "The first step was getting the cabins ready for guests, and the spa."

"Mission accomplished," I add.

He holds up two fingers. "The second step was finding guests. Anyone can come stay at a farm, but I wanted guests who were looking for an experience. Social media is where I started advertising."

His hair lifts in a breeze and pushes through his thick beard as it rushes by. That lightness in him is back and evident in how he talks with his manual labor hands.

"Now the third step." He holds up a third finger. "Give them memories they won't forget."

I rub my palms together. "So…what do you have planned?"

His lips quirk as he lists them off. "Farm-to-table dinners, cow hugging, sleeping under the stars, and horseback riding to name a few." His eyes search somewhere far off. "I want people to see the magic of farm living. Especially people who make their living indoors, staring at work made by a man's hands."

The way he talks about these ventures has me excited, too. I've been on this farm for less than twenty-four hours and have taken some of the deepest breaths in a long time. That could also be because everyone on this farm still has a pulse.

I hold up a hand. "Wait." I chuckle. "Did you say, cow hugging?"

He tips his head back and lets out a deep, rumbling laugh. "It's a thing, I swear. I saw it on social media."

"Do you believe everything you see on the internet?"

He shakes his head. "No, but have you ever hugged a cow before?"

"Uh. No." But I've killed one.

Not really killed, but I do like hamburgers.

"Hugging animals can help both mental and physical health for a person, and I figured, I've got cows, might as well give it a shot. I already have two people signed up this weekend." He leans back on his hands again, bringing his gaze in line with mine.

I can't help but smile. Cow hugging sounds like one step short of putting them in tutus, but I'm here to try new things, so what the hell? "I'll try it."

His eyes lock with mine. "Really?"

I shrug. "I mean, I've never milked a cow so why not lay with one. It sounds oddly less intimate."

His upper lip curls. "Alright, I'll add you to the list then."

He pops a grape in his mouth that materialized from somewhere. I never saw, because I was too busy staring at his mouth. Get. A. Grip.

"You said you weren't hungry, but what about pie?" he asks.

His half-smile causes my stomach to do this weird swoopy thing. "I always have room for pie," I say.

"That's my girl," he says with a devilish grin.

I don't even think he noticed what he just said, but I did. My body does. My heart does. Everything in me reacts to his comment. *My girl.* I've never felt like anyone's girl. I've dated a few guys, but in all honesty, my last serious relationship was a couple years ago, and I had no business being in a relationship when I was still grieving. Needless to say, it was a train wreck. Quite literally since he was in a train wreck. Not a real one.

He was into model trains, and I accidentally broke the steam engine. It was downhill after that.

He sticks his hand in the picnic basket and pulls the pie tin out without tearing his gaze from mine. "Here you go."

I don't look away but accept the fork and tin and peel back the wrapper. My first bite is pure bliss, and I stare at him the whole time until my eyes roll back into my head and something very close to a moan comes out of my mouth. When I look back at Wyatt he isn't smiling anymore.

I cover my mouth. "This is really good. I'm not used to eating homemade pie like this."

He swallows hard, and his eyes drop to my lips, neck, shoulders—I don't really know, but I feel him everywhere. "Get used to it, because Granny likes to make sure there's always pie around."

I stab at another bite and savor the fruity notes of strawberry and the bitter snap of rhubarb. I could absolutely get used to homemade pie, and for the first time since I left home yesterday, I'm glad I said yes to coming here.

I'm not like Tilly who has visited forty-nine states and three countries all before she turned twenty-six. I'm twenty-five and haven't left the square miles that make up the city of Bismarck in more than five years. I tell myself it's because of the curse and while that's true, it's only partially so. I haven't wanted to leave, because going too far would mean I'd be moving on without my parents—without Justice. That's where he's buried and where I feel closest to him.

But here I am. Hundreds of miles away from all my responsibilities, and I'm okay. And the best part is, I'm still breathing.

Nine

Wyatt

"It's so important to do something every day that will make you happy."-Bob Ross

The smell of freshly cut hay and diesel fuel are some of my favorites from childhood.

As a kid, hay baling meant riding beside Gramps in the tractor, stereo tuned to the oldies, and the promise of a cold drink when we finished. As a teen, it meant manual labor and sweat, which were far less appealing. Now, it means seeing a job finished and getting to cool off in the irrigation sprinklers in the next field over.

It never gets old.

After our picnic earlier today, I left Avery to start work on the spa in the cabin's spare bedroom while I started on mowing rows of alfalfa. A job Ronny used to take on before I moved back. I shouldn't have insisted on doing it, but maybe there's a part of me that feels I've got something to prove. I can do this work, even if I'm rusty.

I park the tractor at the end of my last row and hop down as Ronny comes strolling out to meet me. "And what do you call that?" he says in his slow drawl.

I look back over my shoulder. "What?"

He makes a clicking sound with his mouth. "You suck at parking, man."

I scoff. "*You* suck at parking."

And apparently, I'm thirteen again.

He smiles, managing to keep his toothpick balanced between his lips. "Nice comeback. You been workin' on that one?"

Ronny looks like he could be a Jonas brother but with darker skin. And maybe he was since he was adopted at birth and has no ties to his birth parents. I can confirm he has no musical ability, however, and would have to be a backup singer with his mic turned off if he ever joined the boy band.

I ignore him and use the hem of my shirt to wipe the sweat pouring from my forehead, tipping my hat up in the process. The tractor is always ten degrees hotter, especially when the AC stops working like it did five years ago. No one ever got around to fixing it, and now I feel like a melted box of white chocolates.

I rest my hands on my hips. "So, what, you finished your chores and decided to come out here and heckle me?"

He answers my question with a question. I hate when he does this. "You worked up about somethin'?"

I look toward the sprinklers, wanting to be done with this conversation so I can go cool off. I'm crankier than a toddler who missed his nap. On top of the broken AC, I forgot my headphones, and the only radio station that would pick up included a banjo and an organ. Tell me how those two instruments go together.

I fist my hands at my hips now. "Nope."

"No blonde women vexing ya lately?" he asks, mimicking my posture.

We're facing each other, like we're about to draw our pistols and get to hollering about this being our town and needing to get out of here before one of us decides to shoot.

I don't have a pistol on me, but I wouldn't be surprised if Ronny did.

"Nope," I say again. My lips are sealed.

Hard work has always put my mind at ease, and after an hour in Avery's presence, I needed it. I was close to telling her about what happened in San Francisco. I never want to talk about it, or at least not to the women in my family who can be relentless, which is why my dad, Carl, and Ronny are the only ones who know everything.

Ronny tilts his head. "You sure?"

I nod once, keeping an eye on him. "I'm sure. Say, don't you have a concert to get to with your brothers or something?"

He walks closer, and I brace myself for the punch I expect him to throw. Instead, he passes me and claps me on the back. "That's next week, fool," he says. "I'll fix your shitty parking job now, though."

I grunt and wave him off as I head for the sprinklers. Ronny is my best friend. Growing up in a small town, we got to know our neighbors, even if there were acres separating us. I owe him a lot for coming here to help Granny while I was in the city. He took on most of the work after Gramps died while helping his dad on their cattle ranch, too. Granny says that Ronny comes from *good people*, and even if Ronny looks nothing like his parents, Esther and Merv, he inherited their work ethic and heart.

And Merv's affinity for wearing large belt buckles.

The smell of dried hay reaches all the way to the barn as I pass by it. I can feel the pricks of hay stabbing into me as it clings to my sweat-slicked skin. It's the worst part about mowing. The best part is taking my shirt off afterward. Tipping my hat off, I pull up at the hem and tug my t-shirt off in a quick sweep while tucking part of it into my back pocket. Bits of grass stay stuck to my skin, but my eyes are locked on the rotating sprinkler calling my name with every click and sputter.

I don't even notice Avery sitting on the back porch until she calls out to me. "You don't like wearing shirts, do you?"

Her ivory legs hang off the side of the porch, swinging back and forth like a lighthouse guiding me home. I'm sucked into her vortex, the route to the sprinkler completely forgotten.

"I finished mowing and was heading to take a run through the sprinkler," I say pointing at the next best thing to a water park right behind me.

She looks between me and the sprinkler. More like my bare chest and somewhere that isn't my bare chest.

"Why not shower?" she asks, pressing her palms onto the porch beside her thighs.

I brush a few pieces of grass off my stomach and smirk as her eyes follow. "I am showering."

I walk closer to the porch and inhale the sweet scent of lavender surrounding her. The floral scent follows her everywhere, clinging to her hair, skin, and clothes. I can't help but take a hit any time I'm near her. Damn, she's trouble.

I comb out my beard and toss my reservations to the wind. "Have you ever run through a sprinkler before?"

She shields her eyes with her hand and shakes her head. "Not one that size."

Her lips are pulled up in a sweet smile. It's sickening really, what that smile does to me.

I tip my head and start walking backward, needing to cool off more than ever. "Let's go."

Her smile drops. "No. I've gotta get back to work. There are guests coming in four days."

"I do, too," I say. "That's why we have to run."

Tugging my shirt from my back pocket, I toss it onto the porch beside her, then send my hat flying like a boomerang to join it.

"Ew!" she yelps.

I smile mischievously and continue walking backward.

She leaps to her feet. "I can't stay here now that your sweaty shirt is taking up all the oxygen."

"Better hurry then," I say before turning to run toward the water.

I barrel into the cool mist that drenches me in seconds, sighing with how good it feels before turning and running back through it. Avery stops at the edge of the water spray and hesitates.

"Come on!" I wave to her then push the wet hair out of my face. "It feels great."

She looks down at her boots, cut-off shorts, and t-shirt with Bob Ross' face on it. "I'm not really that hot."

If only she knew.

Avery's the kind of woman that doesn't know how beautiful she is. Others might skip over her because she isn't flashy in how she dresses or eccentric in how she acts. She's organic and homegrown. One look into those ice blue eyes and danger signs are flashing in front of me.

She wanted to run through this sprinkler, but something stopped her, and now I can almost see the wheels in her mind backpedaling. Striding back to her, I wipe off the drips of water rushing down my face. On instinct she takes a step back when she sees I'm not stopping.

"Oh no you don't," she says, holding up a hand.

I keep moving forward. "I swear it'll feel so good you'll want to do this every day."

She's shaking her head and backing up faster now like she might run.

But I'm faster.

I snag her by the waist, and she yelps loudly as I run with her over my shoulder back into the wet spray. It drenches us both again in seconds, but Avery has stopped screaming. Now, she's laughing.

She's laughing so hard, I set her on her feet and study her face to make sure she's alright. Throwing her head back, she spins in a full circle. Laughing. I'm laughing now, too. I don't know what's so funny, but whatever it is, it's hilarious.

I'm breathing hard and standing beneath the spray of water as we hold our stomachs and drown in our laughter.

"This is amazing!" she yells, hands still raised in the air.

I have to yell over the drone of the sprinkler. "Worth it, huh?"

"YES!" She spins in place again and again, tilting her chin to the sky, arms wide and eyes closed.

Seeing her like this feels like I'm catching a glimpse of something rare. As if this picture of her, with her face to the sky, isn't how she always acts, even though it looks so natural. Her face is painted in joy, and that small hesitation I'd seen led to this.

My gaze is stuck on her.

Her feet squish inside her waterlogged boots as she trudges over to me. "You were right. It does feel good."

The way her cheeks bloom with color as I start rubbing my arms, chest, and stomach makes me smile. I'm only doing it so I have something to do with my hands. But I like knowing I can create that color on her skin, even if I won't do anything about it. There's water dripping down my face and beard, making it hard not to squint, but I focus on getting all the stray bits of hay off my body.

Her clothes are soaked through, like my jeans, but the outline of her petite form is nothing like mine and causes my skin to grow hot. Her t-shirt is now plastered to her body, the peaks and curves of her figure highlighted even more.

I count to five then force my eyes away so I don't go making another mistake with a woman that will blow up in my face. There hasn't been a successful relationship in my past yet, and I'm not about to ruin everything with a woman I hired to work for me.

She shivers and crosses her arms over her chest for both of our sakes.

"Race you back to the porch?" I ask, scrubbing a hand down my face and offering her my smallest finger. "Loser has to do the dishes tonight."

She studies my pinky finger. "Is this how you make all your deals, Mr. Trapp?"

"Wyatt," I say with a wink. It was probably more of a blink to keep the drips of water from falling into my eyes. "And only with my employees."

The glint in her eyes slightly fades as I say this, and I want it back.

I raise my pinky higher.

She hooks hers with mine and says, "Deal."

I don't let go right away; she doesn't, either. It's a stare down, and also, her skin feels nice. We squint at each other for seconds longer before she rips her hand from mine and takes off. I count to five and watch her race back through the water to the porch.

"Three...four...five," I say, then take off running after her.

She's fast, but I'm highly motivated to get out of dish duty, so I pump my arms harder and quicken my pace. My wet jeans and heavy work boots aren't making things easy on me, but as the field turns to grass, I catch up to her and cut her off, pulling ahead. I've had my fair share of foot races with Ronny out here and know how to play dirty. I beat him in a race from the farmhouse to the cow pasture just yesterday.

I'm panting hard as I stop at the edge of the porch where I found her earlier, resting my hands on my knees.

She slows down, chest heaving with the exercise, and weakly shoves my shoulder. "Cheater."

I straighten at the sound of that word on her tongue and the fact it's directed at me. I want to tell her it isn't true, she's got it all wrong. But instead, all I can manage saying is, "What?"

I'm instantly pulled back to the day in San Francisco I haven't been able to forget for three months. Did Ronny tell her? How else would she know? My chest rises and falls even faster from the added adrenaline coursing me. *I'm going to kill him.*

With hands on her hips, she glares at me and laughs. "You cut right in front of me! I had to slow down."

"Oh," I huff with relief. Ronny's life has been spared. For now.

I run both hands through my hair and down my beard, squeezing out some of the excess water.

The porch door swings open and Granny steps out. "Where's your shirt, boy? Don't tell me it's another one of those thirst traps."

"That was Ronny, not me." I convinced him to make a short video for our social media to go along with the rebrand I still need to tell her about. Looking down at all of my bare skin and back at Granny with a quizzical expression. "How do you know what a thirst trap is anyway, Granny?"

She huffs and produces one of my t-shirts from behind her back, tossing it down to me. "Anyone with wifi knows what they are. You look just like all those half-naked men slicked up with oil and doing just about anything in slow motion."

"Exactly," Avery whispers loudly, and we both look at her. She holds up both hands like a football goal post. "Forget I said that."

Granny goes back inside, letting the screen door slam against the frame behind her. Materializing again, she tosses a towel down to Avery, which she catches eagerly.

"The only difference between ya is the beard," Granny continues, lifting her brows at me.

Only a few steps separate us, but with Granny looking down at me, I feel like a boy again, red-faced and shy, like I'd been caught kissing a girl behind the hay bales.

I palm my beard. "The beard stays."

She waves me off. "I'm startin' dinner."

"I'll help."

Granny and I look at Avery again, the words having jumped out of her mouth before Granny had even finished speaking hers.

"I like making dinner," she says, clutching the towel to her chest.

I take a step closer to Avery and borrow the corner of her towel to wipe the water from my face. And yeah, maybe I dabbed at my chest a bit, enjoying the way her mouth hung open and her eyes followed the movement of my hands.

Smirking, I drop the towel and walk backward. "Avery has some dishes to do after dinner, too."

Granny shakes her head, but I turn and sprint off before she can say anything else.

Making promises I can't keep are one thing, flirting is another.

Ten

Avery

"Don't forget to make all these things individuals—all of them special in their own way."-Bob Ross

The next day passes faster than my goldfish did. I may have underestimated the amount of work and planning it would take to get this spa off the ground and ready for guests. I brought everything spa-like from home including my massage table, aromatherapy, salts, scrubs, and enough sandalwood candles to start my own multi-level marketing business. After a full day of organizing and setting up, I figured the rest of my needed supplies could be picked up in town.

I was wrong.

Town is about the length and width of the farmhouse. When Wyatt drove me through the stretch of buildings, I only had to blink for it to be over. There are a few shops, including a thrift store and post office that doubles as a supply store, as well as a handful of restaurants. Rounding out the tour was a park at the edge of town and a hardware store directly across the street from the grocery store.

Wyatt parks his old truck along the curb in front of the grocery store parking lot, and I grip the handle to try and get out, but it doesn't let me.

I try again.

And again.

Then again, in case it's been lying to me.

"Forgot this door likes to stick." Wyatt stretches in front of me to jiggle the handle and shoves it open with little effort.

His tanned arm grazes my skin and shocks me, as if someone set off a firecracker in the cab of this truck rather than an accidental brush of skin. It's a new and electric feeling that I immediately want to recreate after it ends. *More, please.*

"There you go," he says before exiting out his side.

Swallowing hard, I try to forget the way he smells, like earth, wind, and fire all at once.

"He's your *boss*," I mumble to myself.

It's become my other full-time job to remind myself of this. I've had to move Heaven and Hell to be here, and I don't want to mess this up in the first week. We have guests coming soon, and I need to focus on giving them the best possible experience so I can remain employed for the rest of the summer and secure a future running my own spa. No big deal. As long as no one dies and I don't fall for my boss, I'll call it a success.

I have to pull my legs off the brown leather bench seat, like I'm peeling a banana since the truck doesn't have AC, before sliding out with a thud on the pavement and slamming the door behind me. The interior of the truck is fifty shades of brown. Brown carpets, brown dashboard, brown seats, and brown steering wheel. But the outside is tan and red with rust spots, dents, and scrapes. Wyatt said it belonged to his Gramps, which explains a lot since it was like stepping into a time machine headed straight for the seventies.

My upper lip instantly starts to sweat. Today, we've reached too-hot-to-function temps, and shorts and a t-shirt feel as though I'm wearing a parka. Once we get back, I'll be taking my twenty-third shower of the day and lying naked on the tile kitchen floor.

Wyatt rounds the back of the truck and joins me, keeping a respectable distance while I fan myself.

We've taken two steps along the sidewalk before a woman pops her head out of a small bakery, like one of those whack-a-mole games at the arcade. Thankfully, I startle instead of bopping her on the head.

Her smile is bright and overly cheerful. "Wyatt! How are you?"

Wyatt cements his feet to the pavement and tucks his hands in his pockets. "Good, Helen. You?"

If she startled him, he doesn't show it. Maybe he's used to these surprise greetings.

"Doing alright," says the older woman with gray hairs combed through her black ones. "Who's this?"

Wyatt takes a step away from me, as if our proximity revealed too much and keeps his hands locked in the self-imposed restraints of his jeans. "Avery."

Her smile drops as she does a quick scan of me. "Avery."

No *hello, hi, nice to meet you*. Just *Avery*. I'm really wishing I chose a t-shirt that didn't have Grumpy Cat printed across the front and scowling at her. But there's something in her slight frown that makes me want to give her a list of all the reasons why she would like me. I'm a great friend. Trustworthy, kind, and helpful. But instead, I lift my hand in a wave. "Hi, I'm Avery."

Pretty sure my name has been well established.

I need to remember what my therapist told me before I left: *you won't be everyone's friend*. At the time she said this, I laughed in her face. She didn't laugh. I'm starting to understand what she meant now.

Helen looks between us, a million questions racing across her features, but she only asks one. "What are you doing here?"

The question is blunt, causing me to momentarily stutter while trying to come up with an answer. This is a pass/fail exam, and my wide smile subtly begging her to like me isn't working.

Wyatt morphs from a bearded Clark Kent to Superman and saves me. "She's helping me out on the farm this summer."

"Oh," Helen says. "All summer?"

Wyatt nods but doesn't elaborate. I'm not sure if that's because he'd have to admit he's trying to start a spa at the farm, or if he just wants to be done with this conversation as much as I do.

Her gaze yo-yos between us. "Well, we just made some fresh cinnamon rolls. Want one?"

Always yes.

"Oh, I probably shouldn't." Wyatt pats his stomach that I know for a fact is flat and hard. A cinnamon roll would go straight to his pinky toe.

The smell of risen dough covered in butter with brown sugar and enough cinnamon to warm my entire body is incredibly tempting. I almost tell Helen that I'll take one, even if Wyatt doesn't.

But Helen's smile is loudly shouting *outsider beware*, even when her lips aren't moving. There's a good distance separating Wyatt and me, but Helen seems to be calculating the exact number of inches in her head, like a master mathematician.

"You sure? They're Mabel's special recipe," she says with a wink.

Wyatt opens and closes his mouth like a guppy fish. "I can't," he says, rocking back on his heels. "We're just here to pick up supplies, and then we have to get back. More chores to do."

Mabel? Who's she?

I let out a clipped laugh, as if what Wyatt said was funny. It wasn't, but I laugh when I'm nervous, and I can't help wondering why Wyatt is doing everything in his power to not step foot in that bakery. Does it double as the town jail or something?

"Okay, then," Helen says, reaching to open the swinging door again. "Next time." She points a finger gun at him, and Wyatt's smile fades, as if it were a real one. "Nice to meet you, Avery," she says.

The way my name sounds coming out of her mouth is like honey coating a pickle. Sweet on the outside and sour in the middle.

Wyatt nods politely and tips his hat while I wave a hesitant goodbye. Maybe I should leave that list with her. I'm confident I could sway her into liking me.

Wasting no time, Wyatt picks up the pace after that short but loaded interaction. He peers once over his shoulder, and I follow his line of sight and notice Helen in the window, staring after us. *It's the Wrangler jeans*

Wyatt's wearing, I tell myself. It's always the Wranglers. He wears them better than anything else in his closet, because he owns nothing else. At least, I've never seen him wear anything but his favorite pair of jeans that are now my favorite.

It can't be the fact I'm a new face in a small town, or how I've somehow landed myself on the show *Farmchelor* without even knowing it. I've placed a target on my back for all the other eligible women to hate me.

No, it's gotta be the Wranglers.

Wyatt finally slows when he's satisfied with the distance we've put between us and the bakery. "Helen's been trying to set me up with her daughter, Mabel, since we were in middle school."

"Oh." So, she really was throwing darts at me.

"Yeah. We went to one dance together our senior year, but to Helen it was as good as signing a marriage certificate," he says with a shudder.

I hold back a laugh as a couple linking arms passes us, waving at Wyatt. Does everyone in this town know him? Is this what living in a small town is like? Always running into people you know and staring down your nose at those you don't?

"She's usually not that...cold. But I'm guessing she thought you were..." He shakes his head. "Someone else."

A man walks toward us, and Wyatt tips his chin in hello. He introduces me and explains he's Ronny's dad, Merv. I want to ask Wyatt who he was about to mention before he put on his best town mayor impersonation, but we chat with Merv for a while before crossing the street to the hardware store, and the moment is forgotten.

Everyone we come across inside the hardware store is nice but looks at me like I have a third eye I'm not aware of. Dressed for farm work in my boots and Daisy Dukes, I thought I would blend in, but there's a lot less blending and a lot more...smearing.

"Caroline?" an employee with a name tag reading "Bob" asks.

"Avery," I correct as we step up to the counter.

"Avery?" he questions, then his eyes go wide, as if he realizes his mistake.

I peer up at Wyatt beside me who is slowly shaking his head, eyes just as wide as Bob's.

"Oh," Bob says. "Huh."

Feeling wildly unsure what's happening, I place a hand on Wyatt's forearm. "I'm going to go look around."

He and Bob both stare at my hand and take a moment of silence for the blatant mistake I just made. I look down, too, and snap my hand away with another nervous laugh as I back away. If I could just stop touching my boss that would be great.

Scurrying down the nearest aisle, I bypass potting soil, bird feeders, and bags of seed until I reach the back of the store. I can breathe better back here where no one is watching me with binoculars, like I'm a rare species they've never seen before. It's my first time in town, and I wonder if going with Wyatt was a mistake.

Shaking my head, I focus on my task. I need to find some kind of bin for the foot soaks I'm planning to offer with the pedicures. We had actual massage chairs attached to soaker tubs with jets at my old spa, but that isn't exactly in the budget. I have a small stipend that could rival the cost of dinner out for two with drinks and dessert, and I need to make the most of it.

Watering cans, hoses, and spray nozzles line the back shelves, which all deal with water, so I must be getting close. As I search, my eyes glaze over and my mind wanders. *Caroline*? Who is she? Another one of the *farmchelorettes* I'll be arm wrestling for Wyatt's attention? Based on the way Wyatt did everything short of waving his arms in the air to stop Bob from continuing down that conversational path, I'd say he doesn't like to talk about her.

"Hey."

I startle when I hear Wyatt's voice. I'm so jumpy today but then again that's not really anything new. If it isn't obvious that I was just thinking about him, the heat in my cheeks deposits that check for me.

"Hi, I was just looking for something to use for pedicures."

"Pedicures?" he asks.

"Yeah, I thought it would be a nice addition," I explain. He looks surprised, and I wonder if I should have run this by him first. "Should I...do you prefer me to ask about these things first?"

He shakes his head. "No, no. I was just impressed by your idea."

I play with the ends of my hair. The chance of owning a spa one day has taken up enough of my brain power over the years to provide electricity for an entire city. I have so many lists for supplies, ideas, and services listed in my dream journal. I couldn't just let go of all my ideas when I set flame to my vision board. Seven years worth of plans are in there that I've been waiting to try out. But instead of admitting this, I twirl my hair round and round until it coils too tightly around my finger and gets stuck.

I tug my finger until it's free of the finger cuff I put it in and shift on my feet. "Uh, yeah. I have a few ideas."

A bemused smile plays on his lips as he takes a wide stance and crosses his arms. "Tell me some."

My mouth falls open. He has every right to know. He is my boss after all, but it feels vulnerable sharing them when he has the power to shoot them down. In my head, I'd always been my own boss, making these decisions without anyone else's input.

He senses my hesitation. "I told you some of mine, remember?"

"Well..." I turn and face the back shelf to give myself something else to look at as I pretend not to freak out. "Other than the massages and pedicures, I wondered if we could find something large enough to create an outdoor soaker tub. You know, take the whole idea of nature bathing to the next level."

On my old vision board, the nature bath was going to look out over the water with storm vases full of pebbles from the beach and lit candles. But there aren't any beaches in Montana, and the next best thing I have to work with is a forest.

I bite my bottom lip and wait for him to say something. He doesn't. Not right away, at least. I steal a glance at him, but he's already staring at me.

He nods and drops his arms to his sides. "I like it. Here, follow me."

His stride is twice as long as mine, and I have to shuffle quickly to catch up. He heads to the back garden area, weaving through so many plants I couldn't name if my life depended on it until he reaches a side wall with large, metal bins stacked against it. They could easily fit an adult...or two.

Waving his hand in front of the oval-shaped bins, he asks, "Will a feeding trough work?"

WE'RE BACK ON the farm after our town adventure, and I'm exhausted. Along with the trough, I spotted a couple metal bins on our way out that were the perfect size for foot soaking tubs, so I grabbed those and a bag of Dot's pretzels. I was hungry and regretted leaving town without a cinnamon roll. The smell of them is still stuck in my nostrils.

I thought I'd have energy when we got back to plant some of the flowers Bob loaded into the back of Wyatt's truck—an apology for calling me by the wrong name, I'm guessing. But all I was capable of doing was watching Wyatt unload it all. That activity was sponsored by Wranglers, and I'd like to thank all of the hardworking people who created them. Well done, team, you have my vote.

With the guests arriving on Friday—three short days from now—the pressure to get everything ready is real. Yet, the horrid scent wafting off me was more important. I grunt and roll onto my back where I threw myself on the bed, post shower. It's hot. Every window is open, but it doesn't stop my clothes and bedsheets from clinging to me like duct tape.

The sound of a chainsaw starts up, and I bolt upright. "Leatherface."

My heart is beating wildly, and I settle a hand over it to try and calm down. It's the middle of the day. There's no way he'd be out in broad daylight. Maybe Ronny's just chopping something again. That's probably it.

I slowly pad toward the kitchen and peer out the window above the sink. Sure enough, Wyatt is out back cutting a thin piece of wood over a couple of saw horses.

Shirtless.

"Come on," I groan.

Pulling the back door open, I stand on the porch as he bends over the chainsaw that is really just an electric saw and pushes it slowly through the piece of wood with goggles covering his eyes.

He reaches the edge, and a chunk of the wood falls to the grass, the whir of the saw quieting.

"What are you making?" I ask as I sit on the top step.

He looks over at me, the goggles making him look like a house fly. His beard tugs up in a smile as he shoves them to the top of his head. "I'm making a privacy fence for the nature tub." Standing the piece of wood up, I notice two other sheets are leaning against a tree, waiting to be cut.

In the hour that I laid flat on my back, he was out here working hard and looking like *that*. New paver stones are positioned on the ground in close intervals, leading to a smattering of them snuggled together with the trough resting on top. The flowers I didn't want to plant are sitting beside different pots of varying sizes already half-full of soil.

The cabin backs up to a canopy of trees with streams of light filtering through leaves and branches, casting shadows on the ground. It's secluded enough to make it feel like you're the only one out here but close enough to the cabin to make it a short walk. Though there are half-finished projects scattered around the yard, I can already see the vision I had that Wyatt made happen.

"Wow. You've been busy. Can I get you some water, maybe a whole pitcher of lemonade—"

"Got your tree round," Ronny cuts in, rolling a large chunk of wood around the side of the cabin.

I stand and brush off my shorts. "What's this for?"

Ronny rolls it to the side of the tub and props it upright.

"We had some rounds of wood beside the horse barn that I thought we could put to use," Wyatt explains as Ronny walks closer. "The guests will need a place to put their drink, maybe a candle or two."

Ronny offers Wyatt his knuckles to pound. "Got two more in my truck."

"You really are full of ideas," I say, jutting out a hip and hoping I look thirty and flirty, even if I'm only twenty-five and quirky.

Ronny claps Wyatt on the back. "Once you get him started, he doesn't stop."

I nod and he does, too, both of us prolonging this goodbye into next year.

Ronny chuckles and elbows him. "I've got work to do while you both do...this."

Wyatt produces a shirt from his back pocket and uses it to wipe the sweat off his neck and brow. "I should get back to it as well."

I wave to Ronny as he heads back around the side of the cabin, and Wyatt goes back to cutting. The long lines, ridges, and bulges he has on his body are in all the right places, and my mouth is now full of sand.

Looks like I'll be the one needing that vat of lemonade to cool off.

Eleven

Wyatt

"You can do anything here—the only prerequisite is that it makes you happy."-Bob Ross

N eed anything else before I head up to bed?" I ask Granny after washing the dinner dishes.

She doesn't have a dishwasher and wouldn't let me install one when I updated the sink and faucet. She says doing things the slow and simple way is how we stay humble. I think it's just because I'm the one doing them. Either way, I still try to help with a lot of the household chores as often as I can.

"Yes. One more thing." Granny leans against the counter and crosses her arms while I dry my hands. "The girl."

I know who she's talking about, but I still give her a hard time. "Which one?"

She glowers at me. "You know who I'm talkin' about, boy. Don't make me spell it out for ya."

"Granny." I toss the towel beside the sink and sigh. "Just say what you gotta say about Avery."

"She's pretty."

I nod once, gripping the edge of the sink behind me. "She is."

Though, I won't admit just how much I think so.

"She's funny, too," Granny adds.

And sweeter than a puppy dog. So kind and gentle, not to mention the right amount of quirky. But none of these thoughts will see the light of day.

"Granny..."

She holds up both hands in surrender. "I'm just pointing out the obvious."

"Well, maybe you shouldn't point. It's rude." I need to assure her of this now before she gets any more ideas and passes them off to my mom and Stace like a contagious disease. "Nothing's gonna happen. She's working for me."

I say this as a blanket statement that I hope will cure all.

"Are you still hung up on that city girl?" she asks.

The mention of Caroline makes my blood run cold.

"No. I told you, we're over."

She tilts her head to the side. "Are you, though?"

"Yes."

"So, why'd she call the house today askin' for ya?"

My frown deepens, and the counter behind me is the only thing keeping me steady. "She called?"

Granny nods slowly, twisting her lips to the side.

"Why didn't you tell me earlier?" I ask.

I would've disconnected the landline Granny still insists on paying for and shoved it down the garbage disposal. Or threw it in the wood pile to use as kindling for the next bonfire. There are one-hundred-and-two different ways to destroy the reminder of Caroline running through my head. A woman who can't seem to let me go.

Granny puts her hands on her hips. "You were gone all day, and Avery and Ronny were here for dinner. This is the first chance I've had."

I rub my eyes with the palms of my hands. "What did she want?'

"She left a voicemail." Granny points to the landline that's now linking me to my ex-girlfriend.

Three months has been enough time for me to figure out that Caroline was a mistake. A two-year mistake that cost me a lot. I should've known she'd try calling. When I blocked her number she started sending emails until I blocked those, too. But then she decided to create another email address and beg me to read her long-ass messages.

I didn't.

I couldn't.

Having my life get thrown into a bottomless pit took up too much of my thoughts. Then, there was the big question of what do I do now? A bitter ex-girlfriend was the last thing I cared to worry about.

Granny pushes off the opposite counter and straightens. "Do you want to know what I think?"

I huff out a laugh. "No. But I know you're gonna tell me anyway so go ahead."

She shuffles closer and pats the side of my shoulder. "Cut the ties so you can create new knots."

I exhale. Granny knows the hell I went through in the city but not all of it. I don't regret the decisions I made after everything fell apart, but it would be nice if they didn't follow me. Granny's right, though. Not about tying new knots. I'm not sure I'm ready for that. But I need to cut the line linking me to Caroline and make it clear. I can't ignore her anymore and hope she'll go away.

She hasn't.

She won't.

I stare at the landline for a beat, debating if I should call her now or later. Checking the time on the stove, I determine it's too late to call now. I'm exhausted after the trek into town and building the tub area for Avery. My mind needs to be sharper than a double-edged sword when I take on Caroline.

Granny left the kitchen to sit in her favorite chair in the living room, turning on an old episode of Jeopardy so she can yell at all the half-wits on TV who miss a question. "Don't tell her I say hi when you call her," Granny calls back to me.

I bite back a smile. "I won't."

I know she's just being protective. I'm her only grandson, and she'd do anything for me. That includes letting me live here, help around the farm, and try to make a living out of it so we don't have men in suits knocking on our door, threatening to take the farm.

"Oh, and since the good Lord dropped Avery on your lap, boy, you best be thanking him in your prayers tonight," she says.

I shake my head but also send up a quick thanks. Being thankful isn't a crime.

I finish tidying the kitchen, putting leftovers away, prepping the coffee pot for the morning, and wiping off the counters. Grabbing a glass of water, I pause and stare at the phone once more.

I'll call Caroline tomorrow before the guests arrive. Or next week.

Maybe the one after that.

"GOOD MORNING!" A chorus of overly cheerful voices says as I shuffle into the kitchen.

I rub the sleep from my eyes. "Stace? Mom? What are you both doing here?"

"It's the big day!" Stace says.

"You make it sound like I'm getting married," I grumble.

Stace shrugs. "Oh, we'll make sure to be a lot more annoying when that happens."

I rub my bare chest, wishing I would have known people would be here, so I could've thrown a shirt on. At least I'm wearing pants today.

Mom wraps me in a hug. "I'm so proud of you, sweetie! Your dad is, too, but he had a dentist appointment and couldn't be here this morning."

"Bryan, too," Stace adds. "Not a dentist appointment. He's at work. Jack and Annie are at camp."

"You didn't have to come." My eyes aren't even fully open, and the smell of freshly brewed coffee is calling to me. "Did you get me a trophy with my name on it, though?"

Stace shoves my arms. "You have to earn it first. No handouts, you know that. By the way, I like the sign at the front of the drive. Has Granny seen it?"

There's a twinkle in her eye as she asks, and I shoot her a glare. "Yes, as a matter of fact she has."

"And?"

I shrug and run a hand through my hair. "She loves it."

Love is a strong word. But Granny didn't ask me to take it down so…

"We brought breakfast." Stace flips open the recognizable lid from Happy Donuts. "I got one of every flavor."

I sidestep her and reach for the coffee pot and a mug right above it. "That's not breakfast. That's dessert."

I pour the dark liquid into my favorite mug. The one that Granny had made for me for Christmas last year with her face on it that says: I love my Granny.

"You could use a little dessert, honey. Have you lost weight?" Mom pinches my side.

"Ouch!" I yelp. "No. It's called working out."

Stace grabs a donut and starts talking with her mouth full. "Are you lifting cows or something?"

I huff. "There's no way anyone could lift a cow." I bring the mug to my lips, inhaling the steam. "I lift chickens, as in plural." And only on Wednesdays.

The other days of the week, I use actual weights I have stored in the garage. At least I did before farm work kept me on my feet from morning to night.

Stace rolls her eyes. "I'm going to need to see that." She moves to pour herself a cup of coffee. "Farm life looks good on you little brother."

It's my turn to roll my eyes. Moving back to the farm was Stace's idea and backed by every other family member after drawing options from a hat that all said the same thing. When things fell apart worse than a taco that's too full, I couldn't make any more decisions, so I delegated.

Enter Stace with her always-makes-the-right-decision energy, and she recommended I come back home for a spell. It turned out to be the best decision I could have made, even if I couldn't see it then. But I'm not about to tell her that.

Mom fiddles with the gold cross necklace she never takes off. "How are you feeling about today? Is everything ready? Are you ready?"

I know she's been worried about me. I wasn't exactly in the best mental space when I moved back here and thrust myself into turning the farm into a money-making machine again. I'd just lost everything and couldn't afford to feed myself, let alone live on my own.

I take a sip of coffee before answering. "I'm feeling good. I'll get the chores finished this morning and spend the afternoon getting the final touches completed. The guests will start arriving around three."

"And Avery?" Stace asks.

I pluck a donut from the box and take a bite, talking with my mouth full like she did. "What about her?"

Mom crosses her arms. "Didn't I teach you two any manners?"

Stace takes another bite and starts talking. "No, we're wild animals."

Mom rolls her eyes and sighs loudly.

Stace talks louder. "So, is Avery busy with massages all day, or will she be helping you?"

I give her my back and face the sink, washing the eggs on the counter but don't make eye contact with Stace. She's studying me more intently than she would a *Where's Waldo* book. "She's got one person booked for a massage tomorrow, but other than that, I'm not expecting her to do chores or anything," I explain.

"I like her," Stace says.

I crank the stovetop temperature to quit-asking-me-these-questions. "I know you do."

"I'll like her, too," Mom adds since she hasn't even met Avery, yet.

I scoff. "I'm not surprised. You both like any single woman in my vicinity."

Stace gasps. "Not true. I wasn't a fan of Caroline."

I cut her a look over my shoulder. The kitchen is silent apart from the crackle of the oil in the pan. I turn around fully and study their expressions. They look guilty with gazes studying knicks on the floor.

"You didn't like Caroline?" I ask Stace.

Stace lifts her head to meet my eyes for a brief moment then shakes her head slowly.

I exhale. "Mom?"

She doesn't answer. I turn back to the stove, set my donut down, and start cracking eggs, one by one, into the sizzling pan. I've lost my appetite, but the motions are giving me something to do. I thought they liked Caroline. Sure, they hadn't been in my business as much as they typically had been when I dated someone, but I thought that was because of the distance between us. I'd been in San Fran while they were here, unable to regale me with reasons why they approved or disapproved of the people I dated.

I speak to the eggs, like they can hear me. "I didn't think you both felt that way. Does Granny—"

"What about me?" asks Granny, standing in the kitchen doorway forcing us all to look over at her. "You talkin' about me like I'm not here?"

"Of course not, Gran," Mom says. "We were talking about..." she looks between Granny and me. "Well, we were saying..."

Granny waves her hand. "Go on, spit it out."

I flip the eggs while Mom fumbles to explain. Plating the food, I whip around and face Granny. "They didn't like Caroline. I mean, before we broke up. Did you?"

Granny shakes her head. "Hell no."

"What?"

"Don't act so surprised," she says. "You weren't crazy about her, either."

I hand the plate of eggs to Mom. "What do you mean? Of course I liked her."

We were together for two years. You don't date someone you don't like for that long. There were things about us that made sense, though all of those reasons seemed to disintegrate when I put some distance between me and the city.

Granny shuffles into the kitchen with her slippers and fuzzy robe. "I didn't say you didn't like her. I said you weren't crazy about her. There's a difference."

"I saw it, too," Stace pipes in. "You only brought her home twice, but it was clear."

I rub the back of my neck. "We both worked in the city in another state. It wasn't easy to get home."

Stace holds up her pointer finger. "Correction. You worked in the city. She was a stay-at-home girlfriend."

"She was an influencer." I don't know why I'm defending my ex. Maybe because I don't want to admit to my family, or even myself, that I picked someone like Caroline: self-absorbed and too selfish to notice or care. Not to mention a cheater.

Stace shakes her head. "She was trying to become one. There's a big difference."

I sigh, pinching the bridge of my nose. "Look, I know Caroline was…"

"Stuck up?" Stace offers.

Mom winces. "Difficult?"

Granny grabs a donut. "A hussy?"

"Granny!" I yell.

"Oh, don't act like you all weren't thinking the same thing," Granny says.

I scrub a hand over my face, hoping when I open my eyes again, I'll have teleported somewhere else. I wasn't expecting all of this honesty this early in the morning, and I don't think I'm handling it well. The three most important women in my life didn't like my ex. Add that to the fact they didn't think I was crazy about her. Being crazy about someone isn't always a good thing. You can get lost in them—caught up in a whirlwind romance that doesn't stand a chance of lasting. Caroline was a practical fit for me.

I pivot on my heel and lean against the counter behind me. "Why didn't any of you say anything? I was…" My voice trails off, but I shake my head and keep talking. "I was about to propose."

Mom's exhale could fill a balloon. "Would you have listened?"

I snap my gaze to her. "Yes!"

"Mhm," Granny murmurs, grabbing the plate of eggs from mom and walking to the table. "Sometimes mistakes are better to experience. These two," she points between Mom and Stace as she sits down, "wanted to fly to San Fran and stage an intervention."

I glare at Stace who crosses her arms then to Mom who shrugs. "Mom, why didn't you?"

She opens her mouth to explain, but Granny cuts her off. "Because I told them you needed to figure it out on your own."

I shake my head and keep my gaze locked on Granny's. "And what if I had married her?"

Granny crosses her arms. "You wouldn't have."

"How can you be so sure?" I press.

"Because I know you, Wyatt. If we had swooped in and told you how much that hussy was mooching off ya, you would have dug your heels in. I had confidence you'd come to your senses, even if you were standing up at the altar."

That makes one of us.

"Caroline seemed to have ulterior motives. She always talked about your job and the money you were making. We noticed the designer clothes she had, the fake smile she wore, and the phone glued to her hand, probably buying another pair of Crocs with heels," Stace explains.

We all stare at her.

Stace shrugs. "What? You can't convince me those are cute."

Mom raises her brows and nods in agreement.

Granny is eating her eggs and doesn't care about the love child of lightweight footwear and stilettos.

I rub my beard and trace my mustache as I process all of this. I can't believe they noticed there was something off with us. Hell, I can't believe I didn't see it sooner. I knew when I lost everything and my startup went south that Caroline would be disappointed. And I was right.

So disappointed, she found someone else's bed.

"Well, damn," I say on a sigh. "So does this mean you all are done interfering with my love life?"

"Absolutely not. That was a one-time deal," Stace says, pointing her second donut at me.

Granny picks up her donut again, and she clears her throat. "She wasn't the right one for you, Wyatt. But that doesn't mean there isn't someone out there."

I shake my head and cross my arms. "I'm not looking."

Just then, I hear the squeak of the front door as it opens and closes. Avery walks into the kitchen, hair knotted on the top of her head, wearing jeans and a t-shirt with a picture of Bigfoot on it. She's effortlessly beautiful, even with a forest monster spread across her chest.

Granny takes a bite of her donut, pinning me with a glare as she nods in Avery's direction and talks with her mouth full. "You should be."

I cut her a look and silently plead for her to quit it.

"Good morning," Avery says.

Her eyes widen as her gaze lands on my bare chest. I shiver under her scrutiny, and my nipples go hard, but I resist the urge to cover them with my palms.

"Donut?" Stace offers, as if she's Vanna White.

Avery nods quickly, darting her eyes from me and capturing a donut to shove in her pretty mouth.

"Sleep well?" Stace asks.

"Very," she says with a full mouth, then holds up a finger to finish chewing. "Sorry. Yes, I slept great." She looks up to meet my eyes and thankfully not my hardened nipples. "The best night of sleep I've had in a while."

Three sets of eyes swivel and land on me. Words pass without anything actually being said. I'm not the reason for Avery's good night of sleep, but the raised brows and smirks on everyone's faces say they don't believe me.

I uncross my arms and hold them out in surrender. "What?"

Mom extends her hand to Avery. "It's so nice to meet you. I'm Deb."

"Avery," she says, shaking Mom's hand. Avery shifts on her feet, capturing my attention and my gaze. "Before everything gets busy, I just wanted to say thank you for offering me this job. It really means a lot to me, and it's going to help me learn so much. I swear I'll do everything I can to make the experience the best ever."

Her eyes swim with gratitude, and I smile back at her. "You're very welcome."

Stace repeats the word very in a hushed voice.

Avery's face is washed in a light flush as all three sets of eyes have moved to look at her now.

I point toward the hallway. "I'm gonna go get dressed."

Avery points to the back door. "I'll water something outside. Good to see you all."

Before I can make it up the stairs, I hear the light chuckles from the women I love, and the ones who know me better than anyone else.

I can't go back and change things, but moving forward, I want to make them proud.

Twelve

"They say everything looks better with odd numbers of things. But sometimes I put even numbers, just to upset the critics."-Bob Ross

My jaw hits the gravel drive by the farmhouse, and I leap into her arms. "What are you doing here?"

Tilly instinctively wraps her arms around me. "Surprise!"

Pulling away, she turns back and bends to wave at her Uber driver. "Thank you for the ride!"

The driver is already backing out before Tilly can shut the back door.

She tugs her black bodycon dress down farther and adjusts her cowgirl hat. "He wasn't much of a talker," she says with a shrug. "An hour in the car from the airport, and he said two words. Can you believe it?"

"What did he say?"

"My ears," she says with a laugh. "I thought it was a joke."

I can only imagine how many stories she unloaded upon her poor driver. But she's here, at Trapp Farms, scratch that— *Thirst* Trapp Farms, standing right in front of me. I squeeze her in another hug that's even tighter.

"Nice hat," Wyatt says to Tilly after slinging her bag over his shoulder.

Her eyes rove over Wyatt as I realize what else she's wearing. The bodycon dress is a Tilly staple, but the white cowboy boots, wide-brimmed hat curling around the edges, and flannel shirt unbuttoned and tied in the middle is not. At least she isn't wearing spurs.

I clear my throat and focus on what I really want to know. "Tilly."

She winks at Wyatt, then meets my surprised expression. "Avery."

"What the hell are you doing here?" I repeat, crossing my arms.

She looks beyond my shoulder. "I couldn't let you have all the fun! I'm here to have a good time, of course." She leans closer to me. "And to make sure you do, too."

"She booked a massage with you tomorrow morning, as your very first client," Wyatt says, then extends his hand for her to shake. "Welcome to Thirst Trapp Farms. I'm Wyatt."

"I know." She puts her sultry-watt smile on, brighter than any lightbulb out there. "Thirst Trapp. Hm. That's news to me." Tilly cuts me a scolding look with her bright green eyes since I didn't tell her I was apparently living on a farm with delicious men. Wait until she hears about the shirts these men don't like to wear.

I shrug and telepathically tell her we'll talk later.

Wyatt smiles kindly and nods. "So, how do you know each other?"

I keep my eyes on Tilly, silently pleading for her not to spill any of my secrets. "Uh, yeah. Tilly is my roommate and best friend," I say.

And my human diary.

"It's nice to meet you, Tilly. I'll take your bag to cabin three for you while you both catch up. Dinner is at six, but we'll have happy hour behind the farmhouse in the gazebo at five," Wyatt says, hiking her bag up farther and trying not to wince.

I'm sure now isn't a good time to mention Tilly likes to pack every pair of shoes she owns, which equates to a lot.

"It's a pleasure to meet you, too," Tilly purrs as Wyatt heads down the drive, rocks crunching under his boots as he goes.

She whips around. "That's the cowboy?"

I shrug. "Yeah, I tried telling you!"

"You did not explain how you were working for a rugged lumberjack with forearms the size of actual tree trunks."

I shush her since we are feet away from the farmhouse, and the last thing I need is anyone hearing this conversation. I lower my voice. "I swear it's the Wrangler jeans."

"Those and the flannel. Oh, and the beard. My God, does he shampoo and condition that thing? It's perfect," she says.

"I know," I sigh. "I know, I know, I know."

I peer around her to make sure he's out of earshot. "Tilly," I say and fall into her arms again. "It's so good to see you."

"Wow. You really did miss me," she says.

I pull back. "What do you mean?"

She crosses her arms and juts out her hip. "You've been busy this week and haven't made as many diary entries lately. I just needed to make sure you were being safe with this boss of yours. Now I can see that you are absolutely in trouble."

I scoff and ask again. "What do you mean? Of course I'm being safe. Nothing's going on."

"Mhm, well, either way, I wanted to make sure you had these." She reaches deep into her purse, which is really like a side body parachute, and pulls out a box. "Here."

For the second time in five minutes, my jaw falls open, and I immediately try to shove the box back into her purse. "I don't need condoms, Tilly. Hurry, hide these before anyone sees them!" I scramble to grab the emergency release on her bag. "Why is the box so big? Did you get it at Costco or something?"

She tugs her purse out of my grabbing hands and pushes the box back into my arms. "Yes, actually, I did. Based on everything you told me about that sexy farmer, I figured this supply wouldn't even last the summer."

I hug the box that's the size of a small infant. "Nothing has happened, and nothing will happen. Didn't you read any of my other texts saying I would absolutely not do anything about the hot farmer?"

"So, you admit he's hot?"

I throw my hand up. "You're missing the point."

"The point is that I'm here to help you have a little fun," she says.

My shoulders actually relax hearing her say this. "I love that you're here, but I'm okay, really. I know I freaked out on the phone last week, but things have been going well, even with Wyatt as my boss. I finished getting the spa ready, the other two guests are settling in, and I'm...enjoying this place."

She reaches into her purse again. "Are you saying you'll want this instead?"

I gasp. There really are no words.

The purple penis-shaped vibrator she's holding is waving in the breeze like a flag, staking its claim on the land. I snatch it and shove it under my shirt. "Why did you bring my vibrator? You took this from my room!"

She shrugs. "Because you forgot it."

"On purpose."

She knits her brows together like this is the most inconceivable answer. "Why?"

"Because I'm not here for that."

"You're not dead, are you?" She shifts on her feet and feels my forehead with the back of her hand. "It's worse than I thought. Look, if you don't want to use a condom, or two—"

"Or one-thousand," I cut in, smacking her hand away.

She squints at me. "If you aren't going to use these," she taps the double-wide box, "it doesn't mean you can't use the vibrator. You're here to work, sure, but you aren't in prison. Loosen up. This will help you."

I exhale and stare at the ground. Tilly is always the one trying to get me to harness my fun side. She's taken up the role, like a second job that doesn't pay.

"I may not be dead, but I'm on thin ice as it is by being this attracted to my boss, and I can't veer. No veering! I'm here for the summer to learn," I say. "I quit my job to take a chance and figure out how to start my own thing. By September, I won't be able to buy the letters in the word *fun* if I don't take this seriously. And then there's the..." My words trail off.

"The what?" she asks.

"Nothing."

She rests her hand on my shoulder. "I get it, I really do. It's the curse you're afraid of, right?"

I can't look into her eyes. For a split second, I thought I could pretend it wasn't stressing me out. I thought I could fool myself into thinking the curse isn't waiting for me to mess up so it can serve me with some bad news. Deadly news.

She squeezes my shoulder, giving it a little shake. "Don't you think it's time to break it?"

"If I could, I would," I say.

"No you wouldn't."

I snap my head up to look at her. "What?"

She drops her hand. "Avery, you've been only half-living for years, too afraid to make big changes in fear of this curse. At some point, you have to put your fear aside and live. That's why I came. To remind you to live your life. You've already made the first step by coming here, and I don't want to see you backtracking because you're scared."

Tilly has always lived her life like tomorrow wasn't promised and today was all she had. She's a little eccentric at times, but that's what I love about her. She's so free and vibrant, and everything I'm not. I don't know if I can live like her. But she's right, I did take this step by moving here this summer. It was so reckless that some might even call it brave.

I open my mouth to say something but see Wyatt walking back toward us over Tilly's shoulder. "Oh my God! We have to get rid of these." I thrust the two-pound box of condoms at her as well as the vibrator that likely weighs the same.

She pushes them back on me. "They're yours!"

There's no time to argue. He's going to see me holding this and immediately get the wrong idea. The last thing I want him thinking is that I'm here for different reasons. Not after he told me how important this farm was to his family.

Tilly isn't letting me put them in her purse, so I frantically spin around, looking for a place to stash them. There's access beneath the farmhouse porch steps that my gaze zeros in on and before I can think, I'm rushing over and shoving them beneath the steps and sitting on the top one, as if nothing is awry.

Everything is just fine.

I'm like a cucumber but cooler.

Tilly puts her hands on her hips and shakes her head.

I smile proudly that Wyatt is none the wiser about the sex paraphernalia beneath his porch.

Wyatt approaches and stands between us, looking back and forth.

My legs are crossed, and I'm bouncing my foot, up and down. Tilly is twirling one of her dark brown pigtail braids around her pointer finger. We are the picture of casualness. Easy breezy, lemon squeezy.

Wyatt squints at me. "I'm going to get the snacks ready for the other guests and check on Granny. Ronny is adding the lights to the gazebo. Are you…" He peers over at Tilly, who is smiling like a clown then back at me. "Is everything good?"

"Great!" My voice is way more chipper than it needs to be. I tone it down twelve notches. "Do you need any help?"

He draws out his words, studying me beneath the ball cap he's wearing. "I think we're all set. If you want to relax with Tilly for now, then we'll see you in an hour or so."

"Avery loves relaxing," Tilly pipes in. "By herself, or with other…people."

I would have thrown the vibrator at her if it were still in my hand.

Wyatt looks back at Tilly and nods. "Right. Well, I'll see ya both later." He gives a small wave, pursing his lips in a tight smile before walking up the steps beside me and disappearing inside.

I exhale, uncrossing my legs and slumping over them. "That was close."

"You're right about the Wranglers. You sure you won't need the condoms—"

"I'm sure," I snap. Totally sure that I might just be unsure. But I'm only unsure, because Tilly seems so sure. Eventually, I'll go back to being sure. Or, was it unsure?

With no one around, I bend over to retrieve the box of rubbers just as Wyatt pops his head out the screen door, and I snatch a weed, hoisting it over my head. "Got it!" I swipe a nonexistent hair from my face.

He studies me, and I wait for him to tell me he knows what I'm hiding. "You don't have to weed. Ronny can do that," he says.

"Ronny?" Tilly asks, ears perking up, like a predator sensing nearby prey.

Wyatt nods. "He's my farmhand. You'll meet him tonight."

That look in Tilly's eyes says she's ready to pounce.

I'm ready to cough up a hairball in peace.

"By the way, I put that coconut oil you wanted in your cabin," Wyatt says. "It was the only size they had at the grocery store, so I hope it'll be okay."

"Oh! Thanks! I'm sure It'll be fine." I really need to stop talking in that high-pitched squeaky voice. I sound like the fourth member of Alvin and the Chipmunks.

Wyatt lingers for a second and then escapes one of the top five most awkward moments we've ever had in each other's presence, since I'm waving the weed around in my hand, dirt covering my lap.

The screen door slams, and I sigh heavily and toss the weed to the side. Standing, I walk toward Tilly and point behind me. "I'll have to get those later. In the dead of night wearing all black and night vision goggles."

Tilly laughs. "Mission pleasure."

I shove her shoulder playfully. "Let's go, Cupid. I'll show you the spa."

She claps her hands as we fall into step. "Remind me to tell you all of the ways you can use coconut oil with someone else."

I throw both hands over my ears. "La, la, la. I can't hear you."

She grabs my wrist to try and tug my hands away as we walk to my cabin. "It's great for massaging lots of bits and parts."

I start walking faster, hands still clasped over my ears, pretending I can't hear her.

"It's a good lube…"

I pick up my pace.

"You can eat it."

I start singing the first song that pops into my head. "O say can you see…"

She walks faster, grabbing for my arm. "Or lick it."

She's yelling, but I yell the lyrics louder and start running toward my front door. But I hear the last thing she says as I twist the knob and barrel inside.

"It makes a good hair mask, too," she says, climbing the porch steps behind me.

I turn to face her from inside. "Wait, really?"

"Yes." She walks inside and says over her shoulder, "And it melts quickly…on your fingers."

I throw my head back and groan. I'll never be able to look at coconut oil the same way.

Thirteen

Avery

"Gotta give him a friend. Like I always say, 'Everyone needs a friend.'"-Bob Ross

D oes my ass look like it's ten stories high?" Tilly asks, rushing ahead of me as we walk around the farmhouse.

I slow my pace and drop my gaze to said ass. "I don't even know what that means. What should I be looking for?"

"Never mind. I'm not going back to change."

Again, I think, since we've already been back once. This is Tilly, though. As long as I've known her, she's loved clothes. Putting together outfits, changing often, and trying new styles while I continue to wear the same pair of shorts I bought three years ago from a thrift store. They were mens' jeans, and I cut them into shorts myself.

As we come around the side of the house, the gazebo isn't hard to find since it's completely lit up. String lights are draped around the outer edge as well as to the tree close by, creating a bright canopy beneath it. A food table with snacks, wine, plastic cups, and cutlery stands to the side of the gazebo, and chairs dot the lawn, the smell of fresh cut grass still lingering in the air.

"Wow. Farm Boy really knows how to class things up. This is so sweet!" Tilly squeals.

Another one of Wyatt's ideas strikes again. This whole farm experience is straight from his brain and hearing him describe what he's thinking is nothing compared to actually seeing it.

It doesn't take long to spot Wyatt. He's the one with the mountainous biceps still visible beneath his flannel shirt. He's wearing his signature brown work boots like almost every other day while leaning against one of the railings, invested in a conversation with an unfamiliar face who I'm guessing is one of the guests I haven't met, yet.

"You sure you don't want me to fetch that box of condoms for you?" Tilly asks from beside me.

"Positive."

I'm not positive. Seeing him like this, all easy on the eyes and flannel clad makes me want things. But those are the kinds of "things" with no take-backs.

Wyatt spots us walking closer and tips his hat.

I tip my hat, too, then forget I'm not wearing one. Steering Tilly toward the food table, we grab a small plate and start loading cheese, salami, nuts, and fruit onto them.

"Howdy," Ronny says, approaching the table.

"Hey, Ronny."

Tilly clears her throat and elbows me.

Three cubes of cheese are already stuffed in my mouth when I look up and see the way Tilly is staring at Ronny. It's the same way he's looking at her.

I peer between them, popping another piece of colby jack in my mouth, enthralled by what's going to happen next. It doesn't even look like they need an introduction the way their eyes stay locked on each other, but I give one anyway.

"Tilly, this is Ronny, Wyatt's farmhand and neighbor." I look at Ronny and point at my friend who has gone mute beside me. "Ronny, this is my best friend, Tilly."

"Best friend?" Ronny manages.

Tilly reaches her hand out to him. "And roommate."

He takes her hand, like it's a delicate flower he doesn't want to crush, then reluctantly lets go. "Nice to meet you, Tilly. Are you here as a friend or guest?"

"Both." She teases a strawberry between her front teeth. "I'm here for the weekend."

"We'll have to make it a memorable one then," he says in a sensuous tone I have literally never heard come from his mouth since I've known him, which has only been a week but still.

"Hey, Till?" I whisper.

She keeps looking at Ronny. "Yeah?"

"Do you want me to go fetch that box of goodies for you?" I ask under my breath for only her to hear.

"Maybe," she says, biting the strawberry clean through.

Since they seem to be engaged in some kind of non-verbal eye hockey game and forget about me, I walk over to the gazebo to meet the other guests.

The woman talking to Wyatt is older with ash brown hair, glasses, and bags beneath her eyes. Poor woman looks like she hasn't slept since last year.

Seeing me approach, Wyatt stands straighter and waves a hand toward me. "This is Avery, our spa director."

My heart stops. I'm stuck on the title Wyatt just gave me. *Spa director.* It sounded better than expected, but there's also a panic that starts to fill my chest. Could I do this? Could I be a director? Am I making a mistake, thinking I can handle a title like that? I'll have to if I want to be an owner one day.

The woman extends her hand.

Oh my god, I can't take it. I'm a fake.

But like a Rumba set on autopilot, I take her hand.

"I'm Emery and Colton's mom," she says, shaking my hand and her head. "I mean, Jackie. Sorry, you don't know my kids. I'm so used to introducing myself as their mom, I forget my name sometimes." She laughs a little too long and a little too high.

"Nice to meet you," I say with a smile, but I'm really considering a low-key escape back to my cabin to list out all of the reasons I want to own my own spa, and why I can handle the title of spa director like the grown woman I am. I need a plan.

"I'm going to make sure things are good in the kitchen," I say.

"It's all covered."

Wyatt and all his careful planning to the rescue. *Not.*

"Then, I'll check on the..." I look around the gazebo. "The lightbulbs."

The lines on Wyatt's forehead go from one to five.

Before he can say anything, I add, "It was lovely to meet you, Jackie."

She smiles. "You, too."

Hopefully my hands act more confidently during my massage tomorrow than they are right now. Luckily, Tilly is my first and only client in the morning. She'll have to deal with low budget self-esteem hands that act more like T-Rex claws.

Stepping farther into the gazebo, I pretend to observe one of the hanging lightbulbs and try to make it look like I know what I'm doing when I absolutely have no clue. So, I thank Edison for his ingenuity and inch closer to the other side of the gazebo so I can make a break for it.

It's then I note the only other person there. He's sitting on a bench seat with a plate of untouched snacks beside him, nose in a book. Seriously, his nose is pressed right into the open spine of his book, looking more like he's smelling the pages than reading the words on them.

"Hi, I'm Avery, the...spa director," I say, emphasizing the title to see how it tastes in my mouth. Not bad. Maybe I can do this.

The man doesn't move but keeps his face buried in the cream-colored pages.

He must not have heard me. I clear my throat and speak louder. "Hello?"

The man flails his arms, like an angry Canadian goose set on destruction, and tosses his book in the air until it tumbles to the wooden floor beneath our feet.

"I'm so sorry!" I bend to pick up his book at the same time he does, and we bump heads. I cradle my forehead. "Sorry...again."

He rubs his temple and grabs what looks like a seven-hundred page manual. "I didn't see you."

That much was obvious. "Are you okay?" I ask.

"Fine. Just trying to finish the end of my book," he says gruffly, ignoring me and the plate of snacks beside him.

He looks like a young Stephen King with dark hair, sideburns, and glasses that are barely larger than his actual eyeballs.

"Okay, well, welcome to the farm," I say. "If you need a massage—"

"I don't," he snaps. "I came here to finish reading my book in peace."

You mean your phone book?

He opens somewhere close to the middle and goes back to what he was doing before I interrupted.

I can't help myself. "What are you reading?"

He sighs but doesn't look up. "Horror."

"Oh, as in blood and guts stuff?"

Why is my mouth opening and closing right now, making sounds that form whole words?

He turns the page. "No, but everyone dies."

"Interesting."

He's reading about my life. Great. There's no way I won't be having nightmares tonight.

I tell the man, whose name I still didn't get, that I need water and rush over to where Tilly and Ronny are still standing. What I really need is to scrub my mind and picture unicorns and rainbows until the ghosts go away, then list out at least ten reasons why I'm mostly qualified to be a spa director.

"You okay there?" Ronny asks.

My hand shakes as I try to pour myself a glass of white wine and chug. Wine isn't something that should be guzzled down, like a college student would at a frat party. We are sophisticated adults who eat from charcuterie boards and drink from actual bottles of wine, not the boxed kind.

Even still, I wipe my mouth with the back of my hand. "Fine. Great."

Tilly watches me beneath her narrowed brows, but I only shrug and say again that I'm fine.

Satisfied, she turns back to Ronny. "So, what do you all do for fun around here?"

Ronny's lips pull up into a full smile. "The Thirsty Hippo."

Tilly sips her wine like a respectable adult. "Is that, like, a weird drinking game or something?"

He chuckles, chewing on what I hope is a new toothpick. "No, it's a bar."

Tilly's eyes go wide. "We have to go. Tonight."

I push my body closer between them. "What? No, we can't go to a bar tonight."

I look back over my shoulder at the other two guests, except there is only one. The Soccer Mom. Stephen King is gone, probably confirming the untimely death of too many beloved characters.

"Why not?" Tilly whines.

"Because we have guests," I retort. "And dinner to serve."

Tilly peers over at Wyatt and Soccer Mom. "Look! She's leaving. Likely going back to her cabin to sleep until egg gathering and knitting tomorrow morning."

I glare and hit her with some sarcasm. "Those aren't until the afternoon."

"Exactly."

"I'll talk to Wyatt," Ronny says, setting his beer down and leaving Tilly's side.

I cross my arms and face Tilly. "I don't think this is a good idea."

"You're right, it's an excellent one," she says, tossing a piece of cheese in her mouth.

I groan. "Not what I meant. I'm supposed to be here working. I know you're technically a guest, but you should be helping me succeed at this job, not…not dragging me to a bar to drink and dance."

"Consider it a team-building exercise. You're getting to know your boss," she says with a casual shrug, "and the sexy man he has working for him."

I pick up a wedge of salami and examine it. "I don't need to know if he's a good dancer or likes whiskey more than rum."

She clicks her tongue. "I disagree. You can learn a lot about a person by bringing the defenses down a little."

I shake my head and stand straighter on my legs. "I'm not drinking."

"That's fine. You can drive."

"I don't know how to drive a stick shift," I say. "And Ronny doesn't have a car. He rides his horse here every day."

"Okay, now that is effing hot."

I exhale and set the salami back on the tray, having lost my appetite.

"I'll drive," Wyatt says, walking up behind us with Ronny on his heels.

"Oh. Okay," I say. So glad to know this is now a thing.

Tilly is smiling brightly, and all I can do is glare at her some more. I've been outnumbered. This is going to happen whether I go or not.

Wyatt tucks his hands in his pockets. "Are you up for seeing one of the prized spots in Big Timber?"

I look between Tilly, Ronny, and Wyatt. All of them are waiting for an answer from me. I could stay and fake exhaustion, but then I'd be sending Tilly off on her own. Ronny and Wyatt aren't strangers, but I don't want to be left behind. I know how Tilly can get when she drinks. No table is safe from her dancing on top of it. Plus, going will only solidify how much I like Wyatt in all settings, and that is dangerous territory. On a farm, in a bar, with a horse, or in a car on the way to a place I shouldn't go in case I end up liking him even more.

I sigh. "Alright. I'll go."

Wyatt nods and grabs the meat and cheese platters to put inside while Ronny unplugs the lights. "Meet you at the truck in fifteen minutes," Wyatt says. "I need to check in with Granny and box up dinner for the others who want to eat in tonight."

Tilly claps her hands in excitement, her brown hair dancing around her shoulders as she jumps on the balls of her feet. "This is going to be so much fun!"

I let her grab my arm and lead me around the side of the farmhouse. Tilly is overjoyed at the adventure with the guys, but I'm not. I'm the scaredy cat worried about messing everything up. This last week has gone smoothly, and with the weekend still ahead of us, I don't want to create a list of regrets. My future is riding on this whole summer, and I'm not about to throw it away for a drunken night at the bar.

Even one that's called the Thirsty Hippo.

Fourteen

Avery

"We want happy paintings. Happy paintings. If you want sad things, watch the news."-Bob Ross

O h my god!" Tilly yells.

"Oh my god," I mumble.

"Ladies, welcome to the Thirsty Hippo," Ronny says with a sweeping gesture at the grand reveal.

It's quite a reveal.

If the light-up blowfish hanging from a corner wasn't enough, wooden wall hangings that look like tribal warriors litter every wall. A few large and small taxidermied animals hang between them, including one I think is a jackrabbit and an elk with only one antler. Did I just walk into a Tiki bar or a hunting lodge?

Tilly tugs me toward the bar full of customers twice our age. "It's so small-town-hip."

"Is that a style?" I ask.

My only concern is making sure I don't contract a fatal disease. We should have checked the health rating before coming here. Or, better yet, we should have just stayed at the farm.

Customers don't even look up from their drinks as we walk across the uneven parquet dance floor, which has black duct tape holding it down along the edges.

I'm five seconds from asking someone for a mop and the strongest disinfectant on the market—the black market of cleaning supplies that is.

"Wyatt!" a woman calls from behind the bar. "How are you this fine evenin'?"

The woman has two full arms of tattoos and long gray hair running down her back. Her smile is friendly, thank God, and I release the breath I'd been recycling in my lungs for the last few minutes.

She's the only one in here that doesn't look like she could murder people on the side.

"Hi, Betty." Wyatt lifts a hand. "I'm doing good. You?"

She fills a tall glass with one of the beers on tap. "I'm alright. Been so busy with my grandkids, it's the first time I'm working here this week."

Wyatt smiles and offers me one of the two available barstools.

"Hey, Betty." Ronny tips his chin to her. "Can I pick the music from your iPod?"

Tilly hops onto one of the spinning barstools, doing a full three-sixty as Wyatt and Ronny take up the space—and all of the air—behind us.

Wyatt laughs at Ronny. "Don't make us listen to 'Low' forty times in a row again."

Tilly gasps. "I love that song!"

While they talk music, and Ronny agrees to arm wrestle Wyatt for the pick, I peer next to me at the large man with a large beard and a large frown. He looks like someone named Big Earl with a gold tooth and a switchblade hiding in his pocket.

All I have is bear spray. I bought it in bulk at Costco before coming.

Swallowing and staring up at Big Earl, I smile in case he considers me a threat, even though I'm the size of his bicep. He just grunts and looks straight ahead.

I gulp and swivel my chair to face Tilly, leaning toward her. "If I don't make it out of here alive, tell my parents I'm sorry and make sure to keep bringing our neighbor, Matilda, her fungal cream. Don't forget, okay?"

"Fungal cream?" Tilly scrunches her nose. "What are you talking about?" She feels my forehead as she's taken a liking to doing. "Are you feeling okay?"

"I feel fine," I say, moving my head so her hand falls away. "This place looks as if they are slaughtering the cows out back to make the burgers they have on the menu."

"It'll be a true farm-to-table experience then," Tilly says, looking over the drink menu that's shaped as a giant pineapple.

I lower my voice. "Don't you dare order any food."

Tilly sets the menu down and whispers, "You need to relax. You aren't going to contract some weird disease and end up dead, I swear. The alcohol will kill off any diseases anyway."

"I'm not drinking, remember?" I cross my arms. "I'm still going to use my test strips to make sure your drink isn't laced with some kind of date rape drug."

She smirks and goes back to studying the menu. "You're no fun."

Fun. I want to toss that word in a blender. Fun is overrated. Safety? That's where the real party is.

I sit straighter, and Wyatt places his hand on my back and leans closer. "What do you want to drink?"

I stiffen and shake my head. "Nothing."

"You sure? I'm driving."

Don't remind me. Squeezing all four of us into the cab of Wyatt's two-door truck was an event. Tilly shoved me in next to him before I could protest, and I spent the entire drive into town trying not to melt into his side like ice cream on a hot day. I failed. We were close enough that his sandalwood scent was overpowering proper brain function. I might have nuzzled his sleeve, but I can't remember, because I blacked out. Now, his hand is touching me, and I can't stop thinking about his finger span stretching across my back. He could catch ten footballs in that one hand.

I play with the ends of my hair nervously. "I have a massage client tomorrow. I don't want to be reckless or anything."

Getting shitfaced isn't exactly my idea of a good time. But then again, I've never tried it, so maybe it is my thing, and I just don't know it. I'm not finding out tonight, though. I'm out with my boss. As well as his attractive farmhand that could be a part of a Chippendale troupe if he wanted and my best friend who dances on tables after one sip of water.

Tilly bumps my shoulder. "I'm your client, silly."

I know this already, and Wyatt does, too, but I don't want him to think for one second that just because Tilly is my friend that I'm going to slack off. I'm serious about this job. As serious as Big Earl is about the third beer he's had since we sat down.

I shift in my seat. "Exactly. My hands would be like two hungover giraffe hooves clomping all over your back."

I have now become a master at miming, as I demonstrate what this would look like.

Tilly tips her head back against Ronny's chest and laughs. Wyatt chuckles, too, and I realize just how close he is. I could lean back and feel his laugh if I wanted to.

Ronny orders everyone's drinks and a club soda for me. I never get club soda, but I feel like this is what people order in movies if they aren't drinking.

I immediately regret it after the first sip.

It tastes like air and smells like bubbles.

"How's Granny been doing?" Betty asks Wyatt while she makes the other drinks.

Since there aren't four seats available for all of us, I'm being tortured by the feel of Wyatt's breath moving the fine hairs on the side of my head. I'd like to trade this out for Chinese water torture, please.

He takes the glass of whiskey from her. "She's good. Ronny and I have been able to take on most of the farm work for her, and we've got guests booked until the end of the summer."

"That's fantastic," Betty says, then leans closer, handing Ronny something that likely has rum in it based on the smell. "Any more letters from the bank?"

Well, hello small town living where people ask you deeply personal questions with an invisible microphone shoved close to your face. Even with my back to Wyatt, I can feel him stiffen. The air becomes thinner, and I hold my breath, waiting to hear how he'll answer Betty's question. In my experience, letters from the bank can only mean everything you never want them to. Is this why Wyatt moved back? To help pay off the debts?

He places a hand on the bar top beside me, half-boxing me in. "Nope. The farm's doing great."

"Glad to hear it," she says, then sets Tilly's drink down. "Here you go, sugar."

I stare longingly at the fruity concoction Tilly ordered complete with an umbrella and a pineapple triangle hanging on for dear life off the side. Betty has somehow fit an entire Tahitian island inside that glass, making my mouth water.

I pull out a test strip from my purse and dunk it in her concoction. A quick nod from me confirms she won't die by poisoning tonight.

I sip my bubbles minus all flavor, wondering if I could at least sneak the pineapple.

"You can get that, too, and make it a virgin," Wyatt whispers in my ear, pointing at Tilly's drink.

A shiver runs the full length of my body and back up again. And then down and back up three more times. Hearing the word *virgin* on his lips does not put me at ease.

Forgoing the straw, I gulp my soda water until the tall, slim glass is empty. "Mhm. So good. I love club soda." I raise a finger. "Betty, can I please have another?"

She nods in my direction as she finishes filling a glass of wine.

I glance at Wyatt over my shoulder but don't meet his eyes, too afraid he'll know I was defining the word virgin in my head instead of professing my nonexistent love for bubbly water.

"How about that iPod, Betty? Do I need to beat Wyatt in an arm wrestling contest?" Ronny asks.

Wyatt scoffs from behind his glass. "Like you could."

I'm willing to referee if it comes to it. I volunteer as tribute.

Betty finishes pouring the drink and hands it to someone at the end of the bar, wipes her hands on a towel, and produces an iPod from the early 2000s that should be in a museum and not her pocket. She looks down her nose at Ronny. "No Flo Rida."

"Deal." Ronny circles Tilly with his arms, pulling her against him as they look through the song options.

"That one!" Tilly yells.

Drop it Like it's Hot starts to play, and I groan. "You would choose a Snoop song."

Tilly starts singing every word to the song, and so do I, because even though Snoop isn't my flavor, he is hers. I've been gagged and bound and forced to listen to him since we met.

Tilly grabs Ronny's cowboy hat and puts it on her head as he cradles her hips. The chemistry between them is electric after the few hours they've spent together. Despite there being four of us, I feel like a third wheel.

I swivel my chair to the side and rest an elbow on the bar top so I can try to talk to Wyatt above the pimps in the crib. "So, cow hugging tomorrow?" I say, cradling my replenished soda water.

Bleh.

Wyatt sips from his whiskey, a bead of liquor sticking to his mustache. I reach up and swipe it away like this is what I do. I wipe grown men's mouths with my bare hands.

What is wrong with me?

The club soda has gone straight to my head.

"Sorry," I say in a rush.

He continues to stare down at me as the most aggressive blush climbs my neck and fills both cheeks. I'm so hot, I want to press my cool glass against my face or dump it straight over my head. Damn those intrusive thoughts.

"Thanks, for that," he says and clears his throat. "We won't be able to do cow hugging tomorrow. One of the girls came down with something, and I need to get the vet out to look at her first."

"Oh no. That's terrible. Is there anything I can do?" I ask.

He smiles behind the rim of his glass. "Unless you know how to administer antibiotics."

"Definitely not. Though, I do know how to flush a goldfish down the toilet when it dies."

Why am I bringing up such a sore subject? Here? Now? The lights in this bar are dim but feel like they are boring down on me and preparing to investigate the far too early death of Goldilocks. Two days has to be a record.

Wyatt laughs, the deep rumble reverberating in my bones at a stronger pitch than Snoop Dogg's beats. "I've never flushed a fish before."

I let his laughter pull me in, and I join him. The smile beneath the dark, rough hairs of his beard is easy to see when I'm sitting this close. I silently curse Tilly, who is already ordering her second drink, for bringing me here and forcing me to admire Wyatt.

Ronny chooses the next song, "Shivers" by Ed Shereen, and pulls Tilly to the scuffed dance floor. Drink in hand, he twirls her around slowly as she rolls her hips.

"Do you know how to two-step?"

I look up at Wyatt. "What? No."

But apparently Tilly does.

Ronny tugs her in and spins her out all while making her drink slosh but never spill.

"I could show you," Wyatt says.

"Oh, it's okay." I wiggle my feet. "Giraffe hooves, remember?"

It's not that I don't know how to dance at all. The month before prom, I decided to teach myself how. Unfortunately, with little money and no way to afford classes, I decided on the next best thing: Dance Dance Revolution. I spent hours at the arcade practicing with Justice, who became some sort of a master at it, but they didn't have a two-step. I'd be a fish out of water.

"That's only if you have alcohol, right? You should be good with that soda water."

I stare down at my tickly water and curse it for not being stronger.

"I'll lead," he adds, offering me his hand.

My gaze moves to his calloused hand that was on my back earlier. Robust and solid and so *him*.

I look away from his hand before I start drooling. Ronny seems to be leading Tilly expertly around the dance floor. My instinctual response is to say no, but watching Tilly and seeing what a good time she's having, reminds me why she's here.

Fun.

Dancing with my boss is probably fine. I can handle that.

Throwing back the rest of my soda water, I set it on the bar. My nose burns, and my eyes start to water from all those damn bubbles, but I slap my hand in Wyatt's. "Alright. Let's do this."

He takes me by the hand to the duct-taped floor where I'm about to build a bonfire of regrets then faces me. With a wink and smirk—classic flirty Wyatt face—he raises our clasped hands and spins me in a full circle before he smashes me against his chest and dips me backward.

What. Just. Happened? He spins me away from him, and I do my best to copy everything he's doing, and as promised, he leads me through each move.

His hands are always on me. Gripping and turning me, tugging my shoulder to manually twirl me, and cradling my elbow as we move. As promised, my hooves stomp on his feet a few times, but he doesn't wince like I do. He just keeps going, smiling the whole time through the curtain of his beard.

It's when his hand finds my waist and the song ends that I think I might faint. He folds me into him, the hard lines of his body pressed close to the fleshy parts of mine. For a minute, I think he'll say something, but he doesn't. He drops his hand two inches, entering the danger zone, while his eyes stay locked on mine. Then, he squeezes.

It's only the two of us in this tiki bar now with a blowfish lamp setting the mood lighting until words rush from my mouth, marking this moment. "I have to pee."

I peel away from him and shuffle toward the bathroom, as if my hair is on fire.

This is exactly what the curse needs: more ammo against me. Being around Wyatt is only going to make it harder for me not to catch bigger and badder feelings. If and when I do, the curse is going to remind me just how foolish I'd be to make yet another change and let him in.

I push through the single bathroom door covered in stickers and stand in front of the mirror. After downing two glasses of straight water, I really do have to pee, but first, I force myself to see what Wyatt sees. When he looks at me, what does he notice?

Does he see someone who isn't as fun as Tilly?

A woman who doesn't know her way around a dance floor?

Maybe a girl who lost her brother at age twenty and is cursed for all eternity because of it?

It's likely a combo of all of those things. But when I look at him, I see someone who's well-built, reliable, and likely not missing any parts beneath the hood. I could be describing a tractor by the sounds of it, but I'm not. There's a confidence in Wyatt that makes him sturdy and sure-footed.

Add in the reminder of his full lips, which curve in all of the right places, and my limbs start doing this weird tingly thing, and I have to steady myself with my palms on the counter.

What is happening?

It's probably just the club soda.

Fifteen

Wyatt

"Talent is a pursued interest. Anything that you're willing to practice, you can do."-Bob Ross

I knock furiously then wait.

My watch says it's 1:12 a.m., barely thirty minutes since we got back from the Thirsty Hippo. Tonight was one of the best nights I've had out in a long while. I didn't want it to end, and the way Avery lingered outside my truck when we got back, I don't think she did, either.

She's probably fast asleep now. I'm sure she is. That's what people do in the middle of the night. *Sleep.* Except for me, because apparently farmers don't sleep.

I knock again and check my phone. No new messages. If Ronny would just answer his phone, I wouldn't be trying to wake Avery up like I am, which is seeming more like a booty call with every knock.

Ronny always answers except for right now when I really need him. Granny's in no state to help me, and by the time my parents got here, it would probably be too late. Stace would remind me of the duty she's already performed by birthing two humans. She'd say she doesn't need to witness any animal births. I can hear her now, been there, done that.

But I need help.

Tapping my thigh, I say into the night air, "Come on. Please answer."

I start making promises I may not be able to keep if she opens the door.

I promise I won't punch Ronny. I'll quit singing in the shower like Granny asked. I'll even stop looking at Avery's ass. Though, I might have to tape my eyes shut for that one. I'll pinky swear it.

Before I can make any more empty promises, footsteps pad softly on the other side of the door, and I start thanking every animal on this farm by name. Thanks to Avery, they all have one now.

"Avery? It's me, Wyatt."

"Wyatt?" I hear her say from behind the door.

"Yes, it's just me."

"What are you doing here? I thought you were a burglar!"

I narrow my brows. "Even though I knocked on the door?"

"It could happen."

I shake my head and rest a flat palm on the door frame. "Can you open the door?"

There's a pause and then the clicking sound of a lock releasing. She cracks the door open, so I can only see one of her wide blue eyes. "Yeah?"

I sigh. "I need your help. Can you get dressed and meet me at the horse barn?"

I'm already retracing my steps down the stairs.

"Wait!" she calls. "Why? What's going on?"

"I need help with one of our horses. Ronny isn't picking up, and I can't do this alone," I explain in case things go wrong, though I omit that part. "Hurry."

I spin on my heel and start jogging to the barn, hoping she isn't far behind. The fear in her eyes said there's a chance she might not come, but I can't waste anymore time. After we got back from the bar, I went to check on the horses. One of our mares, Daisy, was well into labor and is having her baby tonight, and I need to be there for moral support. For her, not me. That's a lie. I need it more than her.

Curving inside the barn door, I make my way to the last stall where Daisy is flat on her side drenched in sweat. I snatch the bucket of water and look around for something to dunk in it to help cool her off. There's nothing nearby, and considering the way she's grunting, I don't want to leave again, so I yank off my t-shirt. Dunking it in the water a few times to soak it, I use it to gently rub along Daisy's neck. Her light brown coat is usually the color of the hay, but between the water and sweat, it looks several shades darker, as if looking at her through sunglasses.

"Is she okay?"

I snap my head up to see Avery standing in the stall door with silk pajama shorts, a tank top, and boots. I'm not used to seeing her like this. All hazy with sleep, hair thrown up on her head haphazardly, and more vulnerable than ever. I like it too much.

Didn't she hear me say to get dressed first? If my calculations are correct, she's not even wearing a bra. But then again, I'm half-dressed, too.

Daisy kicks her hoof against the stall and calls my attention back to why we're here. "She's in labor. Probably has been for the last couple hours. It won't be long now."

Avery throws a hand to her chest. "So, she's not dying?"

I look between her and the horse as I dunk my shirt again and wring it out over Daisy's warm body. "Dying?"

"Never mind." Avery walks in and squats beside me. "What can I do?"

Her shimmering shorts are catching every bit of light, like a mirror on a sunny day. *Eyes up, Wyatt.*

"Uh, can you grab the gauze in the cabinet just outside the stall? I need to wrap her tail."

She jumps up, moving swiftly to grab the roll. I force my eyes to heel and focus on Daisy. She's the only girl I should be looking at right now. Horse. Labor. Need. Focus.

Trudging back through the thick pile of hay, Avery kneels down near Daisy's neck and hands me the roll. "Why do you wrap her tail?"

I blindly take the gauze, refusing to look at those blasted short-shorts, and shuffle down to Daisy's hind to start wrapping. "It keeps her tail out of the way and clean during birth."

She watches me for a beat and nods. "How many times have you done this?"

"Never." I've witnessed plenty of births, but I haven't done one on my own.

"Never?"

I shake my head and move back to Daisy's flank. "I watched my Gramps plenty of times, though, and we shouldn't need to do much if it's a normal birth." I'm sure it'll come back to me in the off chance I do need to intervene. Like riding a bike, or a...horse. "Ronny's done it plenty of times. I just can't get a hold of him."

"Wyatt."

"It'll be fine. You have your phone, right? In case we need to YouTube something?"

"Wyatt."

I brace my hands on my thighs. "I swear, you can learn how to do anything on the internet these days."

"Wyatt!"

I look at Avery. "What?"

She doesn't have to answer since her lifted brows and finger pointing at the hooves protruding from Daisy's backside say enough.

I leap up and hover over the scene unfolding before my eyes. The picture quality of my eyeballs is top-notch, because at this distance, this angle, I can see it all.

And I do mean *all*.

"What do we do?" she asks.

Hands on my knees, I marvel at the two hooves that turn into legs and then the top of a muzzle. "We watch a miracle happen."

Daisy's body tenses, and she grunts as she continues to push.

"Good girl, Daisy. That's right, keep going," I encourage.

I'd clap if I thought it was the appropriate time but pushing anything of that size and girth out can't feel great.

Avery moves closer, mouth falling open as knobby knees become visible. "Wait..." She tilts her head to the side. "Is that the—"

"Front hooves," I say quickly and point. "And that's the nose."

"Ohhhh."

If the birth goes as it should, we won't need to interfere at all until the very end. Gramps used to say that animals are more confident in birth than most humans are. Daisy knows what to do and so does her body, despite this being her first birth. And she's doing it. All on her own.

A few more pushes, and the foal's flank and rear are born fully encased in the amniotic sac. Daisy lifts her neck to peer back at her baby but stays lying down, her fur slick with effort.

Avery tugs at my arm. "She did it!"

"She did it!" I yell.

My adrenaline and pride are on overdrive. I wrap my arms around Avery and spin her in a full circle, laughing loudly. I'm so happy I could kiss her—Daisy and Avery. Not only was this the first unassisted birth I've helped with since my earlier years with Gramps, but it was successful. I needed this. A slice of success that felt even better than analyzing profit margins.

I can picture Gramps in his Carhart overalls, standing quiet in the background as he watches thoughtfully. Maybe he is here, smiling and watching over me as I try to step into his big shoes. Would he be proud? I think so.

Feet back on the ground, Avery bounces on her heels, but I can't seem to let go. Her voice cracks. "I can't believe I got to see that."

The sac around the foal breaks, and the youngen nuzzles the ground, figuring out what to do with all these new body parts.

Avery is tucked into my side, and I squeeze her shoulder, feeling everywhere we're connected and the warmth she brings to my bare chest.

Bare chest?

I look down and confirm I'm still half-nude, Avery's hand resting on my skin.

She looks at her hand and stares at it like it has a mind of its own and she didn't know it had escaped to come frolic in my chest hair.

She pulls it away and takes a step to the side. "Sorry."

"It's okay." More than okay, but I'm sure my creepy grin said as much.

It's been months since someone has touched me like this. Every layer of my skin is hot and bothered. Was it like this with Caroline? No, I don't think so. God, I can't believe I'm thinking about her right now, but that's what two years with someone buys you.

An hour passes, and after delivering the placenta, Daisy is on all fours again. The foal is testing out her legs as well and begins searching for milk. She attempts to suck at anything in sight, including me, which I promptly have to shut down. I lead Daisy to her newborn, and the foal is finally satisfied with her first few suckles.

We both coo at the pair like a couple of proud horse doulas.

"Now what?" Avery asks, redoing her bun.

I peer around the stall at the afterbirth and blood coating the straw. "I need to finish cleaning this up."

"I'll help," she says.

"You don't have to. It's late, and I'm sure you're tired after I woke you. You can head to bed, and I'll clean out the stall."

She's already gripping one of the rakes outside the stall. "I'm helping."

I like when she talks dirty. Or clean, in this case. "Okay, I'll get a wheelbarrow," I say.

We work together to muck the stall and replace it with new hay for Daisy and her foal to bed down for the night. Neither wastes any time getting comfortable.

Avery is already rubbing her arms, teeth chattering, like a couple of maracas.

"I think we're done here. I'll walk you back," I say.

"Can we stay?" she asks in a rush. "Just for a little longer?"

If she thinks I can say no to her, then I'm not the man she thinks I am. "Of course. I'll go grab a few blankets."

The best I can do are horse blankets, but they're at least made out of thick wool. Draping one over her shoulders, I lay the other one on top of the fresh bed of hay and point for her to sit down near the wall. I found a flannel jacket I had left in here, too, and put it on.

When I sit beside her, resting my back against the stall, I'm surprised at how comfortable it is. Or, maybe that's just because I'm tired enough to think anything would be. My eyelids bounce up and down, but I force them open. Her shivering has lessened, but I continue to rub her arm anyway.

I like touching her.

I like the way she feels under my arm.

I like how she smells.

I like all of her.

"Tell me about your family," I say, realizing I don't know enough about her. "I'm guessing you didn't grow up watching live births for fun on weekends."

She laughs and leans her head back. "No, definitely not. Though, this is probably more exciting than how I used to spend my time."

"Let's hear it."

"Well, before...um, before I moved out, my brother and I would do a lot of biking. We'd go everywhere. It started as short trips to the gas station and graduated to biking the miles to downtown. Sometimes we'd pack a lunch and sit at one of the parks for hours. Other times, we'd find a bookstore and read in a quiet corner together."

Her voice is wistful like she's reliving the memories more than just telling them.

"This was in Bismarck?"

She nods. "We lived about fifteen miles outside the city center. Once we got better on our bikes, that distance was nothing."

"Mhm," I hum, a lazy smile perched on my lips.

My eyelids are so heavy. I can't keep them open for much longer, and hearing Avery talk lulls me, but I don't want to miss anything. I want to keep listening, keep learning.

"Do you still like riding bikes together?" I ask through a slur.

The pause before she speaks is long enough to make me think I fell asleep.

"No," she finally says.

It's so quiet and small, I'm sure I dreamt it. I search my dreams for her voice, but I can't find it. I want to find it. But I...just...can't.

"WYATT, HEY MAN, wake up."

I feel a nudge on the bottom of my boot and just like that I'm back in the world of the living. Blinking rapidly, I try to focus on the face hovering above me.

The cowboy hat.

The dark hand, waving in front of my face.

"Daisy had her foal."

That voice.

I lift my head. "Ronny?"

"It's me," Ronny says. "Don't get up too fast."

I rub my eyes with my free hand. Wait, free hand? I look at my other arm, which is pinned beneath Avery. She's lying on her side, curled against my chest, her fingers stretched out over my stomach. We must have fallen asleep and laid down at some point.

I peer around the space. "Where's Daisy?"

"Her and the foal are outside in the pen."

The sun is shining through every slit of the old barn. We've been asleep for hours.

"We were here last night when it happened," I whisper. "What time is it?"

I don't bother moving. Not when Avery's soft breaths tickle the dark hairs of my chest. She's still fast asleep, and after dragging her in to help me last night, I resist waking her.

"It's eight in the morning." Ronny scratches the back of his neck. "Sorry I missed your calls last night. I was…I, uh…"

Tilly pokes her head inside the stall and snaps a picture of Avery coiled around me, like an octopus with eight appendages instead of a human with only four. Her leg is draped across my thighs while the other curls behind my calf. The hand on my stomach is resting dangerously close to my belt, and the other has a death grip around my bicep. I hate that we woke up with an audience or else I could have really enjoyed this.

Ronny brackets his hips with his hands and doesn't meet my eyes. "We…uh.."

Tilly snaps another picture in landscape orientation. "He was with me."

So, he was on the farm all along. I'd punch him if the night hadn't gone better than expected.

I lightly shake Avery awake. "Hey," I say softly. "We have to get up."

She hums at a pitch that stirs my body and wakes me up in more places than I already am. It isn't helping that one of her hands is now rubbing back and forth across my abs. I have to cover it with my hand to keep her from starting anything I know we can't finish.

Ronny covers his mouth with his fist, and Tilly bites her lip to hide a laugh as Avery burrows farther into my side, like a hibernating animal.

I scoot to the side and carefully pull my arm from under her, saying her name the whole time to try and get her to wake. The bare leg draped across my thighs tries to keep me pinned to her, and I have to use the arm not propping me up to tug it off me.

Ronny and Tilly can't hold it in any longer, and their laughter bounces off the wooden beams surrounding us.

Avery's lashes flutter against her cheeks until she's staring up at me. Then Ronny. Then Tilly. Then where our bodies are still connected.

She pulls her leg off quickly, retracting her hand from beneath mine to cover her mouth. "Oh no."

"Morning," I say with a smile.

Sitting up, I work on the buttons of my flannel quickly before standing and offering a hand to Avery. She shakes her head and pushes up to sitting and then standing on her own.

"What happened?" she asks, brushing stray pieces of hay off her clothes.

I pick a piece of hay out of her hair then pull my hand back, leaving the other fifty pieces for her to handle on her own. "Nothing. Nothing happened," I reply.

"How did you both end up in the barn together?" Tilly asks, leaning against the stall door.

Avery gapes at her friend. "The...horse. Daisy. She was having her baby."

Ronny crosses his arms. "A successful birth, I'd say."

I scowl at him, promising to add a knuckle sandwich to his order later.

"I have to get ready for my massage. I should go," Avery says.

Tilly raises her hand. "I'm your client, remember?"

Avery widens her eyes and tries to mouth something to Tilly that looks a lot like *stop*.

"Me, too," I say to bail her out. "I have to get breakfast ready for everyone."

Blonde strands stick up everywhere on Avery's head, like we had a good romp in the hay last night. Even though I know we didn't sleep with each other in one sense of the word, we still slept next to one another in a different sense. I'm still wrapping my head around this. Not because I can't believe it, but I want to remember every detail of how she felt.

Avery looks in my direction but avoids my eyes. "Did anyone else sign up for a spa service?"

I open and close my mouth then shake my head.

"Oh." There's disappointment written on her downcast features. She swallows and peers around at all of us once more. "Okay, bye."

She hurries past us, and Tilly chases after, calling her name.

Ronny swings his gaze to me and raises his brows.

I run my hand through my hair and beard, realizing I probably have hay stuck there like Avery did. Pointing a sharp finger at him I say, "Nothing happened."

"You said that."

"I'm not lying," I say defensively.

Ronny walks out of the stall, calling behind him, "I believe you."

He doesn't.

"You gonna tell me what happened with you last night?" I yell after him.

"Nope."

I scrub both hands down my face and scratch at my beard.

Nothing happened.

But also, enough did.

Sixteen

Avery

"That's a crooked tree. We'll send him to Washington."-Bob Ross

B reakfast was...awkward.

I disappeared in my cabin afterward until Tilly threatened to claw through the window if I didn't open up and tell her everything.

But there wasn't much to tell.

One moment, I'm slipping my feet into my rubber boots and running to the barn, expecting the curse to have struck again, and then I'm leaning into Wyatt's side as the sounds of rustling hay sing us to sleep. I was still finding straw in my hair as I recounted the night to Tilly.

Thankfully, she dropped it.

Only because she fell asleep during her massage.

I left her in my cabin to snooze, passing Soccer Mom on my way to the horse stables.

"You're the massage lady, right?" she asks.

I smile and cross my fingers behind my back. "Yes, did you want to schedule one?"

Her eyes go wide. "Oh, god no. Between my husband and kids, there's always someone touching me. I came here to not be touched." She holds up a finger. "But I would like to take a photo with the man of Thirst Trapp Farms and his pectorals. Any ideas where I can find him?"

"Nope." I'm trying not to run into him and his pecs right now. I spent too many hours with my cheek pinned to one.

She adjusts her fanny pack. "I'm going on one of those farm tours with the guy who looks like Aladdin but with a cowboy hat."

That's a freaky accurate description. "Ronny?"

"Sure."

"Well, I hope you have a great time. There are some fantastic views," I say.

"As long as I get one of those mugs with the barn and farm animals on it," she steeples her fingers like the pitch of a roof, "I'll be happy. Promised my kids I'd bring them home something. Free is always the best price!"

Soccer Mom is already walking away before I can say anything more, so I shake my head and continue toward the barn. It's past lunchtime, which means Wyatt is likely sunbathing at his "spot" near the creek where we first met. It's why I have the guts to venture out of my cabin at all. I'm not ready to look deep into his eyes and explain my wandering hands that he woke up to this morning and how I'd attached myself to him like a leech. The photo Tilly took of us said one thousand things. None of which were: *this is your boss.*

While I have the chance, I want to check how the new foal is doing and to ensure the night sleeping with my superior was worth it. Ronny said she was as healthy as any foal he'd seen, but I need to see her with my own eyes to be sure.

As I approach the fenced area behind the barn, I spot the young horse immediately. She's pressed into her mother's side with legs like stilts that are too long and gangly for her small body. Daisy is bent over, chomping on a patch of grass and has that post-birth glow.

Leaning my forearms on the splintered wood and propping my foot up on one of the bottom rungs, I watch them move together as one. The foal shifts on her feet but doesn't stray far from Daisy's side, as if she's still scrunched inside her womb. Her ears are standing straight up with tufts of brown and white fur surrounding them. I pull out my phone from my shorts and snap a picture of the two of them. The angle is weird, but I can't help tipping my phone slightly whenever I take a photo. At least

I'm not crouching like usual. Tilly says I take pictures like an overzealous dad. I say it's all in the angle.

It's only been a week since arriving at the farm, but this might be one of my favorite moments so far. This new birth feels like a weight lifted off my shoulders. Maybe the curse has been lifted, too.

"Hey."

I startle and whip around.

Wyatt holds up both of his hands. "Sorry, I didn't mean to scare you."

"You should bang some pots together so I know you're coming," I say, coaching my heart rate down.

He smiles. "That's fair. But since I don't walk around with a pocketful of pots, how about I whistle next time."

His expression is devilish and sweet stirred together in a concoction I like. "What are you doing here?" I ask.

He was supposed to be somewhere else that isn't here. Not sneaking up on me wearing his sexy "Thirst Trapp Farms" hat and those racy Wrangler jeans, looking like he just stepped out of a farm magazine. Is he selling seeds? Tractors? Dirt? Doesn't matter, I don't care; I'll buy whatever he's selling.

"I wanted to come check on the foal," he says, resting his forearms on the top of the fence beside me.

There are enough corded muscles to send my heart into a gallop. I'll respectfully decline the heart palpitations, thanks. I turn my eyes back to mother and daughter. "She's perfect," I say in a wistful tone.

All babies are cute. It's this theory I have that all animals are cuter as babies. An opossum leaves much to be desired but a baby opossum? I'll adopt ten.

Wyatt laces his fingers. "I was hoping you'd name her."

"Me?"

He nods. "Yes, you. I know how much you like naming the animals. Figured you might even have one picked out already."

I smile and dip my chin. "I don't but give me the day to think on it."

"Alright. How about a ride in the meantime?" he asks. "I want to go scout a potential spot to take guests camping."

I hesitate. The last thing I need is more alone time with Wyatt. "I should probably get back to my cabin. Tilly fell asleep facedown during her massage, and I should check on her."

"After?"

"What about the farm tour? I ran into Soccer Mom, and she said Ronny was giving her a ride around the property and a free mug. Don't you need to go with them?"

He turns to face me, one elbow resting on the fence. "Wait, who? Soccer Mom?"

I scratch my neck. "Sorry, I meant, Jackie."

He laughs, then shrugs. "That's a pretty good name for her but no. I don't need to go. Ronny's got it covered."

I face him, too. "What about Stephen King?"

"You mean, Joe Hill, as in King's son?" Wyatt clarifies. "He's been in his cabin all day. I haven't seen him since yesterday."

My mouth drops open. "Wait, Joe is really Stephen King's son?"

Wyatt nods. "That's what Ronny said."

This explains so much. "He was really into his book," I say.

Wyatt peers back at the cabins. "He said something about coming for the *quiet*."

And he thought a farm would be quiet? "What about Granny? She doesn't need help with anything?" I ask, turning to face him.

Wyatt pushes off the fence and starts slowly walking to the front of the barn. "Granny is fine. Plus, she doesn't like it when I hover. Any other excuses?"

I turn my back to the horse pen and lean my elbows on the fence behind me. "I have to water my plants."

He turns and puts his hands on his hips. "You don't have any plants."

"I need to water the grass."

He shakes his head. "Try again."

I tap a finger on my chin. "I should water...my car."

"Are you trying to avoid me for some reason?" he asks with a laugh and a wink that could slay me. "Wait, Avery, have you been on a horse before?"

I bounce my hand and lower my voice, drawing out the word, "No...and also, no."

He claps his hands together then walks toward me to grab my wrist and tug me toward him. "Then, let's get you on a horse."

I'M TRAILING WYATT up the mountain on horseback like I do this all the time. It's one thing to throw on a hat and think of yourself as a badass cowgirl but another to be her. Now my actual ass is sore in so many places, I have to bite down on my lip to keep from screaming out in pain with every jostle of the saddle. Ten out of ten do not recommend saddles.

Wyatt let me ride his horse, Axel, since I trusted him more than a horse named *Trigger*. It might as well spell Danger. But now that I'm too many feet off the ground, staring down at the rocky path below, and at the mercy of a horse bigger than me, names don't matter. Horses don't matter. Safety matters.

"How much longer?" I ask as Axel's hoof slips on a rock and my tailbone jabs into the hard seat.

Axel is powerful. He's also as bullheaded as they come.

Reins? What reins? He's ignored my pulling and not so friendly jabs to his side since we started on the path. And speaking of asses, his nose keeps finding Trigger's crack, giving him playful bumps that Trigger isn't laughing about. Wyatt said they're brothers, which makes a lot of sense since Axel seems to take his job as a younger sibling very seriously.

"Not long. We're almost to the top."

I can't keep my groan inside any longer and cry out in pain with the next bump. Leaning forward in the saddle and closer to Axel's ears, I pat his neck. "Look, I know you're just trying to do your sibling duty and annoy Trigger, but please get me to the top and back down in one piece," I beg.

Wyatt turns in his saddle. "Did you say something?"

I sit straighter and wince at the bruise developing on my left butt cheek, matching the one on the right. "Nope."

He turns around, and I lean forward again, saying for Axel's ears only, "Don't forget what I said."

I exhale and clench my thighs, standing slightly in the stirrups to relieve the ache happening down below. Axel seems to have heeded my plea and is keeping his nose up and his hooves on solid ground.

It's warm this afternoon, but I still wore joggers instead of shorts to avoid any chafing, as Wyatt suggested. Trust a man that wears Wranglers regardless of the weather.

I need that embroidered on a pillow.

The sky grows wider the higher we climb until we're mostly horizontal again. Wyatt slides off Trigger and leads him around the flat ground, where trees are sparsely shooting up here and there, and slings the reins around a low-hanging limb.

"I think we could fit a few tents up here." He looks up at me. "What do you think?"

The area is huge and flat, and the wind isn't nearly as bad with the protection of the trees and shrubs speckled around the area. It's when I look out through the opening of the trees, where the land runs straight off the cliff and faces a big sky painted with every shade of blue that I forget about my sore muscles and tender places.

"Wow."

"Beautiful, huh?"

"Breathtaking."

Except, somehow I still have breath in my lungs.

"Good job," Wyatt says, leading Axel to where Trigger is grazing. "Stand up in the stirrups and swing your other leg over. I'll help you slide down," he says.

I stand like he says. At least, I think I'm standing. My legs are flimsy pieces of paper and shake uncontrollably as I swing my leg over.

"That's it," Wyatt says, and grips either side of my waist.

Since my legs are no help to me anymore, I slide or fall or some combination of the two into his arms. He holds me close until my feet are on the ground, and I can feel the blood re-enter my legs.

"You alright?" he asks in a low, steady voice.

I nod, feeling every glorious inch of him on my back. Biting my lips and closing my eyes isn't helping brush off how good he feels. One hand is splayed on my stomach while the other curls around my hip.

My body is turned on and ignoring my pleas to turn off right this instant!

He straightens and takes a step back, each hand falling away. "You might be a little sore tomorrow."

"A little?" I ask, turning around and tugging my shirt down.

Wyatt laughs, the hearty sound traveling on the next breeze that passes through, tickling my spine. "I like your shirt."

A chill rushes over me under his intent stare, skating along my skin and causing the fine hairs on my body to rise. I'd forgotten which shirt I was wearing between trying not to fall off a horse and being caught up in his arms. "Tilly got it for me when I graduated from massage school."

We both look down. There's a cat curled up beside a stack of rocks with the words: *Relax, I'm a Meowssage Therapist.*

His eyes snap up like he's seen something he shouldn't. "She has great taste."

Are my nipples as hard as they feel? I look down and immediately confirm my worst nightmare.

Yes, yes they are.

I should have changed out of my bralette. They're like an unruly aunt with a cigarette hanging out of her mouth and can't be trusted. Luckily, Wyatt strides to the saddle bag draped over Trigger's backside and pulls out a rolled hammock. "Here, help me set this up."

He shakes it out and walks to a couple of trees that are closest together, wrapping a strap around each hearty trunk and pulling to make sure they're taut.

That looks like a one-butt hammock to me. "You're going to set up a hammock? Right now?"

"Of course. We need to make sure the guests have a good view from every angle."

Right. The guests. It's all for the guests. "Okay." I walk over looking like the hunchback of Notre Dame until my nipples can quit their shenanigans. "Could I borrow your flannel?"

Without question, he slips off his flannel, tossing it up as I catch it in the air. At least now my inappropriate nipples will be covered. And I'll get to smell Wyatt while keeping my distance.

Holding one end as he secures the other, I attempt to wrap mine around the tree, and Wyatt does the tug test to make sure I've got it secure. He stands in front of the hammock and waves me closer. "We should sit at the same time," he says with a smirk. "It's easier that way."

So much for distance. I walk over and stand beside him, the hammock hitting behind our knees. "Okay, Hammock Master."

He smiles and holds up one finger at a time. "One...two...three."

He sits before I do, and the edge of the hammock swings forward, knocking me off balance. I fall into Wyatt's lap with a yelp. "I thought we were sitting on go!"

"You always go on *three*. Never *go*."

He doesn't make a move to push me off his lap, and I'm not trying to rush off either. But when the socially acceptable time to be sitting on your boss' lap expires, he finally shifts me, sliding me off his lap and positioning me beside him. "There."

I brush the light wisps of hair from my face and take a few breaths to gain the composure I just lost. Or, maybe it was never there in the first place. His arm is still draped around my shoulder, and I stare at it, trying to make sense of what is happening and those warm feelings swirling deep and low inside me.

He's not letting go. I'm not moving. We're both here, staring down at the valley of trees reaching to touch the sky and is like the view from the farmhouse, Wyatt's creek, or the old tree. It's the same but also new. A different angle and perspective that gives it new beauty. I don't care that the whole world shares one sky. It's this particular slice I'm falling in love with.

"Do you want any dinner?" he asks in a low drawl that makes my toes curl.

He brought dinner?

I shake my head, not wanting to disturb whatever is happening. "I already ate." My brain is asking questions that I'm swallowing just as fast. I go with a simpler conversational approach. "I thought of a name for the foal," I say, suddenly.

He kicks at the ground to swing the hammock. "Oh, yeah? Let's hear it."

I clear my throat and do a drumroll on my thighs. "Britney Spurs."

He throws his head back and laughs.

I start laughing, too, and pretty soon the hammock is shaking, not swinging.

Wyatt combs through his beard. "That's good. How do you come up with these names?"

I shrug and peel my eyes away from his amused face. There's that hollow feeling beneath my breastbone. The one that is empty and aching but still full of memories that echo loudly off the loss. The missing piece inside me.

"It's uh...this thing I used to do with my brother," I explain, my laughter from minutes ago sobering up and taking a hike back to the dark side.

"Used to?"

I should have known Wyatt would ask more questions. It's nothing new to talk about Justice in the past tense now, but for weeks and even months afterward, he was always in the present. *Justice loves hiking, too. Justice likes pizza more than hot dogs. Justice will laugh about this one.* He still existed all around us, even when he wasn't physically there.

But now, my body, my brain, my days without him texting me memes from The Office are fully aware of the lack of space he once took up in my life.

Tears sting the backs of my eyes, and I contort my face to keep them from falling while looking away. I scrunch my nose and stare down at my lap. "Yeah. He…"

I can't even bring myself to say it.

Wyatt stays quiet, rocking the hammock back and forth as I train my features, tamp down the rising emotion, and tell myself not here, not now. My brother died five years ago, but the grief is still fresh at times, acting as though it happened last week.

"He died."

"How?"

I suck in air through my nose. "He was…hit…by a car." The emotion is so thick in my throat I have to clear it before continuing. "On his bike."

When was the last time I'd even told this story? I don't talk about it often. I spend most of my time talking to my neighbors, friends, and coworkers about their lives, not mine. I offer pieces, but none that look and sound like this truth. Death, curses, and crippling fear don't make for good small talk.

I'm not sure the gaping hole of his loss will ever be filled. Or, that it will ever get easier to talk about. It forces me to relive his death all over again.

This is the part where I remember his bike. The bent wheels, broken handlebar, and the pedal that was hanging off. It was recovered from the scene and given back to us, mangled and unrecognizable. If my brother had looked anything like this bike, I didn't want to know. Not seeing him one last time, to say goodbye, is my biggest regret; but at the time, I just couldn't do it. I couldn't see him laid out in that hospital bed—dead—with a body that had been crushed beyond repair.

The arm around my shoulders squeezes a little tighter, as if Wyatt can feel me start to sink. "Memories are what we have left of them. Not even death can take those," he murmurs in my ear.

I nod and dip my chin lower and lower until the weight of my tears, the pang in my chest, is too much, and I let them out.

With tears dripping from my eyes, an arm around my shoulders holding me together, and the memories I collected over so many years, I let myself remember.

Seventeen

Wyatt

"The secret to doing anything is believing that you can do it."-Bob Ross

Granny, I'm back."

"Didn't know you'd left," she says from her recliner.

So much for being around to help my ailing grandmother. She's as healthy as a sprightly newborn kid. The goat kind, not the human one.

"I already made some dinner. Want some?"

She cranes her neck to look at me. "I ate dinner hours ago. It's time for pie."

After the time spent with my arm around Avery, her tears soaking my shirt before I eventually dropped her back at her cabin, I'm ready for dessert before dinner. "Pie it is."

She meets me in the kitchen as I pull the familiar tin out of her hiding spot in the cabinet with other fancy dishes that never get used. I think it's more so Ronny doesn't find it. Granny doesn't take chances with her pie falling into the wrong hands.

"Where are all the city folk? Laying eyes on a cow for the first time?" she asks.

I laugh under my breath and plate a piece of pie for each of us. "Back in their cabins after a tour with Ronny. I'm going out soon to make a fire tonight after everyone else eats dinner."

She points at the freezer, and I walk backward to retrieve the ice cream. In the few months I've been here, I've learned how to speak Granny. It involves mostly hand gestures, like pointing and finger snapping with an occasional grumble thrown in to make things interesting.

"So, if you aren't giving them a tour, then what've you been doing?"

I hesitate. The moment Avery's name rolls off my lips, I might as well be setting out a suggestion box for her to offer her comments and opinions.

I scoop out a spoonful of vanilla bean ice cream onto her plate, and she takes the spoon from me and serves herself two more. "I was scouting out a good camping spot," I explain.

She licks the spoon clean. I guess I'll just get a new one to dish myself some.

"You're taking people camping now are ya?"

Using a new spoon, I dish a heap of ice cream on top of my pie. "They paid for experiences, so that's what I'm going to give 'em."

"Speaking of payment." Granny walks around the counter to the stack of mail piled beside the home phone. She says she knows exactly what's in that pile, which makes me wonder why we still have it.

She hands me an envelope that's already been opened. The local bank's logo is printed across the front with the familiar address stamped on the top left corner. I've personally visited that location on multiple occasions.

I set my spoon down, sensing I'll need both hands to handle what the letter says, and slip the folded sheet of paper out of the envelope. Without reading word for word, I scan the harsh Times New Roman font that says the same thing every time then skip to the end where an unforgiving number is written along the bottom.

We'd long since run out of get out of jail free cards with the bank and owe them a sum that neither Granny nor I have. Ronny did what he could after Gramps died to keep the farm profitable, but it wasn't until I moved back that I found out Granny hadn't paid on the loan they had taken out to start their meat business. Call it grief over losing her other half or simply not knowing the ins and outs of the bills since Gramps always took care of everything, but here we are. My parents pitched in where they could but running another business on top of their day jobs wasn't feasible. No one had the funds.

Selling cuts of chicken, beef, eggs, and other garden vegetables to local spots around town, Bozeman, and Billings was barely enough to make ends meat—pun intended. Add in the fact Granny didn't ask for help with the loan when she realized there was one and figured her longtime friendship with the bank manager would be enough. It was for a while but not forever.

I fold up the letter and drop it on the counter. "We should have enough by the end of the summer to pay at least half this amount. I'll go in and give them what we make this weekend so they see we're trying. That's all we can do."

"Thank you, Wyatt." Granny raises her brows and looks down at her plate again. "I trust you. Even after I—"

Her voice catches, and she drops her head. I reach across the counter and lightly squeeze her shoulder. Those words mean more than anything. She knows what I went through. From one financial emergency to the next. I'm surprised Granny even wanted my help after forfeiting my share in a business partnership. I came here with nothing but sheer determination for it not to happen again. We've both been trying to climb out of financial ruin, but now we're doing it together.

She spoons another bite then asks, "And Avery? What's she been up to?"

I drop my hand from her shoulder and take a large bite of my dessert, chewing it slowly and thinking of an answer that will satisfy both of us. "You know, Ronny's around here, too. Why don't you ever ask about him?"

"Because Ronny doesn't have as cute a smile as Avery does."

True.

She spoons a bite of ice cream in her mouth and swallows. "And Ronny checks in. I know how he's doing already."

I forget how close the two of them have become. Once, Ronny was just a neighbor, then my best friend who was my sidekick in all things spelling trouble. Now, he's family.

She holds up a hand. "You know what, say no more. I don't need to know about what you two were doing in the barn together last night."

I swallow a bite too large for my throat. "How'd you know we were in the barn last night?"

"I've got cameras on the house. It sent me a text alert when it sensed movement."

"What? Since when do you have cameras?" And get text alerts?

"A year ago when Gramps died."

The statement is like a punch to my conscience.

Another reason I should've been here sooner.

But I wasn't.

I grab a glass and fill it with water. "Nothing happened with Avery in the barn...with a candlestick and Mr. Green."

"Mhm. You keep telling yourself that," she says. "It was on the back of a horse with a pistol and Miss Blue Eyes."

Leave it to us to use our favorite board game, Clue, to make a point. Gulping down my water, I set it back on the counter, a little too hard. *Here we go.* "We were there to help Daisy deliver her foal. And tonight, we were up there on a scouting mission."

"Is that what the kids are calling it these days?"

I pick up my plate and keep shoveling more bites of apple goodness into my mouth.

"And what about after she helped deliver the foal?" she asks.

I shrug. "We fell asleep."

She raises her brows.

"On accident," I clarify with a tilt of my head.

She sets her spoon down with a clank. "You can't punish yourself forever, Wyatt."

Her words are strong and loud, like she's saying them through a megaphone while hitting a triangular dinner bell and yellin' for me to come in and eat. I stand straighter, my own act of defensiveness.

"Eventually, you're gonna need to suck it up and be okay with the fact that things didn't work out with that hussy, Caroline. It doesn't mean they never will with anyone else, though."

Her steely eyes and years of wisdom have me pinned. But she doesn't get it. "Things are still...fresh," I say.

It's only been four months since my dad had to drive me home, like I was a kid coming home from college. I sold my car so I wouldn't default on my rent. My startup was sold, and I broke up with Caroline on the same day.

I lost everything, which is enough to know I don't want to lose anything else.

She shifts on her feet, angling herself to face me. "Honey, I'm about to tell you something you're gonna wanna hear." She puts both hands out in front of her. "Failure is subjective."

I scoff. "Not when you lose it all: money, girlfriend, job, security. Seems like a pretty universal failure to me."

"Maybe you needed to lose all of that to find out who and what you really want. I don't see those things as failures. I see them as growth. But the only way you will, too, is if you learn from them and keep growing," she says.

I turn my eyes toward the TV that's still casting Jeopardy at a low volume, needing something other than her hard stare to look at.

"You can beat yourself up every time you try something and it doesn't work out. Or, you can do something else." She takes a bite and talks around a mouthful. "Or someone else."

"Granny!" I scold.

She shrugs. "What? You forget I was your age once."

My ears are bleeding.

She swats my shoulder, and I raise my hands to protect myself. "Okay, okay, but don't you think that's oversimplifying things a little?" I ask.

"About doing someone else?"

"No," I say, drawing out the word. "About failure."

She pretends to swat a fly away. "There's no sense trying to make life more difficult. There are enough mysteries in this world without us needing to create more. Live your life, Wyatt, grow and learn. That's all there is to it." She claps her hands. "And go tell Avery you want to make her your gal."

"Granny!"

"You're foolin' nobody trying to dance around the issue. It's pure misery being in the same room as you two right now. Just ask her to go steady and call it a day."

I bite my cheek to keep from smiling as Granny turns and heads back to her recliner to crank the volume back up to a level that requires ear plugs for anyone else.

The next bite of crust is usually my favorite, but it tastes like it's lost all its buttery flavor. Just like my mood.

I run through every reason why I shouldn't start something with Avery.

I just got out of a long-term relationship.

I'm her boss.

Too busy trying to save the farm.

I might not be here in two months.

Afraid to lose her.

And there it is.

Losing someone like Avery is the last thing I want to sign up for. If I never have her, I can't lose her. But if Granny is right—Lord knows she's got enough wisdom to go around—and failure is subjective, then maybe things aren't as hard as I'm making them out to be.

"Damn it, Granny," I mutter under my breath at a pitch I know she'd never be able to hear.

Maybe I could do more than move on.

And I could do it with someone like Avery.

THERE'S SOMETHING ABOUT sitting around a fire that recharges my battery. Inhaling the scent of burning wood, stoking the coals, and staring into the dancing orange flames is the best kind of therapy. Add in the charred scent that ingrains itself into every fiber of my clothing that I can smell days later, and I'm in.

I'd bathe in the scent if I could.

But that would be weird.

I built this fire pit with cinder blocks when I was a teen. It's a ways behind the barn, which blocks a lot of the noise and light, and is partially up the hillside. I used to have my friends over late at night, well after my grandparents went to bed, and we'd get into some trouble out here. I had to fix one of the four wooden adirondack chairs when a couple of my knucklehead friends decided to drunk wrestle on top of it. Those dumbasses were Ronny and me.

And those chairs? They're the very same ones we're all sitting in tonight, weather-worn with more scratches and gouges than when Gramps helped me build them. Avery's sitting in the one I had to fix. She probably can't tell the chair pitches to the right slightly, but I can see the slope that causes one of her hips to dip lower.

The sun has dropped low behind the mountains, leaving us in pitch black darkness. There are a few blankets draped on the back of the chairs I brought out that Avery and Tilly put to use the moment they sat down, burrowing beneath it, like mice bedding down for the winter.

Avery's eyes find mine across the fire. Normally a cool blue, they are sharper in the glow of the yellows and oranges, her silk hair looking, as if it's caught flame.

Ronny interrupts and pulls my attention away. "I'll grab another log." He braces himself on the armrests.

"Sit," I demand. "I'll get it."

I'm still feeling spicy after my conversation with Granny.

Ronny gives a low whistle. "Want to wrestle for it?"

I stand. "No. That never goes well."

"True," he says, then stands anyway. "But I'll help."

I shrug and walk to the side of the barn and strain to hear the voices that turn into low whispers as they pass between Avery and Jackie. I haven't seen Joe, our other guest, since yesterday. Hopefully that means he's enjoying himself.

Preferably not lost and definitely still alive.

I make a mental note to check in on him in the morning.

Ronny jogs up beside me. "You doing alright?"

"Yeah, for sure."

"Okay." He drags out the word and adjusts his hat. "So, now that you've gotten the lie out, how about the truth."

I bend down for the small hand ax and set to chipping away at a quartered log in order to make more kindling. We don't need it now that the fire is going strong, but I'll have it for next time. And hopefully avoid Ronny's interrogation in the process.

Ronny stands, looming above me with his hands on his hips.

I peer up at him. "What?"

He sighs and drops his hands. "Look—"

I hold up my hand. "I really don't need another pep talk." Shaking my head, I add, "Do you and Granny coordinate or something?"

"Yeah, every Saturday." He gnaws on his toothpick and shoves his hands in his pockets as I glare at him. "Fine. No, we don't. But we know you."

I stand abruptly, ax hanging at my side. "And what do you know?"

He takes a step closer. "I know what it looks like when you're holding back."

"Ah, hell. Here we go."

"It's about time you wake up and smell something other than cow shit," he spits back.

I narrow my gaze at him. "What's that supposed to mean?"

"It means, you didn't move back here to rebrand the farm, try all this stuff, hire a beautiful woman—"

"That was an accident." And half his fault, too.

He shakes his head. "The point is that you're scared."

I scoff and drop the ax next to the log I mutilated.

He won't be dissuaded. "You can't see past all the shit you went through to even see all the good in front of you. You're just...existing. Wake up and smell that pretty lady, would ya?"

I drop my eyes to the grass beneath my scuffed work boots I've lived in for the last three months. They're nothing like the custom leather loafers I wore to work every single day in the city. Those are no good out here. They're just taking up room in my closet now. I don't know why I'm keeping them. Is it because I actually think I'll move back to the city one day? That one day, Trapp Farms will get out of the red, and Granny will keep running things after I leave again?

Is that what I want? Is that why I'm keeping those shoes?

All of my questions are stuffed in a pair of damn shoes.

I kick at the piece of wood on the ground and clench my jaw before blurting out, "What if I'm not meant to run the farm? What if I can't? What if she leaves? What if—"

"Exactly. *What if*," he says, cutting in. "But the Wyatt I know isn't afraid of a couple what ifs."

I'm starting to see bits of myself again as he talks. The parts that have been ingrained inside me with super glue. This farm, these experiences are all experiments. But I'm doing them, even if I succeeded and failed epically when I tried before, it doesn't mean it'll happen again. Maybe I'm scared to let go just as much as I am to stay.

I let out a deep breath. "Alright. I get it."

He nods. "You still want help with the wood?"

I glare at him with an amused smile. "I never needed your help. But you always know when to give it anyway."

He smiles and tips his hat before pivoting to head back to the fire.

It's then I have another idea worm its way into my brain.

"Ronny!" I yell after him.

He turns, eyebrows scrunched in question.

I grab a few logs and stalk toward him, transferring the load to his arms. "Can you bring these back? I have an idea."

He laughs. "Of course you do."

"Cover for me?"

"Anytime."

Eighteen

Wyatt

"Water's like me. It's lazy. Boy, it always looks for the easiest way to do things."-Bob Ross

K eep your eyes closed. No peeking," I whisper in her ear.

Avery's so close, I can smell the lavender she has to be rubbing all over her body every day. Or, at least on everyone else's. I'm cupping her elbow and steering her through gravel, grass, trees, and cabins, like the surprise is making it through an obstacle course.

"I swore I wouldn't. Just make sure I don't run into anything," she says. "Or get eaten by a wild creature."

I'd likely turn into a wild animal myself trying to protect her if that happened.

"Are you going to tell me why you're kidnapping me?" she asks.

I cup her other elbow when she stumbles. Now my arm is around her, and I'm drowning in her floral scent. "I told you, it's a surprise."

"Mhm. You told me there'd be chocolate. It's as good as luring me in a van with the promise of candy," she says.

"It worked, didn't it?"

"True," she says with a shrug I can feel against my chest. "Do Tilly and Ronny know where we're going? And can you even see where you're going?"

"No, they don't, and I'm not the one with my eyes closed," I chuckle. " I could draw a map of this farm with lines of latitude and longitude if I had to."

"Careful. I might test you on it," she teases.

My tone turns deep and gravelly, which is my sultry voice that only comes out to play when I'm really into someone. I guess that makes sense here. "I'd accept the challenge."

"Do I get a hint?" she asks.

"Nope."

"What? Why not? What if you're taking me hiking in the woods with bears? I don't have my bear spray on me."

"That's not happening," I confirm. "No hiking. No bears."

She snaps her fingers. "Or shooting soup cans off a log? I've got horrible aim, you know."

"It's dark." I laugh. "And it's cute if you think I'd let you shoot my gun at all."

"Good point." She stumbles again, and I grip her waist on instinct. Now that my hand is here, it has no plans on leaving. "You could be taking me swimming in the creek," she says.

I don't answer right away. "Good guess, but I don't swim."

"You just run through sprinklers."

"Exactly," I say and squeeze her waist. Damn, it feels good. "We're here. You can drop your hand now."

She slowly lowers her hand and blinks against the lights I hung over the outdoor tub.

Her voice is quiet when she speaks, and I feel it everywhere I shouldn't. "You finished."

"I did."

Her gaze darts from one end of the space to the other, taking it all in.

Hooks are hung at different intervals inside the privacy fence with robes and towels hanging on them with slippers beneath. More stepping stones have been added, and the large tree round is situated by the tub with different colored glass jars atop it. The tub is filled nearly to the top with steam billowing off the water. I'll need to figure out how to connect the hose to the faucet inside to get hot water for the future, but tonight

I had to fill five-gallon buckets from the bathtub and pour them in just to make this happen.

A candle is lit and positioned on top of the smooth slab of wood that stretches from one side of the tub to the other, and I move from her side to pick up one of the jars. "These are bath salts. Granny had some in the farmhouse, but you can use your own if you want." I grab another jar with liquid in it and turn it over. "This is soap...I think."

She gapes at the jar of soap I'm holding, like it possesses the answers to world hunger, or at least what's happening right now. "You did all of this?"

I set the jar back down. "I figured you could be the first to test it out. I know there weren't many massages and spa treatments this weekend, but there will be. I already have requests for next week. A couple people from town even asked about booking. And after the horseback ride today, I knew you'd be sore. Axel isn't exactly known for his light feet."

"When?" She meets my eyes for the first time since opening hers. "When did you do all of this?"

I shove my hands in my front pockets and rock back on my heels. "Tonight."

She looks back over all the hard work. The work I did for her, and maybe the guests, but mostly to let her know I see the sacrifice and hard work she's put in, the late nights and willingness.

"This is amazing, Wyatt. I can't believe it. The guests are going to love it...I love it."

Her wide mouth and wider eyes tell me she isn't used to people doing these things for her. Like she's shocked by the effort I put in. But once I knew this was her vision, I wasn't going to stop until I finished so she could be the first to enjoy the fruits of her idea. I needed to finish, and I wanted to do it for her.

"I'll leave you to enjoy it." I nod once in her direction. "Oh, and I added a drain on the side, so all you have to do is open it when you're done."

I start walking backward, but she stops me. "Wyatt."

"Yeah?"

She bites her bottom lip then rubs them both together as a soft glow highlights portions of her face. After all the work and stress over the past week, late nights, and tired muscles, I can finally exhale, knowing what this meant to her.

"This is..." She waves a vague hand around the entire space. "This is really, really kind of you. I don't feel like saying thank you is enough. But, thank you."

My lips stretch wide. "You're welcome." I study my feet then look at her face one last time. "I'm really glad you're here."

Then, I disappear into the night to let her enjoy the space. It's as I turn and walk away that I hear her faint response.

"Me, too."

Nineteen

Avery

"Be so very light. Be a gentle whisper."-Bob Ross

I have minutes before I'm positive someone will find me and make this the most embarrassing moment of my adult life.

Nothing could top this: standing in the entryway of the farmhouse, a vibrator and a small crate of condoms under each of my arms with a hose around my neck. I'm either hiding something or into some really kinky stuff. To add more fuel to this bonfire of embarrassment, I've started to sweat, which means the vibrator is ready to bail out of my armpit to find greener pastures.

Pleasure hasn't exactly been on my radar when I'm constantly walking around, hoping a tree doesn't fall on someone if I decide to get bangs. That never happened. Bangs are reserved for breakups only, and seeing as I haven't had a boyfriend since dinosaurs roamed the earth, I've dodged the bang train.

Even though it hasn't been on my mind, Wyatt had to go and fill a tub with some salts and offer a soft robe to make me feel like the most amazing version of myself. I wasn't expecting him to finish the space this weekend, and I definitely wasn't expecting him to do all of that for me last night. The fact he did made me swoon something fierce. It did not bode well for my heart and the feelings I am taking an active role in trying to quell.

Which is why I need to hide these items of pleasure somewhere else so no one accidentally finds them, or I don't accidentally use them. I meant to take them to my cabin after dropping off the hose—a random item I plucked from the side of my cabin to have a reason to come to the farmhouse—but I heard commotion coming from the side of the house. A deep, resonant voice was singing a Taylor Swift song (Ronny, obviously), and I darted inside out of sheer panic of being caught. Granny is at Esther's house, I know that much, and Wyatt is...well, that's the problem. I don't know where he is, per usual, but the house sounds quiet. For now.

Ronny is still outside and looks to be settling in for a weeding sesh. I can't just waltz outside without him seeing what's in my arms and going out the back won't help since my cabin is the opposite direction. I need to deal with this cooler-sized box and Purple Pecker of Pleasure.

I look up at Moosifer who is looming over me with his one judgmental eye. "You really need to stop with that."

I'll need to hide these things somewhere in here before I'm caught and until I can steal them away to my cabin and throw them in the trash. Wait. That wouldn't be a good idea; someone could find them in there.

I'll give them a proper burial in the backyard.

Well, maybe just the condoms.

I stand, my gaze landing on the stairs just off the entryway and past the formal living and dining rooms. *Bingo...was his name-o*. Perfect. Hiding them on the main level would have been easier for someone to find like Granny whose room is near the kitchen. Putting these items anywhere near her space seems close to sacrilege.

I toe off my boots and head toward the stairs. What I don't account for are the creaks I confront on every step. All of my dance-dance-revolution skills don't stand a chance here. Every step I take, or don't take, sends up an alarming cracking noise that is probably alerting the neighbors miles away.

I peer behind me. Somehow Moosifer is still looking in my direction, silently scolding me. A phenomenon I can't quite explain and don't want to.

One full flight of stairs stands between me and a discreet place to bury the evidence that my best friend wanted to pimp me out with. I just have to do it.

I run up the stairs, taking them two at a time until I'm standing at the top, heaving more from fear of being caught than the exertion.

Just get rid of them, my brain yells.

Looking to my right, a bedroom door stands ajar and a floral comforter in hues of pink and green stares back at me from its creased corners and taut position across the bed. It must be a guest space. I tighten my hold on the box slipping from my arm. I can't hide these in there. There's no way. What if someone comes to stay in this room like his sister or...oh god. His mom.

I shake my head and look to my left. The door is swung wide, and a paisley-patterned bedspread is bunched and rumpled at the end of the bed. Jeans, of the Wrangler variety, lie discarded on the ground and a belt hangs on the outside door handle.

Wyatt's room.

If I hide these things in his room, I'm sure he'll find them. But, then again, based on the disarray of the space, maybe he won't.

Unsatisfied with those two options, I look straight ahead at the third and final door: the bathroom. Neutral ground, with cabinets that could easily hide a small tugboat and a brightly colored meat tenderizer.

It's also my last option since I hear a door swing open downstairs.

"Granny? You home?"

Wyatt!

"Shit, shit, shit!" I whisper-yell.

Darting into the bathroom, I silently shut the door and begin rummaging through the cabinets below the sink. Towels, cleaners, extra rolls of toilet paper, a scale with dust on it, and a bin, which is large enough to house one-hundred and fifty hotel-size bottles of shampoos and conditioners. The musty floral scent that accosts my nose when I tug the soft-sided bin closer has me questioning why?

I don't give into the smell and shove the box of condoms into the fabric bin, following it with the vibrator.

"Granny?"

Pushing it back into place, I can just barely see the top of the condom box, but it's enough to see a photo of one of the rubbers gracing the side.

I tilt my head. "Is that the actual size?"

Tilly must have purchased the extra-large, and now I can't unsee that.

The same creaks I tried dodging on the way up begin to sound off like firecrackers. I'm out of time in three...two...

I whip open the door and startle Wyatt.

One.

"Hi."

"Hey."

I don't offer an explanation for why I'm here, but he isn't going to let me off the hook that easily. "What are you doing here?" he asks.

Fair question. It makes a lot of sense since I've literally never been upstairs in this house before, and I have my own bathroom. So, I say the first thing that pops into my head.

"My toilet is clogged. I had to use yours."

Really, any other explanation would have been better than this one.

"Oh." He widens his stance and crosses his arms, going into Bob the Builder mode. I like this setting. "You didn't have a plunger in your cabin?"

Another Pulitzer Prize-winning question from Bob.

"I...don't know."

"You don't know?"

"I don't know...what a plunger looks like. I've never had this happen."

I want to curl up and die under the bathroom sink with the XL rubbers.

He hooks a thumb behind him. "I could show you."

Of course the first time Wyatt and I have really had a chance to talk since yesterday when I cried on his shoulder and told him stories of my deceased brother then sat in his love bath would be now. We're completely alone with condoms equivalent to the size of a hot air balloon only feet from us.

Yeah, definitely a lot to unbox here.

"It's fine. I'll Google a picture and figure it out. You know, since I'm an independent woman who doesn't need a man to plunge her toilet."

I'd laugh if every word I just said wasn't so suggestive.

"Avery, you don't have to—"

"No," I say abruptly, standing straighter in the doorway. "I do."

He closes his mouth and nods, like plunging toilets is the greatest of my worries.

Deciding this embarrassing moment has lasted long enough, I nod and try to move past him, but I don't account for the fact his body takes up the entire width of the stairwell. He's standing at the top, but he doesn't leave me any room to move past.

"Can I..." I point behind him.

"Uh, sure," he says, moving to the side. "Sorry."

He rubs the back of his neck as I pass by, one inch separating our bodies. Dried sweat and dirt mingle together, telling of the hours he's spent working outside. It's intoxicating. So mind-numbingly delicious I might even prefer it to my sandalwood candles. It's total blasphemy, but I can't seem to find a care when he's this close.

I make the mistake of looking up at him, and I want so badly to hold his face between my hands and kiss his mouth to see if the salty flavor extends there, too. For research purposes only, I swear.

He doesn't seem to have the same qualms of keeping his hands to himself and rubs a piece of my hair between his fingers. "Are you at least going to come horseback riding with the group today?"

"I'm still pretty sore." I pause. "And I might need to water my ficus."

That garners a laugh from him. "What if I ask nicely?"

My mouth curves into a smile and without being able to stop myself, I'm now whispering sensual things in stairwells. "Say, please."

His smile is molten lava covering every square inch of my body. But he doubles down and leans closer as he twirls the lock of my hair around his finger. "Pleeeease."

I pull my bottom lip between my teeth and nod. "Do I get to ride Axel?"

He smirks. "Only if you ask nicely."

I lean back against the wall, giving our bodies some space to cool off from this inferno we built in milliseconds. "Pretty please?"

"Good girl."

My mouth falls open, and I shove his shoulder and pretend, like his response didn't go straight to my loins. He leans closer, lips hovering dangerously close when we hear...

"Wyatt?"

Granny.

He pulls back, like a teenager that was just caught making out with his girlfriend in his room with the door shut. "Be right there. Just giving Avery a tour up here."

There's a pause and then Granny says, "Sure ya are."

He closes his eyes and rubs his forehead. "So, horseback riding..."

"Horseback riding," I repeat, clasping my hands behind my back.

He opens his eyes and rests his hands on his hips, making me wonder if he's trying just as hard as I am to not touch again. "You can ride Axel."

I'm still whispering. "I forgot I had a last-minute massage booked."

"By who? Everyone's going on the trail ride," he says.

I open my mouth but get cut off again.

"Wyatt!"

He keeps his eyes on me like I'm going to vanish into thin air. "Yeah?" he yells down to her.

"Esther sent me home with some of those dishes you wanted for your big, fancy dinners. Help me get them out of the trunk would ya?" Granny says.

"Be right there." He sighs and pushes a rough hand through his hair. "I should help her before she decides to do it herself."

I laugh, my voice coming out all low and sultry like. "You should."

His eyes roam my face and drop to my lips. Seeming to catch himself, he finds my eyes again. "For the record, Axel does like you. A lot."

"A lot?" I ask. "How do you know?"

His expression is serious. "He told me."

"Do you speak horse now or something?"

He shrugs with that boyish smile of his. "I speak Axel."

I cross my arms. "Tell him…"

There are two courses of action here. Set up boundaries like Wyatt really is my boss and I respect him too much to start something when he is clearly trying to help his family, and I am even more clearly trying not to be afraid of my own dreams. Or, I could play the game.

"Tell him I like him, too," I say.

Wyatt's grin is the size of an obnoxiously huge billboard. He waves a hand toward the stairs for me to walk in front of him. I will, but first, I lift up on my toes intent on one thing.

His lips part, and the closer I get the more the smell of straw infiltrates my senses. My chest skims his as I raise my hand and pluck a stray leaf from his hair and hand it to him.

He swallows and takes the leaf as I walk downstairs. I can feel the weight of him on the steps behind me and the warmth prickling across my skin, making me sure we weren't just talking about the horse.

"DO YOU HAVE to leave?"

After running into Wyatt in his own house, raising questions that I'll never answer, I came back to help Tilly pack. She keeps tossing her clothes into her suitcase while I sit on her bed and fold them for her. She didn't ask me to do this, but I can't help it.

"I only had enough time off for one weekend here. Tis the season for drastic color changes and bangs at the salon." She throws a pair of jeans over her shoulder, and I catch them in the air. "If I could stay here the whole summer, you know I would."

My voice is sad, and I hope she hears it. "Yeah, I know."

We packed in a lot this weekend. Between the bar, foal birth, bonfire, rides around the farm on the Cougar, and a couple of horseback rides, Wyatt made sure there was something for everyone. Well, except for Joe who we literally never saw for the rest of the weekend.

I hope his book was a five-star.

"You'll have other guests here next week, and you'll forget all about me," she says.

She smells the t-shirt in her hands and deeming it clean, she trades it for the one she's wearing. It's such a Tilly thing to do. I feel a pang in my chest at the thought of her leaving.

"It's supposed to be a busy week," I say while rolling the shirt she discarded and tucking it inside one of her shoes for space-saving purposes.

She starts packing up her makeup. "Ronny said the rest of the weekends this month are booked out, and you even have a group staying for a week in August."

I try to keep my composure and not burst at the seams over how happy and relieved I am that this summer is shaping up to be a busy one. There are more bookings coming in from people around town, and I plan on offering package deals to continue incentivizing folks to sign up for services. Thank God, I won't have to resort to offering pedicures to the cows.

I lean back against the fabric headboard and cross my arms. "You and Ronny, huh?"

Her back is to me, but I can see her roll her eyes in the mirror. "It was just a one-time thing."

"Except, I know for a fact he stayed in your cabin last night, too," I say.

Her mouth falls open. "How do you know that?"

I lean down and pick up the leather belt with a buckle the size of North America attached to it, holding it up for her to see.

"That could be mine," she says.

"It could be," I say with a laugh. Tilly would probably wear something like this. "But Ronny wears this one every day."

She spins around and walks closer to the bed to grab the belt, looping it through her shorts. "I think I'll keep it. As a souvenir."

"He might come after you if he figures out you took it," I say with a wink. "He loves that one."

"There are worse things that could happen," she says, hands resting on her hips. A sad look hijacks her features. "I'm going to miss you, Avery."

I tilt my head. "I miss you already."

And it's true. Tilly adds a vibrancy wherever she goes. Sometimes it's messy, like splattered paint on walls, but most of the time she's creating works of art with those colors. Ones that I've been lucky enough to be a part of.

She wraps me in another hug. "It's a good thing you'll have a hunky farmer to help you forget about me."

I scoff. "I could never forget about you. Hunky farmer or not. You're my best friend and completely unforgettable."

She laughs at this and pulls back to hold me at arm's length. "Promise me something."

"Maybe."

She drops her hands. "Come on. It's my last request before I leave you to fend for yourself."

I twist my lips and chew on the inside of my cheek before finally nodding.

"Don't be afraid to grab life by the balls."

I sputter out a laugh. "Thanks for the delicately worded encouragement."

"Anytime." She hugs me again. "But seriously, it's time for you to have your moment. Even if you have to do it scared."

The air that whooshes out of me leaves me light headed. I cling to my best friend. When she's around, I feel braver. Like I could stick up my middle finger to all the pesky reminders that tell me I don't know what I'm doing and that I'm a fraud. But then I think of how I've proved to myself I am capable of doing this on my own. I'm here, aren't I? I just need to remember the progress I've already made and keep taking one day at a time.

While also grabbing some balls.

Twenty

Avery

"You need the dark in order to show the light."-Bob Ross

The weeks pass with a routine I could set a timer to. Waking, eating, flirting with Wyatt, feeding the animals, and choring (yes, it's an action). There haven't been any more trips to the Thirsty Hippo since Tilly was here, but she reminds me of it almost weekly.

And asks how Ronny's doing.

I tell her he's moved on to greener pastures. Literally, since he's been working out in the fields more while Wyatt takes the lead with the guests. It means we've had less time together, and I notice.

She sent me a stern face emoji.

And I sent her a cow emoji, because it's cute.

In between all the adventures Wyatt has planned, I've been up to my eyeballs massaging mass amounts of sunburned skin and knots the size of baseballs. The spa has been booked solid most days, even in between guests, since a lot of the locals caught wind of it and have been making treks out here. Gone are the quiet days of twirling my thumbs waiting for someone to show and using pillows to practice massage techniques on. Now, I'm a full-on spa director. Pedicures, nature bathing, massages, and facials have been my constants.

Wyatt and Ronny spend the majority of their days mending fences in the August heat, moving cows, and plowing. Mostly sans shirts. When the guests are tucked in for the night, Wyatt makes a fire, and we stay up late swapping ghost stories that make it impossible for me to sleep. Other nights, we go for a ride in The Cougar and don't talk at all. The farm seems to do most of the talking for us. It feels like those first few days of awkward interactions are behind us, and we're building something stronger now. A better working relationship, friendship...I don't know, but I won't forget the door on the birdhouse this time.

The weekends are constantly booked with guests, a few weekdays too, as we give them an experience they won't soon forget. I've told my diary (aka Tilly) about every single one of them. Dinners beneath the stars, cow hugging, and the sixty-minute Swedish massage are our most popular activities. The reviews on Experiences R Us tell us as much.

Today, a whole month and one week after stepping foot on this farm, I'm preparing for another group to arrive. We've managed to reserve every cabin, including the spare room in the farmhouse for this whole next week. Since our social media following has multiplied, we've leveled up and become an Experience Master, a place vetted for their outstanding hospitality on the site with the amount of positive reviews and bookings.

Since early this morning, I've had one massage client (Esther from next door), done laundry, baked more cookies, and wiped every surface twice. To think, a month ago I was desperate for one client that wasn't my best friend, and now, I'm booked solid with a waitlist.

Two knocks sound on the door as I fluff the couch pillows and karate chop them in the middle. I don't know why I've taken to doing this, but the internet has influenced me.

I walk to the door and open it. Wyatt's beard greets me. "Hi."

"Hey." I stare down at him since he's standing just below the steps.

"I had someone ask if they could schedule a massage today at four. Are you okay with that?" he asks.

"Let me check my schedule."

Pulling out my phone from my back pocket, I navigate to my calendar. Eventually, we'll need to implement a scheduling app. Phone calls, texts, and messages through the vacation rental site are making more work.

Eventually.

As in, a time that goes beyond this summer. Is that what Wyatt wants? This was only supposed to be a two-month trial, but so far, it's been a huge success. And I'm not just talking about the spa. The social accounts for Thirst Trapp Farms have blown up since the feature that someone did in a small travel magazine. Sure, Wyatt had his shirt off with the farm in the background in the spread, but Granny was so proud she ripped out the centerfold and framed it for the family photo wall.

Wyatt has only hinted at continuing the reservations through the fall, winter, and spring months, but soon I'm going to have to ask for an answer. If I move here permanently, I'll have to give Tilly a heads up. If I don't, I'll need to figure out a different job. A sour feeling fills my stomach at the thought.

"Looks like four will work," I say, pocketing my phone.

"Great. I'll let them know."

"Perfect."

He shifts on his feet. "Well, I'll see you later then."

He turns to walk away, and I catch myself calling for him. "Wyatt, wait."

Pivoting back around, he searches my face. "Yeah?" He's on to his next work task, and I can't just bring up all that's on my mind right now. I should come up with a plan first. There's a month left in our deal after all.

"I'm finished in here. Is there anything else you need help with?" I ask.

He looks to the edge of the cabin, considering my question. I take the moment to study the vertical lines in his neck, making guesses as to the strong jawline he likely has hiding beneath that full beard of his.

There have been stolen moments, looks shared but never acted on, and plenty of harmless flirting. I've become better at it, I like to think. If I'm leaving in a month, I don't want to leave with strings. If I'm staying, I'll have to keep working with Wyatt for a lot longer than a summer.

"I was about to go check in on the horses and make sure we have everything for the rides tomorrow. Want to join?"

I nod. "Okay. I'd love to. Let me grab some shoes."

"And you might want something cooler than that sweatshirt. It's getting hot out here." He wipes his brow with the back of his hand.

I stare down at my sweatshirt and without thinking, I pull my arms through the hoodie and lift it over my head, revealing the black spaghetti tank I have on underneath. I slip my feet into my sneakers and walk out onto the first step, closing the door behind me. "Ready."

He looks like he's in the middle of a lake without an oar as his mouth falls open, and he rubs the back of his neck. "Yup."

I jump off the last step and stride past him. "Let's go, Farmer Wyatt."

"What did you just call me?"

"You heard me," I say without stopping.

My ears might be playing tricks on me, but it sounds like he says *I like it.*

He jogs to catch up. "We're planning another camping trip at the end of the week for anyone who wants to join," he says. "Are you interested?"

I've missed out on a lot of the adventures since I've been so busy.

I study him as he stares forward. "What about the spa?"

He shrugs one shoulder. "We can clear your schedule, block out those days."

I match his strides. "I've never been camping."

He swings his head to look at me. "Seriously?"

"Never. Most of our family vacations involved a cabin or hotel, never a rock bed and sleeping bag."

"You have to come then," he insists.

"It's supposed to be for the guests," I say as we reach the barn. "Not me."

"They may need you after a day of horseback riding."

My grin widens. "Should I pack my massage table?"

"No, but I'll pack an air mattress for you." He slides open the door. "Everyone else has to sleep on foam pads."

My insides melt like cheese in a microwave. Apparently air mattresses are the way to my heart. "Okay, I'll go."

Wyatt smiles. "I didn't even have to offer to bring you your own sleeping bag. Guess we'll have to share."

My heart stops beating at the mere thought of sharing a sleeping bag with Wyatt.

He doesn't seem fazed at all other than the small laugh.

It's just flirting, I scold my heart. He isn't actually serious.

"Hey, buddy."

Axel swings his head over the barn door to say hello as we walk in. He nudges Wyatt with his nose, urging him to open the stall faster.

"Hang on, hang on," Wyatt says.

Axel doesn't seem to care and knocks Wyatt's hat off and begins nuzzling his hair. It pulls a laugh out of me. The two of them are quite the pair.

Wyatt finally unlatches the stall and uses his hand to push Axel back so we can get in. I slip behind him.

Wyatt smirks. "He's a little needy if you couldn't tell."

"Only a little."

Axel is huge, tall and fit like his other half (Wyatt), and seemingly a big softie, too. I run my hand along his muscled neck. The hair looks coarse, but it's like silk beneath my fingers. The Big Friendly Giant shifts on his hooves, but I don't startle like I did the first time. His movements seem exaggerated because of his size, but we're friends now.

"How long have you had him?" I ask.

Wyatt rubs circles into Axel's chest while the horse's head hovers over his shoulder. "Since I was sixteen. Most kids get cars for their birthday, but I got a horse."

A shiver causes Axel's skin to twitch and ripple.

"So, when you were gone, did anyone ride him?" I ask, lifting a hand to finger-comb through his chestnut-colored mane.

Wyatt's expression turns serious. His lips that were once peaked on either side fall to a straight line, and the creases in his forehead multiply. I must have hit a nerve.

"Ronny did every so often, for training and to keep him exercised, but I think he was just as lonely as I was."

This kind of admission wasn't what I was expecting. Wyatt doesn't like to talk about his time living in the city. I've steered our conversations away from it, but maybe I should ask. Maybe by not asking it's made him lonelier.

"Do you miss it?"

"Miss what?"

I scratch Axel's jaw then follow the line of his neck. "The city. Living somewhere that isn't here. Being away from your family."

He continues to rub long strokes on the other side of Axel's neck, but he answers immediately. "No." There's a steely look in his eyes as he says this. "And yes. I miss swimming in the ocean, the salty air, and the food. I had a purpose and a title, and I won't lie and say those didn't feel good to have. But I thought being away, living in the city, and having a good paying job would make me happy. What I've realized is that it never could. Things aren't capable of that. People are. And when I got back to the farm, after losing everything I'd worked so hard for, my people were here for me."

His words take a shovel to my heart, removing more layers of dirt that have been covering the tender parts hiding underneath. I want to cry. Big ugly tears could come pouring out of my eyes if I let them. How many years did I wait and wish for my parents to notice me? They lost Justice but not me. I was still there. I could've made them happy. I still could.

Wyatt has that: people.

And I want that. The family, the support, the joy.

Wyatt's hand covers mine on Axel's neck, and I realize I'd stopped petting him at some point. I stare at our hands and then look into Wyatt's eyes.

"Hey, what is it?" he asks, touching my wet cheek with his other hand.

Apparently those big tears decided they couldn't hang on any longer. "Nothing. It's just…" I pause. "You have a beautiful family. Sometimes I wish I could experience one like yours. Maybe I wouldn't be so afraid all the time."

If I'd had the kind of support Wyatt has, maybe I would've tried something big and crazy like him. I could've moved away, started my spa business sooner, or joined a traveling circus as a trapeze swinger. Younger me would have loved that. Instead, I've been paralyzed. Stuck. Jilted.

He steps out from beneath Axel's neck and stands behind me, curving his other arm around me until I'm boxed in by the safety of his arms. His chest is sturdy, and I find myself leaning into him, as though he could support me. Maybe he could.

"You can borrow my family," he says with a gentle laugh that I can feel everywhere. He leans closer, whispering in my ear. "We all wonder what if. But all we have is now. You're living now, Avery, and that's what matters. What would you do if you weren't afraid?"

Loaded question for $500, please.

If I weren't afraid, I'd kiss Wyatt. I'd tell him I want to stay longer. I might even make a new vision board for the future spa. And, if I weren't afraid, I'd try using a chainsaw.

Nope, still doesn't feel right.

He begins to move my hand along Axel's neck again while the other rests on the horse's shoulder. Here, in the circle of his arms, I don't question why I didn't start on my dreams sooner. I don't think about all the ways I could make my parents notice me. I don't even think about the curse. The only thing I'm focused on is the rhythm of Wyatt's heartbeat on my back.

Twenty-One

Wyatt

"Go out on a limb—that's where the fruit is."-Bob Ross

Avery's back is pressed up close to my chest as I guide her hand across Axel's neck.

We take long, slow strokes down his coarse chestnut hair and start again. I love this about the farm. Life slows down, multiplying the moments that matter and deleting the ones that don't. Hearing Avery talk about her family has me choreographing a gratitude dance for mine and feeling like they might be exactly what she needs right now. Stace has already asked me for Avery's number, and my mom practically hogs her during family dinners. I hate it for me, but love it for her.

This last month has gone better than expected. We're drawing in more customers from different parts of the U.S. and most who haven't ever been to a farm before. I don't doubt the spa has lassoed them in. Avery has gone beyond what I'd thought up, and if I weren't so damn proud of what she's accomplished and how hard she works, I'd steal her away every chance I could. What I told her about San Fran was all true. The question I didn't answer was: if not San Fran or the farm, then where? I have no clue what I'll do. What I do know is, I want Avery all to myself in the meantime.

Axel shudders under our touch as he nibbles some hay, working his jaw in a circular motion. His eyes are soft and round, indicating he's as comfortable with Avery's hands on him as I am.

The hand she's using to graze over Axel is the one that was on my stomach once upon a time. I can still feel the phantom touches. Warm with firm pressure as she stretched her hand across my skin when we woke up in the barn together. This hand is the one I've held when helping her out of The Cougar or worked beside me drying dishes while I washed. It's the hand I've come accustomed to trusting will be there when I need it. The memory of her hand alone sends a message to my body I've been trying not to answer since the future of Thirst Trapp Farms is hanging on by one of Gramps' zip ties. I have a month to figure out if the potential off-season profits will sustain the farm—and me.

I shamelessly inhale the smell of lavender on Avery's skin. Floral and sweet, like her, with enough earthy undertones not to overpower. The new guests are arriving within the hour, but I push that aside as I think of doing more than just smelling her. If I leaned inches closer, I'd be close to her ear. Maybe I could lean in and lick the outside edge of that ear, nibble her lobe until she threw her head back with a moan. I could kiss her delicate skin until it went from cream to red, leaving a mark to remember me by.

Do I need all the answers to my future questions to kiss her? Couldn't we just give in and see if we like the flavor of one another? Maybe I'd find she tasted like grape—a flavor that actually makes me sick. Or, she could taste like cherry Chapstick, in which case I will propose marriage today.

I lean closer until my breath is hot on her neck, causing the hair on her outstretched arm to stand. The tip of my nose traces the edge of her ear, and she tilts her head to the side, exposing her neck and sending me a personalized invitation to continue.

My lips hover above her skin, making my mouth water and blood rush below my waistline. I place a feather-soft kiss where her neck and shoulder meet then tug her waist until she's flush against me. Another kiss to her neck, and my tongue follows, tasting the sweet honey flavor that is Avery's skin.

She grips my hand at her waist to steady herself as my phone starts to vibrate in my pocket. I silently curse the interruption and choose to ignore it. I'm busy. There's always something else to do, but once we exit this barn, this moment will be nothing more than that—a moment. A blink. A dessert that you savor only for it to disappear. I like dessert too much.

"Are you going to answer that?" Avery asks, clearing her throat and standing straighter in my grasp. "I can feel it vibrating on my leg."

No. "Yeah." The moment fizzles, and I close my eyes adjusting so I can grab my phone. Dropping my arms and stepping away from her and Axel, I answer. "Hello?"

"Guests are here," Ronny says in a flat tone.

I'm used to him getting straight to the point. He never says hello or goodbye.

Avery continues to pet Axel with her back to me. It makes me smile seeing them together like this. Or, maybe it's because I'm positive her mouth won't taste like grape. "We'll be right there," I murmur, so focused on the scene in front of me I almost hang up.

But Ronny lowers his voice and speaks directly into the phone, drawing my attention. "Prepare your heart."

I snap out of my trance and laugh. "Did you get that from Oprah or a fortune cookie?"

"I'm not playing with you. It's…" Ronny pauses. He doesn't laugh like I do. There isn't a lightness in his voice like mine. "It's Caroline."

My entire body tenses, and it feels like something ruptures inside my chest. I turn around again, so my back is to Avery and growl into the phone. "What?"

He sighs and keeps his voice low. "She's here."

Avery's talking in a hushed tone to Axel. But even without seeing her face, or being in her presence, her voice is loud as my past and future pull out lightsabers. "Now?"

"Yeah."

"At the farm?" I ask.

"Yes."

"And she's real?"

A pause, then he says, "No, she's a hologram, clearly."

This option seems to make the most sense.

"Of course she's real. I'm staring at her right now," he says.

I rub my forehead. "Have you talked to her?"

"She just arrived. I didn't waste my breath talking to her before I spoke to you," he says.

If I ever picked a fight in a dark alley with some shady characters, I know Ronny would have more than my back. He'd take the lead.

The idea of Caroline being here sends a knife through my perfectly curated bubble surrounding Thirst Trapp Farms. I liked my bubble. Even more, I liked who was in it with me.

I don't bother saying goodbye and tap to end the call. Closing my eyes, I inhale through my nose. I should've assumed this would happen after ignoring all of Caroline's calls and emails. Did she really pay to stay here for an entire week just to talk to me? How did I not notice her name when she booked? Did she use a different one? I need answers to these questions, and then I need to figure out how to get her to leave so I can blow another bubble.

I allow myself one more steadying breath then become like a sloth walking back to Avery's side. "The guests just arrived."

My voice is solemn like someone just died. Maybe they did. Maybe I did.

"Oh, great. Let's go," she says, twisting to look up at me as she tucks her hair behind both ears. "Is everything okay? You kinda look like you've seen a ghost."

Basically. My ex showed up and is about to ruin everything when I thought I ghost-busted her months ago.

I drop my chin to my chest and shake my head. "I'm fine."

She places a hand on my arm. "You sure?"

I stare down at her hand on my bicep and swallow. If Caroline is here for the week, everything just got more complicated. This thing with Avery, the flirting, the lingering stares, the newness of floating with someone else is grounded by a paperweight the size of King Kong. It probably smells as bad as he did, too. I'm not ready for that. I don't want Caroline getting in the way, and now I'm positive I'll end up throwing myself on the ground and banging my fists into the dirt.

I study Avery's delicate hand and then her face. The flush on her cheeks, the soft pink of her lips, and the narrow width of her nose. I've just become the most dramatic person in this space, apart from Axel, because he really is a drama queen, believing that I won't be able to look at her like this again until Caroline is gone. I told myself I wasn't ready for this—for Avery, but I can't ignore the tug I feel when I'm with her. I should stay away until I figure out my damn life.

"I—"

I'm stepping closer, placing a hand on her waist again before I can finish my thought. Her eyes flicker as the weight of my hand doesn't leave her side. I keep it there, wanting her to know I notice. Even if all of my past mistakes and unknown future try to get in the way, I still see her.

She swallows, the smooth skin of her neck moving with the motion. "You're looking at me like you either want to hurt someone," she pauses, "or, you want to kiss me."

Her words start to inflate the bubble. Maybe it doesn't have to break. Could I make it stronger?

My gaze drops to her lips, and I lick mine. "I don't want to hurt anyone."

I just don't want anyone else to hurt me.

Bending closer, my lips are only centimeters from hers. I have to know if her mouth is as sweet as her. The way her lips part and her crystal blue eyes are only half visible beneath her lids is now my favorite view. I lean in like I did when kissing her neck, but this time, I brush my lips against hers, pulling her flush against me in one motion. There's so much pent up need packed inside my 6'2" frame, and all of it gets funneled through my mouth. The kiss could be eager and sloppy based on how long I've wanted her, but it's slow and languid as I tease her lips with my tongue then hide her mouth behind my beard.

I'm holding her close and squeezing the soft flesh above her hip as my other hand finds its way into her hair, gently angling her head back and tasting the most delicious dessert I've ever had. She doesn't taste like cherries. It's better. It's honey and lavender, lazy Saturday mornings, and iced coffee on hot days. Kissing her is more of a rush than pushing Axel to his top speed and feeling the wind push my hair back. Avery's fingers digging into my scalp is better. Her lips are so pliant and warm as her hips press into mine and hushed moans erupt from the back of her throat, sending me into a deeper spiral.

"So, this is what you've been doing," a familiar voice snaps.

I break away from Avery and jerk my eyes to Caroline who's now standing outside the stall, her voice already grating on every nerve. She's not holding a machete like I expect her to be, but the scowl on her face matched with her long, intricately painted fingernails does the trick. When I look back at Avery, she's turned toward Caroline, her fingers covering her now red lips. The moment is gone, burning off like the morning clouds.

Ronny rushes in behind Caroline, hat pressed to his chest while he shakes his head and mouths an apology.

I nod at him. I can only deal with one thing at a time and right now it's *her*. Resting my hands on my hips so I don't reach for Avery or throw hay at my ex, I say, "Caroline. What are you doing here?"

She crosses her arms, dark from the self-tanner she likes to use. Her thick lashes are taller than I remember, fanning the space between her eyelids and eyebrows like spiders. Add that to the canary yellow jogger set she's wearing that makes her look like she's a talking banana.

She flips her dark hair over her shoulder. It's shorter than the last time I saw her, but the cut only reveals more of her sharp points. Sharp jawline. Sharp collarbone. Sharp nose that she's looking down at me from.

"I thought it was obvious," she says with a slow lilt to her voice as she studies her nails.

Every part of her is fake. I don't know how I didn't see it before. How had I missed this? Avery's gone still beside me, but she's taking steadying breaths through her nose.

Caroline juts out one of those sharp hips of hers and says the four words nobody wants to hear. "We need to talk."

Twenty-Two

Wyatt

"However you think it should be, that's exactly how it should be."-Bob Ross

As much as I love reunions—I really loathe them—we have to cut this one short.

"You're Wyatt's..." Avery starts to say with wide eyes.

I hold out my hand. "Now, hang on a minute."

"Who's this, Wyatt?" Caroline asks, crossing her arms.

"Avery."

Avery catches my eyes and tips her head toward Caroline like I forgot something.

"Oh. And Avery, this is Caroline," I say.

Avery nods. "Caroline."

"Avery."

Ronny raises his hand. "Ronny."

Caroline pins me with a harsh glare. "Wyatt, we need to talk," her sharp voice rings again.

I sigh and pinch the bridge of my nose. "We do, but I don't have time to talk about this right now since the other guests are here. Ronny can take you to cabin four, and we'll talk later."

Caroline scoffs. "I think it's important. I've already waited four months."

Her words sound as if she's clipping a tag on my ear, like we do to identify the cows.

My eyes are the size of bowling balls. "And I don't have to talk to you at all after what you—"

"Wyatt," Ronny cuts me off with a warning.

Caroline cuts him a look over her sharp shoulder, and he holds up both hands.

I owe her nothing, but I want closure, too. Everything happened so fast, and I never said the things I wished I would have. I exhale slowly, letting my rigid posture relax some. "We'll talk later."

Partially satisfied, she turns on her heel—high-heeled Crocs, that is—and leaves the barn, Ronny following after her. Cabin four is the farthest one from Avery, but it still doesn't seem far enough.

This isn't good.

Avery clears her throat.

I'm seconds from crashing into her two icebergs staring back at me. "I...that...she..."

"You don't owe me an explanation." Avery waves me off and steps out of the stall. "Let's just go meet the guests."

"But—"

She whips around. "Really, Wyatt. It doesn't matter."

She's out of the barn before I can tell her that it does matter. To me. She matters and until my lips were on hers, I didn't realize how much. As her boss, I should keep the boundaries clear. But as a man, I want to obliterate them with a grenade.

I slap my thigh and rest my hands on my hips. Axel blows air through his lips and aggressively nods.

"I know what you're thinking," I say to him. "I made a bigger mess."

He turns his head, and now we're eye to eye.

I point at him. "Don't tell Granny about that kiss."

I'll never hear the end of it. I'd been avoiding her attempts at hosting a pop-up wedding with Avery as much as I'd been ignoring Caroline's calls. But now, I have to deal with all of it. The feelings sitting high in my chest for a woman who is my employee and the sour memories of how everything ended with Caroline. And with only a month left of the summer, I need to start making some decisions.

I stomp out of the barn and take note of the few people speckled about the front drive. I spread my arms wide as I approach. The Wyatt of one minute ago is gone, and now I'm a circus instructor with a big ol' grin and magic hiding up my short-sleeve shirt.

Time for me to grow up and focus on what matters: making money to keep the farm.

"Welcome to Thirst Trapp Farms," I say, darting my eyes between the five guests.

"Oooo, goodie," a woman in heels and a small dog in her arms says with a wink. "I'm Nikki."

Her eyes scan me from head to toe, and now I feel like I'm standing naked in front of everyone. Okay, maybe Stace was right. Maybe *Thirst* wasn't the right addition to the rebrand. But we have guests, and that's what matters.

"Hi, Nikki. Welcome."

A middle-aged woman is furiously texting and adjusting her hat every few steps, darting her eyes from left to right while the man beside her has entered full incognito mode, wearing all black. Black pants, shirt, shoes, black hair, black aviators. It's at least eighty degrees out here, but he's managed to find a patch of shade to huddle under.

"What's the Wi-Fi password?" a young man with a fedora asks.

I rub my hands together. "All of that information is in your cabins. Why don't I help you all get settled before the happy hour starts."

"Do you, like, own this place?" Nikki asks as her dog begins to bark. "Peaches, quiet!"

I clear my throat to make introductions. "No, but I help run it. I'm Wyatt Trapp. Ronny is another employee, but he's tending to another guest right now, and this is Avery, our spa director."

I try not to stutter when I say Avery's name, her lips on mine still a fresh memory. She bites her lip and fans herself, like maybe the memory is engraved in her cells, too.

I pull out my phone and navigate to the Experiences R Us app that has all of the reservations to figure out who I'm talking to. "Butch?" I call out.

The man in black raises his hand without saying a word. If he's looking at me, I wouldn't know it.

I read on. "Bobbi and…" I reread the reservation to make sure I'm not wrong. I'm not. "Ross?"

Well, isn't this a happy little accident.

"I'm Ross," the guy in the fedora says. "This is my sister, Bobbi."

A girl in baggy pants and star-shaped sunglasses has her cell phone high in the air. "Oh my god. How are we supposed to upload our videos? Does this place even have electricity?" She whirls on Ross. "I thought you said this farm has Wi-Fi and shirtless men!"

"We do," I say.

"They do!" Ross adds at the same time.

"Not shirtless men," I rush to clarify. "But the Wi-Fi password is in your cabin, I promise." Maybe I should consider leading with that.

"You have to, like, hold it higher," Nikki says, mimicking the motion with her phone.

Coming from someone in the dial-up era, I wouldn't trust her, but Bobbi raises her hand higher, using Ross' shoulder to steady herself.

They'll figure it out soon enough.

"Nikki?" I call.

The woman raises her dog's paw in the air. "Here! Oh, and Peaches." The dog barks. "When are we, like, going to see the cute little farm critters?"

"Tomorrow," I confirm. "We'll see the…critters tomorrow."

"Did you hear that Peaches?" she asks the dog. "You're going to love making friends!"

The small rodent in her arms begins aggressively licking her entire face. Lips, eyes, nose, everything.

I shudder and look down at my list. "Rachel?"

"It's Rach," she says, adjusting her hat so it covers her eyes more and moves closer to whisper something to me. "Say, uh, how's your security system in the cabins?"

I stare blankly. "There is no security system. Only a lock on the doors."

She sucks in air through her teeth. "Mhm. I see. Well, it'll have to do."

I immediately want to ask a follow-up question, but Ronny's back now from depositing Caroline.

I scan the luggage. "We can take each person to their cabin with their things. They aren't far. Butch, you'll be in the farmhouse this week."

He twirls his finger in the air. "Yippee."

"How far is, like, not far?" Nikki asks as her miniature chihuahua burrows in her neck. "We don't hike."

I point to the cabins that line the drive. It's a short walk, but luggage on gravel doesn't work so well. "We'll drive you over in The Cougar."

Nikki makes a growling sound, and I close my gaping mouth and change the subject immediately. "Just a reminder that all meals will be served in the farmhouse at six, but tonight we have a special happy hour behind the farmhouse in the gazebo at five. At the end of the week, we'll have a large farm-to-table dinner near the gazebo as well." I tuck my phone away. "Oh, and Nikki, you've got a massage tonight at four with Avery."

"And don't forget Peaches," Nikki coos.

Do we offer dog massages? I should know this.

Avery tilts her head to the side, studying Nikki and Peaches likely trying to determine the same thing.

Bobbi is still holding her phone high in the air to locate that elusive bar of service, while Nikki walks on unsteady feet in those platform wedges of hers toward The Cougar.

Ross scans The Cougar like it's personally offended him. "We can walk," he says and grabs Bobbi's arm to get her attention. They both stare in disgust. "I'd rather not be the cause of global warming. You should really think about an electric one of those," he says, pointing judgmentally at my whip.

I give him a pinched smile and nod. "I'll consider it."

Once everyone is carted to their cabins, Avery included, I head back to the farmhouse to show Butch to his room, shower up, and check in with Granny. She's sitting in her favorite rocker, doing another one of those Sudoku puzzles she loves so much.

"Hey, Granny."

"Wyatt? What are you doing back so early? I didn't expect you until close to dinner, since all those city folk are coming in."

I shove my hands in my pockets. "They've all arrived and are settling in."

"Lord, help us all." She draws a cross in front of her as is customary for Catholics.

We aren't Catholic, but it seems like she wants all the help she can get.

"I need to shower and get a head start on the snacks. Are you going to join us?" I ask.

She doesn't look up from her puzzle. "Do I have to?"

I bite my cheek to keep from smiling. If there's one thing Granny could do without, it's being around another group of strangers. "If you want to eat."

She cuts me a look above her reader glasses. "I'll starve, thanks."

I start to back out of the room. "You sure? I'm making your favorite."

"Chocolate cake?"

"Lasagna."

I take the steps two at a time but not before I hear her voice ring out from below. "Shoulda made chocolate cake."

Twenty-Three

Avery

"You have to allow the paint to break to make it beautiful."-Bob Ross

Caroline's name glares up at me from my phone screen.

Of course she scheduled a massage the day after arriving. Looks like avoiding her isn't actually going to work like I'd hoped. After finding Wyatt and me lip-locked in the barn, I told myself I needed to keep my distance this week. They clearly have some things to work through. But at least I know who the mysterious Caroline is.

This isn't summer camp where we start as friends and turn to frenemies when we find out we like the same guy. So, why do I want to beat her in a tug-o-war and rub mud in her face?

I need to be like a caterpillar, emerging from its cocoon, and morph into a professional butterfly—I mean human being.

Someone knocks on the door, and I consider hiding under the couch cushions, but that will only prolong the inevitable. I'm here to do a job. I'm being paid for this. Moping on the couch isn't going to help. I need to drag myself to the front door and answer it.

I stand and walk to the small, tiled entryway and look at the mirror hanging on the wall.

"You are a badass butterfly," I murmur to myself. "You can do this."

I grip the handle and swing open the door with a smile that is a big, fat f-word: fake. "Hello there."

Caroline jumps.

It only makes me smile wider.

"Come on in." I gesture for her to walk past me as I shut the door. "Cookie?"

She makes a disgusted sound in the back of her throat. "I don't eat carbs or sugar."

I scan the length of her while she types away on her phone, and I confirm there likely is not one granule of sugar inside her body. She's thin and tall with dark hair and brows that make me want to shave mine off and make a wig out of hers; they're so perfect.

"Water?" I try offering instead.

"I don't drink tap water," she says, then flips her hair like there should be more of it. "Where do you want me?"

In a cauldron of fire sounds great.

I smile at the thought and then scold myself for the jealousy hijacking my mind. "Down the hall, first door on the left. You can undress, slip below the sheet, and let's start you face down. I'll knock in a couple of minutes."

She turns and stalks toward the room, dropping her purse on the coffee table, then slamming the door behind her.

I scoff and walk by the side table to grab a cookie and shove the whole thing in my mouth. Someone should eat it if she isn't going to.

Swallowing, I inhale to steady my heart rate. Then exhale, telling myself I won't elbow her in the back too hard. But her ass is fair game. It's probably tight and taut and sugar-free like the rest of her.

Sticking a finger toward the back of my throat, I pretend to gag.

This is just lovely. Exactly how I wanted to spend my afternoon. Feeling up the ex of the man I kissed in the barn yesterday. My skin heats at the thought while a pit forms in my stomach, knowing her showing up like this has changed everything. It didn't help that she witnessed our first kiss, either. I was one tongue swipe away from the take-me-here-and-now-mode, and there's no way she didn't see how Wyatt completely unraveled me.

I rub my temples. It feels like I've just signed up for a game of capture the flag, a summer camp favorite. In this scenario, I suppose Wyatt is the flag, but who has it—him? Do I start off with the flag since I kissed him last? That seems fair. Why am I thinking like this? I've never been a jealous person until Wyatt had to go and kiss me. Now my heart is practically screaming *mine*.

My fingers stop pressing firmly into my head. Wyatt kissed me. I kissed Wyatt. It's been twenty-four hours since I flew back to my cabin after meeting the guests, leaving track marks on the gravel on my way, and hiding out until my massage with Nikki. It replayed in my head nine-hundred times. I didn't even complain when Peaches curled up on Nikki's ass and gave me the stink-eye every time I rubbed her back.

Ask me how his lips felt, how he tasted, and I'll provide a very detailed report. Probably with some graphs, and maybe a pyramid chart showing the greatest and worst kisses I've ever had. Spoiler: Wyatt would be at the top.

I need to stop thinking about this. Going into that room with Wyatt's lips on my mind will help me zero percent. Channeling Becky Stringer from middle school summer camp who put a dead fly in my water is more like it.

Walking to the room, I knock twice. "Caroline, are you ready?"

"Yes. I've been ready," she says with a scoffing tone.

Maybe I should see if there are any dead flies outside first.

I open the door and stride into the room. "How is the temperature in here?"

I'm so freaking professional.

"I'm sweating. Be a doll and open that window." She's face down on the table but waves a vague hand toward the window she so desperately wants me to open.

How about I throw a bucket of water over her head instead? She's acting like I'm "the help" and nothing more. Is it because she knows I mean more to Wyatt? I'm not going to shrink back and let her stomp all over me. Finally kissing Wyatt yesterday gave my swirling feelings a place to land. It felt right, and I won't feel guilty about it. God, who am I? Tilly? She'd be so proud.

"Of course. That's no problem." I stalk to the window and push it open even more then shut the curtains. "Better?"

"Much."

Walking back to the small dresser with all of my aromatherapy and massage oils, I lather up my hands and turn back to Caroline's tanned back. I hesitate.

I can do this.

"Do you have any problem areas?" Besides all of you, since you are now my problem.

"No."

"Great." Looking to the ceiling and back down, I press one hand to her spine and push upward while the other follows. "Let me know if this is too much pressure."

"I will," she grinds out.

A few rolls of my thumbs on her shoulders and firm presses of my palm on either side of her spine, and I'm feeling confident I can get through this fifty-minute session. As long as she doesn't want to talk, I'll be fine.

"So...are you and Wyatt dating?" she asks in a pinched tone.

I'm kneading circles into her neck as quickly as my heart is beating. I'd rather talk about the details of our periods more than this. Do you have a heavy or light flow? Pads or menstrual cups? Anything other than Wyatt.

I hesitate. These are exactly the kinds of questions I wanted to avoid. But they won't go away by changing the subject, either. I take a deep breath before saying, "No."

She grunts into the headrest as I work her back, then asks, "How did you and Wyatt meet?"

I chew on my bottom lip. "Well, we didn't really."

"It was online then?"

I tilt my head. "Sort of?"

"How?"

Talk about an inquisition. I could tell her this isn't the time to talk about it or direct her to ask Wyatt, but what am I afraid of? Telling the truth and her getting upset? That makes no sense. I'll just stick to the facts.

"Actually, yeah, we did meet online," I say with a confidence I'm still waiting to show up. "I heard about the job through social media and reached out."

"Hm," is all she says, which is more of a sound and can't really be counted as saying anything.

I follow it up with, "He's a good boss."

If I didn't have coconut oil all over my hands right now, I'd slap a palm to my forehead. Really? This is the foot I'm going to lead with? After almost a month of boss-zoning Wyatt, I'm going to do it in front of Caroline?

I need a better strategy if I'm going to keep this flag.

"Right," she says. "Did he tell you how we met?"

Go ahead and send my thoughts through a cheese grater, because none of them are kind. "He didn't."

I begin to knead her shoulders and neck harder than before, but she doesn't complain, so I continue. She won't be leaving here with the flag, just a few bruises.

"It's a great story," Caroline says in a snide but muffled tone thanks to the face cradle.

"I bet it is," I settle on saying.

Maybe now is the time I should fake a phone call. *Oh, look, my doctor's calling.* Nah, too weird. I could just pretend Wyatt's calling. If that doesn't scream jealous non-girlfriend, I don't know what does.

One manicured hand moves around in circles as she starts. "We were at a bar. I was dancing with a friend, and he kept watching me, so of course I had to say hi."

Of course.

More neck kneading.

"He bought me a drink, and we talked for hours. I can't remember laughing so much. And at the end of the night, I went home with him. The rest was history."

"Mmm." Someone please shove cotton balls in my ears so I don't have to hear any more.

Her telling me this story is for no other reason than to try and piss all over Wyatt to stake her claim. I mean, if we were animals that is. I've never been the kind of girl to fight over a guy, even someone like Wyatt, which is why the next words out of my mouth sound like strangers.

"We met online, but did he tell you about the first time we met in person?" I ask, not even knowing why my mouth is saying such things.

Silence, and then she mumbles through a grunt, "No, he didn't."

The fact she can still say words, considering how hard I'm pressing is impressive. Tracing her spine with my palm, I keep kneading my way back up to her shoulders and harder this time. My hands are on autopilot, working muscles and loosening knots without much conscious effort. I'm too busy fabricating a different story—a more interesting one—in my head.

I really don't know what I'm saying right now, but my mouth starts moving. "Well, he had his shirt off for starters." Another grunt is all I get from Caroline. Good. "He was sunbathing and asked if I could rub sunscreen on his back, so I took that tube and slathered it on every square inch of his body. You know, so he wouldn't get burned."

Caroline lets out a strained groan. She's trying to grit her way through this deep tissue massage she didn't ask for. She still doesn't tell me it's too much. So, I press harder. "He then told me all about the farm while applying sunscreen on me," I say in a dreamy tone. "Twice."

Someone give me an Oscar for that performance.

She groans a word that's too muffled to understand.

"What was that, Caroline? I can't hear you?" I use my forearm to push into her shoulder blade.

"Sto—"

"What?"

She snaps her head up. "Stop!"

With a smile, I lift my hands from her back. "I'm sorry, was that too hard?"

She's breathing heavily and moving as slow as the clouds in the sky. Once she catches her breath, she drops her head to the side. "I didn't think Wyatt wore sunscreen?"

"He does now."

She grabs the sheet and clutches it in the middle of her chest. "I'm done with this massage."

I wipe my hands on the towel and head to the door, saying, "I'll let you get changed," over my shoulder.

The door clicks shut, and my smile fades. I start to panic. What was I thinking telling Caroline that lie? What was the point? All she'd have to do is ask Wyatt or Ronny or really anyone on the farm to confirm my story was a fake. It felt good to put her in her place, but now I'm left with the rubble of my jealousy to sort through.

I don't know what came over me. Telling her Wyatt and I rubbed each other down makes it sound like we are more than what we are. What makes me think there's more going on? One kiss doesn't prove that. Though, I wish it did.

Twenty-Four

Wyatt

"We don't make mistakes. We just have happy accidents."-Bob Ross

H as anyone here been horseback riding before?"

No one raises their hand.

"Great. Okay." I scratch my head. "Ronny and I are here to teach you. First things first, we need to get on the horse."

"What? That, like, doesn't seem safe," Nikki says, scrunching her nose and curling her lip.

Probably not in the heels she's wearing, or with the dog she's holding.

"Does the horse really want us to climb on its back?" Bobbi asks. "If it were me, I'd say hell no."

Fedora Ross adds, "Have the horses given their consent? Is this animal cruelty?"

"Uh," I swing my gaze to Ronny, looking for help and to confirm I'm actually hearing all of this right now.

He nods and strokes his horse's neck. June nuzzles him back. "We made sure to ask them before saddling up."

Bobbi and Ross squint at Ronny and June then nod.

"Alright, any other questions before we get started?" I ask hesitantly.

Nikki's hand shoots into the air. "Will there be, like, cell service?"

"No, unless you have a pager." I laugh, but I'm the only one.

Nikki's nose scrunches. "I left mine in, like, the late 90s."

"What the hell is a pager?" Bobbi asks.

"Maybe the dinosaurs invented it," Ross snickers.

"I heard that, GenZ," Nikki says in protest.

"My name is Ross."

I hold up both hands. "Okay, okay. Let's keep it friendly. We are generation positive here at Thirst Trapp Farms."

Did Nikki just stick her tongue out at Ross?

Rach raises her hand, and I point at her like we're in class and not outside a barn. "Are there any roads? You know, that cars and...people could follow us on?"

I cock my head to the side. "Uh, no. It's just a trail. In the woods."

She relaxes with a sigh.

"Anyone else?" I ask.

Butch raises a finger. "Can I ride the black horse?"

"We don't have a black horse."

He scowls. At least, I think he does. He really just has the same expression at all times.

I rock back on my heels, waiting for someone else to say something. No one does. "Alright, let's get on the horses."

"Wyatt!"

That voice grates on me. I swivel around and give Caroline a tight-lipped smile. "Yes?"

She bats her lashes at me, but they are long enough that they look like small fans cooling off her eyeballs. "Can you help me get on my horse?"

I look over my shoulder and lock eyes with Avery, who is leaning against the barn and watching everything play out. She smiles brightly at me, and I realize how greedy I am for her smiles. Two days later, and I still haven't forgotten how she tastes. The fact I haven't ripped her bodice and taken her on the bar top is staggering, but then again, we aren't in an old western movie. This is real life with people and guests needing things that prevent alone time. I'd rather stay back with her and Granny instead of taking my ex-girlfriend on a trail ride, but here we are. Maybe Caroline will get lost, or her horse, Achilles, will take her off a cliff instead.

I'm a horrible person.

"Wyattttt," Caroline coos, dragging out my name.

I sigh and look back at Caroline who's wiggling her fingers at me.

Three strides and I'm in front of her, pointing and saying gruffly, "Put one foot in the stirrup."

"So bossy these days," she says, then leans closer. "I like it."

I glare down at her and try not to roll my eyes. We still haven't talked since she arrived unannounced, but we need to, if only to get her out of my hair. Going through the rest of this week with encounters like this one isn't going to work for me. I've been busy with the guests, but I have to find the time. Being kind to her in front of everyone is starting to grate on me.

For now, I point at her foot and the stirrup once again to make it clear.

She lifts her leg and rests it in the stirrup while running a hand up my bicep to settle on my shoulder. I try not to grind my teeth so much that I'll get a headache. Looking behind me at Avery would only confirm what I already know. She's seeing all of this. What does she think? Does she know how I really feel about Caroline? I need to tell her. I can't have her thinking for another second that there are any residual feelings on my part.

The kiss changed things between us, and I decided to take my own advice of living in the moment. And hell if I don't want to kiss her again.

"Grab the pommel," I say to Caroline through a tight jaw.

"Ooo," she purrs. "Dirty talk."

I cut my eyes to hers. "What? No. It's the horn on the saddle. Grab it to help pull yourself up."

She grabs the pommel without saying anything else and hoists herself into the saddle. If this was Avery, I would have enjoyed the view. But with Caroline, I look away so her purple spandex doesn't burst like a grape. It's like the veneer she wore for so long when we were together has completely worn off, and I see her through the eyes of my mom, sister, and Granny. How was I so blind? How was I so color blind?

Once she's settled, I hand her the reins. "Pull back to stop, otherwise keep the reins loose. Achilles knows what to do." I turn away and start walking over to where Ronny is helping Bobbi. "How are we doing here?"

Ronny nods. "Nikki went back to her cabin to change shoes."

"Good. And the dog?"

He shrugs. "Told her she couldn't bring her."

"Alright. I'll put her on the Palomino horse today since he's docile enough," I say, pointing behind me.

"Smart choice. Henry's the oldest horse here. Don't reckon he'll make it far from the back the whole time. I'll keep close."

I nod and move on to help Ross take hold of the reins that he informs me feel too much like genuine leather, to which I told him no animals were harmed in the making.

Butch stares at his horse, like it has two heads and twenty-seven legs, and is some creature from another planet, but at least he's on it.

The only one we're missing now is...

Nikki and...Peaches.

They both come strolling down the drive, Nikki wearing sneakers as instructed, but with Peaches still in her arms. More like strapped to her chest in a baby sling.

Ronny sidles up to my side as she approaches.

"Ready!" she chirps.

I smile at her, and then Peaches whose straw-colored fur sparkles in the early afternoon sun. Or, maybe that's just the diamond-encrusted collar she's wearing.

I look at Ronny and nod once. "I'll help you two get on the horse."

"God, I hope this isn't a bad idea," I say under my breath as I trail Nikki to the last horse and point at the blonde Palomino. "This is Henry."

"Ew."

"What?" I ask.

"Henry is such a boring name." Henry stands there looking like Eeyore as she taps her chin. "I'll call you Felix."

Henry (aka Eeyore; aka Felix) shifts on his feet, caring little about this trail ride and even less about his name change.

"Let me help you up." I run through the instructions for mounting four times before Nikki decides she's ready to try.

She grips my shoulder with the strength of an ox, steps into the stirrup, and raises her other leg. But she's too short to swing her leg over the saddle while also trying to stay mostly upright so Peaches doesn't fall out of the carrier.

Grunting and swearing, Nikki digs her fingernails into my shoulder, lifting and pulling.

It's not working.

And now I've got shoulder piercings, so that's great.

"I'm going to give you a boost," I say.

"A boost?"

"Yeah, just keep hanging on." I stare at her backside and wonder where the least intrusive spot would be to put my hand. There aren't any, but I at least try to avoid scraping my hand on her bedazzled jeans' pocket. "I swear I don't mean anything by this."

She tries to look down at me. "What do you mean?"

"I'm going to push you up."

"Okay—"

I cup the center of her ass—which sounds better than saying crack—with my palm and hoist her up. She squeals either because of the surprise of my touch, or the fact she is now sitting in the saddle.

She screams so loud that Henry's (aka Eeyore's; aka Felix's) ears stand up. I hold the bridle so he doesn't bolt before remembering who I'm dealing with. The fact that this horse's ears stand up is a big deal.

Nikki adjusts Peaches then winks at me. "Next time I'm going to make you buy me dinner first, cowboy."

I pull my sunglasses from the collar of my t-shirt and put them on, slinking away before she can see the blush creeping up my neck. There's laughter of a particular pitch that catches my ear. *Avery.* Her hand is covering her mouth, and I point at her, which only makes her laugh more. I'll get her for that later.

I head over to Axel and place a foot in the stirrup to swing my body up and over. "Are we ready?" A few grunts, groans, and agreements ring out. I reiterate the instructions for leading a horse. "The horses will want to stick beside one another. If you need anything, you can ask me or Ronny in the back."

Bobbi takes my picture.

"Can you send that to me?" Caroline asks.

"Ohhh, me too!" Nikki exclaims.

Bobbi shrugs. "I guess. He's not even smiling."

Nikki points at my chest. "Maybe like, take your shirt off, too?"

"No, it's the hat. Could you put it on backwards?" Ross tilts his head to the side. "Or hold an ax over your shoulder, like you're going to chop wood."

I narrow my eyes at him. "I'm on the back of a horse."

Ross nods. "Right, right. So, maybe a...sword?"

I shake my head.

"A pitchfork?"

I have completely lost the ability to speak.

"No, no. He needs a face tattoo," Rach says. Everyone looks at her and she shrugs. "What? Face tattoos are badass—very Prison Break."

"I loved that show!" Nikki says with a screech that sets Peaches to barking. "Shh-shh, Peaches. Don't worry, they break out."

"A cape," Butch says. "He needs a black cape."

With that, I steer Axel toward the trail, giving Avery a salute before leading the group away from the barn and toward the trailhead. If we all make it back without anyone falling off or a thirst trap of me ending up on the worldwide web, I'll call that a win.

Caroline flips her hair. "He needs a woman on his lap."

Scratch that. If Caroline fell off, I wouldn't mind too much.

Twenty-Five

Avery

"Isn't it fantastic that you can change your mind and create all these happy things?"-Bob Ross

D ear Diary, Wyatt kissed me."

"Tell. Me. Everything!" Tilly exclaims through the phone. "How? When? Do you want to do it again? Of course you do. Was he a good kisser? Spare no details."

I throw myself back on my bed. "I don't kiss and tell."

"Hellooo, I'm your diary!"

She makes a good point. I've always told her everything. But right now, I need Tilly to be the voice of reason. Someone who will tell me that I have an underwear line or a booger hanging out of my nose. Not the one who gives me a shipping container full of rubbers.

"This job ends in a month, and I have no idea what comes next. The kiss should have never happened," I say through a sigh.

A cabinet shuts on Tilly's end of the line. "Psh. That's still a month you have together, though. Who knows? Maybe it doesn't have to end. You said he might extend the trial through the fall and winter, right?"

"Yeah, maybe. He mentioned it offhandedly once. But what if he doesn't?" I exhale and roll to my side. "I haven't had a chance to talk to him much since *she* got here." Or kiss him again for that matter. "His ex-girlfriend showed up completely unannounced while we were lip-locked and isn't making it easy to get any time alone with him. She hangs all over him and flirts shamelessly."

194

"Ex-girlfriend?" Tilly screams after opening a wrapper. "She just showed up out of the blue? What did he say? He told you he doesn't like her, right?"

"I mean…not in so many words." Just with his mouth. "I've been trying to avoid them as much as possible, but Wyatt asked me to go on the camping trip at the end of the week. I can't decide if I should go or not. Caroline will no doubt be there since she's a paying customer."

"Are you?"

"What?" I ask.

She starts whisking something. "Jealous."

My sandalwood candle burns from my bedside table. It smells like him. But like my candle, he'll eventually be gone, too. What right do I have to be jealous of someone who was temporary and never mine to begin with? I groan loudly and let that be my only response.

She starts pounding something and raises her voice. "I think you should go, Avery. Don't let this woman stomp all over you. If Wyatt invited you to go, you have every right to be there. Plus, maybe he'll want you to share his tent."

I can't help laughing. "I'm sure whatever happens in a tent is PG at best."

She stops pounding and a buzzer goes off. "You don't think your mountain man has some hidden talents up his flannel shirt?"

I roll my eyes and flop to my back. "You're supposed to tell me I need to distance myself from him now so it doesn't hurt so much. That I should have enjoyed the feel of his tongue sooner before she showed up and will never get the opportunity to do it again."

The background noise quits. "Wait, he used tongue?"

"I don't kiss and—"

"Tell. Got it," she says, finishing my sentence while clanking pans together. "It's like you're saying you don't want to eat the cake, but you definitely want chocolate with strawberries and ganache. It doesn't make any sense. You can't have it both ways. Plus, you know I'm not the one who's going to tell you to play it safe."

"Oh, I want the cake," I say.

She hollers and makes some whooping sound. "Get it girl!"

I have to pull the phone away from my ear until the racket dies off. "But I'm torn. I don't know if I should lean in or pull away. I really, really like being around him." If he wasn't so kind, hardworking, loving, tender, and sporting actual ab muscles there wouldn't be a problem here. He'd be like every other guy I tried dating, which is the sum total of three, two of which were in high school.

I groan loudly and cover my eyes with my forearm.

Tilly opens the fridge, the quiet purr reminding me of home. "You've got it bad," she says.

"I really do."

"Avery, this is good. Past aside, you deserve this. You deserve him. You've spent a lot of your life holding yourself back and trying to make everyone else happy. Well, what makes you happy?"

I don't even hesitate. "Being kissed by Wyatt."

"There you go," she says with a full mouth. "I say go for it."

"Go for it?"

"Yes. GO FOR IT!" she practically screams in my ear.

I drop my arm from my eyes and stare at the ceiling. "I don't even know what he wants. Maybe he's only interested in something casual."

"Would that be so bad?" Tilly asks, the queen of casual.

"Yes? Maybe? I don't know. I'm not really a casual person." I'm either it's nice to meet you, or, will you marry me? Avery's Curse has taken a backseat for the time being, but what happens if I make a change to this delicate ecosystem of existence? Flames, doom, heartbreak.

A water spigot gets turned on from her end. "What would be worse, leaving and wishing you'd taken advantage of every second with him while you could? Or, leaving and regretting the time wasted?"

"Doesn't that make me a rebound girl if his recent ex is here?" I ask.

"No, it makes you a woman going after what she wants," Tilly says. Before I can respond, a knock sounds on the front door.

"Hey, Till, I gotta go. My next appointment is here."

"Maybe it's him," she says as something metal falls to the ground. "Oops."

"It's not, but I still have to go." I shake my head. "What the hell are you making, by the way?"

"A cake for my half-birthday," Tilly says. "Don't forget to GO FOR IT. Byyyyye."

I pull the phone away from my ear and laugh. "Happy half-birthday."

Standing, I tuck my phone into the back pocket of my shorts, walking to open the door for my next client. I'm still not convinced I want to follow Tilly's advice. It's a byproduct of playing it safe my whole life and rarely going for things I really want.

I swing open the door and see the slight old woman scowling up at me. "Hi, Granny."

This is the first time she's stood outside my door. She pulled me aside while Wyatt was making breakfast this morning to ask about getting a massage. Now that she's here, she looks smaller and almost out of place. Like seeing your teacher at the grocery store or someone from your past a decade later.

It's weird.

She squints at my chest. "What in the blazes is on your shirt?"

I look down. "A wolf."

She tilts her head. "But what's he doing?"

I tug my cropped shirt down so the picture is more visible. "He's howling...at the moon."

"Like a werewolf?"

"No...like a wolf."

She shakes her head and changes the subject. "Still have time for me?"

"Yes, come on in."

I step aside so Granny can pass me into the living room. When she said she wanted to book an appointment, I was surprised since she hadn't shown any interest before.

I shut the door behind her. "You can head to that room to undress and lay flat on your stomach or back, whichever is most comfortable for you."

She doesn't go to the room, though, and instead, sits on the couch. "Oh, I'm not here for a massage."

"You're not?"

She shakes her head. "Nope."

I sit on the chair across from her. "Okay...so why are you here?"

Please don't say you're sick and don't know how to tell your family. Please.

She doesn't answer right away but looks around the cabin, like she's seen a ghost. Her voice is low and gravelly when she speaks. "I haven't been in any of the cabins in a long time."

I follow her gaze. Painted wood cabinets in the kitchen, laminate floors throughout, a fresh coat of white on the walls, and mostly matching furniture are all Wyatt's upgrades. But it's the intensity behind her stare that speaks of the memories living beneath them, as if she's digging up layers of dirt to find the treasure beneath.

"Walter built these cabins," she says more to herself than me.

"Wyatt said he built them for the family to come and visit."

She nods and drops her eyes to her lap. "He did." Dabbing her cheek, she continues. "Hell, we couldn't get them to leave after that. They only lived a few miles away but would come for the weekend and end up staying the whole week."

Her laugh is feeble, but I smile anyway.

"I miss him," she says, looking past me into the kitchen.

Tears spring to my eyes. I can feel the strength of her loss in the heartbeat of mine. I know my brother is free of his pain. He's probably riding his bike on streets of gold or throwing a football with Jesus. It's always harder for the people who are left behind.

"But telling you how much I miss my dead husband isn't why I came," Granny says.

She swipes beneath her eyes, and I blink back my own tears. "So, you aren't here for a massage, even though you booked a time slot, and you don't want to talk about your late husband?"

She crosses her ankles. "That's right."

"Then, why are you here?" I ask, leaning over my thighs.

"What I came here to talk to you about is Wyatt," Granny says.

"Wyatt?"

"Wyatt."

I manage to ask. "Okay, what about him?"

She sighs and shakes her head. "I don't want you going and thinking that because that hussy is here, he's off the market."

"Hussy?"

"Caroline."

Right.

"He's a good man, but he's been through a lot in the last year," Granny says. "I know he's trying to find his way right now—and he will—but don't give up on him."

I pinch my lips together and drop my gaze to the floor. "Look, Granny, I really like Wyatt."

"Even with the beard?"

"Even with his beard," I say with a laugh. "But I don't know what the future holds for both of us. I'm just trying...trying to..." What am I trying to do? Live without this crippling fear? Move on with my life and start finding things that make me happy? Those all sound about right. "I'm trying to get through the next month before my time here is done."

She holds up a hand. "It doesn't have to end."

I scoot to the edge of the chair, this small movement taking so much energy. "Yeah, but Wyatt hasn't said anything different. I don't even know if he's planning to continue with the spa, the guests, and every-thing else."

I'm not sure why I'm unloading all of this on her, but it's fresh on my mind after talking to Tilly. I can't say I haven't worried about what the future holds, either. My contract ends here, and it's the first time in my life I don't have a plan for what's next. It's terrifying and weird but also relatively freeing. The idea that I could do anything or go anywhere is as enticing as it is unsettling. Change is starting to sound better than it did a month ago since Avery's Curse seems to be on vacation.

Granny's brows draw together. "You know, when Wyatt first moved back here, I wasn't sure if he'd be ready for the farm, even though it's been ready for him. After living in the city for close to a decade, I was afraid his calluses had gone soft."

I can confirm they are anything but soft.

She continues. "But what I've noticed since he got here is he's risen to every challenge like he has all his life. Maybe he lost his way there for a while or got stuck in a different kind of cow pie, but that's one thing I can always count on Trapp Farms to do—help you find your way back to yourself."

My expression is blank, at least I hope it is, because everything she just described is what I've experienced in the last month of being here, and her words are like a square peg fitting into a square hole. The farm has helped me rediscover my first love of owning a spa and in many ways, I've found parts of myself that were hidden. The parts that came before Justice.

"You alright there, Avery?" Granny asks, snapping her fingers.

I shake my head and stand abruptly, needing a distraction from the effect of her words. "Do you want a cookie?"

She's just as startled by my outburst as she leans back with wide eyes but recovers faster than I do. "What kind ya got?"

I swallow all the emotions my musings have brought to the surface. "Chocolate chip."

"I'll take all of them," she says with a smile.

I match her grin, even if it's forced, and pad into the kitchen, calling over my shoulder, "Do you like milk?"

"Does Dolly Parton sleep on her back?"

Grabbing the cookies from the shelf, I realize they aren't cookies but crackers, so I put them back, get the right container, then open the fridge saying, "I don't know, does she?"

"Of course she does. Don't make me explain why."

Ohhh.

Shutting the fridge, I retrieve two glasses and pour the milk as my hand shakes and causes some to slosh over the edge and onto the counter. What Granny said reminds me of how much Wyatt and I have in common. We're both scared shitless. I didn't put it together before, because Wyatt seems as confident as a surgeon holding a scalpel. But maybe he's scared of his future here. It's been hard enough trying to get him to confirm what comes next after the trial.

Granny yells, "Everything okay in there?"

I clean up the milk mess on the counter and call back, "Almost done."

The small tin of cookies feels like a weight in my hand as I enter the living room, and I drop it onto the coffee table a little too hard. Handing Granny her glass of milk, I clutch mine in my hand and try to keep up with the thoughts running around like wild horses inside my head as I sit.

She takes a sip and sets it on the coffee table. "It wasn't but five months ago Wyatt knew nothing about turning out cattle in different fields. Walter always took the lead. But now that boy is orchestrating everything from grazing to slaughter," she says with a proud lilt to her voice.

My skin is warm and clammy, and my mouth has fallen down and can't get up. *Slaughter.* That word brings even more fear than Pennywise the dancing manic clown does.

I pull the lid off the cookie tin. "Yeah, but Wyatt hasn't," I almost choke on the word, "slaughtered any animals recently...right?"

Granny nibbles off a corner of her cookie. "Oh no, that happens in the fall."

I exhale my relief and nod. But as I pick up my cookie, Granny's next words stop me cold.

"Can't help when the coyotes pick a few chickens off like they just did, though. Such a shame."

"What?" I yell, startling Granny.

"Jiminy Crickets," she says, one hand flying to her chest.

"Coyotes k...ki...killed the chickens?"

"Not all of them." She shakes her head. "I shouldn't have opened my big mouth. Wyatt knows I can't keep quiet."

My heart starts racing. "What happened?"

She grabs another cookie for her other hand. Double-fisting them, she dunks both into the milk and takes a big bite of each one.

"Granny..."

She talks around a mouthful. "Wyatt said he'd talk to you. I figured he already had."

The cookie crumbs taste like cardboard in my mouth, so I drop it on the table and stare her down as intently as the wolf on my shirt is staring at the moon. "How many chickens died?"

She takes a sip of milk. "A few."

"How many?"

"A dozen, maybe?"

"Twelve chickens!" It's not even a question but a frantic statement of fact. Twelve chickens lost their lives. I can't even.

She holds her hands up. "Now just a minute here. To be fair, we account for losses in our numbers, and while it's sad, there's a natural order to things."

I cover my mouth with my hand and think of all the chickens I'd named.

Oh my god.

Avery's Curse is back from vacation.

I stand again and start pacing the room. My head feels like it's about to explode, and my warm skin is now the temperature of a thousand Hot Pockets.

"Avery," she says, but I tune her out.

No. Why? How could this happen? I shouldn't have been so naive. Of course this would happen. Wyatt said as much. But this...hurts. These animals were as much my friends as anyone else, and I believed they'd be spared. I believed Avery's Curse couldn't touch them, but it did. It got them right in the jugular.

"Avery!"

"What?" I scream, throwing up my hands then take a deep breath to calm down. "Tell me something..."

She sets both half-eaten cookies down and sits straighter.

I'm breathing hard and place a hand over my heart as I ask, "Was it Hennifer?"

She tilts her head and nods slowly.

I throw my head back and cover my face with my hands, groaning loudly over the loss.

Her voice drops low. "I know you're upset. Wyatt said you would be, which is why I know he wanted to tell ya. I'm sorry for spilling the jelly beans. He probably would've said it better."

I shake my head. "I'm cursed."

"Cursed?"

I drop my hands and nod. "Cursed."

"How do ya figure?"

"Every time I make a change, someone dies. It's been happening since Justice, my brother, passed away. Avery's Curse has been on a killing rampage ever since."

I drop my chin to my chest and lean a hip into the loveseat, unable to hold the weight of this curse and my sadness. Liking Wyatt has terminal consequences.

"Ah, I see what's going on here," Granny says, brushing crumbs from her jeans.

I lift my head to stare at her, blinking back tears. "What do you mean?"

She shifts in her seat and laces her fingers to cradle one of her knees. "Grief likes to whisper stories in our ears to help make sense of things when they don't."

"But people died…" I shake my head. "My goldfish died and all after making a change. Hennifer wouldn't have died if it weren't for me."

"Honey, those chickens have a short lifespan anyway, and if it wasn't coyotes, it could've been coons or the butcher. That's life—that's also death. It doesn't always make sense. And our grief," she blows out a gust of air, "it's just as confusing." She pauses before continuing. "I'm gonna tell you something I've never told another living soul."

I gulp then plop back on the loveseat. I sink as far back as it will let me until the cushions curl around my shoulders, and it's swallowing me.

"After Walter died, I didn't know what I'd do without him. We'd been working this farm together for decades, and his death took some of the shine outta this place. I saw him everywhere—still do—and I wished the Lord woulda just taken both of us, but He didn't." She drops her gaze to the table between us. "So, every night and most days after he was gone, I crawled onto his side of the bed and slept there. It smelled like him—a mix of wood and straw—until one day it didn't. It started to smell like me. But even today, I still sleep on his side, not because I want to smell him on our sheets. Rather, I feel closer to him. Like his arms are wrapped around me. And you know what, I swear to you I feel his arms some nights, and that's what gets me through the days without him."

A tear falls from the corner of my eye, but I don't swipe it away. I let it streak down my cheek, curve around my jaw, and trail down my neck. I've never been so close to someone else's grief that felt so tangible. As if I could reach out and touch it like another person in the room.

She picks up her glass of milk and then both of her cookies. "Death is cruel in how it takes, but it can also give. Don't let fear rob you from receiving, Avery."

I sniffle. "What did death ever give me?"

She raises her glass of milk and nods once. "That's for you to find out."

Twenty-Six

Avery

"Just let go—and fall like a little waterfall."-Bob Ross

Another knock.

I wipe my wet cheeks and peel myself off the couch to answer it. Granny just left fifteen minutes ago, is she back again? I smooth my hands over my blue summer dress and open the door saying, "Granny, did you change your mind—"

Wyatt stands with one foot propped on the top step, one hand on his hip while the other holds something wrapped in a brown paper bag. He's wearing his favorite hat that shields his face, but I can still see the sweep he does from my head to my toes. I feel it in every pore of my body.

"Hi," I say with a strained voice, hoping my eyes don't look as puffy as two inflatable pool tubes. "I thought you were Granny."

He definitely is not.

"Um, hi," he says. "You look...different." I look down, overly conscious of what I'm wearing now. He waves a hand in front of me. "The dress...I've never seen you wear one."

Smoothing a hand over my dress, I say, "Oh, yeah. I only have one."

All of my graphic tees are dirty. After Granny dropped her wisdom on me, and I had to grapple with the fact that Hennifer and Hilary Fluff are no longer with us, my emotions were charged and jittery. I spilled ketchup down the front of my shirt, making it look like the wolf was bleeding.

He stares up at me, a look of pure steel. "I wanted to come by to see if you were busy."

Did Granny send him here? His guilt? Why hadn't he told me sooner? "I'm not busy." Upset is more like it.

He shifts from one foot to the other then grips whatever is in the paper bag with two hands before extending it out to me. "I brought you something."

I peer down at the bag and wonder if I should walk back inside and slam the door. I'm angry, but I know that's only on the outside. On the inside, I'm sad. I blame my therapist for teaching me that anger is really a secondary emotion.

Grabbing the bag with one hand, I realize immediately how heavy it is and have to use my other hand to grab it. "What is this?"

He nods at the package while tucking his hands in his back pockets. "Open it."

I look from him to the bag then reach inside to find what feels like a cold but smooth rock. It's as heavy as one, and as I pull the bag away, I notice etching on the front of this flat, rectangular piece of stone, which reads: *Hennifer, the greatest chicken there ever was.*

My chin drops open, and I trace the words with my finger before looking up at Wyatt. "You did this?"

"Yeah."

I exhale. "Did Granny..."

"She told me that she told you. Look, Avery, I'm so sorry. I was planning to tell you first, and then it all happened so fast. Caroline showed up, and then Granny went and told you, and with everything else going on, I was worried you'd...hate me." He finally takes a breath and drops his hands to his sides. "Do you hate me?"

I stare down at the gravestone once more and read Hennifer's name a few times. It's not like he was the cause of her demise, but it still stings. Without Wyatt, or this farm, I'd never have known her. That has to count for something.

I inhale through my nose then say, "I don't hate you, I just wish you would have told me sooner. It was a surprise I wasn't ready for."

His shoulders drop, and his other foot joins the one on the top step, putting him just outside my door and staring down with relief written in the semi-hidden smile lines behind his beard.

"You're right, I should have." He pushes my hair off one shoulder. "I'm sorry, Avery. I don't like that you were surprised or hurt, and I had something to do with it."

To know he cares just as deeply as I do is making my stomach flutter as the anger melts away. "Thank you," is all I can manage.

He hooks a thumb through his belt loop, his voice low and gravelly. "Do you think...well, maybe, since you're not busy...and you don't hate me..." He glances up briefly and then back down at the porch where our feet almost touch. "Do you think we could talk about something else?"

He's rambling, and a flustered Wyatt makes me smile. But I know exactly what he wants to talk about apart from Hennifer (and the event that shall not be named). I don't think I'm ready for this last-minute conversation about Caroline. I need at least three business days before I can discuss this. "I don't think that will work. I have another client in an hour."

It's true, but I don't mention that the client is his sister.

He tilts his head. "How about a...massage then?"

He sounds nervous asking this and yet, maybe he just wants to spend more time together like I do. But the idea of placing my naked hands on his naked back is making me feel like I'm standing here naked right now. "Uh..." He's never asked for a massage before, though he'd have every right. "Sure, a-huh, I can do that."

I open the door wider and invite him in. He shoves both hands in his pockets and steps up and over the threshold. He immediately removes his boots as I wonder how the hell I'm supposed to do this. *He's my boss.* I need to remember this when my hands are touching parts of him I've never touched before. If I don't, I'll think about what his lips felt like on mine—tender and soft, a little bit wet, and a whole lot of trouble.

Every part of Wyatt commands attention. His height, the width of his shoulders, the size of his boots. His body is loud when he enters a space, and right now, he's practically screaming at me. The air in this cabin is charged, and I'm afraid touching him will be like touching a lightning bolt, or at least a hot toaster.

Pulling his hat off, he hangs it on a hook before running hands through his wet, flattened hair. Freshly showered Wyatt is a favorite of mine. I'm aware of every movement he's making and every one I'm not.

Is my mouth open? I snap it shut. "Follow me when you're ready."

He trails me into the room, and I spin around, the massage table between us. The room feels smaller all of a sudden, as if it shrunk to the size of a dollhouse while I was gone. "You can remove your clothes down to your…underwear," I choke out. Definitely need to make sure he keeps those suckers on.

Visions of his bare body on my table are making me sweat in places that I'm not okay with. I'll be shoving tissues in my armpits just to survive the next hour and will need a cold shower pronto, possibly an ice bath, or a last-minute trip to Antarctica to cool off with the polar bears.

His hands bracket his hips as he takes in the space with a few nods. "So, you want me to remove all of my clothes?"

"Mhm." I drop my gaze to his jeans and think of what's under them before quickly shaking my head. "Most of them."

One of his brows lifts. "Just not my underwear?"

My gaze has turned molten. I need to start thinking of Freddy Krueger if I want to make it out of this session alive. "Mhm."

"Alright. I can do that," he says with a smirk.

My eyes widen when he reaches for the hem of his shirt. "Wait! I'll give you privacy." I walk toward the door and catch the smile tugging at the corner of his mouth. Thank God he'll be face down on the table, smirk hidden and mouth trapped.

I step out in the hallway, closing the door behind me and breathing hard, like I'm just coming up out of the water after several minutes. I pull my phone out of my dress pocket and shoot Tilly a rushed text. *He's getting undressed as we speak so I can give him a massage.* As I expected, she replies within seconds. *Get it girl!!!!!!*

There are so many exclamation points, I don't even have time to count them all before Wyatt calls out, "Ready," from inside the room turned sexual tension torture chamber.

I huck my phone into the air as I startle, and it lands with a thud on the ground.

"Get it together, Avery," I say quietly, bending to grab my phone and connect it to the bluetooth speaker.

I can do this. I'll go in there, rub him down with oil, and call it a day. It'll be fine. We'll be fine. It won't be weird at all. Or hot, or hard, or heady.

Time to lasso my thoughts out of the gutter.

I push the door open and come face to back with his bronze, chiseled skin. He's face down, which I figured would be easier for me to handle. Wrong. His sculpted upper body is every bit as jaw dropping as the parts of him visible through the sheet. I close my eyes in a rush.

"Do you prefer waves or calm music?"

He lifts his head. "Got any Mozart?"

I scroll through my music. "No, but I'm sure I could find some—"

He laughs, the sound instantly causing my head to snap up and look at him. It's a Pavlovian response at this point. "Avery, I'm kidding. Any music is fine."

I go with the calm music, because I could use some zen in my life, and set my phone down beside the tub of coconut oil. My tranquility dies a slow death. *Coconut oil.* Oh god. Tilly's voice comes marching back into my head.

Remind me to tell you all the ways you can use coconut oil with someone else.

Shoving the thoughts aside, I rub it on my hands and stare down at them, like they're coated in blood. But it's worse. It's oil. Slick, smooth, and slippery. I've massaged plenty of men. But this is Wyatt lathered in coconut oil by my hands. Can the women in a one-hundred-mile radius even handle this? Can I? I have to think of something else.

Buttons. Peacocks. Palm tree. Coconuts. Oil.

Shit! Not working.

I turn around. "Okay, I'm going to get started."

Cup. Walnut. Cadillac.

"Ok," he says, then his back flexes. It *flexes.*

Hands hovering over him, I slowly lower them like a crane. "Here I go."

Peanuts. Walrus. Zoo.

He groans into the face cradle, and I pause, my insides becoming mush. "So, uh, what kind of pressure do you prefer? Firm or soft?"

"Uh...I've never had a massage before," he admits.

He's a massage virgin. *Great.*

I blow a hair out of my face. "Never?"

"Nope. But I guess firm is probably what I'd prefer. I'll let you know."

He'll let me know. Mhm, yes. As he should.

Desire pulses low in my belly. "I can do that."

Balloons. Cat. Dirt.

I lower my hands to his taut shoulders that twitch beneath my touch and begin kneading. I knead some more. Then, I drag both hands up his spine.

Knead, knead, drag.

Drag, Drag, Knead.

Look! I'm doing it! I'm massaging Wyatt without thinking about what's beneath the sheet.

At least, I was.

Now I'm not.

Dresser. Window. Blinds. Chair.

Wyatt's clothes are on the chair. Wranglers.

Damn it. I shake my head.

His skin is as soft as I assumed it would be. But the knots in his upper back and neck are anything but. I spend a few minutes pushing my fingers into the tightest ones and working my way down his spine, relying on my hands and not my thoughts to carry me through.

"How does this feel?" I ask.

He grunts. "Amazing."

The low growl of his voice fills my stomach with heat, and my knees are practically knocking together, making it difficult to stand. Twelve new heartbeats have sprouted inside my body, so that's great. Despite my attempts at distracting myself from this overwhelming attraction, made even more so by his thoughtful gift, he seems to be enjoying it. He deserves to relax. Every knot I'm working has a different name: Granny, Trapp Farms, his family, the future, the past, Caroline. And me. Hennifer, too. He carries so much for everyone else. Taking care of him like this is the least I can do to alleviate some of that pressure weighing down on him.

It's why I love massage. Our bodies carry our stories inside them and being able to pinpoint and alleviate some of that pressure is what got me through losing my brother. I spent countless hours on a massage table, letting someone else work out the grief I couldn't handle myself. I'd already started and quit massage school once after Justice died but going back felt like the only option for me. It was a part of my healing, and I wanted that for other people.

"This feels so good," he says.

Pride settles high in my chest. I continue to rub down each arm until I reach his rough hands where I apply a rocking pressure to his palms. I manage to massage his calves and thighs without needing to call in reinforcements that don't exist to take over for me. I must have been transported somewhere else in order to make it through.

Then, the unthinkable happens.

Siri cuts off the birds and the bees nature sounds and begins reading a new text...from Tilly. "You are so getting some!" says the robotic voice. I rush to the dresser and grab my phone, but my hands are struggling to grab it since they're drenched in blood—oil. "Don't forget the coconut—"

I manage to press the button on the side after multiple attempts before the rest of her message is read, saving me from Tilly's exuberant support.

Wyatt clears his throat but says nothing.

I bite my lips and stare at the ceiling. Another reminder to put my phone on silent while I'm rubbing down my boss and someone I also shared a moment with and maybe sort of like. Okay, someone I'm totally into and makes my palms sweat. I choose to ignore the entire event, turning the sounds of nature back on while silencing all communication with the outside world. Bees are the only ones welcome here.

I clear my throat so my question doesn't sound like it's been baked in a hot oven set to twelve-thousand degrees. "Are you ready to turn over so I can work on your neck and shoulders more?"

He moans into the headrest as I prepare to face him.

"I'll hold the sheet up so you can turn," I say, a little breathless.

He makes a noise that sounds an awful lot like agreement but hesitates.

When he does push up, I hold the sheet, so it creates a wall between us as he twists and lays flat on his back. I swear I saw nothing, but when his thigh bumped into mine, my stomach did a backward handspring into a somersault before ending in the splits. At least I landed it.

His hands cover his bulge, and I widen my eyes until they are the size of dinner plates and no smaller. It really has been a good massage. Plenty of male clients have informed me it's a simple matter of blood-flow that just...happens, yet with Wyatt, I wish it weren't.

Pigeons. Steak. Pizza.

I should be used to seeing his chest and back, but now it's glowing in this faint light coming through the sides of the curtains, and something about that makes my blood heat to an uncomfortable temperature. Sitting on the chair near his head, I work out the tight spots in his neck.

Pretty sure my boobs graze the top of his head at one point and pretty sure he smiles.

"Your hands are magic," he says as I trace his collarbone.

His eyes are closed as he says this to the ceiling. I take the opportunity to study every part of his face. The scar near his left eye and the longer one on his pec tell stories I don't know, yet. I run my thumb along the one on his chest as I push my palms forward.

The silence stretches around us like a fitted sheet hugging a mattress for a full thirty minutes. "All finished. I'll step out so you can get dressed."

He blinks rapidly and rubs his brow. "Wait, Avery," he says, and I stop near the foot of the table. He sits up, clutching the sheet to his bottom half as he props himself up with one hand. "Thank you."

Perfume. Flower. Tractor.

Keep your eyes up. "You're welcome."

I turn to leave, but he says, "Stay."

That one word is felt in all of my now tingling places. I couldn't even move if I wanted to. "Okay."

He shifts until his bare feet graze the floor. "I know this isn't exactly the best time." I meet his eyes, and he gestures toward the slim sheet covering him. "But I really need to talk to you, privately."

I clasp my oiled hands in front of me so I don't reach out for him. He's all lazy features and rumpled hair—a new favorite. "Alright."

My heart is hammering away, like a woodpecker set on taking down a tree.

"Caroline and I...she...we." He sighs and rubs his chin. "Sorry, I'm not good at this."

I want to move closer and bridge the gap The Kiss has created—the gap Caroline has built between us—but I hold my ground for a moment longer. Until I meet his rounded eyes and gentle smile, forcing my feet to walk around the table and put my hand on his arm. "Hey, it's okay. I told you before, you don't have to explain anything."

And I mean it. Whatever happened between them clearly labeled them with an "It's Complicated" status. My intention was never to add to that label, changing it to: It's complicated and also even more complicated.

"No, I want to explain because the barn…" He looks from my hand to my lips. "The kiss. I didn't want you to think I'd just kiss you and then forget. But after Caroline showed up—"

"I get it. She's your ex-girlfriend. It's okay to still have feelings for her and maybe be confused—"

"I'm not confused." I start to pull my hand away, but he captures it before I can. "I don't like Caroline. In fact, if one thing has become more clear to me, it's that the idea of her was always more appealing than the reality. She went with the lifestyle I had before, like cufflinks to a custom suit. But that's not who I am. Not really. I like…" He grabs my other hand and tugs me closer, his knees bracketing my thighs. "I like who I am with you, Avery."

This whole boss/employee thing is crumbling. It's dust under a bookshelf—completely forgotten. The ground is shaking under my feet, and a low-ringing noise hisses in my ear. It's actually just the bird sounds coming from the speaker, but it's so loud, I can't hear myself think. I should think about this. What does this mean? What is he saying? What am I thinking?

I can't think when I'm thinking so much.

And those damn birds are really distracting.

Still beneath his intense gaze, he lets go of my hands in order to hold the outside of my thighs. The thin material of my dress is no match for the warmth of those manual labor hands. He lazily runs his palms up to settle on my hips where he uses his thumbs to rub slow circles into my sides. Tingles shoot down every one of my limbs, causing me to shiver under his touch.

Nothing makes sense.

Bullet. Potato salad. Pillow.

He licks his lips and stares at mine. "What would you say if I asked to kiss you again?"

Consent looks so sexy on him that I want to immediately agree to everything running through my mind. But first, I lean closer until my lips are hovering over his. Unable to do anything else, I'm sure of my answer and sure of the man I'm giving it to. "I'd say yes."

Twenty-Seven

Wyatt

"Didn't you know you had that much power? You can move mountains. You can do anything."-Bob Ross

Her perfect mouth slants over mine, and I groan. I can't stifle it. She's so soft beneath my grip, which is exactly opposite of how I feel right now. I've envisioned her lips on mine plenty more times since the barn. But no daydreams have come close to this.

She's as ready for this as I am.

As her hands meld to my back, my arms, my chest, I'm reminded of all the reasons I'm going a little crazy over this woman. She's attentive. Everyone she's with gets her full attention. She's caring. Always asking what she can do to help. And she's beautiful. The kind of beauty that makes my mouth feel like it's stuffed with a handful of marshmallows every time I see her. When she opened the door in her light blue summer dress with skinny straps and a flowy skirt, my mind became as small as one of the freckles on her collarbone.

Avery doesn't wear makeup or spend much time styling her hair, but everything about her is so deliciously feminine, I could lap her up like a thirsty animal.

Slow it down.

She gave me permission to kiss her, not devour her, though I'd very much like to do that, too. I open my mouth wider, tasting more of her, as my hands trail up her back and cradle her face. I weave one hand through her hair and twirl a silky strand around my finger. She smells like her signature lavender scent—or maybe that's me? It's earthy and floral. Grounding yet, lose-your-mind kind of intoxicating.

I drop my hand to her shoulder and trace her collarbone with my hand and then my mouth.

Her head tips back, and she's breathing heavily as I kiss my way across her chest.

"I don't usually do this," she says, placing steadying hands on my shoulders.

I hook a finger beneath the small strap of her dress and let it fall off her shoulder. "Do what?"

"This." She presses closer, the flimsy sheet hiding what she can now feel against her stomach. "Sleep with my client. Or, more accurately, my boss."

I find her lips again and press light kisses against them. Hovering an inch above her mouth, I ask, "Is that what we're doing? Sleeping together?"

She pulls back, eyes wide. "No! I mean…no. Sorry, I didn't mean to assume."

I grip her waist and tug her back to me. "Please. Don't be sorry. I'm not." I brush her hair out of her face so I can see her better. I don't want anything between us. "I didn't come in here assuming this would happen, but now that it is, I'm more than okay with it. Are you?"

She stares into my eyes, and I stare back, my innermost thoughts clear of hang-ups, reservations, second-guessing. I want this. I want her. I want us.

She answers me by lifting her hands to my bearded face, running her fingers over the coarse hair before tracing my lips with the pad of her thumb. First the top then the bottom. I take her finger into my mouth and suck gently before pressing a hot kiss to the inside of her palm.

Then, I lean closer and run my tongue just below her jaw where her heart rate is fast and pulsing while I pull the other strap of her dress off the other shoulder.

"Wyatt," she whispers.

I hum against her skin and continue to kiss and nuzzle her neck. Blood rushes to my head, which is surprising that there's still some left in my body after all of it feels like it's going straight to my dick.

"Wyatt."

"Yeah?" I say against the expanse of skin just above her breasts.

"Can you do something for me?"

"Anything."

Easy answer. Next question.

"Can you..." She tips her head back as I lick the full length of her neck and start peppering kisses near the base of her ear. "I can't think when you're..." She can't even finish her thought, and that feels about as rewarding as winning first place in a pie eating contest. I've won enough of those to know.

Placing her hands on either side of my face, she lifts my head until I'm staring straight into her glassy blue eyes. "If Caroline asks, can you tell her we rubbed sunscreen on each other when we first met?"

I'm momentarily stunned. This never happened, because I would have remembered it in scary-accurate detail. I would have replayed that memory in my mind until the cows came home on their own. Now, all I can think about is rubbing sunscreen on her.

"Yes. Done."

She seems to relax further into the Spiderman grip I have on her waist. "Thank you. I didn't mean to lie, but she told me how you two met and I just...I got carried away."

I knit my brows together. "Were you jealous?"

Her lashes skim her cheeks. "Maybe."

I outline her lips with my finger then tip her chin up. "You have nothing to be jealous about."

"Okay, I believe you," she whispers. Bending closer, her mouth dropping closer to mine. "One more thing."

I swallow hard and want to reiterate my thoughts on this, but she turns in my arms until her back is to me, revealing a zipper. Scooping her hair to the side, she looks back at me, resting a chin on her shoulder. "Help me with my dress."

I fumble to grip the microscopic zipper and my fingers slip against the smooth fabric. My body wants to rush, because Avery is everything it wants. But I don't. I need to take things slow. I want to show her just how much I appreciate every part of her.

I'll tell Caroline I met Avery in my dreams if that's what she wants. It wouldn't be far from the truth. This feels like more of a dream right now anyway. Unzipping her dress, the only thing left is her light blue, lacy underwear, which is enough to make me forget how to spell the word *slow*.

I take a deep breath and let her shimmy out of her dress until it meets the floor, and my eyes memorize every angle and contour of her backside. I'm pretty sure I let out a gruff laugh while shaking my head, because this woman. Damn. Trailing my hands back up her arms, I lean in and kiss the center of her bare back, pressing light kisses against her spine. She shivers as I reach the base of her neck then below her ear.

I'm already out of breath. "Do you have any extra coconut oil?"

She murmurs, "Yeah. Why?"

I trace the outer edge of her ear with my nose. "Let me show you."

She leans forward and grabs a tub—an actual tub—of coconut oil off the dresser. The one I got for her. At the time, I didn't see it being used for this. "Is this enough?" she asks.

Honestly, I'm not sure it is considering all the things I want to do to her. I'm glad I splurged for the jumbo size tub of oil, though.

"For now."

I take the oil from her and lather my hands with it. Starting at her shoulders, I knead them like she did for me. Pushing my thumb into the base of her spine and following it all the way to her hairline. I try to mimic her earlier movements, though I know I'm not as good. I've never given a human a massage before, which sounds like I'm into some weird shit.

I'm not. But I hope this feels as good for her as it does for me. Just having my hands on her is enough.

Her hips graze the insides of my thighs, and my body feels like it could self-destruct. "How does that feel?" I ask her.

She lifts up onto the table until the soft curves of her ass meet my rigid lines, making me even harder. She rolls out her neck. "So good. Don't. Stop."

Her words and the fact she's nearly sitting on my lap make me pulse with heat and want. Slathering more oil on my hands, I press my palms into her stomach and pull her even closer. She rests her head back on my shoulder, and I kiss her cheek, rubbing repetitive circles into her core, then beneath, between, and over her exposed breasts. Her rib cage flares out as she arches her back, and I dip my finger lower just below the hem of fabric at her waist, sliding back and forth in a teasing motion. She's breathing hard and repeating my name, the sound reverberating in my ear and down to my cock. I slide my hands back up, slipping curious fingers beneath each breast and framing them with my palms.

With her head still resting on my shoulder and my chin resting on hers, I stare down at her and groan into her ear. She is everything. The hills, valleys, and textures of her body make my blood pump faster and my breathing erratic. She is a landscape waiting to be appreciated. Slack in my arms, I know I'm holding more than her body. I'm holding her trust.

My hands aren't far behind my eyes, and I trace the roundness of her chest, squeeze their fullness, and pay special attention to her hardened nipples as she pulses beneath my touch. The oil makes her skin feel fifty degrees warmer and so slick with a gleam that catches every bit of light coming through the covered window. She is putty beneath my touch, panting and writhing. We could stay right here and ride this out together. I won't last long. But I want more with Avery. I want everything.

Her back curves even more as I whisper against her cheek. "Can I?"

I'm begging and I know it, but she nods emphatically, and I can feel her body shaking under my touch.

"Wyatt," she says on the heels of a moan, and I grunt as my only response while she spreads her legs wider, and I continue massaging circles lower and lower until I reach her center.

She covers my hands with hers, and I slow my rhythm. I kiss her neck, savoring the sweetness of her skin and let my hands keep exploring, pausing when her moans and shudders become more intense. I take notes in my mind. The sounds she makes, the way her body vibrates at my touch, the things she asks for—*more, here, right there*—and those she doesn't since pleasure steals the words from her mouth. I won't forget a single part, because there isn't a piece of Avery I could forget.

"Stop. Please," she begs.

I stop and rest my hands on her stomach, concern thick in my throat. "What's wrong? Are you okay?"

She lifts her head and spins around to face me, my hands heavy on her hips. "I want to watch you," she says against my lips, then kisses me hard, biting my bottom lip as my fingers dig into her sides.

I pull back and with panting breaths ask, "Watch me?"

She nods. "Watch you lose it, too."

Twenty-Eight

Avery

"No pressure. Just relax and watch it happen."-Bob Ross

Both my hands creep down his chest, sliding lower and lower over his strong frame. I kiss his neck, feeling how he swallows until I skim the edge of his briefs. Then, he goes completely still, and I watch him. My eyes lock on his face as my finger dips below the hem, stretching the elastic at his waist to hold his length in my hand while he inhales sharply and closes his eyes.

I nearly shattered like a glass swan that's been sitting on the shelf too long when he had his hands on me. I could have given into the euphoric feeling and followed the bright swirls of color behind my eyes, but instead, I wanted this. I wanted to see Wyatt come undone. To know that I affect him the way he does me.

But his mouth is magnetic, and I lean in to part the seam of his lips with my tongue. Our lips and hands become frantic and our kiss turns sloppy, diving head first into this new territory and finding places to explore and touch that incite new sensations and louder sounds.

He bites my bottom lip, egging me to move my hand.

So, I do.

"Avery," he says against my mouth. "Shit." I press closer, our bare chests touching. One hand stroking him while the other plays with the hair at the nape of his neck. His breath tickles my lips. "Hang on. I need a minute."

I stop working him with my hand. "You okay?"

He bends and presses a kiss to one of my breasts, beard scraping my sensitive skin. "More than okay. But I won't last long like this."

I smile, wishing I'd gone back for that box in Wyatt's bathroom. "Do you have a condom?"

He nods. "In my jeans."

I let out a breathy laugh. "You came prepared?"

He guides me backward as he stands, the sheer breadth and height of his body making me ache for him even more than I already am. "I've been ready," he says, walking to his discarded jeans on the chair in the corner.

I repeat his words in my mind. *I've been ready.*

His tented briefs tell me just how true his words really are, and the pulsing heartbeat below my waist is evidence enough that I believe them, too.

"Since the kiss?" I ask.

He shakes his head. "Before that."

I blink rapidly, watching him search his pockets. "Since the Thirsty Hippo?"

"No," he says, locating the square package. He's so sure—so confident—as he says, "When you stood over me near the creek while I was taking my break. Your hair was glowing, eyes sharp and seeing. It was then."

I watch as he drops his jeans back on the chair, my breath just as irregular as it was when his hands were on me. "But that was the first time you saw me."

"I know." He walks back to where I'm standing and pulls me into him. "You're so beautiful." He kisses me deeply, and I stand on my tiptoes to meet his eager mouth, melting into him. "I want you so badly," he murmurs against my mouth.

Wyatt has been wanting to do this since the first time he saw me? I can't even believe it, but then again, the way every muscle in my stomach pulls taut like a slingshot assures me I can.

I press feather light kisses to his cheek. "You have me."

He cups my breast, massaging gently and lulling me back to that sweet spot of want and need and everything in between. My body responds by pushing closer and closer. He rocks his hips against me and my body folds, and I coast on a wave of pleasure. It's intoxicating. It's new. It's Wyatt.

I've been ready.

He holds me upright so I don't topple over. "Should we go to your room?"

I nod, head still in a daze from the thrumming and pounding happening in long neglected places. He grabs my hand and leads me around the massage table toward the door of the room. We walk down the hall, and he pulls me behind him just as we hear three knocks.

"Damn it," Wyatt says under his breath. He looks back at me.

That door. I'm going to cover it in balloons or...or sanitary pads. That'll keep everyone from knocking. There are still twenty-two minutes before Stace's massage, and she's never early, so it can't be her.

The desire in his eyes and mussed up hair say he's not ready for this to end. It's too soon. We were just about to...maybe I don't have to answer it. Maybe they'll go away. I hold a finger up to my lips and stay still.

Whoever is on the other side of the door knocks again, and I release my breath. My mind starts to race with the possibility of a last-minute booking I missed, Granny, or one of the guests. Could something be wrong? Does someone need help?

"I should probably answer it," I say in a hushed voice.

His lips form a thin line, but he nods, roaming his heated gaze over all of my exposed parts once more. "I'll get dressed and slip out the back door," he says in a thick voice.

I close my eyes, swallow, and yell, "Just a second," to the person at the door.

He pulls me into his arms and kisses the tip of my nose, my forehead, my lips. "One more kiss for the road," he says with a sheepish grin.

I tickle his side. "That was more than one."

He captures my hand and crushes me against him, our skin still bare and warm, mine still slick from the oil he rubbed on me. "One isn't enough."

I bite my lip then follow him back into the massage room to quickly slip my dress back on. Wyatt zips me up, and though my underwear managed to stay on, it's wet with the reminder of exactly how he unraveled me.

Smoothing both hands over my hair to put it back in place, I shuffle down the hall, through the living room to face the door. I wait until I hear the squeak of the hinges on the backdoor and a click of the lock as it shuts.

I exhale once then open the front door.

"Ronny, hi. I was just…" I point behind me, "finishing a massage." At least that part is true. My heart is still erratic thinking of Wyatt's hands on all of my tender places.

He looks at my shoulder, and I follow his gaze, seeing that one of my straps fell again. I lift it back into place and stand half behind the door as I clear my throat. "What's up?"

He rocks back on his heels. "Have you seen Wyatt around? He isn't answering his phone."

It's not like I can say that Wyatt was busy completely destroying me with his mouth, his hands, and his beard seconds ago. That he brought me a freaking plaque in remembrance of my favorite chicken and told me *I've been ready*. Heat slithers across my skin until I'm positive I look like a tomato. Blasted fair skin.

I look down. "I, uh. Hm. I don't know. Haven't seen him. Is he in the barn?"

Ronny squints at me. "Already checked there."

I scratch my head. "Oh. Well, maybe check the farmhouse."

"I'll check there again." He tips his hat at me and smirks. "If you see him, let him know I need to talk to him." He turns, his heavy boots thudding down the porch steps. He waves a hand in the air without turning. "Have a good one, Avery."

I gently shut the front door, leaning my head back and exhaling all of the air in my lungs.

He knows. Ronny knows.

There's no way I played that cool enough. Why did I have to answer the door? I should have ignored it or snuck out the back with Wyatt.

Padding back to the massage room, I look around. It's empty now, Wyatt's scent still lingering in the air. The rumpled sheet on the table is all that's left of him, reminding me of what just happened between us. I smile and bite my thumb nail, blushing uncontrollably.

Just thinking about it sends ripples through my body all over again. If we hadn't been interrupted, I can almost bet I'd be curled into his side in my bed, hot and sweaty from more than just the weather.

Maybe Granny was right.

Life can come from death.

Twenty-Nine

Wyatt

"If we're going to have animals around, we all have to be concerned about them and take care of them."-Bob Ross

C ow hugging?" Rach asks from the opposite end of the breakfast table.

"Yeah. It's great for regulating the nervous system and reducing anxiety," I explain. Again.

"What if I don't have anxiety?" Butch pipes in.

His all-black ensemble is causing him to sweat something fierce.

I rub my neck. "Then you get to hug a cow."

Caroline groans and stomps her foot. "What if cows give you anxiety?"

I try not to roll my eyes and force a smile. "Then don't join us."

Nikki takes a bite of bacon. "So, like, all I have to do is just sit there...by the cow."

"Yup." I'm acting like I know all about this form of therapy when in reality all I can offer is what the internet taught me, which is both surprisingly a lot and also nothing at all.

"Does anyone want any more eggs or bacon?" Avery asks, stepping into the farmhouse dining room with a spatula and a pan of scrambled eggs.

She has never been sexier.

Bobbi raises her hand, and Avery loads up her plate. I had to take Bobbi and Ross on a full chicken coop tour to convince them all our chickens are humanely raised. Pretty sure I had Bobbi convinced once I introduced her to Mother Clucker.

"I think it's a great idea. I've heard of cow hugging, too," Ross says.

"You have?" I ask, nearly toppling over in my chair.

He shrugs. "Of course. It's all over social media."

"It is?" Bobbi adds. "Why haven't I seen anything about it?"

He leans forward on his forearms. "It's probably not on your *for you page*."

Avery heads into the kitchen, and I scoot my chair back and stand, announcing to the group, "I'll meet you out at the cow barn after breakfast. Ronny can show you the way."

I dart into the kitchen to avoid any more questions as Avery sets the pan on the stove. There's no one else in here, and I take full advantage, sidling up behind her and circling my arms around her waist.

I kiss her neck and tug at the hem of her shirt. "I like your shirt today. Did I tell you it's my favorite?"

On the front, Beethoven has a pen and paper, composing what will be some of the most famous classical music, wearing red, heart-shaped sunglasses. It's timeless.

She leans her head back on my shoulder, mimicking our position yesterday. "I thought Bigfoot was your favorite?"

"They all are." Pulling her hips back against me I whisper, "I especially like what's underneath—"

Someone clears their throat, and I jump back, putting a football field's distance between Beethoven and me. "Morning, Granny. You're up early."

"Damn right I am. Where's the bacon?" she asks with a smirk.

"I'll make you a plate," Avery offers. "Can I get you some eggs, too?"

"Please." Granny smiles then sits at the small eat-in table. "What do you both have planned today?"

I walk to the coffee pot to fill my thermos. "Cow hugging."

She stops opening her Sudoku book. "Cow...what? I know you didn't say 'hugging.' Is that what you've been doing with my cows?"

Avery dishes a plate for Granny in silence then slides it in front of her.

I wink at Avery, my eye having a mind of its own. "Want to join, Granny? It's great for reducing stress and anxiety."

"The only stress I have is how much manure these folks are about to come in contact with. Are they prepared for that?" Granny asks around a bite of bacon.

"I cleared an area outside the barn and laid down fresh hay. I sprayed off a few cows yesterday to make sure they were ready for the big day," I explain.

Granny stabs her eggs. "And the tutus?"

"The what?"

Avery laughs and Granny waves me off.

"We should get down there before the guests. Right, Avery?" It looks like I have something in my eye based on how aggressively I'm winking.

"I was just going to do these dishes—" She meets my eyes, which are now wide with unsaid words. "Oh. Got it. Yeah, I should go with you and make sure the hay is...comfortable."

I give her a sly thumbs up. "Need anything else before we go, Granny?"

"Nope."

"Okay, we'll see you later."

Avery heads out the back door first, but before I can sneak out, Granny stops me. "Wyatt?"

I falter. "Yeah?"

She points her fork at me. "I'm gonna ignore any text alerts I get from the barn cameras. But just remember, this isn't a brothel."

Woah. Zero to sixty on that one.

I raise my brows then relax them and wink. "Thanks, Gran."

Avery's talking to the chickens when I meet her outside. "Dora the Eggsplorer, you can't peck at Mother Clucker. She did nothing to you."

"Do you like where I put the gravestone?" I ask, walking up to the fence.

Avery startles and clutches her chest, scattering more seed in the process. "What happened to whistling a warning? I could've whacked you in the head."

"But you didn't."

She crosses her arms. "Maybe my reflexes have short-circuited since you're always scaring me."

I step closer, invading the invisible wall of decorum. "Do I scare you, Avery?"

"A little." Her eyes settle on my lips, and she leans in. "And yes, I think Hennifer would be very pleased with her placement near the coop."

Our noses knock together. "Good, now follow me," I say, tugging her arm and heading to the barn. "Granny said she'd turn off the cameras."

Avery squeezes my hand and laughs. "I don't believe you."

I pick up the pace. "I'd let you ask her yourself, but there isn't any time for that. I need to rip that shirt off—"

We reach the edge of the house, and I stop abruptly as Caroline cuts off my path, blinding me in her asparagus colored costume of a workout tank and bike shorts.

I drop Avery's hand instinctively and keep my eyes on the vegetable in front of me, knowing Caroline will play dirty before Avery will.

I'm sandwiched between them and wishing I weren't envisioning myself as deli meat.

"Wyatt," Caroline says.

"Caroline."

She peers around me. "Avery."

"Caroline."

And now that we've established each other's names yet again, I say, "Avery and I were on our way to the barn to get the last things set up."

"Oh." She rests a hand on either one of her sharp hips. "I was hoping we could talk."

"Talk?" I ask.

"Talk."

Avery clears her throat. "I think she wants to talk."

I look from Avery to Caroline. "Can it wait?"

Caroline drops her hands to her sides. Her tanned midsection and green ensemble have her looking too much like an avocado right now for me to take her seriously. "Please, Wyatt. We haven't gotten a chance to talk all week," she says.

Because you've been too busy trying to make Avery jealous, I want to say but hold my tongue.

Avery squeezes my bicep. "You go ahead. I'll get to the barn to meet everyone."

"But...no cameras," I say, knowing just how whiney my voice sounds.

"Later."

I nod once and watch Avery walk away while Caroline stands firmly planted in front of me. This conversation has been a long time coming, and it'll be better if we just have it out now.

"Okay," I say with a sigh. "Let's talk."

NOTHING COULD HAVE prepared me for this. I wish I could have warned the cows beforehand, but I didn't know it would come to this.

"Aren't you just like the cutest whittle cowsy!" Nikki coos while scratching behind his ear. Peaches barks so loud, blood trickles from my ears. Not really, but it feels like it could.

Nikki nuzzles the cow's neck. "I just want to pack you up and take you home with me."

Not in that little baby carrier of hers she won't.

My nerves are on edge after my "talk" with Caroline, which really turned into her asking how I'd been before Ronny interrupted us. I must have been giving him the "help me" look since he made up some excuse about needing to braid the cows' tails.

We've never done that before, but it worked.

I clap once. "Alright everyone, gather around for a minute."

Bobbi and Ross walk through the hay like there are snakes in it. Rach is scoping out the exterior of the barn for hidden cameras. Butch has his arms crossed, scowling at everyone, cows included, and Nikki is...well, Nikki. She's hugging all the cows and kissing their faces that no one could pay me to put my mouth on.

I mean, I am a little desperate for pocket change. I probably have a price.

"We've got a few of our most chill cows here and thanks to Avery..." I point at her and smile, forgetting what I was about to say. I snap myself out of it. "Thanks to Avery, they now all have names."

I was hesitant about this at first, because what the guests don't know is that these cows will most definitely become hamburger meat at some point. My Gramps would roll over in his grave if he knew we were naming them. We're a beef supplier first, therapy-hugging cow sanctuary second.

"Rach, you'll be with Deja-Moo." I point, and her hand instinctively grabs for her pocket. "Nikki, you'll get Cowabunga." She's already petting the cow like a house cat. "Butch, we've got Holy Cow for you." Was that a hint of a smile on his face? That's a first. "Bobbi and Ross," I gesture toward the back, "That's Cockadoodle Moo."

Bobbi scoffs. "Does that cow like being referred to as a chicken?"

"Uh..." I'm not really sure how to respond to that.

"It could be offensive," she adds.

Avery jumps in to help me. "Did he say Cockadoodle Moo?" She slaps her knee. "That's Moo-la-la."

In the words of the famous televised artist, Bob Ross, f you make a mistake, just add another tree. Or, in this case, if you choose a chicken name for a cow, just choose a different one.

Bobbi squints at us, deciding if we're full of shit or not. We are, but I'm hoping she'll buy it.

"Look," Ross points at Moo-la-la, the chestnut brown cow. "She's lying down."

Moo-la-la, tired of all the chatter, lays down, chewing her cud and blinking sleepily.

"Aw!" Bobbi clutches her heart as if it's exploding inside her.

"I think I'll start a cow sanctuary in CA," Ross says from beside Bobbi.

"Brilliant," Bobbi says.

I lean in, placing a hand on Avery's back and whisper, "Thanks for saving me."

She shrugs. "Anytime."

Caroline steps between us, slipping her arm through the crook of my elbow. "Who do I get, Wyatt?"

I lead her over to the brown cow with white ears and pull my arm back from her death grip. "Meet, Moo York."

I make a sweeping gesture while beaming, and she scowls down at the cow like it's going to lunge at her.

They could use some bonding time, so I stride back to Avery while pointing at Ronny who is leaning against the inside of the barn. "You've got Winnie the Moo."

He pulls his toothpick out and holds up both hands as he slowly walks over to the cow he has personal issues with for reasons I don't understand. Good. Hugging should help them iron out their differences.

I look at Avery. "I saved the best for you."

"That could only mean one thing."

"Sir Loin," we both say at the same time.

I stare into her endless blue eyes, brighter than any summer sky I've seen. Looking away isn't an option until I'm forced to.

"So, like, what do we do now?" Nikki asks, adding a bedazzled scarf around Cowabunga's wide neck. Peaches is curled against her new friend, having deemed him a friend and not a foe ready to eat her. TBD.

The cows are all lying down now, and Ronny and I spread a few blankets near each one. "You can scratch them, rub your head on their fur, close your eyes when they do, or try to match your breathing with theirs."

I feel Ronny's gaze on me. Turning my head would only confirm he's trying to bite back a smile. He thinks this is ridiculous and has been clear about it since day one. I think it has some merit.

The guests greet their cows, testing the waters with a few hesitant back scratches.

Avery moves from my side and heads straight for Sir Loin, laying her back against his side, relaxing into him while closing her eyes like she's done the last couple of weeks. I wasn't planning on staying, but when Avery pats the ground beside her, I can't resist.

I glide toward her, dropping to sit close enough that our thighs touch. Sir Loin twists his head and rests it on my shoulder.

"He likes you," Avery whispers.

I whisper back. "He likes being in the shade."

Sir Loin swishes his tail and rubs his head against mine, messing up my already wild hair.

She laughs heartily. "Agree to disagree."

I scratch Sir Loin's neck, and that seems to satisfy him. "Is she looking over here?"

Avery peers around the cow's rear end, knowing who I'm talking about. "Yup."

I groan and lean into the soft but solid flesh behind me.

Avery picks the stray bits of hay from her jeans. "Did you guys have a good talk?"

"No. We didn't get the chance. But we need to. I just…" I shake my head. "Never mind. I don't want to think about her right now."

I rub a knuckle along the outside of Avery's leg.

She hooks her pinky with mine, and it's enough to let me know she's still with me. I haven't scared her away and neither has Caroline. For now. I need to have a firm conversation with Caroline and set her straight. But

I'm not going to waste my minutes with Avery. They're already too few as it is.

I inhale the scent of grass and dirt. It's earthy and smells exactly like I do at the end of every day. It's the smell of my childhood and Gramps. Familiar and calming in a way I can't fully explain but feel in my marrow.

I lull my head to the side, resting my cheek against Sir Loin's soft fur to look at Avery who's been staring. "What?"

"You look...relaxed," she says.

I close my eyes and focus on the feel of her pinky hooked with mine. "I am."

My body slumps farther into the hunk of beef behind me as my eyelids get heavier. The last words I hear are Avery's and sound so close, I swear her lips graze my ear. "Good."

My eyes don't open again, and I let the magic of farm life, or Sir Loin, carry me from one dream to the next.

I HEAR SNICKERING.

"Avery?" I whisper.

More laughter.

My face feels wet.

"Avery?"

"Mhm."

"Is that you?" I ask.

"Mhm."

Something rough, slimy, and warm rubs against my cheek.

I blink rapidly, trying to focus my eyes. "Avery, why are you...licking me?"

I don't remember her tongue being this...big and...moist.

Even more laughter.

I know who laughs like that.

I fling my eyes open wide to find Ronny bent at the waist, trying to contain his laughter and failing at it. His face is bright red.

"What the hell?" I mutter, lifting my head.

Another warm, wet kiss is planted on my cheek, but this time I can see Avery isn't the one doing it. I widen my eyes as a glob of drool lands on my forehead.

I bolt upright until I'm vertical again, wiping my head. "What the hell! You could have woken me up before Sir Loin got to second base!"

Ronny gasps for breath. "And miss...that? No...way!"

My pants are covered in hay, so I brush them off. "How long have I been asleep?"

Avery scratches her head. "Oh, uh...hours. Two, maybe?"

"Shit," I whisper, holding my slimy hands away from my body. "I need to get to town to pick up a few things for the camping trip tomorrow. Where is everyone else?"

"Resting in their cabins." Avery checks her phone. "We still have time."

"I didn't get a chance to muck the stalls or fill the water troughs this afternoon," I say, as laughter still reverberates off the barn walls. My sharp tone lights into him. "Ronny."

His laughter gets shot from the sky and dies before hitting the ground. "Yeah, boss?" His shoulders shake trying to hold it in as he points to his chin. "You got some...you got...right there."

I find the piece of hay stuck in my beard and pull it out quickly. "Alright, just get it all out. Laugh it up."

Ronny slaps his knee, and Avery bites back a laugh, still trying her best to show some camaraderie. It isn't until the loud lowing of Sir Loin startles us all that Ronny says, "Your boyfriend wants us to shut up."

The makings of a smile crawls across my mouth. "You done?"

"Yes." He can't even keep a straight face. There are actual tears pooling in his eyes. Wiping at them, he stands straighter and clears his throat. "Okay, I'm done."

"I need you to do the afternoon chores while I head to town," I tell him, smoothing my hair down. "Avery, do you want to come?"

"Sure, just have to change into my *udder* shoes," she says.

Ronny barks out another laugh.

I gesture for them to keep the jokes coming. "Clearly, you're not done."

Ronny wipes the tears from his cheeks. "We've gotta *milk* it for all it's worth."

"You're such a *cowmedian*, Ronny." Avery goes to give him a high five, but I intercept it.

"Man, Sir Loin really put you in a *moooood*." Ronny walks past me, and I sock him in the arm.

He rubs his bicep as he keeps walking. "I think it's *pasture* bedtime, man."

I point a finger at him. "Get on those chores before I tan your hide."

"Good one." Ronny indulges in more laughter and leaves the barn, swaying on his feet.

Avery offers me her fist, but instead I pick her up and throw her over my shoulder before leaving the barn while she squeals.

Thirty

Wyatt

"This is a happy place; little squirrels live here and play."-Bob Ross

All the guests are huddled around the front steps of the farmhouse ready to venture into the great unknown. But it is known since I scouted the camping site with Avery, set up all the tents ahead of time, and cleared out the trail even more.

Granny and Stace are swinging on the porch swing while Ronny prepares the horses. Avery should be here, but she isn't. Yet. I hope she didn't change her mind. Caroline has done everything possible to come between us.

Not today, Satan. Or tonight, rather.

Since I was in charge of packing and setting up the equipment and supplies, I made sure we didn't have enough tents for everyone. Meaning, there won't be an extra tent for Avery. But mine's a double, and I already set up an air mattress.

Just call me a genius.

"You sure you don't want me to poison her food?" Stace asks.

I follow her gaze to where Caroline is setting her timer to take pictures of herself in another matching workout set. She chose bright orange for reasons I couldn't begin to imagine unless she has a thing for looking like a traffic cone. At least she'll be easy to spot.

I sigh and look at Stace. "I'm sure."

Kind of.

Stace crosses her arms. "Let me know if you change your mind. By the way, where's Avery? She's coming with you, right? I wasn't able to book a facial with her since the spa will be closed."

"She's comin'."

Stace gives Granny a side-eye glance.

"She is. Don't worry." Because I'm definitely not worried.

Stace gives a pinched laugh. "Oh, I'm not. I'm more worried that the orange creamsicle over there is going to break a bone and need to be airlifted off the mountain."

I look back at Caroline. "I should bring another first aid kit."

Jumping off the porch, I head for the barn to see if there are any more gauze wraps and antiseptic, but Ronny blocks my path.

"We're down a horse," he says, resting his hands on his hips.

"What do you mean?"

"I mean, we don't have enough saddles for everyone. Henry isn't doing well. He's lying in his stall and refuses to get up. Could be the heat or something else. I called the vet, but for today, someone's going to have to share."

I can't even hide my smile. I'm sure I look maniacal. "I'll ride with Avery."

Ronny scrunches his nose. "Don't look so smug about it."

I go to shove his shoulder, but he deflects with his hand. "You'd be smug, too, if you were in my position," I say.

"Oh yeah? And what position is that?" He shifts his toothpick to the corner of his mouth. "Top? Or bottom?"

I peer behind me and see Avery's here now and chatting with Nikki while Peaches licks her nose. Visions of Avery and coconut oil fill my mind. The things I still want to do to her.

"On my knees," I say, lifting my brows.

Ronny whistles low as I redirect my path toward Avery.

She's wearing jeans today since we'll be riding. Sensible light blue denim that covers more than her standard cut-off shorts do and somehow still emphasizes every curve right down to the new pair of leather boots.

"Hi," I say, approaching.

It's only been a month since Avery came to the farm, but it feels like ten years. I drop my eyes to her shirt, per usual, to see what graphic tee she has on today. It's cropped to the top of her high-rise jeans with a picket fence beneath the words, *Thirst Trapp Farms*.

I forget Nikki's there until she says, "I need to go get my carrier for Peaches, BRB."

Instead of focusing on the fact Nikki used the acronym for "be right back," I keep my eyes laser-focused on Avery's chest. "New shirt?"

She looks down and back up. "Yup. Figured it was time we had more merch besides coffee mugs and hats."

I meet her eyes but still haven't managed to breathe. "I think you're right."

She walks past me and bumps my shoulder. "Don't worry. I got another one from my favorite online custom t-shirt shop for you, too. Now we can match."

Before she can get too far, I spin to follow her, like a purebred Golden Retriever who only wants one thing: a sock. Or, in this case, a woman. "I like your new boots, too."

She pops a heel back as she walks. "Thanks. Stace took me shopping in town, and they spoke to me."

"The boots...spoke to you?"

"Yes."

I shake my head. Can't say any of the clothes I've bought have spoken to me. "Hold up a minute." I circle a hand around her forearm gently so she'll stop walking, but now that my hand is here, why pull it away? "We're down a horse this trip. Ride with me?"

A pretty smile stretches across her lips before she bites her bottom one. "Sure. But I hold the reins."

I want to sink to my knees right now hearing her say this. "You got it."

"Wyatt!"

Almost a full week of that voice, and I'm ready to feed her to the coyotes.

I shoot Avery an apologetic look and then turn to Caroline. My patience with her is wearing thin and I snap, "What do you need?"

Her matching set is giving off strong carrot vibes. Couple that with her hair in a high ponytail, and it makes it look like she's protruding from the earth.

"It's my wrist." She holds it up between us. "I don't think I can ride."

How unfortunate for her.

"I'll ask Stace if she can bring you to urgent care."

I'm already walking toward the porch when she grabs my arm. "Don't!"

I look at her hand on my forearm. The very same one that was hurting milliseconds ago.

She pulls it back and cradles it against her chest. "It's not broken or anything."

Crossing my arms, I squint down at her. "What are you saying then?"

"I should ride with someone," she says.

"Ride with Ronny."

"I don't trust Ronny."

I scoff. "And you trust me?"

"Yes, believe it or not. You may have run out on me, but I didn't stop—" She cuts herself off. The emotion in her voice almost makes me want to believe her. "We need to talk, Wyatt. You can't just keep ignoring me. That's the whole reason I'm here."

To talk, right. She's said that so many times, but so far, all she's done is make my life more difficult. I finally have something good going on, and it feels like Caroline is trying to sabotage it. But I've been avoiding this conversation only because I don't want to morph back into the dick human I was when I was with her.

"Fine. We'll ride up together and talk."

She nods. "Thank you."

I stride over to the porch where Avery, Stace, and Granny are engaged in conversation.

"Wyatt, just in time," Stace says. "I was telling Avery about the last time we went camping together, and you thought that pile of wood was a rabbit."

I'm in no mood for this. "It was early in the morning. I didn't have my glasses on."

"You don't wear glasses," Stace says with a laugh. "He woke us all up and said, look at the size of that rabbit!"

Avery bites her cheek so she doesn't laugh too hard, while Granny and Stace giggle like a couple of hyenas.

"Just hilarious," I say before tugging Avery aside.

"I believe you, I swear," she says, lifting a hand.

I shake my head. "It's not that. It's...Caroline."

Avery's smile drops into a frown. "Is she okay? Please tell me she isn't terminally ill and wants you by her side until the end. But also, if that's the truth, I totally understand and don't want her to be alone when she dies."

My eyes narrow. I'm not even sure where to start. Do I dive into the terminally ill comment, or the fact Avery would be selfless enough to want Caroline to have my support?

God, this woman is amazing. But that also would never happen.

"No, nothing like that. But remind me to circle back to this conversation later."

"Got it."

"Caroline's wrist is hurting, and she doesn't think she's able to hold the reins. As much as I want to ride behind you for an hour, smelling your hair and kissing your neck, I should ride with her. I think she's lying, but I'd rather she didn't make a scene in front of the other guests," I say.

Her shoulders drop. "As relieved as I am that no one is dying, I'll miss you creepily smelling my hair."

I smile down at her. If I wasn't a thousand-percent positive Granny and Stace were watching us, I'd kiss Avery until my lips were sore and we were gasping for air.

I settle for linking my pinky with hers. "Next time?"

"Next time," she confirms through a half-smile.

I drop her hand and feel the regret slicing through me seeing her disappointment. But everyone here is counting on me. Turning to face the group, I whistle loudly to gather everyone's attention.

"It looks like we're ready to go. Make sure to grab your backpacks with personal items. We have water and some food in the packs strapped to each horse," I say.

Nikki flings her hand in the air.

I point to call on her. "Yes?"

"What about the beds? We aren't, like, sleeping on the ground, right?"

Her eyes are wide, as if this is the worst possible scenario. We'll have to save sleeping under the stars for another time. "I took the gear and some food to the campsite already. You'll have a foam pad."

Bobbi clutches her chest. "Thank God we won't have to hunt for our food."

Ross pats her on the back. "I would rather eat my shoe."

"On that note, let's saddle up," I say, clapping my hands together.

"One more question," Butch says from behind his black sunglasses. "Did you bring any garlic?"

Avery coughs from behind me, disguising what she says. "Vampire."

But I hear it and have to hide my smile behind my fist.

Everyone turns to look at him.

Butch shrugs. "I just really don't like garlic."

"All meals have been pre-prepped and are simple. No garlic," I say.

He sighs in relief and nods.

"Good luck, brother," Stace says from behind me.

I squint at her over my shoulder. "You sure you don't want to go?"

"I would, but I have to pay taxes."

Facing her, I say, "It's not even tax season."

"I know."

I shake my head and find Ronny behind the group, giving me a nod. With no other questions, Ronny and I help everyone get on their horses before heading back around the farmhouse and down the trail cutting between the cow pasture and the alfalfa fields.

Ronny is leading the group while Avery brings up the rear with Caroline and me just in front of her. I'm hyperaware of Avery behind us, and so is Caroline, but she sees this as an opportunity and braces her hands on my thighs.

I grit my teeth and want to tear her hands from me, point fingers, and yell that she's poking me, just like Stace and I used to do in the backseat of our mom's car.

Instead, I remove her hands and grind out, "We need to talk."

She yawns and leans back into my chest. "We will."

I push her forward and lean back, dodging her like she's covered in mud and will get me dirty if we touch. I'm starting to think that no matter what I say, Caroline isn't planning to listen.

Thirty-One

Wyatt

"Talk to the tree, make friends with it."-Bob Ross

We made it to camp just before dinner. It took us longer than expected since most everyone is new at riding. Nikki was beside herself when we spotted a black bear a ways off and was convinced Peaches would be eaten, demanding we take her back. Butch was perfectly content on the back of Betsy, an all-white Lipizzan horse that belongs to Ronny's family until he got a mosquito bite and screamed *bloodsucker* so loud while flailing his arms, he nearly fell off his horse. Ronny rode back down with them and will follow the path back up to meet us later.

Bobbi and Ross spent half of the time creating social media content until they realized Wi-Fi didn't work up in the hills then proceeded to tell us all how bored they were every five seconds. Rach was also checking her reception incessantly, holding it up to the sky with an outstretched arm but instead of finding service, I think she was trying to make sure we don't have any.

As expected, Caroline deflected every time I tried to bring up why she was here and what she wanted to talk about. She kept mentioning the good times we had, like she needed to remind me of who we'd once been. But I don't know that guy anymore, or the one I'd been when I found out she cheated on me. The guy with the fancy shoes and suits plus a good amount of swagger. These days, I'm a guy who wears work boots and walks through shit every day. Still with swagger, though.

She sat in Axel's saddle while I straddled the back of it, giving us as much space as possible. I still held the reins, though, and had to reach my arms around her.

She smelled the same. Like walking into a boutique clothing store with designer perfume drenching the whole place. I used to like it. Now, it tasted sour every time I inhaled, which happened to be often.

I wished Avery were riding with me on Axel.

I have to make Caroline listen somehow. There's only so much more I can say that hasn't already been said. The more I've thought about what I would tell her, the more I realize I just don't care. We've been over for four months, so my brain has only come up with one-word responses so far: never, nope, nah, get lost. That last one is two words, but the sentiment stands. She's supposed to leave in two days, but there have been moments I think she's fishing for an invite to stay longer. Not happening. I'll be saying sayonara and puffing on a cigar before she reaches the end of the driveway.

Now that we're at the camp getting settled in, I've stolen no less than one-hundred looks in Avery's direction as she skillfully hangs the hammock—our hammock—between the same two trees. That might have been the moment a month ago that changed things for us. I mean, I walked away with snot on my shirt. It's basically the new third base. What I wouldn't give to have that time alone with her again.

The spot is still as beautiful as ever. We have a perfect view of the valley with the farmhouse, barns, and animals in the distance. It's windy but not unbearable.

"I'm going to get a fire started and cook up some dogs. Who's hungry?" I ask the tired travelers.

Ross gasps. "You savage barbarian!"

Can't say I've ever been called that before. I do my best to hide the annoyance in my voice. "Not actual dogs—*hot* dogs."

His nose scrunches in disgust. "Ew. Those might be even worse."

"Suit yourself," I say, lifting the soft-sided cold bag.

"I can help," Caroline offers.

My gaze finds Avery, wondering if she heard. She glances up at me as she tightens down the strap even harder. She's yanking it like she heard what Caroline said. Is it going to be like this the whole time? Caroline butting in to "help," and me looking around for Avery to help me?

I keep my eyes on Avery then answer Caroline. "Fine. Help me grab those rocks to create a fire pit first."

We continue working, though I say little to Caroline the whole time. I'm stewing in my regret of letting someone who looks like the innards of a papaya force me to ride horseback with her. What is wrong with me? Why do I keep being nice to her? She wasn't nice to me. Every crumb of feelings I had for her have been vacuumed up already. But making a scene isn't my style, either. I didn't even blow up when I found her with him, my business partner. I just left.

I shove the thoughts into a suitcase and focus on making a fire, using wood and kindling from the nearby fallen tree branches before pulling out the hot dogs. I brought enough food for the group, but it's simple compared to the fanfare everyone has been enjoying all week. Hot dogs, jerky, plenty of water, and cereal. We'll be home by lunch. Mom and Stace have that covered.

Avery finishes with the hammock and sits in it. I'm craving that seat beside her. But I'm stuck making dinner now.

"Are these hot dogs Kosher?" Bobbi asks, interrupting my thoughts.

I pull out the discarded package they were in. "Yes."

A happy accident for sure. Had Bobbi even mentioned she ate only Kosher food?

Before I can ask, Ross chimes in. "Do we have s'mores?"

"Do bears shit in the woods?"

Ross stares blankly. "I don't know. Do they?"

I go with the simplest explanation. "Yes."

"So, yes bears shit in the woods? Or, yes, you brought s'mores?"

"Both," I confirm.

He blinks rapidly then rolls his eyes.

I continue to stoke the fire, sneaking looks at Avery and wondering when I can steal her away from here for a few minutes or maybe twelve hours.

"I'm going on a quick hike," Rach says.

She's got a white-knuckle grip on that backpack she's wearing and for good reason. It's huge. Where did it come from? She didn't have that on the ride up here.

I stand. "Do you want to leave your pack—"

"No!" she snaps, then softens her features. "I mean, no thanks. I got it."

"Alright then." Whatever she's got in that pack, she doesn't want anyone messin' with it.

"Do you have bear spray?" I ask her.

"I have pepper spray."

I shake my head and reach into my pack for bear spray. "That doesn't work for bears."

She snatches it from my hand. "Thanks. I'll be back. Don't come looking for me."

I sew my brows together. That's not usually what people say when hiking in the woods.

Ross comes to sit on one of the blankets around the fire, grabbing a hot dog and one of the sticks I gathered. "I found the perfect dance for us to do."

Dance?

"Dance?" Caroline echos, sitting on the other side of me—the spot that had Avery's name on it.

I scoot closer to Ross. "Is it a two-step?"

Bobbi laughs and sits on the other side of Ross. "Uh, noooo."

"Then, I can't dance," I say with a quick shake of my head.

Bobbi isn't buying it. "Everyone can dance."

"Not me." There's no way this is happening.

"It's easy," Ross starts. "All we have to do is find a trending song and practice it until we can slay." He does some snappy thing with his fingers, flinging his arm from left to right.

I pull out the hot dog buns. "I'll film you."

"That's what tripods are for," Bobbi says, skewering a dog.

I pull my knees in and rest my arms on them. "You brought a tripod?"

Bobbi shrugs. "Of course. It goes everywhere with me."

Huh. That's new. I only carry a few things with me everywhere I go: a knife, my wallet, a picture of Granny—her doing, not mine. A tripod doesn't even make the top ten.

Avery joins us and sits across the fire from me. She's too far, and it's making me grumpy.

"What are we talking about?" she asks, decidedly not looking at me.

"Dancing," Bobbi says, pulling her hot dog out of the flames and sliding it into a bun.

"I don't dance," Avery says immediately. "Unless it's at an arcade."

That's my girl.

Caroline looks at Avery sideways. "I don't get it."

Ross waves her off. "Wyatt said that, too. But you have us to help you."

He points between him and Bobbi. Even though it's dark out, Bobbi still has her signature pink, star-shaped sunglasses on while Ross's fedora now sports a feather. Did he get that from the chicken coop? He's been spending a lot of time there lately.

"I like to dance," Caroline says. She nudges me with her shoulder. "I'll teach you."

I can think of plenty of other things I'd rather do. All of them including Avery.

Bobbi claps her hands. "Okay. Everybody up!"

Caroline leaps to her feet, like a carrot being plucked from the ground. At least if we need an emergency flare, she's got us covered.

I drag my feet to standing, rounding the fire to offer my hand to Avery. "I'm good, really. I was going to take a walk," she says in a hushed tone, pointing behind her toward the woods.

"You shouldn't go alone," I say.

"Why not?"

"Because—"

Arguing from the group steals our attention.

"Behind? I should be in front. I have more experience choreographing dance routines," Caroline says.

Bobbi mumbles, "NSYNC isn't exactly the kind of dance routine I had in mind."

Caroline crosses her arms. "What did you say?"

"Nothing. Just that as a millennial, you definitely have more experience than the rest of us," Bobbi says, blowing fake smoke from a fog machine up Caroline's ass. Caroline doesn't seem to notice.

I yell over the competing voices and point toward the trees. "We're going to go chop...something." No one looks at me, so I turn back to Avery and tip my head toward the trees. "Shall we?"

She hesitates first then smiles and grabs for my extended hand. "Hurry."

We both slink off, slowly at first, and then we burst into a run once we're in the trees. I'm breathing hard and laughing harder when we manage to put a good distance between us and the group. Hands on my knees, I catch my breath.

"Do you think they'll come looking for us?" Avery asks on an inhale.

I shake my head. "I think we're far enough out."

"I'm glad we dodged whatever choreography Ross had in mind."

Standing straighter I laugh and say, "Me, too."

It's so quiet and peaceful up here under the cover of the trees. The sounds of nature are the loudest. Birds flit from one tree to the next, leaves rustle with the push and pull of the wind, and the underbrush crunches and swishes underfoot as I step closer to Avery.

The familiar loose-fitting flannel, which used to be mine but looks better on her, falls off one shoulder, and my hand itches to pull it up. So, I do.

She watches my hand and then meets my eyes.

"I brought chocolate," I say, dropping my hand away slowly and pulling out the chocolate bar from my back pocket.

Her eyes light up as her mouth widens. "You're my hero."

I laugh and hold it out to her. Before she can grab it from my hands, I pull it back. "First, a game of Truth or Dare."

She glowers at me. "Aren't we a little old for that game?"

"You're never too old."

She huffs an exaggerated breath and crosses her arms. "Fine. Truth."

I tuck the chocolate in my back pocket for safekeeping and smooth out my mustache in a show of thinking up what I want to ask her. I already know.

"Were you mad about me riding up here with Caroline?"

She crosses her arms and swallows. "No. I was...disappointed."

I nod once and take a step closer. If only I could wipe away that feeling, like it's a smudge. I don't like that I made her feel that way, and that Caroline keeps coming between us.

"My turn," she says before I can say anything else. "Truth or dare?"

I cross my arms. "Truth."

She doesn't say anything for a beat, but I wait. Her eyes find the ground. "Do you like me?"

"Yes."

"Not, you know, as a friend," she says hesitantly.

"I know. I like like you...a lot." I'd absolutely check "yes."

She lifts her head, and my smile is already waiting to ease her nerves. It's the fastest *yes* I could've given, because Avery has invaded all of my thoughts since the moment she arrived.

"I see," she says. "Well, okay then."

I take a step closer. "Truth or dare?"

Her lips part, and the word comes out on the back of a pinched breath, "Dare."

I close the distance between us until her chest is touching mine. "I dare you to do exactly what you're thinking right now."

The smooth column of her neck shifts as she swallows, her skin a creamy texture that is begging for my mouth. The thought of kissing her again, holding her, touching every part of her has a rippling current skating across my body.

She keeps her eyes locked with mine as I feel her hands slink up my sides, spreading across my pecs, then over my shoulders and down again. My body tingles at her light touch, and I want to grab and touch and fondle, too. Not quite so lightly. But, I wait.

Her hands reach around my waist, lifting the back of my shirt and touching my skin in a way that has me settling a hand on the tree behind her head just to steady myself. Soft and slow, the tips of her fingers drag up and down before flattening on my back.

Our chests are smashed up against each other, and I know she can feel how much her touch is turning me on right now. Even just the mention of kissing her again has my blood boiling to a degree I won't recover from.

There's a quirk in her smile that I notice right away. Her eyes are on my lips, and I swear she's going to kiss me, but instead, she drags her palms down my back, over my belt, and cups my ass. I press my forehead to hers and groan.

She pulls her hands away and holds them between us, a full-size chocolate bar now standing in the way of kissing her full lips.

I lift my forehead. "You tease. Truth or dare?"

She laughs, and I want to capture it with my mouth. "You can't steal my turn."

I roll my eyes playfully. "Fine. Your turn."

"Truth or dare?" she asks.

"Dare."

"Good."

She wraps a hand around my neck and slams her mouth against mine in hot pursuit. The seam of our lips part on contact, and my tongue is frantic to find hers. To taste the sweet and sour parts of her again. I'm not as gentle as she was when her hands roamed the skin beneath my shirt, or when I massaged her shoulders and cupped her breasts in her cabin.

My hips thrust forward, aching for something only she can give, and she grinds against me. I grasp her ass and pull her closer on instinct.

"Avery," I say, groaning into her mouth.

My name is a whimper on her lips. "Wyatt."

I pull away and stare down at her in a haze of my own desire. "What if I can't stop thinking about you? About our kiss and...everything else? The way you feel in my arms? Your smile?" My breaths come out so fast, I'm panting. "Am I the only one?"

She closes her eyes briefly, her bare lashes fanning across her cheeks. "No."

Say less.

I seal our lips, and her fingers dive into my hair, tugging me closer and deeper into her mouth. My hands fall lower, gripping her tighter against me so I don't lose her to another interruption. Not this time. I pin her against the tree with my hips. She moans when my hard length meets with her pliant center.

"You," I say into her neck. No other words follow because none feel as right as this.

She's all I see. All I want.

Avery shivers beneath my touch, tugging at the hair hiding my chin and crashing her lips into mine. My hand trails over her hip and down her thigh, lifting her leg and wrapping it around me, pressing farther into her. The sounds she makes as I rotate my hips, needing to feel all of her with all of me, have me moving even faster.

Our jeans are stiff and restricting. This isn't enough. Our tongues twirl together in a furious pattern between nips and pecks. Her fingernails scrape down my arms as I rock into her. She grinds her hips closer, and I sputter out a curse.

I kiss her harder, faster, as my hands find the hem of her shirt and explore the skin beneath it. Cupping her breast and running my thumb over the taut nipple beneath her bra, I murmur, "Too much fabric."

She pushes me back, removing the bulky flannel separating us and tossing it to the side. "Better?"

"Almost."

I lift her shirt and press my mouth to the edge of her bra, kissing my way to the peak where my tongue swirls around one nipple hidden behind a thin layer of silken fabric. Her head lulls back to give me more access to torment her shuddering body with my mouth.

I use the tips of my fingers to stroke the small valley between her breasts, pressing my lips to what I swear is the smoothest part of her. I need to fact check this. I hook my thumb into the loop of her jeans at her lower back, spreading my hand to accommodate the width of her perfect ass as I kiss her harder.

She arches into me. I pull away again and look down at our bodies pressed tightly together, her hair disheveled, eyes hooded. I can't think of anything I want more. I can't think, period. Her heaving chest, the t-shirt shoved up in haste, and her hips melded into every crease and curve of me fills my vision completely.

Reaching between us, I unbutton her jeans. "This okay?"

She nods furiously.

I kiss my way down her neck and over her ribs, reaching below her belly button where I taste the part of her stomach that is always visible beneath her cropped shirts. Her muscles contract, but that doesn't stop her from threading her fingers through my hair and guiding my head lower.

I remove each boot and her hips shimmy as I pull her jeans down and then her underwear, tossing them aside and admiring all of her laid bare before me. She leans back against the tree, panting and whispering my name as I marvel how beautiful she is. How the moon highlights the contours of her stomach, her hip bones, the pliable flesh between her thighs that's wet and waiting for me.

I'm in complete awe of her right now, unable to move for too many seconds.

I hold her steady with my hands at her waist and sink a kiss on the inside of her hip bone, humming as I move my mouth across her and feel the vibrations on my lips. "You're so beautiful."

"You're so beautiful," she says in a throaty response.

I look up at her from my knees, and the molten gaze she gives me urges me on. Lifting one of her legs over my shoulders as she leans her head back against the tree behind her, I kiss my way around her clit, feeling her quake with every flick of my tongue.

"Wyatt," she says, moaning.

"Avery," I murmur against her folds.

Nothing more is said, because no other words are needed, as I indulge in the woman who has managed to make my heart beat faster every time I'm with her.

Thirty-Two

Avery

"I think each of us, sometime in our life, has wanted to paint a picture."-Bob Ross

At some point, when the sun has dipped below the horizon, my weightless body slumps farther into the tree. A lazy smile is covering my lips, and I feel satiated and full, as if I've just eaten the most deliciously filling meal. I didn't really. But Wyatt did.

He looks around at my discarded clothes on the earth's floor, using the back of his hand to wipe his mouth, then decides to pull his shirt off.

"What are you doing?" I ask through the haze of pleasure I'm currently lost in. Someone call for a pack mule to take me home, because I officially have no bones left in my body.

He uses his shirt to tenderly clean me as my legs fight to stay standing. The echo of Wyatt's mouth is still bouncing off my thighs and the thousands of nerve endings in my clit. He lifts one of my legs at the ankle, threading my foot through my jeans slowly and then slipping my boots back on.

"You don't have to dress me. I can do it." I absolutely cannot. I'm ready to curl up on the ground and sleep until next spring.

He peers up at me with hair sticking up in every direction as I brace my hands on the tree behind me. Did I do that to his head? Damn. Just the sight of him all ruffled and shirtless has my insides yelling for more. There are drums and maracas, maybe a tambourine or two, egging me on for round two. I don't know if more exists with someone like Wyatt, because even more never feels like enough. Apparently, I like my men how I like my pie: bottomless.

Pulling my jeans over my ass, he reaches around to button them. I grip his hands. "Wait. What about..."

He tilts his head in question and says in a rough voice, "What about..."

I lick my lips. "You," I say quietly then thread my arms around his neck. I need the support just as much as I need to touch him. "You can't lie and tell me that's comfortable."

We both look down to the front of his jeans that are currently stretched to their farthest capacity, restraining his erection.

"About that," he says with a small laugh. He leans in to give me another stomach-dropping kiss. "I'm not done with you, yet."

I smile against his lips before he bends to grab my flannel, which is actually his, and puts it on. Grabbing my hand, I trail behind him, doing my best to tame the actual bird's nest on my head. Bark, small twigs, and something sticky I'm positive doesn't belong to me resides there now, making it the perfect place for a robin to make a home.

As we reach the edge of the camp, Wyatt ducks behind another tree. Bobbi, Ross, and Caroline are still deep into their choreography. Hands are raised, hips swivel, and there's even a hair flip involved as the music plays loudly for the current audience that is left speechless: rocks.

Ronny and Rach are nowhere to be found.

"Follow me," Wyatt says, putting a finger to his closed lips and tugging me toward the far side of the camp. He unzips the tent and waves his hands in a sweeping motion to gesture toward the air mattress inside. "Ladies first."

I lower my voice and waggle my eyebrows. "Is this my tent?"

His smile turns wicked. "And mine."

I hold up a hand. "Wait, did you plan this?"

He peers around to make sure we're still alone. But how alone can one truly be as "Toxic" by Britney Spears begins to play in the background?

He bites his lip before saying, "Yes?"

I take a step closer and sing with Britney. "A guy like you should wear a warning."

His tongue pushes his cheek out, but I duck inside the tent before he can say anything and sit on the edge of the mattress to remove my shoes.

Wyatt slips off his boots outside and climbs in beside me, shirking off his flannel, too, his bare skin gloriously exposed. The tent is big enough to fit one queen-size air mattress, creating a cocoon around us and making it feel like we're protected from the outside world. Or, at least, from the dance troupe on the other side of this thin slip of fabric. It's dark in here with only a light glow from the fire near the center of camp where all the tents are circled around. However, I hadn't noticed until getting in that Wyatt's tent is set back into the brush more than the others.

I peer over my shoulder as he scoots himself up, laying his head on the pillow and patting the one beside him. "Come here."

I don't waste time with words, and instead, flip over to my knees and try to balance on this tightrope filled with air. Reaching him, I lay beside him and try to search his face, but it's too dark to see every feature I'm used to. His hand finds my waist and tugs me closer until our faces are inches from each other and his breath is hot on my lips.

"I want to do this all night," he whispers.

"In a tent?" I ask with a short laugh.

"Everywhere. A tree, a tent, a house, a tractor..."

I pull back slightly. "A tractor? That's a new one."

"I've never tried it, but," he kisses me once, "could be fun."

He cradles the back of my head and pulls me closer, kissing me slowly. I take note of how everything feels. The way his lips are warm and soft while the inside of his mouth is hot and inviting. The smell of campfire emanating from every part of him—his hair, breath, bare skin. And the coarse texture of his beard against my raw cheeks and chin, telling of the time he's already spent devouring my mouth tonight. The flavor of me is still on his tongue.

I press closer until it isn't close enough, and I swing my leg over his hip and push myself up until I'm straddling him. "How about we start in the tent and upgrade to a tractor next time?"

He doesn't respond but shifts to his back as his hands rake up my stomach and over the bra beneath my shirt. "This is officially my favorite view."

With a half-smile, I lift my shirt up and over my head and toss it to the side.

He sucks in a sharp breath. "Just kidding...this is."

I bend down and kiss him, plunging my tongue into his mouth and swirling it with his as I rock my hips against his hardening length. His chest feels better than I remember, and I take my time dragging my hands over his shoulders, down his pecs, and lower across his tightening abs.

He reaches behind me for the clasp of my bra and skillfully unhooks it while pulling the straps slowly down my arms and tossing it aside. The muted light isn't enough to highlight the subtleties of his expression, but the way his mouth falls open as his eyes study me and his hands roam my bare breasts tells me he can see everything he wants.

"Shit, Avery," he says in a gravelly voice as he rocks his hips upward. "This view is...unmatched."

I laugh. "Really? I don't know. I think we can beat it."

"Impossible," he mumbles as his fingers circle my hardened nipples.

The air mattress provides a flexible rebound as he thrusts his hips up to meet my needy center in a slow motion that could make me lose my mind again. But I refuse to leave this tent without showing him the same kind of otherworldly pleasure he showed me.

I shift backward over his thighs, trailing my hands to the edge of his jeans to undo his belt. His face is covered in shadows, but his chest rises and falls with every heavy breath.

I undo the button and then the zipper, which makes a louder sound than anything else. Tugging at his belt loops, I hover above him as he wiggles out of his jeans and then his briefs. I sit back on his shins and run my hands up and over his muscular thighs. I'm so turned on by the sight of him that I momentarily gawk. To finally see what I've only felt against me is a heady feeling.

I wrap one hand around the base of him and work him slowly. He moans loudly, and I stop, moving up to my knees to cover his mouth. His hands grab my breasts while I'm here, and I shoot him a warning glare I hope he can actually see before sitting back again. But I don't feel like sitting anymore.

In fact, I'm tired of it.

Instead, I move to all fours and catch my balance on the trampoline we're trying to maneuver on. Then, I crawl backward until my mouth is hovering above his throbbing cock. I take his length in my hand again and then my mouth.

Wyatt grips a handful of my hair and speaks in a ragged tone. "Did I mention this is my favorite view?"

I laugh with him still inside my mouth, and he shudders for seconds that turn into minutes. I lick and taste and touch until my tongue is tired, and Wyatt is mumbling, "I can't...this...I...I'm gonna..."

He reaches his finish as I do one final lick from base to head. The muscles in his stomach are pinched tight as he traverses his way back down the mountain. I smile in satisfaction and peer around for his t-shirt he cleaned me with earlier and do the same for him.

"Avery," he whispers as I finish cleaning him.

My name on his tongue has me sighing heavily and ready to float away on this cloud we're surfing on. This night went nothing like I thought, yet it was perfect. Britney has stopped singing in the background, and the camp is quieter now as Wyatt feels around for his briefs and slips them back on. I stand, which really just looks like an upside down L, and peel my jeans off before tossing them on top of Wyatt's backpack...and mine. He really did plan this out. I guess what I assumed was a mixture of flirtatious teasing was a serious notion in Wyatt's mind.

I find my t-shirt and underwear to put back on as Wyatt grunts from his side-lying position on the Macy's Day float he's on. "Don't put anything else on," he says in a hushed voice.

I curl my lips inward, hiding a smile he can't even see and then crawl over to curl into him. He tugs a sleeping bag over us that's already fully unzipped and tucks my back against his chest, like a jigsaw puzzle piece he'd lost. Well, he found it.

He buries his face into my neck and inhales deeply while I memorize how he feels circling all of me in his arms and hoping this isn't the last time but the first.

Wyatt's breathing slows, and his body becomes heavy as I whisper a confession in the silence. "It's dangerous...I'm falling."

Thirty-Three

Avery

"Remember how free clouds are. They just lay around in the sky all day long."-Bob Ross

Have I been cast out to sea?

My eyes are closed, but I'm starting to feel seasick with the up and down motion. I open one eye, and then the other one to see a shirtless man sitting at the end of my bed.

Correction: my air mattress.

Other correction: his air mattress.

It moves in waves as Wyatt tugs a shirt over his head.

"Don't do that," I mumble.

He looks back at me. "You're awake."

"Your shirt is on."

He looks down at the moss green t-shirt—the one that makes his eyes look like a lush field of unplowed grass—and whips it off, almost rocking me off this ship as he climbs back up to me. He kisses me soundly on the lips as he hovers above me, then kisses his way down my body until his breath is hot against my stomach.

I pull him up by the shoulders and whisper, "Wyatt! Not here, or now."

"I had you pinned to a tree last night," he says, the hair on his head askew. "And you had your way with me right here last night. What's the difference?"

I try to sit up, but he doesn't make it easy with his sasquatch-size body on top of me.

"Yeah, but that was all to the soundtrack of what is arguably one of Britney's greatest hits. No one could hear us. I'm not sure all the guests would enjoy waking up to the noises you like to make."

He smirks and slowly nods. "So...we should go back to the tree?"

I laugh a little too loudly and cup my mouth with my hand. "No, we can't go back to the tree." But we definitely need to at some point.

He rolls over to his side and props his head in his hand. "You're right, it's probably for the best. I was going to get a fire started and set out breakfast for everyone."

I stroke his beard. "Later, okay?"

"Okay," he agrees, but that doesn't stop him from leaning in to kiss me until I'm breathless and close to begging him to put me out of my misery. The familiar swipes of his tongue in my mouth remind me what it felt like to have him spell his name on my inner thigh.

Wyatt finishes getting dressed and leaves the thin fabric walls of our tent, so I can do the same. I need to let this flush on my face and the second heartbeat between my legs fade before I go out there and face everyone, especially Caroline.

She's gonna know.

Nothing says, *I slept with your ex-boyfriend* like climbing out of his tent with sex hair—not to be confused with bed hair. They're way different.

How am I supposed to look at Wyatt and not picture one of my legs slung over his shoulder? Or, how he pulsed inside my mouth? I cradle the sides of my face, still hot to the touch. The amount of hope I have running through my veins now is lethal. I let myself want, and it led me here, to Wyatt's air mattress.

I can't help thinking I let myself get lost in the moment with Wyatt because of the conversation I had with Granny about Hennifer, yes, but also about Wyatt. He's been through a lot, too, and has grown just as much.

I take my time putting my—his—flannel back on since I didn't end up sleeping in it with Wyatt's body heat curled around me all night. Who knew he was so into snuggling? I sure didn't. I moved, and he followed all night across the seven seas (or lumps) of this inflatable ocean.

I finger-comb through my hair and hope it isn't a neon sign pointing to where Wyatt's hands ended up last night. Exiting the tent, I stand tall for the first time all morning to stretch out the kinks, relishing how good I feel in my own skin.

Would it really be so bad if Caroline found out what happened last night? Maybe it would clear things up for her and for me. But as I bend around the tent and spy the first flames of a fire on the ground, I see Caroline draped over Wyatt's back as he sits on a stump, pressing herself into him so naturally, it sends a pang through me that I'm not expecting.

I turn my back on them immediately. There was a time they probably did this every morning. Her waking up and running manicured nails over his broad shoulders and down his chest. He probably turned his head and kissed her like she was the love of his life.

The thought has my feet moving forward. I don't want to see them kiss, but it feels like I already have since the vision in my mind is so clear. At the edge of the tent corner, I look around and try to figure out where to go. I don't have my own tent that I can escape to and going back to Wyatt's Den of Desire doesn't seem like a good option, either.

Worried about being noticed, I quickly turn the opposite direction. I don't know where I'm going yet, but I tell my heart to be afraid. Very, very afraid, because Wyatt Trapp has found a way to coax my heart out of hiding, and it scares the living shit out of me knowing what he could do with it.

I'M STRETCHING OUT my neck when the two zippers on the tent slowly separate, and a pair of hiking boots comes into view.

"Rach?"

She squats lower, lifting the tent flap. "What are you doing in my tent?"

My eyes turn to saucers. "I–I thought we were sharing."

Lies. There's no way two people could fit in here, but it was the only vacant tent that wasn't Wyatt's, so I borrowed it.

Her brows lower. "Oh, okay." She points behind her. "Well, I just had to pee."

For over an hour? I want to ask her but think better of it. She was gone when I showed up. I don't need to know about her bathroom habits, especially considering she has dirt smudged on her cheek, and there's sweat on her brows. The next thing I know, we'll be talking about how regular we are and bonding over poop jokes.

"I'm done in here," I say. "I was just heading out for breakfast."

Surely Caroline is done fawning all over Wyatt, and surely he has responded in whatever way he deems appropriate. I don't need to know. I told Tilly I could handle casual. But then casual drowned in the depths of the ocean when Wyatt kissed me last night. Now, I'm floating on a makeshift air mattress raft in the middle of turbulent waters.

I need to text my diary. Damn the trees and their interference with cell reception.

I contort my body to exit the tent and realize something. Did Caroline just steal the flag back? Have I lost the game? Do I want to lose?

Ah, hell no.

I march around the tent and back to the campfire only to ram into Ronny. He grips my shoulders. "Woah, woah. Take it easy, turbo. Where are you off to with that jetpack and scowl you're wearing?"

Am I really that transparent?

"Yes, you are."

My eyes go wide. "Did I just say that out loud?"

He nods and drops his arms from my shoulders while twirling his toothpick.

I rub my forehead. "Oops."

"You okay?" he asks. "You seem…"

Bobbi passes us. "Morning!"

I jump out of my shoes, and if Ronny weren't there to keep me firmly planted on the ground, I'd be scaling a tree right now.

"You seem...jittery," he finishes.

I press a hand to my heart. "I'm fine. Everything's fine. Great, actually."

He studies me for a beat, and I can feel the warmth rushing to my face. We aren't close enough to the fire to blame it on the heat. "Did Wyatt do something I need to punch him for?"

"No!" I practically yell. Training my tone, I try again. "No, I just...well we...and then..."

His lips split into a wide grin, but he keeps his toothpick sandwiched between his teeth. "You two had some fun last night, I reckon."

"Well, I...he..."

"Avery."

My shoulders slump with my sigh. "How'd you know?"

He points at my neck and both my hands race to cover the hickey I now know is there. I don't need a mirror to confirm such things. I can remember Wyatt giving it to me just by touching it.

He follows my gaze to Wyatt who is currently throwing jabs at Ronny with his eyes from his spot in front of the fire while Caroline sits beside him, chatting into his other ear.

Ronny turns back to face me and smiles before cupping my cheek and planting a kiss on the other. He pulls away and passes me. "You're welcome," are his only parting words.

I'm too stunned to do anything but stare straight ahead at Wyatt who is stalking over to me with fiery arrows darting from his eyes at Ronny's back.

"Good morning," he grinds out.

I close my gaping mouth. "Morning."

"Sleep well?" he asks. His voice is taut as he continues to glare past me.

"Great," I say.

Eyes on me now, all the rage in him seems to dissipate. "Hi," he says again.

I smile and tuck my hair behind my ear. "Hi."

Half of his mouth turns upward. "Did you fall back asleep?"

I open my mouth to speak but then close it to consider my words. "No, I got up and came out here but then…"

His expression falls. "Caroline."

I nod. "Caroline."

He shakes his head and reaches out to loosely hold my fingers. "She came out right when I did. When I tried to bring things up with her, she threw herself on my back. But I pushed her away." He closes his eyes briefly. "Please tell me that you saw when I pushed her away."

"No, I didn't," I say in a feeble voice that almost topples over.

He drops his chin to his chest then tries to catch my eyes with his. "Caroline and I are over, Avery. I swear it. I wouldn't have…" He pauses and peers around to see if anyone else is around. They aren't, for now. "I wouldn't have kissed you the way I did last night otherwise."

I'm blushing something fierce at just the mention of last night. Funny, since I don't seem to blush at all when he's looking at my body, like a person studying the sunset.

"I'm going to have Caroline ride down on your horse," he says. "Axel wants you to ride with us."

"He does, huh?" I ask. "Did he tell you this?"

He leans in and kisses my other cheek that Ronny's lips didn't touch. "I told you, he tells me everything." Then, he strides over to his tent, winking back at me before disappearing inside.

I bite my lip and whisper, "You're dangerous…I'm lovin' it."

Thirty-Four

Wyatt

"We artists are a different breed of people. We're a happy bunch."-Bob Ross

I've been in the kitchen all day cooking for a crowd. I'm sweating in a few places I'd rather not mention, and I burned my finger on the cast iron like a dimwit. I never do that. But I want this dinner to be perfect. I want the biggest group of guests we've had yet to rave about it to their friends and family, and for them to bring everyone back here for the prime rib that could rival any they'd eat in the city.

"It smells amazing in here," a voice says from behind me.

I glance over my shoulder while preparing the charcuterie boards. Doing a double take, I spin around and wipe my hands on the denim apron Granny got me that has a picture of her throwing up finger guns. I should have never showed her the internet.

The apron is nothing compared to what Avery's wearing. She changed into a flowy white dress that exposes her shoulders and hits mid-calf. It hugs the smallest part of her waist, and now I think I'm drooling. "You look..." I can't even finish my sentence as my eyes drink her in.

"Is it too much?"

I begin aggressively shaking my head. "No. Not at all. It's...perfect." And it is, because she's wearing it, and the more I get to know the heart beneath her skin, the more she consumes all of my thoughts. It feels like I'm falling for her.

"I found it at the thrift store in town this morning," she says.

I'm in trouble. Our situation hasn't changed. I'm still her boss. Caroline is still here. The summer is still ending, and I still have to figure out what comes next. But when we rode down that mountain, her in my arms, I knew things were different.

I step closer. If I weren't positive I smell worse than a full day working outside, I'd eliminate all the space. Hell, I'd take her upstairs and use the lock on my door. "You're beautiful, Avery. All of you."

And I really mean all of her. The inside, the outside, her backside, her left foot...

Her cheeks flush as I stare intently. I want her to hear everything I'm not saying. That I'm glad we met. That I like her so damn much it's kind of scary. That I want all of her kisses. That I don't want her time here to end.

"Thanks," she says, biting her lip.

I can't help myself. I reach up and tuck her hair behind her ear.

Taking a step back, I wave a hand in front of my outfit. "How do I look?"

She takes in Granny's gleaming smile sprawled across my chest in full color. "Like you'd make your Granny proud by cooking a phenomenal meal while I give facials and listen to gossip."

I laugh. "What are people saying?"

She lifts her brows. "You don't want to know."

"I do."

She purses her lips in thought. "For starters, your abs are usually a hot topic of conversation."

I step closer. "Oh yeah?"

She nods. "And your arms."

I kiss each of my biceps. "Which one?"

"That's not a fair choice."

I take another step and lean closer, my lips a fraction away from hers. "Wyatt?"

Caroline.

I'm considering changing my name to Bug Off, so everyone will know how I really feel.

Avery clears her throat and turns to face the front door Caroline just walked through. "Caroline."

She looks at me. "Wyatt." Then to the woman at my side. "Avery."

"Caroline."

Someone throw us a life preserver to rescue us from this greeting loop we keep getting stuck in.

"Stace said you were in the barn, but when I only found Ronny, he told me you'd be in the chicken coop. And guess what?"

"I wasn't in the chicken coop."

She crosses her arms over her hot pink spandex dress situation that makes her look like a stick of bubble gum. "No, you weren't. But that weirdo who speaks in code during her phone calls told me you were in one of the cabins."

"You mean Rach?" Avery asks.

"Yeah. Her."

Avery and I share a look. That checks out.

"I went to Avery's cabin, but no one answered," Caroline says. "So, I came here."

I give her my best jazz hands and forced smile. "You found me."

She shoots a glare to Avery, looking her up and down. "What are we doing?"

I was planning to kiss Avery, maybe convince her to get ready twice after showering with me, but clearly that idea is out the window and swept up with the tornado that just rolled through.

"We're just finishing up. Can you open the wine in the dining room?" I ask Caroline.

There's only a few things left to do, and if she's offering, I'm going to put her to work. Because if Caroline is working, she isn't bothering me.

Caroline uncrosses her arms and sways her hips as she walks to the room nearest the front door where a few different wine bottles sit ready and waiting.

Avery swivels to face me when she's gone. "What can I do?"

I turn back and take inventory of what's happening in the kitchen. I barely know. The prime rib is in the smoker. I'll boil the potatoes soon and then warm the bread Esther dropped off earlier. Granny's six pies are cooling on the counter. I told her she didn't have to bake that many, but she told me once people taste them, they'll want more. No one ever complains of having too much pie.

I assess everything strewn about on the counters. "I'm going to go take a quick shower, and then we can take all of this out. Can you get the water boiling for the potatoes while I'm gone?"

She nods. "No problem."

I link her pinky with mine and squeeze. It's like a promise I haven't voiced yet. But I feel it, and she's the one who brings it out of me. Maybe I'm promising her that when this week is over, I want more weeks with her. Or, maybe I'm promising that despite Caroline's best attempts, anything I felt for her is in the past, and when I look to the future, it's all Avery.

She squeezes back, and I move past her, peeling off the apron and setting it on the counter. Then, for practical reasons only, I remove my t-shirt and walk closer to the laundry room, tossing it into the bin. I strut like a peacock past Avery and smirk while she openly appreciates me.

"I'll be back," I say, trying hard not to flex too much. But I make sure my abs and biceps aren't in a seated position, I'll say that much.

I take the stairs two at a time and quickly finish undressing in the bathroom. Before the water can warm completely, I remember I'm out of soap, so I squat down and check below the sink. I rarely look down here, but I vaguely remember there being extra bars of soap in here somewhere.

I feel my way around until my hand circles something rubber that reminds me of a...

What the...

Pulling my hand out with said device gripped tightly, the sex toy stares back at me.

It's purple and ribbed in certain places. *Specific places.* I should drop it or bury it back beneath the sink, but I only tighten my hold until it begins doing the unthinkable in my hand: vibrating.

It's when the possibilities start rolling through my head that I drop it. How did this get up here? Why is this here? The vibrating only continues its steady rhythm, gyrating in a circle on the bathroom floor. I can't just leave it there, so I pick it up carefully between my thumb and pointer finger, find the "off" switch, and huck it back into the bin I found it in.

It bounces against a box peeking up, and I recognize the logo, so I pull that out next and stand, grasping it between my palms like I would a full-grown chicken.

Damn.

I've never seen a condom box this big before. It has to equate to a lifetime supply. I scratch my head. Is it even possible to use this many in one's life?

I shrug and set the box on the counter to search for what I was actually looking for. The vibrator can stay buried beneath the bathroom sink for all eternity, but I think I could put this unopened vessel of condoms to use.

Hopping in the shower, I scrub with the ferocity of a man that wants to impress a woman. I even shampoo and condition my beard and use beard oil when I get out and dry off. It smells like evergreen trees and citrus (aka: my secret weapon).

Dressing quickly and giving myself a once-over, I head down the stairs and back into the kitchen in record time. It's Avery's turn to spin on her heel and scan me from head to toe. Her eyes linger everywhere, all at once, and I feel heat flood my gut.

"Well?" I ask.

She smiles wide. "Satisfactory."

I walk close and rest my hands on her waist now that I can't be mistaken for a dumpster.

"You smell even better," she says, combing her fingers through my beard.

She drags the tip of her nose across my chest. My breath stops completely as her hand replaces her nose and creates a path up my neck and behind my head. She leans in closer until her nose follows the line of my jaw. "Oranges."

"Hm?" I mumble. I'm currently on vacation and sending out of office emails to whoever dares interrupt us.

She pulls back, her eyes hooded like mine must be. "You smell like oranges."

All I can think about is the box.

The box that could have its own zip code.

The zip code that leads to my room.

I thread my fingers through the hair at the nape of her neck. "Avery."

"Mhm."

The water starts boiling over, and she jumps out of my arms to turn the temperature down and remove the lid. I'd forgotten about the potatoes I asked her to start and the dinner I'm supposed to be making for the guests, and apparently that this isn't a private residence.

Someone clears their throat from behind me. I whip around lightning fast. "Mom. Hi."

She looks between me and Avery with a large smile. BigMac level large. "Hi, honey."

Stace is standing beside her and looks back and forth so many times, I'm just waiting for her to call us out. Instead, she asks with a cotton candy sweet smile, "Avery, how are you?"

Avery places a hand on her stomach and waves her other hand. "I'm...great. And you?"

My dad walks up and places a hand on mom's shoulder as she says, "Just super. Wonderful, really." Her eyes still bounce between the two of us, attempting to decode any secrets with the power of her mom-sense, which is like a spidey-sense but way stronger. She points to Dad. "We brought whiskey."

Dad reaches around and hands me the bottle. I accept the amber-filled glass, gripping it tightly so my sweaty palms don't drop it. "I told you guys you didn't need to bring anything."

"Oh, but we wanted to. You're doing everything else. It's the least we could do," Mom says.

I bend closer and kiss her cheek then welcome my dad with a hug.

"Can we do anything?" Mom asks.

"You can bring these cheese boards outside to the table. I set it up by the gazebo out back," I explain.

My parents each grab a large wooden board and head out the back door.

"Sorry," I say sheepishly to Avery when we're alone again.

"For what?" she asks.

"For the interruption," I say with a clipped laugh. "They have a way of doing that."

Avery steps closer, reaching to grab the bottle of whiskey in my hands and another bottle of wine beside it. "I like your family."

"You say that now."

My comment makes it sound like time exists outside of now. As if there is a future. Does she want that? I do. I have an entire box of condoms to get through with her.

"I'll think that tomorrow, too," she says. "Probably the day after that."

I shrug and brush a piece of hair off her bare shoulder, letting my fingers trail across her collarbone before dropping back to my side. "I hope so."

Her breath catches, and she swallows, staring deep into my eyes. I don't break contact. I want her to know I'm serious. I've never been more so.

She clears the desire from her throat while I let mine choke me. "I should take these out there," she says, lifting the alcohol slightly.

I nod, because she's right. She should. I need to finish up here and then head outside to greet and mingle with everyone. But I part my lips and trace hers with my gaze. "I'll be out there soon."

Avery stands on her tiptoes, still gripping the whiskey bottle, and presses a light, feather-soft kiss to my cheek. I close my eyes and savor every feeling that rushes through me at warp speed.

"See you soon," she says before pulling back with the restraint of a saint and patience of a fisherman and walks out the back door.

I comb through my beard and stay standing in the same spot for a few more beats of my throbbing heart. I want Avery. I want her so badly, my pulse is erratic with the feel of her light touches branded all over me. I want her in my bed, yes, but I want her in my life more. I want her to stay.

The future has yet to work itself out, but for now, my present looks pretty damn amazing in a white dress.

I STEP OUTSIDE, and my gaze immediately lands on the strands of hanging lights strung from limb-to-limb of what was once our favorite climbing tree as kids. It's far enough away from the chicken coop that you can't see or smell them, but the sporadic clucking still reminds you you're on a farm. And if that doesn't do it, the endless stretch of land in the backdrop littered with cattle will.

I walk up, prime rib plated, my parents trailing me with warm loaves of bread. The guests clap. *Clap.* And I indulge them with a bow once I place the meat on the table.

"Thank you all for coming tonight. Please eat, drink, and enjoy," I say.

Nikki claps her hands and pulls out a chair next to Stace, settling Peaches on her lap. I don't even care that she's at the table. This dog is about to enjoy the best damn prime rib of its life. Bryan sits on the other side of Stace, while Bobbi and Ross, who are wearing matching blazers, sit across from them and next to my parents.

Butch is at one end of the table, and I take the other with Avery on one side and Caroline, unfortunately, on the other. Rach is the last to sit and gives the chair a full pat down first.

Nikki taps her long nail on the side of her wine glass. All heads swivel in her direction. "I just wanted to make, like, a special toast to Wyatt for hosting us this week. This is like, the best fucking farm in all of America."

There are actual crickets in the background.

Her face is beaming with joy as she raises her glass. "To Wyatt."

Everyone grabs their glass and raises it. We all drink to that. Even Peaches gets a taste of white wine from Nikki's glass.

"Thank you, Nikki."

She winks at me before sitting again.

I reach for the knife to start cutting the prime rib when Caroline pushes her chair back, struggling to slide it across the stone pavers. She pulls her dress down and smooths her hands over her hips. Her eyes are wide as she scans the group, and we all wait for her to speak or sit down so we can eat. Preferably the latter.

She grabs her glass of wine and fills it to the top, slurping it a bit before raising it high and facing me. "Another toast."

Oh God.

The lights strung behind us have her backlit, making the features of her face dark and mostly unreadable. Blame it on the lights, or the fact that I can't read her like I used to. Maybe I never could.

"Wyatt," she says.

I'm willing her to hurry up with my eyes, so I can serve the food before it gets cold.

"Wyatt, I just wanted to say, thank you..."

"You're welcome. Shall we eat?" I say, staring longingly at the prime rib getting colder by the second.

"...And that I love you."

Mom spits out her wine.

Stace gasps.

Granny murmurs *hussy* under her breath.

Dad looks around at everyone like he missed something important.

Then, everyone looks at me.

But the only person I'm looking at now is Avery.

Thirty-Five

Avery

*"If I paint something, I don't want to have to explain what it is."-Bob
Ross*

Oh no she didn't.

But also, yeah, she just did.

Caroline just admitted, out loud, in front of all of us that she loves Wyatt. His mouth is currently hanging open and staring at me like I can somehow do something about this.

Maybe I can.

I push my chair back and stand tall, strangling the neck of my wine glass while I grip a handful of my dress in the other. Caroline is still standing and glowering at me.

"I have a toast also," I say, raising my glass higher than Caroline's.

I have no idea what I'm going to say, but I have to say something. I'm standing up and demanding everyone's attention as their eyes burn holes clean through me. My mouth is suddenly filled with sand, and my thoughts race faster than any Kentucky Derby horse in history. I don't think I've ever been more terrified.

I'm literally staring at my greatest fear: love.

It's love that was taken away when my brother died. Love that was withheld by my parents when it ran out, and now love will either propel me toward everything I want, or the fear of it will keep me quiet. Is this the moment Avery's Curse and my fear come to die?

Maybe it's time to put this fear six feet under.

The realization makes me stand taller. This is my moment, and I don't want to be afraid anymore.

"I like—" The word gets caught in my throat. "—love Wyatt, too."

I stare down at him, the admission ripe on my tongue, and his softening gaze releasing thousands of doves inside my chest. All that flapping and fluttering takes its toll and before anyone can say anything more, I speak directly to Wyatt and let my heart do the talking. "I love you."

Holy shit!

Did I really just say that? I did. I can't believe I just said that out loud. I feel lighter and heavier all at once.

He smiles so big and starts to stand when Caroline yells, "You bitch!"

I snap my head to look at her.

"You can't steal my moment!" she yells.

I scoff and start to say something when two dark figures stroll toward the table out of nowhere, quite literally.

"Hello?" one of them says.

I'm ready to huck a glass at the intruders when Wyatt stands and says, "Helen?"

"And Mabel," she calls back as they come into the dim light.

"What are you doing here?" Deb asks, looking between her son, to whom I just professed my love, and the bakery owner in town.

Helen thrusts the pink box into her daughter's arms. "Mabel brought cinnamon rolls."

"Hell yeah! We, like, LOVE cinnamon rolls!" Nikki says. "Don't we, Peaches?"

Peaches barks, and Helen peers around the table at all the familiar and unfamiliar faces. "I'm sorry to barge in," she says, pushing her daughter forward who looks shyly at Wyatt before dropping her gaze back to the box. "Mabel wanted to make sure you had these this weekend. We haven't seen you in town, Wyatt."

"I—" he starts but is cut off.

"I'll take those for you," Ross says, standing and plucking the box from Mabel's hands.

He sits back down, and Bobbi glares at him while we all gape. He pulls his phone out and takes a few angled pictures of the pastries. "What?" He shrugs. "Calories don't count on vacation."

"Helen, Mabel," Wyatt says. "Thank you for the cinnamon rolls—"

"Homemade cinnamon rolls," Helen corrects.

Wyatt continues. "We all appreciate it very much, but—"

"Enough to ask Mabel on a date?" Helen asks, raising her brows.

Caroline crosses her arms. "Oh, fuck off!"

Helen raises a hand to her chest, mouth falling open. "I beg your pardon!"

Deb shifts in her seat and holds her hand out to Caroline. "Okay, okay." She addresses Helen. "I'm so sorry, Helen, but now really isn't the best time."

"It's, like, always a good time for cinnamon rolls," Nikki says, then looks at Wyatt. "If it doesn't work out with any of these babes..." She holds her hand up to her ear like a phone and mouths, *call me*.

Stace stands suddenly and clears her throat. "I have an announcement to make." She scans the table quickly then grabs her water cup and lifts it higher than Caroline's or mine had been. "We have an announcement."

Bryan tugs his wife's arm. "Honey, I don't think now's a good time."

She yanks her arm back and whispers to him, "It's the best time. We need to steer this ship somewhere else before it crashes." Water sloshes out of her cup as she straightens. "As I was saying...Mom, Dad."

Deb's eyes are wide, and her head is tipped to the side. She grabs her husband, Carl's hand, who looks as if he's going to be sick.

Stace is positively glowing. "We're pregnant!"

Deb screams and stands so fast, her chair falls with a clatter. "Oh my god! I knew it!" She slaps her husband on the shoulder as she hops up and down. "Didn't I tell you?! I knew it!"

Stace is jumping up and down, too, as Bryan rubs his forehead.

Bobbi stands, deciding there is no time like the present to announce, "Since we're all sharing exciting news, I just wanted to let you know that our dance video from the camping trip is going viral!"

Ross talks around a bite of cinnamon roll. "No way! You're lying. Tell me you're lying, or I'll pee my pants RIGHT NOW!"

Ew.

"I'm totally not lying!" She whips her phone out. "See! One million views and counting."

Ross high fives Bobbi, and they look like they might shed happy tears like Stace and Deb are.

"You have to go shopping for baby clothes with me! And Granny, you're going to love being right down the street and so close to the baby." Stace claps a hand over her mouth and slowly peers down the table at a fuming Wyatt who has his hands on his hips. She speaks through the cracks in her fingers. "Forget I said that."

He clenches his fists at his sides. "What?"

And just like that the secret is out.

"Uh, sweetheart," Deb drawls.

Wyatt cuts her a look.

She laughs nervously. "There's something we need to tell you."

What in the blazes is actually happening right now?

Granny stands, resting her palms on the table and leaning into them. We all watch her, waiting for her to put us out of our misery. She doesn't look at Wyatt right away but speaks to her plate. "I'm selling Trapp Farms."

Resounding gasps leave everyone's mouths. I sharply crane my neck to look at Wyatt. I can't take my eyes off his hardened face as he stares Granny down with more fire than I've ever seen. He's reaching a roiling boil beneath his button up shirt that isn't fully buttoned all the way.

His heart is breaking bit by bit and taking mine with it.

"What the fuck—"

Granny holds up a hand and finally stares him down. "Before you get your unders all in a bunch, I'm not selling the farm to just anybody."

"Who is it?" Wyatt snaps, hands on hips.

She laughs. Actually laughs while everyone else looks like they've swallowed a piano.

"You don't already know?"

"Ronny?" Wyatt asks.

"Hell no," Granny spits back, then looks across the table at Ronny. "No offense, Ronny."

He tips his hat. "None taken."

"Dad?"

Granny looks at her oldest son, sitting two seats down from her, cradling his head in his hands. "No, farm life wasn't for him. He never wanted it."

Carl, Wyatt's dad, nods in agreement as he rakes his hands down his face.

Wyatt steals her attention back. "Who is it, Granny?"

"You."

I'm bouncing my eyes between the two of them so fast. Wyatt looks like a cold bucket of ice water was just dumped over his head. "What?" he whispers.

Granny throws both arms in the air. "I'm selling you the farm, boy!"

Wyatt swallows and runs a hand through his hair, staring intently at his feet. I want to reach out to him and provide some semblance of comfort or steal him away and kiss him until he's ready to talk.

"Well, this'll be news to share at the bakery," Helen says, elbowing Mabel.

"Now, you just hold on a minute, Helen." Granny pins Helen with a hard stare and a straight finger. "You don't go spreading rumors around town before Wyatt has a chance to decide." She looks back to Wyatt. "This is your choice, Wyatt. If you don't want the farm, we'll figure it out."

"Why?" he asks so quietly it's a wonder Granny could hear him. "Why me?"

"I'm dying," Granny says.

Wyatt snaps his head up to look at her.

"Mom, what are you saying?" Carl asks.

Deb places a hand over her heart, while Stace circles a hand around her belly.

Shit. I hold my throat, feeling like I'm going to barf up the cookies I just had to finish before dinner.

Granny waves us all off. "I'm not dying, yet. But I'm old, and I won't be around forever."

Everyone around the table takes a giant exhale in unison.

Ronny stands. "I just want everyone to know I do not have an announcement to make."

I look at him sideways. It might be the best news of the night.

Butch raises his hand.

Nikki points at him. "Yes, Butch? It's your turn."

He's finishing a bite of the roasted Brussels sprouts he snuck onto his plate before he starts aggressively clearing his throat. "Are there..." More throat clearing. "Are there onions in this?"

"Of course," Wyatt says, like the thought of leaving them out would be savage.

"I...I'm...allergic...to..." His eyes cross as he grabs his throat.

My mouth falls open. He really is a vampire!

Deb rounds the table to slap Butch's back while yelling, "Carl, call 911!"

Carl fumbles for his phone in his pocket as worry erupts around the table.

"Oh my god! Is he dying?!" Bobbi screams.

"I don't know CPR!" Ross covers his mouth and starts shouting, "DOES ANYONE KNOW CPR?"

I shake my head, frozen in place with my wine glass still in my hand. "No. No, no, no. He can't...he can't...die."

The curse was supposed to be broken. I sacrificed my voice to an evil sea witch for a chance at walking on land to be with my one true love. Wait, no, that's The Little Mermaid. But I did admit my feelings for Wyatt, which should be good enough to have broken Avery's curse. This can't happen.

Caroline takes this opportunity to point toward the front of the house. "Are those...wow, that was fast! The ambulance is here!"

Wyatt moves from his place at the head of the table as red and blue lights create a frenzied light show on the front of the farmhouse.

"That's not an ambulance. Those are cops!"

Rach, who's been quiet this entire time, bolts from the table, tripping over her chair and scrambling to gain purchase. She rams into Wyatt, knocking him off balance, and he bumps the table, and Ross, a little too hard. Wine glasses clank together as plates clash. Ross collides with the perfectly set table, and the momentum is enough to tilt it. The prime rib jostles, then slides, then...

"No!" Wyatt yells, but it's too late.

The prime rib surfs the edge before landing facedown on the ground.

A voice comes through a loudspeaker, rattling my eardrums. "Come out with your hands up!"

All of us raise our hands on instinct except for Butch who looks to be breaking out in hives. And Rach who is frantically searching the area for a place to run.

Two more dark figures circle the house. "Hands up! Put your hands where we can see them!"

With precious time wasted, Rach decides to do the exact opposite and takes off at a dead sprint toward the cow pasture and away from the farmhouse. Nikki is screaming *oh my god* on repeat while Peaches yelps, as if she were the one being chased. Shock hits us all. Some of us freeze, like me, others hide under the table, like Bobbi and Ross, a few try to help the dying vampire, and others—only one of us—decides to run.

Rach is barely to the edge of the fence, pumping her arms and running like a bad guy on an episode of Cops. The soundtrack immediately starts playing in my head, and it will now live there on repeat for five-hundred hours.

Unfortunately, the two cops are faster and throw themselves on top of her before she can leap over the fence, like a gazelle with a secret to hide. It's too dark and the grass too tall to see what's happening. But when I look over at Wyatt, his chest is heaving, and he's looking straight at me.

God, I hope this doesn't make it into the reviews.

Thirty-Six

Wyatt

"In nature, dead trees are just as normal as live trees."-Bob Ross

S he robbed a gas station," cop one says, while cop two leads Rach to his vehicle.

I've already forgotten both of their names, but I'm not freaking out about it since there are bigger things to wrap my head around. Like housing a robber on the run on my property for a week.

"Are there any other questions for me?" I ask.

Not like he didn't already ask me every question he could think of, including my favorite color. Alright, not really. But almost every question.

"We're good for now but call that number." He points to the card in my hand. "If anything else comes to mind, or you find where she stashed the money."

I nod. "You got it."

All the guests, my family, and the town representative, Helen, are all still here, watching. To be fair, there hasn't been this much action around these parts in a while. I'm surprised the rest of the town hasn't shown up yet.

"Hang on," Rach says to the cop detaining her before he can lower her into the backseat. "Wyatt, thank you for your hospitality this week."

"Uh, yeah...you're welcome."

The cop nudges the back of her head to get her to bend over and sit, but Rach isn't ready.

"Sorry about all the fuss, but other than the...well, you know..."

I know.

"It was a great week," she continues. "I'll write a good review when I get out."

With that, she's lowered into the backseat when cop two decides he's had enough of her rambling.

I mumble, "Great," as the cop car pulls down the gravel driveway.

The lights are still spinning, but the sirens stopped a while ago when the ambulance arrived with theirs on at full blast. Two medics dashed out to help Butch just as Rach was being hauled to her feet again.

The town gossip will have a heyday with this one. I know they say all publicity is good publicity, but I don't think that applies to small towns. Only time will tell.

Turning around, I'm met with too many eyes, and I immediately want to go hide in my room. Caroline, Mom, Dad, Granny, Stace, Bryan, Helen, and Mabel are watching for what I'll do next. Hell if I know. None of the other guests are here and neither is Avery, making me think she might have taken them all back to their cabins.

We didn't even get to eat the prime rib.

Mom reaches out first. "Honey."

I let her rub my shoulders, even though she kept all of these secrets from me.

Stace launches into an apology. "I didn't mean for it to slip out. They wanted me to keep it a secret. I would have told you."

I hold up a hand. "Just...congratulations on the baby. Can you guys clean up some of the food for me?"

Stace closes her mouth and nods her agreement.

"I'm going to bed," I say.

I pivot and start walking toward the farmhouse, hearing Granny say, *give him time*, under her breath.

I'm ready to throw myself onto my bed, like a breach whale jumps out of the water, when I hear my name from behind. Yup, I'm changing my name.

Caroline follows me up the steps and inside.

"What now?" I bark out.

"Can we talk?" she asks as I spin around.

"Now you want to talk?"

Her eyes fill with tears and she nods. Well, I'm a dick. "I'm sorry." I rub my temples. "Tonight was...not what I expected."

"I know, I know," she says, looking at the ground. "You haven't exactly been easy to share things with."

I cross my arms, resisting the strong urge I have to tell her she lost the chance to talk to me when she cheated, but I'm giving her a chance to say what she needs to say to finally end this once and for all.

She looks up and studies me. "I didn't mention this before, but I like your beard, by the way."

"Caroline."

"Okay, okay. Sorry, you're right." She sighs and puts her hands on her sharp hips that could poke an eye out. "It's just...hard to rehash everything."

If that isn't a complete understatement...

"I hate how we ended things," she says with a shrug. "You just...left. I had to pack up the whole apartment myself and broke four nails in the process. It was bad enough having you leave, and then my nail tech scolded me for my carelessness."

I clench my hands into fists at my sides. "You cheated on me, Caroline. With my business partner. I wasn't about to stick around and try to play nice with you and Jake."

That was a dark time for me, and to think, it was only a few months ago. So much has changed since then, but as I look at Caroline in her bright pink costume, askew on her shoulder, smearing makeup, and sad expression, I can see what I couldn't before: she's a mess in a candy wrapper.

"I didn't get a chance to say my part. Everything just ended so suddenly. We were living together, Wyatt, and you tossed me out like a sack of donated clothes. I didn't mean for..." She stops herself and shakes her head.

"There was so much happening in my head, I couldn't even think straight. You didn't just bang anyone. You banged Jake, the guy who owned half of my company."

"Okay, maybe *banged* isn't the right word here," she says, raising a lime-green tipped finger in the air.

I throw my hands up. "Then, what is? Please, enlighten me."

She exhales. "You're right. What I did was messed up. But I didn't stop loving you after you broke up with me. I didn't stop loving you when I...and he..." She spins one of the rings on her fingers. "Lots of couples get over infidelity. I shouldn't have done it, but I was feeling lonely. You had your job and were doing so well and would sometimes just forget I existed. I hated feeling like that."

I lost a lot because of her. The stress I was under was more than I'd ever carried at once. The business was growing, but life was limping along. I'd lost Gramps nine months before and was spinning out. Work was all I had. Until I didn't. Until it was taken from me when I sold my half of the company to the sleazeball who slept with my almost-fiancée.

At least he saved me from that fate.

"I thought if I came here, we could work on ourselves and remember what we had. I thought you just needed some space for a while, and then we'd figure it out," she says, hopeful.

I pinch the bridge of my nose. "But there was a lot more between us that led to our breakup."

She stays quiet, bouncing her leg as she wraps her arms around her middle.

I drop my hand. "We were so different, you and me."

She meets my eyes, her lip quivering under the weight of her emotion. "I know. I just...it killed me."

I reach for her shoulder and tug her closer. "It killed me, too."

More than I even know. Now, I know what I want. Who I want.

"I'm so sorry," she says into my chest.

"Me, too."

I'm not sorry for leaving or breaking up with her, but I am sorry for how everything happened. I wish I didn't know what it felt like to be stabbed in the back. But, then again, I wouldn't know what it felt like to be stitched back together and survive that injury if I hadn't.

She pulls back and wipes below her lash line. "Do you love her?"

This is the last question I want to answer coming from my ex-girl-friend, but honesty is where I need to land.

"I do."

She nods and shrugs one shoulder as more tears fill her eyes. "I could tell. She's...nice. Her nails are horrible but—"

"Caroline," I say with a warning edge to my tone.

She holds up both hands.

I'd give her a speech about how she'll find someone nice one day, too, if I thought it would help. But I keep my mouth shut. More words won't make the truth hurt less.

She points at the door. "I'm gonna go. This is super awkward now."

I laugh and tuck my hands in my pocket as she slowly makes her way to the front door.

"Caroline?" She cranes her neck back to look at me, hand on the door knob. "Safe travels."

Half of her mouth turns up into a smile. "Enjoy all the...cows."

With that, she walks out the front door and leaves me standing in the entry. I want to rush out and tell Avery the news, tell her I love her, too, and that I want her to stay at the farm and work here until...well, forever. I want to kiss her senseless and break into the gigantic box of condoms tonight.

But on the other side of that door are more prying eyes and more questions than I have the stamina to deal with tonight. I need to sleep, and in the morning, I'll find her.

Thirty-Seven

Avery

"Make love to the canvas."-Bob Ross

*D*ear diary, I went down on my boss in a tent. No, I'm not joking. Oh, and I told him I loved him.

I shoot off my text to Tilly, even though it's eleven at night and I should be sleeping, but I can't. Not after the display that was dinner earlier this evening. I still can't believe Rach was taken down by the cops and hauled off to jail. I mean, she did ask me if I knew anyone who made passports. At the time, I thought she just wanted to know where to get one. So, I told her to go to the post office. Now, I think she might have been talking about something more nefarious.

My phone dings with a new text. *You're shitting me.*

I type back, *I'm definitely not.*

Instead of responding, Tilly calls my phone.

"Did I wake you?" I whisper, like this will somehow help.

"Of course you did. I have that special ringtone just for you."

"I'm sorry." I sigh and roll to my side. "Wait, what's my ringtone?"

"In Da Club."

I smile. "Classic."

"50 Cent just gets better with age."

"He really does," I say. "Anyway, I'm sorry for texting and waking you up."

"Don't you dare apologize. Just make it worth it and tell me what-the-cheese happened?"

I recount my time with Wyatt in the woods…and then the tent. We both visited another galaxy that night but falling asleep in his arms and staying there all night was delicious. As a souvenir, I've got a scratch on one of my ass cheeks from the tree bark that I had to douse in lavender oil, and I got sap in my hair that took four rounds of shampooing to get out. But somehow, retelling the story only reminds me of how feral I become when I'm with Wyatt.

"Don't be stingy now. How did you end up confessing your love?" Tilly asks. I can hear the whir of our fridge in the background as she opens and closes the door.

This small reminder whacks me in the face. Not because I'm homesick, but because I'm not. I don't admit this out loud, because I'm too lazy to reach my wooden nightstand to knock on it, but I think the curse has been broken. I think I did that by coming here, and for that, I'm more grateful for this place than even I know.

I take a deep breath and flip to my other side. "His ex-girlfriend decided it was the right moment to admit her undying love over dinner. So, naturally, I needed to as well."

"Oh my god. That's so unlike you."

I close my eyes. "I know. I still can't believe I said it."

"What did Wyatt say?"

A knife lodges itself in my chest. "Nothing."

This might be the worst part. I never got a response since he was busy talking to the police, and I was bouncing between answering unknown questions about Butch to the paramedics and easing the worries of the other guests.

"You have to find out," Tilly says.

"I don't think I want to know," I say in a hushed voice.

"No, no, no. You have to talk to him. I'd put money on him loving you back."

I pause. "Have you? Bet on it?"

"No, not yet."

"Tilly."

"Avery! I get that you want to hide after totally putting yourself out there but don't you dare."

I laugh. "Is that a threat?"

"Absolutely it is."

Flopping over onto my back, I stare up at the ceiling and consider what she's saying. The hardest part is over. I've already told him I love him. Sure, he didn't say it back, but with the shit-show that followed, he didn't exactly have a chance. And I need to see him. I want to make sure he's okay after tonight.

I bolt upright. "I'm going to go talk to him."

Tilly screams.

"I'll call you tomorrow," I say, slipping on my boots at the end of my bed.

"You better! Don't forget the box of condoms. Byyyye!"

She hangs up before I can tell her I don't have the box anymore, and there's no way I can unearth it from Wyatt's bathroom like a great archaeological find. Not tonight.

I race to my door and unlock it, swinging it open and pausing when I remember how dark it gets out here. It's a different kind of dark since no buildings or street lights cast a glow. My phone's flashlight lets me see about five inches in front of me, so that's not helpful.

Remembering the headlamp hanging on the coat hook, I snag it and shove it on my head, pressing buttons until the ground becomes clear. Tilly's right, I should talk to him, but I want to see his face and see all the subtleties I will be trying to decode, like someone dismantling a bomb. A text or call won't tell me these things.

If my calculations are correct, Wyatt's room is on the right if I'm facing the back of the farmhouse. I considered just walking inside, knowing the door would be open, but I don't want to startle or wake Granny. And I know Wyatt has a gun, and I don't want to see it.

Not that kind anyway.

I grab a few sticks and start tossing them, but his room is on the second story and my aim is about as good as a walrus'. I can't explain how that makes sense, either.

The sticks aren't working, so I move on to pinecones. When those aren't successful, either, I stare at the small bed of rocks around the garden beds. One of them probably won't do much damage.

I pick up a handful and pinch one small pebble between my fingers. A hooting sound makes me jump, and I almost lose all the rocks and my nerves. Tossing one up, it lands with a sad *plink*. I throw the next one harder but hit the siding and not the window.

I try again at the same time the window opens and end up nailing Wyatt in the head.

He yells and grasps his forehead. "Avery?"

"Wyatt!" I scream-whisper.

"What are you doing? Other than throwing rocks at my forehead."

He leans farther out the window, revealing a lot of skin. Arms, hands, face, and chest. My mouth runs dry, and I have to remind myself why I'm here.

"Are you okay?" I call up to him.

"What?" he says quietly, then shakes his head. At least, I think he does. "You know what, just come around front."

I nod and maneuver carefully around the farmhouse in the dark toward the front. I take the steps quietly, avoiding the creaks I know of now. All of that bare skin I saw in the window is now holding the screen door open for me.

"Hi," I say, once inside.

He smiles and says with a raspy voice, "Hey."

I peer up at Moosifer who seems way too intent on what I'm about to say. That makes three of us.

"What are you doing here?"

"I...I..." I start, but Moosifer is making me sweat. "Can we go somewhere private?"

I glance up at the moose head, and Wyatt follows my line of sight. "Yeah, follow me."

Instead of curving left into the living room, he takes the stairs, and for reasons that make sense in my body and not my head, I follow him.

He leads me into his room and shuts the door behind him. His bed sheets are bunched together, but the crease of where his body once was is still there. That and the window is still open.

"This is...better." Or worse, I'm not quite sure yet.

"So, what brings you to my room at midnight?" he asks, grabbing my hand and staring down at me, his face cast in the moon's glow.

His hair is rumpled, and I don't even think he's put it together yet, that he's only in his briefs. But I have. I've solved that equation four times since walking into this house.

"Do you think maybe you want to put some clothes on first?" I ask hesitantly.

He looks down, drops my hand and cups his crotch. "I wasn't expecting a guest."

His words cause me to exhale. He'd been clear about where he and Caroline stood all week, but her admission of loving him at dinner tonight rattled me.

"I can see that."

His lips twitch like he'll smile, but he just asks, "What can I do for you?"

I can think of a few things I'd like him to do.

I scratch my head and shift on my feet. "Um, I guess I just wanted to see how you were doing after...everything?"

Wyatt loves this place. That much has been clear since taking the tour with him and seeing his face light up as he pointed at different places and shared stories that went along with them. But does that mean he wants to stay? Does he want me to?

He laughs under his breath. "I haven't stopped thinking about it. I've just been tossing and turning, trying to fall asleep, but I can't."

"Me, neither." I'm seconds from stress-cleaning his room.

He walks back and sits on the end of his bed, putting his head in his hands. "I wasn't expecting any of that, especially Granny wanting to move in with my parents and leave me the farm."

I shiver and rub my arms. "What do you think you'll do?"

The question isn't entirely selfless. I've wanted to know the future plans since I arrived. But I also want to know where his head is at now.

He sighs and rests his elbows on his thighs. "I'm gonna stay."

My shoulders lift. "Stay on the farm?"

He nods, and though the room is dark, I can see the movement of his head so clearly. "I'm gonna buy it."

A weight lifts from my chest hearing him say this. He's perfect for this place, and I'm just glad he's noticing.

I swallow hard, my words barely above a whisper. "And Caroline?"

He looks up. "She's leaving tomorrow."

"Ah."

"For good," he clarifies.

"Oh." I'm not even sure my lips moved to form that single word.

Caroline is accounted for, but what about me? "And the spa?"

He stands and strides closer to me. The chill I'd once felt is replaced with his body heat.

"I want you to stay on as our spa director," he says, stroking a thumb over my cheek.

"Huh?"

"I want you to stay."

"I heard you," I say. "I just like hearing you say *spa director.*"

"Avery," he whispers.

"Yeah?" I'm not even sure if I said this out loud or just in my head.

"*Spa director.*"

The way he says "spa" makes it sound like there are forty-one "a's" in that one word. I can't even answer him, I'm so turned on.

"Avery?"

His hand is so warm, so…I shake my head. "What did you say?"

He skims my bottom lip with his thumb. "I want to kiss you."

"Oh." There's that sound again.

He slides his other arm around my waist, up my back, and around my neck. His bare thighs press against mine and are so warm.

"It feels so good to hold you," he says against my mouth. "Can I?"

Liquid fire runs through my veins, and I nod.

He takes my mouth with his, stealing my next breath. His hands explore, raking over my skin and sparking heat all over my body. His length is full and needy as it presses into me.

Oh no.

No, no, no.

I shove him back with my hands. "Wait!"

He holds both of my wrists, not ready to let me put any distance between us. But I can't keep kissing him, feeling his body on mine, and not make sure he's really okay.

He shakes his head. "What?"

"So, you're not upset?"

He smiles and tugs my wrists so our chests are touching again. "Oh, I'm upset," he says, wrapping his hands around my waist and forging a trail beneath the hem of my shirt. "Just not in the way you think."

"Then how?"

His hands are hot irons, searing my skin in ways I'll never forget.

He bends to kiss the side of my neck. "I'm upset it's taken me this long to figure out what I want."

"And what do you want?"

A hot kiss presses into my cheek. "The farm."

I'm a statue, waiting to see what he'll do next as he kisses his way around my face.

"This life," he adds.

"Uh-huh."

He kisses my bottom lip, then the top, asking and telling me so many things at once, but all I hear is the one word he whispers into my mouth. "You."

"Me?"

"You, Avery. I want you. I want to kiss you and make love to you, wake up and fall asleep next to you. I want long days and even longer nights around the fire with you," he kisses my forehead, "I love you back."

I'm completely speechless. So, instead of speaking, I push up on my toes and kiss him fully, plunging my tongue into his mouth and letting him know exactly what I think.

Lifting my shirt off, he tosses it across the room and continues to hungrily kiss me like it's been a while. We did this yesterday. But it's like I've remembered and forgotten. Our bare skin touches, leaving the feel of him emblazoned on all my exposed places and even those that aren't, because that's what Wyatt has done to me. He's made himself unforgettable.

I take as much as he gives and find myself pressing my hips into his, wanting to meld to every curve I can find. His mouth moves to my neck, and he trails hot kisses down to the peaks of my breasts. I angle back, inviting and asking for all he's willing to give. I'm out of breath already as he takes one nipple into his mouth while cupping and massaging my other breast.

I moan into the quiet space that's filling up with our noises of pleasure. I want him and me and us together like I've thought of too many times since we got back from the camping trip. Pulling his face up, I stare at him and gasp when his hand drops beneath my silk shorts and he grabs my ass. He doesn't pause there and swoops me up until my legs wrap around his waist, and he lays me back onto his bed where he hovers above me on hands and knees. It's still warm where his body once was, but nothing compares to the heat emanating from him. From me.

My hands roam the hair on his chest, his broad shoulders, and then back down to his boxers. When I slip them down his hips and lay eyes on him, I don't want to wait for anything else, I want his weight on me.

But Wyatt has other ideas.

He lowers himself down to his elbows and cups my face, studying me. "I love you."

I'm melting farther into his mattress and becoming a puddle on his floor. His response to my truth bomb at dinner unlocks another level of my heart. The caution that has been my security blanket for years doesn't feel necessary anymore. It falls off when the man holding me so gently is covering me in safety while I stand out on the ledge.

That's how it is with him. Taking risks while completely safe.

"I love you, Wyatt. I want Thanksgiving and Christmas on the farm. I want family dinners every week. I want to feed the chickens every morning. I want to make love to you after long work days. I know that's a lot, and it doesn't all have to be now. We can take things slow and—"

"Avery." He smiles and presses his forehead to mine. "I want all of that, too."

I swallow and drag a hand down his chest. "I want other things, too."

He continues to look at me until his eyes flutter closed, and his breathing picks up as I touch him over his briefs. He lays down beside me, running light fingers up my stomach, over my bare chest, and down again while curling his tongue around mine. Dipping lower into my underwear, his hand massages me until I'm at the edge of my control.

"I want you," I manage to say.

"You want me?"

I shake my head. "Inside."

My breathing is raspy, and my thoughts have all been thrown into a mixer.

"Condom?" I ask.

"Plenty."

My eyes widen as he rolls over and lifts the small car-size box of condoms up, yanking the flap open and grabbing one. He rips it open with his teeth and slides it on all while I'm frozen in shock.

Did he...were those...they are.

He found them. But there isn't time to tell him the story now as he's back to kissing my neck and touching me where I want him most. He gently pushes every inch of himself in, thrusting slowly at first and then faster with my urging.

Our bodies move together in unison, delighting in every morsel of passion we can take from this moment. There will be more, I'm sure of that, but for now, I let my desperation for him take over. I moan into his shoulder, grip his neck, and arch my hips higher until we both crumble in a contended heap of love and want.

Thirty-Eight

Wyatt

"You too can paint almighty pictures."-Bob Ross

W yatt!" an incessant voice calls. "Wyatt, time to wake up, boy! You've already slept past your alarm."

Wyatt is tired. Wyatt doesn't want to come to the phone right now, but if you leave a message, he'll wake up later and let the chickens out, gather the eggs, and make some breakfast. If I could change my name, it would be to Czeslaw or Ermenegildo, because they are impossible to spell correctly and even harder to say.

Czeslaw is perfectly content wrapped around this dime piece in his bed.

Dime piece?

I really must be dreaming.

Shifting in bed, I go to stretch and realize my arm is pinned and I can't move it. Not another dead arm. Every time I sleep with my arm above my head, all of the blood rushes out of it, and I'm left with a floppy, no-good noodle that works about as well as a dead fish.

But as I make a fist with that hand, I don't have the same tingling sensation.

I peel my eyes open and look beside me.

Lo and behold, there really is a dime piece sleeping next to me. Her blonde hair is fanned across my pillow, her head heavy on my shoulder, and breath tickling my neck.

I use my other hand to feel my way down her leg and note it's slung over top of me again. Oh, wait. That's my leg slung over her. If I could see us right now, I'm sure Avery and I would look something like a fortune cookie bent and twisted around each other.

"Wyatt, I'm gonna come up there!" Granny yells from downstairs, and I snap my head up from the pillow. *Granny.* "Last night didn't go as planned, but that doesn't mean you have to hide in your room all day," she says.

I shake Avery awake, and she moves closer with a low murmur of unintelligible words.

"Avery, we have to wake up."

"Not yet," she says with her eyes closed.

Of course it's as she moves closer that I remember just how bare and naked she is beneath my sheets. "Avery, come on. Granny's awake."

Her brows crease, but she still doesn't open her eyes. "Hm?"

I try to move, but then one of her hands drops below my waist and I pause.

Last night was incredible. It was everything I'd hoped it would be, and I'm not just saying that because Avery's hand is currently curled around me.

"Mhm," she hums lazily, making me more alert. "I guess it is time to wake up."

I close my eyes and stop her hand. "Avery!"

She lets go and blinks up at me. "I'm sorry. I—"

"Don't be sorry," I say, planting a kiss on her forehead. "But we can't do this now. It's...Granny."

"Wyatt!" Granny pounds on my door.

Avery bolts upright, clutching the sheet around her and stealing it all from me until my morning wood is exposed.

She whips her head from the door to me and whispers, "What do we do?"

I stand up and wave her off the bed. She rolls across it, becoming more of a burrito and struggling to stand. I help her up on my way to the closet.

"I'm sorry to have to do this but—"

She pulls the closet door shut before I can finish and do it for her.

"Okay, then." I look around my room. "Pants…" I pick up a shirt that looks like underwear then toss it aside. Next, I grab a shirt with Mario and Luigi frolicking in what looks like a field of banana peels.

What?

Definitely Avery's.

Locating a familiar pair of black basketball shorts, I tug them on just as the door swings open.

I cover the front of my shorts with my hands. "Granny."

Granny stands in the door frame, one hand on the knob, one on her hip. She peers around my room. "Wyatt."

"Sorry, I slept through my alarms. I'm getting ready and will be right down."

She nods once. "You aren't avoiding me?"

I see the extra lines in Granny's forehead materialize, and my shoulders slump. "No. I want to talk things over with you. Let me get dressed, and then I'll be right down."

After I let the naked woman in my closet free.

"Okay," she says, taking one more gander around the room. "I'll meet you downstairs."

She goes to shut the door, and I exhale in relief a little too soon.

The door swings open again. "And thank Avery for taking her shoes off downstairs. Helps not having dirt tracked all over the house."

With that, Granny shuts the door, and I scratch at my beard. "Avery?" I say.

The closet door opens slowly, and Avery peeks sheepishly around the corner. "My bad."

I can't help but smile, then I stalk over to the closet and push her back inside so I can kiss her good morning properly.

***

"DON'T WORRY, SHE already knows you're here," I say to Avery as we head downstairs after getting dressed. And then getting undressed again before we got dressed for real.

She stops me by the shoulder in the middle of the stairs. "Yeah, but won't it be weird? I mean, she knows I stayed the night."

I turn to face her and cup her face in my hands. "It'll be fine. We are two, consenting adults who love each other."

She sighs. "You're right."

Damn right I'm right.

"Granny really likes you," I reassure her.

She wouldn't have spent all these weeks trying to push us together if she didn't. It's a sign she's on board with Avery and I becoming an *us* and also that she really does know what she's doing.

"Okay, I'm ready," Avery says on an exhale.

But I'm not. I kiss her once more and whisper, "I love you."

She smiles. "I love you, too."

I grab her hand, and we head down the stairs. Together. "Granny?" I call out as we hit the last step.

"In here," she says from the kitchen.

We head down the hall and enter the kitchen. I stop short when I see three sets of eyes staring back at me. My mom, Stace, and Granny are all seated in the breakfast nook, cradling cups of coffee and staring laser beams at where Avery and I are joined.

I clear my throat. "Uh, hi...everyone. I didn't know you'd all be here this morning."

Mom's eyes skate between us, and I can feel Avery tense up beside me, her hand squeezing mine harder.

Stace sits straighter in her chair and studies me through a lowered gaze.

Granny looks back down at her Sudoku puzzle. "So, Avery slept over," she says before scratching a number into the grid.

Mom stands abruptly. "Coffee, anyone? Avery?"

Avery holds up a hand. "I'm good for now. Thank you, though."

Mom nods and sits back down before waiting for my answer.

It's Stace's turn to stand up. "Wyatt, can we talk about last night? I feel horrible, and I hated leaving here knowing how upset you must've been."

She's talking with her hands like she does, but the worry lines on her forehead and between her brows tell me how bad she feels for spilling the news about Granny.

"And good morning, Avery," Stace says before sitting.

Avery waves at her but doesn't say anything.

I blow out a breath. "I'm not mad."

Mom and Stace speak at the same time. "You're not?"

I shake my head and drop Avery's hand so I can move closer. "No. I'm...surprised and maybe a little confused about how it all happened, but I'm not mad."

Stace's shoulders lower a good three inches.

"We knew how much you already had on your plate," Mom says. "But we shouldn't have kept the news from you. Right, Granny?"

Granny taps her pencil on the page as she looks up at me. "That's right." She shifts in her seat to cross her legs. "Talks of selling the farm have been going on for a while now. Even back before Gramps died."

I stiffen. "Really?"

That shocks me. Trapp Farms was my Gramps' pride and joy. He would've rather sold a kidney than sell the farm. Had it really gotten so bad that he'd considered it?

"Now, hear this. Walter didn't want the farm sold with a realtor and fancy pictures posted around town advertising to the highest bidder." She shakes her head. "Oh, no. He wanted the farm to go to you, Wyatt."

"Me?" I point at my chest. "But I don't have any money."

She nods. "He told me before he died that if I needed to sell the farm, that would be okay, but it had to stay in the family. He said your name a dozen times, and I finally told him to just put it in writing, so when the time was right, I'd let you read the letter."

I think my heart has stopped completely. Is this what a heart attack feels like? Or, maybe just what it feels like for my world to split in two.

A small part of me has been holding on to the city version of myself. But honestly, I didn't like him all that much. I didn't like the pressure I was constantly up against to try and fit into shoes that weren't boots. I like my boots. And now that I've walked around in them a little more, I don't want to take them off. This is me. This is Wyatt.

Granny stands and pulls out an envelope from between the pages of her Sudoku book and extends it for me to take.

I pinch the letter between my fingers, waiting for it to vaporize before my eyes. But it doesn't. It's solid and smooth between the pads of my thumb and pointer finger. As I look down at it, I see my name scrawled across the front in that familiar font that could only belong to one person.

Right now, I couldn't be happier to have the name Wyatt. I wouldn't want to be anyone else. Not when my Gramps addressed a letter to me. To Wyatt. A letter that will probably make me cry big, ugly tears until my eyes are red-rimmed and splotchy and I can't see anything but the chicken scratches of my Gramp's handwriting.

"The farm is yours, Wyatt," Granny says in a low voice. "But I'll let him tell you that."

"And what about the money? I can't afford to pay you what this place is worth, Gran. And you can't afford to sell it to me for nothing," I say.

"Money has a way of working itself out. For now, we'll work out an arrangement for you to lease the farm. If you keep attracting all these city-dwellers, you'll be able to pay some rent and keep up with everything."

I shake my head. "Wow, I...don't know what to say."

She nods at the letter in my hand, and I clutch it tighter. My voice is thick with emotions just below the surface. "Thank you."

Mom stands again. "We love you, honey."

Stace's chair scrapes on the linoleum as she stands again, too. "If anyone should have the farm, it's you, brother. Not because you're better at mucking stalls," she says with a smile. "But because this is where you come alive."

Tears start forming in my eyes, and the letter becomes nothing more than a blur. Avery takes my other hand in hers again as my dad walks into the kitchen asking what he missed. Now, all I'm focused on is the man I idolized growing up—who I wanted to be like more than anything. The footsteps I knew I'd follow at the moment I changed shoes.

Granny's arms wrap around me first. Avery tries to let go of my hand, but I don't let her. I hang on like our hands are glued together. Mom and Stace are on her heels, and they all smother me like they've been doing all my life. Dad, too.

I wipe my eyes. "Thank you for this letter, Granny. I'm going to read it, I promise, but my answer is the same."

Everyone is collectively holding their breath, even me.

"I want the farm," I say. "We'll have to figure out the financing and hope that we have a profitable off-season, but I want it."

Another round of hugs ensues, but this time, they are accompanied by squeals of laughter and joy. Even Dad's voice rises an octave above his usually low tone as he pulls me in for a hug and claps me on the back so hard that I know it'll leave a bruise. I don't even care.

"Now, before you go tending and watering all those guests—"

"Granny," I interrupt. "They aren't flowers."

She pins me with a stare.

Maybe she's at least a little bit right.

"As I was saying, before you go..." Granny turns to face Avery who hasn't left my side and leans in, whispering, "Avery, your shirt's on backward, dear."

Avery looks down at her shirt. The plain red tee doesn't pass the vibe check of the woman wearing it. She swivels to try and stare at her back where Mario and Luigi are all smiles.

And at this moment, with all of my family here—Gramps included—I am, too.

Thirty-Nine

"I really believe that if you practice enough you could paint the 'Mona Lisa' with a two-inch brush."-Bob Ross

D ear Wyatt,

You're probably wondering why you're reading this letter. Well, I'm dead. But you probably already know that.

Hopefully you've been getting on fine without me. Granny, too. That woman is as tough as jerky, but I know she'll need the help. You know what family means to me. It's less about the mistakes we each make in our lifetime—and Lord knows I've made a few—but that we're there for each other when they happen.

You've had to find your own way these past few years. I told Granny when you graduated high school that you were a dreamer. Those big goals you had, well, they were gonna take you somewhere, I knew that much. Wherever you find yourself reading this letter, whether it's in San Francisco, another country, or selling beauty products for a pyramid scheme, I want you to know I don't expect you to stop dreamin'.

But I also know it's time to ask.

By now, I know you're reading this letter because Granny is tired. The farm has been our livelihood for so long, our joy, too, but now it's time for her to move on—to rest. Now, hear me out. I'm not expecting you to drop everything in your life with what I'm about to ask you. But I do want you to consider it like you would any job offer.

You can buy the farm on one condition: you have to want it.

You know what it takes to keep the machine well-oiled and running. I don't need to bore you with the details. Anything you don't remember, I know you'll figure out.

Indulge a dying (dead) man and promise me something, though. If you take on the farm, I don't want you to stop dreaming. This isn't a life sentence. It's an opportunity. Your opportunity.

Remember when you created that lemonade stand at the edge of the gravel driveway when you were eight, only to realize we were out in the middle of nowhere? No one came by that day. But when you packed it in and sat on the porch with your head in your hands and all sad-like, you started thinking.

Thinking led to dreaming, and dreaming led to, well, you know the rest. You took your first idea and gave it wheels, literally. You made fifty dollars by dragging your lemonade stand around town in that wagon. How's that saying go? Making lemonade out of lemons? Well, you did that and then made some hard cash out of cold lemonade. I don't doubt you'll do great things, boy.

I'm proud of you no matter what. I hope I said this enough while I was still breathing. I think you could make some magic with this old place. That's my dream.

When you're ready, come on home.

Love,

Gramps

Epilogue

"See how it fades right into nothing. That's just what you're looking for."-Bob Ross

C an you pass the popcorn?"

Tilly grabs the bowl and hands it to me without peeling her eyes away from the TV.

I laugh. "You can look away from the TV, you know?"

She pops another skittle, or five, into her mouth. "No, I really can't."

A high-pitched scream comes from the screen of many colors, and Tilly jumps and scrambles into my arms, knocking over the popcorn bowl in the process.

"Tilly! What are you doing? It isn't even that scary," I say, trying to unlatch her talons from around my upper arm.

She unravels her hand one finger at a time and helps me pick up the popcorn. "Sorry, you know how I get on Monday nights."

I can't help but laugh. "The Bachelor is nothing compared to a horror film."

She pauses the show and sits back on her heels. "Says who? The woman who's found her one true love and isn't worried one bit about being single and alone for the rest of her life?"

I lean back against the couch. "Tilly...what's going on?"

She sits beside me, drawing her knees up. "Nothing I can't figure out without a fresh cut and color, and a Sex on the Beach. The drink, not the..." She waves a vague hand.

"What ever happened with Ronny?" I ask. "Didn't you both go on a hike the other day?"

It seemed like earlier this week when Tilly arrived, I couldn't find either of them for two straight days. Now, every time they're in the same room, it feels like one of them is going to combust into a mess of confetti.

She makes a disgusted sound. "He was so last week."

I'm not buying it, but I don't press, either, and settle for poking her side. "Are you afraid you'll end up like twenty-four of these twenty-five contestants and go home without a rose or a proposal?"

She doesn't meet my gaze. "Maybe. A little…" She covers her face and groans into her hands. "Okay, yes! There. Are you happy?"

"Am I happy that Amelia got sent home after that horrible group date where she showed up in a dolphin costume that was really a shark? Yes, without a doubt," I say. "Am I happy that my best friend in the entire world feels like she will never fall in love? Fuck no."

Tilly whips her head to look at me. "I can't believe you just said *fuck*."

"Don't get used to it."

"I'll try, but you sound way badass when you say it, for the record," she says.

I wrap my arm around her and tug her close. "And for the record, you're a catch."

"But not the dolphin kind, right?" she asks.

I throw my head back and laugh. "Definitely not."

We devolve into a fit of laughter on the floor when something like a tapping sound starts on one of the windows in the house.

We aren't laughing anymore.

"What was that?"

More tapping.

Tilly looks at me and swallows. "I don't know. Could it be Amelia in her dolphin (aka shark) costume?"

I swat her shoulder and hold back a laugh as something close to scratching is added to the tapping noise. Neither of us are smiling anymore.

"Tilly."

"Avery," she whispers. "Please say that was a tree on your window?"

I shake my head but don't dare look away from her face. "There aren't any trees touching this cabin."

The tapping picks up, louder this time, then stops.

"We're going to die," Tilly squeaks.

"Don't say that!"

I peer around the room. The TV is paused and not making any sound. I can see the front door from here, and it's locked.

The tapping turns urgent before quitting again, and Tilly clings to my arm again as I wait for my impending doom. There's probably a reasonable explanation for this. The wind or change in the weather is my first guess, but if that was the case, we would have heard it earlier.

"I can't die alone. Please, don't let me die alone," she says on repeat.

I reach for my phone and tap the screen. Dead.

Well, that's just great. "Where's your phone?"

Tilly, breathing heavily, looks around for her phone. "I don't know. Oh, shit. I don't know!"

There's a level of panic in her voice that is higher than I want it to be right now.

I need to stay calm.

"Okay, we should figure out where that noise is coming from. Right? I mean, we won't know until we check it out."

Tilly holds up a finger. "Or...we could hide in your room and lock the door."

I stare at her for a beat then leap to my feet. "Okay, I like your plan better."

She rushes to stand, and we both quickly tiptoe toward my room down the hall. But as we pass the kitchen, the tapping starts again, but this time it's knocking.

We both jump into each other's arms, and we don't have far to go since we were already grasping one another in an attempt to hold onto our lives.

"Avery."

I keep my eyes trained on the back door off of the kitchen. "Tilly, did you just say my name?"

Tilly's cheek is pressed against mine, so I can feel her answer when she shakes her head.

"Avery, it's Wyatt."

"Wyatt?" I ask the murderer outside my door.

"Yes, me. You know, your boyfriend."

I exhale and start to move toward the door before Tilly gathers me back into her arms. "Wait just a minute," she whispers, facing me. "How do you know for sure that's really Wyatt out there?"

I shrug. "It sounds like him."

"He could be using a voice mimicker," she retorts.

"Is that a thing?"

"Probably."

I start walking toward the door again, and she grabs my arm. "We need to confirm. Ask him something only he would know."

"I'm not going to do that," I say, crossing my arms.

Tilly looks from me to the door. "If you are really Wyatt, what is my favorite color?"

The voice is clearer now and less muffled by a whisper. "Blue."

Tilly makes a buzzer sound with her mouth. "Wrong. It's yellow."

I slap her arm. "Yellow is your favorite color. Blue is mine."

She snaps her fingers. "Oh, right."

"I'm going to open the door," I say, but she still doesn't let me.

"One more."

I sigh and throw my head back. "Fiiiiine."

"If you're really Wyatt, tell me something about your girlfriend that no one else knows."

"Tilly!" I scold.

There's a pause. "She has a birthmark...below her left butt cheek that looks like Mickey Mouse."

My mouth falls open, and I fling my gaze to Tilly.

Tilly's mouth is just as wide as mine. "Well, we're going to need to confirm this."

She reaches for my leggings and is two seconds from pulling them down before I spin out of her grasp and head for the door, yelling back to her, "You're just going to have to trust him."

"Oh no...I'm going to need to fact-check this," she says, chasing after me. "Or, should I say, fact-cheek!"

I shake my head and open the door to find Wyatt in all his rumpled glory, staring at me like he knows his way around my left ass cheek.

"Hi," I say, biting my lip.

He steps up and kisses my cheek, his cold lips causing shivers to skate down my arms. "Sorry to interrupt Bachelor night—"

"Girls' night," I correct.

"Girls' night," he says. "But I have a surprise for you."

"A surprise?"

He nods.

I shove a finger into his chest as he tries to get closer. "Is anyone giving birth?"

"Not that I know of."

"And no one's dying?" I ask, lowering my brows.

He puts a hand over his heart. "I swear it."

I grab both of his front pockets and pull him toward me. "Then, lead the way."

"Ew."

I look back at Tilly who has resumed her popcorn-eating and is now watching us instead of the TV.

"We'll be right back," I say with a wave.

"Wait!" Tilly yells. "You're going to leave me in this haunted cabin? Alone?"

Wyatt pulls out his phone. "I could text Ronny to come by."

"No! Don't!" she yells even louder this time.

Wyatt and I both look at her.

She pops a piece of popcorn in her mouth. "I'd rather be stolen by Sasquatch and become his wife, thanks."

I squint at her. Definitely need to talk about what happened between the two of them. But for now, I want to see this surprise.

***

Wyatt

I reach for her hand again. "Follow me."

While Avery spent her evening curled up on the couch watching trash television—fight me on this—I was preparing a magical oasis for her in the backyard.

The outdoor tub is lit up all around with hanging lights and candles. I had to borrow every one that Granny, Mom, and Stace had, but it was worth it to bring my vision to life.

"You did all of this?" Avery asks.

I peck her cheek and pull her around the privacy fence. "Of course."

Her mouth drops as she studies the area. Rose petals dance across the surface of the steaming water, and soft music accompanies the cows intermittently lowing in the background. The joy that lights up her face makes it all worth it.

She bends to trail her fingers through the water, and I come up behind her and set a small, leather pouch with drawstrings on the wooden slat lying across the tub. I start massaging her shoulders.

She points at the satchel. "What's that?"

I wrap my hands around her waist and begin lifting her shirt over her head. "Let's get in and find out."

She slips out of her yoga pants and underwear while I help with her bra and get a little distracted in the process. After kissing her neck, shoulder, spine and then back up again, I finally let her climb into the water. I've never gotten undressed so quickly. Not only because there's a beautiful, naked woman in the tub, but also it's cold out here. Nighttime temps have been dipping low while daytime has been picking up slow, or however the song goes.

Her skin glows beneath the hanging lights and warms me all the way through as I slip in behind her, pulling her between my legs and into my chest while kneading her shoulders. She moans at my touch, and I tell her to cover her mouth if she doesn't want me to haul her out of here and make sweet love to her. We've already tried it out here once and I banged my knee on the metal side, giving me a bruise the size of a bowling ball.

She grabs the pouch and feels it. "Is it chocolate?"

I kiss the edge of her ear once. "Nope."

"Condoms?"

I laugh. "No. But I think we might need to start putting the rest of our unopened stock in the guest cabins with a note that reads *Love, Tilly*."

She rests her head back on my shoulder and laughs. "I'll get right on that."

She finally told me where the five-gallon bucket worth of condoms came from, which also led to more questions about the vibrator I found with it. The Purple Pecker has earned a spot in the bedside drawer to live out its days...or battery life.

She shakes the pouch. "It kinda sounds like beads. Did you make me a necklace?"

"No, but the way you sounded so excited makes me wish I'd thought of that."

She continues to rub the velvet pouch between her fingers.

I'm starting to sweat with nerves and can't take this turtle pace any longer. Snagging the bag from her hands, I open the drawstrings and place my hand below hers to cup her palm so I can dump the contents out.

"Impatient much?" she asks with another laugh.

I can't even respond but wait for her to put the pieces together.

Holding up the small packet, she shakes them again. "You got me...seeds?"

I point at the picture on the front. "They're flower seeds. I figured we could plant them in front of your cabin. That way, we'll always have them, and they won't wither away and die like cut flowers do," I say.

We stay in Avery's cabin every so often and make good use of the massage table after business hours, but since Granny is still living in the farmhouse, preparing to move to my parents' place by the end of the month, I try to stay there as much as possible.

Avery picks up the small Ziploc bag next that looks like it belongs to mice and holds it up to the light. "And this is...shiny rocks?"

"Diamonds," I correct.

She holds it in her flat palm to study them more closely. The iridescent gems are simple at this point since they aren't set in any jewelry, yet. But that's the point.

"You got me diamonds?"

"I got you a promise," I say.

She turns her head and shifts to the side so she can look back at me. I stroke her cheek as I explain. "These diamonds were in the ring my Gramps gave to Granny when they first got married. I had them removed from the band so you could choose how you want them set."

Turning completely so she's on her knees in front of me, she sits back on her heels and grabs my face between her palms. "Are you asking what I think you are?"

The moment I look into her eyes, my nerves take a hike. This isn't just any woman I'm asking to spend the rest of my life with. It's Avery. "I think so...unless you think I'm asking you to make waffles in the morning."

She wraps her arms around my neck and squeezes. "Yes."

I cradle her waist and pull her onto my lap so she's straddling me. "But I haven't officially asked you, yet."

Pulling back, she rests her forehead on mine, and I notice the sheen of liquid on her cheeks. "Wyatt, you could ask me to make waffles, or to marry you, and I'd say yes."

"So...you'll marry me?" I whisper.

"Tomorrow."

I laugh and pull her as close as physical space allows, kissing the tip of her nose. "Don't you think we'll need more time to plan?"

She shakes her head. "No. I mean, yeah. I never envisioned a big wedding, but that's mainly because I never spent time thinking about those things after Justice died."

I run a hand up her spine and cup the back of her head. The fact she just said those two words—Justice died—is something I don't take lightly. They are forever felt by her and me.

I pull her mouth to mine and kiss her like I mean it. I kiss her wet cheeks, her jaw, her neck, and now I'm getting way too distracted. If I go any lower, I'll be a goner, and she will be, too.

"We can take the planning slow and think about who we want to invite," I murmur against her skin. "There's no pressure. I just want you to know I'm dead set on you, Avery. It's only you."

She leans in and kisses me again, combing the hair at the nape of my neck before pulling away suddenly. "Tilly can be my maid of honor!"

I cup some water and pour it over her shoulders. "And I'll probably ask Ronny to be my best man."

She raises her brows. "I'm sure she'll love that."

I furrow my brows. "What's with those two?"

She shrugs. "No clue." Gasping, she adds. "We should get married here, at Thirst Trapp Farms!"

I hold up a finger and shake my head. "I think we're going to go back to Trapp Farms. I had a bachelorette party try to book recently, asking if the male stripper was included or paid separately."

Avery covers her smile with her hand. "We can't. It's forever Thirst Trapp Farms in my head now." She rotates her hips slightly, and I suck in a breath. Maybe doing it in the water wasn't as bad as I thought last time. I could probably find some knee pads somewhere. "What better way to become a Trapp than to be married here," she adds.

I grip her hips, which quickly devolves into grabbing her ass. "I like that idea. We'll keep it Thirst Trapp Farms, but I'll have to tell the bachelorette party we only have one stripper available."

"Ronny?" she asks.

I rub her shoulders. "Obviously."

She smiles, and it's brighter than the hundreds of candles around us. "We're going to get married."

"We are."

Her lips find mine, kissing me hungrily until my fingers are threaded in her hair, and my name is nothing more than a plea on her lips.

She hovers her mouth over mine. "I love you, Wyatt."

Pressing my hand to her heart, I feel it beating steadily. "I love every part of you, Avery."

"Even the weird parts?'

"Those don't exist," I say quickly, framing her face with my hands.

She nips at my bottom lip, then says, "Good thing I have forever to prove you wrong."

***

Thank you so much for reading! If you enjoyed this story, please consider leaving a review on Amazon, Goodreads, and your social platforms. It helps indie authors so much and would mean everything to me!

You can register for my newsletter at authorchristinahill.com to stay up to date.

I also love connecting with readers on Instagram and TikTok: @authorchristinahill.

Acknowledgements

Welcome to the end of the book where I'm hoping you feel at least a little bit sad, maybe slightly hungover from the story now that it's done. By the end of the writing and editing process, these characters became so dear to my heart and hopefully yours as well.

I owe so much to the people who helped me hone this story into what it is today. It was a book I'd written during National Novel Writing Month and ended it at about half the length of what's in your hands. Time and help played a vital role in molding this story!

Many thanks to my writing group gals: Hannah, Haley, Paige, Marie, Krys, Jill, Kathryn, and Amy. You've faithfully stood by me as I first started writing this one and saw me through to the end. The multiple texts, emails, phone calls, and in-person chats allowed me to run my ideas by you, vent about characters, and ask for help with plot. You've been there through all of it. I appreciate your brutal honesty more than you know. Long live coconut oil.

To Erica who read the very first, very different, very rough draft of this book. You make an excellent alpha reader, and helped me guide the story to where it needed to go. Your eyeballs always catch so much, and for that my books have benefited immensely.

Mom and Dad, though there are a few parts of this story that your eyes will never see (hello, camping scene), thank you for your unending support as I've written and talked about this book. It has given me the confidence to write what flows from my heart.

A huge bundle of gratitude to all of my ARC readers who signed up and blew my mind with your excitement and thoughtful words. Knowing how much you loved this book helped me get through the final stage of labor to birth it into existence for the rest of the world to experience. You're the best.

My editor, Krys, we've completed yet another story together. From conception to the final word, you were there. I've had the privilege of working with you for a few books now and always appreciate your attention to detail. Thank you for responding to my many questions about grammar rules and the like. You are so patient.

To the Fab Four and my husband, Samuel, who had a front row seat during this whole process. You've seen the good and the hard and all of the other subtle emotions that come with writing. Not every day was laugh out loud funny, others were, but you were there in all of the in-between. I appreciate and love you all to the moon and back...times one million.

Everyone else that had a hand in this book, a HUGE thank you to you! Erika for the stickers you printed for me, Dylan for the fantastic illustrations on the cover, and my dear friend Angela for your always honest, always enlightening conversations about vibrators. Lastly, to every reader who has picked up this book, I love you. Thank you for laughing out loud at my jokes, reviewing, and sharing.

If you are interested in seeing my inspiration for some of the characters, scenes, outfits, etc. discussed in this book, you can find me on Pinterest @authorchristinahill.

I also love connecting with readers on Instagram and TikTok: @authorchristinahill. If you loved the book, please consider writing a review on Amazon and Goodreads. This is such a tangible way to help authors and for this book to reach more beating hearts.

With all of my love,
Christina

Thirst Trapp Wedding

Chapter One

Tilly

I wouldn't do this for anyone else but her, my best friend, the woman getting married in a week, and the new mother of two, rambunctious kids...of the goat variety.

I blow a piece of hair out of my face. "Avery, we've been in this position for long enough."

Sweat builds on my brow as I do my best to balance in a table-top position with one leg extended backward and a yoga mat beneath me. Oh, and a goat on my back, which Avery named Vincent Van Goat. I will scream like a rabid animal if his cloven hooves dig into my spine one more time.

Avery lets out a slow breath, careful not to move quickly. "I'm afraid to move. I don't want to hurt ScapeGoat."

Honestly, I passed concern and care a long time ago when Vincent Van Goat head-butted my leg while I was in a downward dog position. If he doesn't kill me, this hot summer day in Big Timber, Montana will. Bismarck, the city I'm from and where Avery and I met in high school, gets hot, but only for the five minutes of summer we get every year. Otherwise, it's ball-freezing cold, like my heart. Just how I prefer it now.

I've been visiting Trapp Farms for the last two summers since Avery decided to move here and start a low-key spa for visiting guests. Not only do said guests get a facial, but they also have the once-in-a-life-time opportunity to hug a cow for an hour. In between lying with a smelly ogre and a foot soak, Avery decided to fall in love with a sexy, bearded farmer, which explains why I'm here: it's wedding week.

Also the week I've been dreading. Not because her fiancé, Wyatt, is stealing her from me, though I have had words with him about this. But because this week is all about the power of two people falling in love and reminding me I'm no good at it.

I lower my leg and drop into a few cat-cow stretches, providing unstable footing for the wannabe tap dancer on my back. Eventually, he decides this rollercoaster ride is his worst nightmare and jumps off. But not before his bony hooves dig into my skin and make me scream like a wolverine.

I sit back on my heels, grabbing at my back as if I've been stabbed—it would probably hurt less. Coaching myself through a few deep breaths so I don't murder the livestock here, I ask, "Remind me why we're doing goat yoga in their pen? Can't we just do it in the farmhouse? You know, where the cool, conditioned air lives."

"Tilly." Avery grunts just as ScapeGoat jumps off her back. "You know Wyatt isn't a fan of having the animals in the farmhouse."

I rotate my neck side to side, working out the extra kinks I ab-solutely blame the goat for putting there. "That's never stopped you before."

She places a finger to her lips as she sits up on her knees. "Shh! Don't say that so loudly. Wyatt could be lurking. He can't know Mother Clucker spent the night indoors that one time."

I furrow my brows and push myself to stand before slipping my sandals back on. "You said it was twice."

She peers around us, looking for eavesdroppers. "Three times. But only because Wyatt was meeting with his new financial advisor for the farm in Billings, and I was lonely."

I tip my chin up and cross my arms. "Right."

She rocks back on her heels and stands in one fluid motion. "I told Wyatt that if we got goats, I'd teach them yoga so when guests come, they can enjoy—"

"Stabbing pain all over their body?" I fill in. "How about the smell of their—"

"You really aren't an animal person, are you?" she asks, shaking her head at me.

"I don't hate-hate them. But loving them is weird." Love is weird. Period.

Attaching yourself to one person and hoping they'll reciprocate those feelings for all of eternity? Weird. It doesn't help that my parents are divorced. My list of grievances about love was ten pages long by the time I turned sixteen.

She narrows her eyes at me. "It's my wedding week. You have to do everything I say."

I throw my hands up, then bend to roll up my mat, which is now covered in what I'm going to tell myself is dirt and *only* dirt. "Since when does becoming a bride mean I have to exercise with animals and do whatever else you've romanticized in your head? It's not written in that rulebook you gave me, is it?" The one I had to confirm she didn't need me to sign a blood oath just to read.

She shakes her head and bends to grab her mat, too. "If you had read my wedding planner I gave you, then you'd know it wasn't a rulebook. It was a carefully written list of instructions, details, and my color scheme."

I tuck the rolled mat beneath my arm and shoot her a glare. "Isn't your color scheme called *nature* since it's outdoors?"

She closes the small gap between us, tucking her somewhat rolled-up mat under her arm, too. "Yes, with pops of red to match the barn."

The sound of a shovel sinking into gritty earth steals my attention, and I turn toward the noise before I can respond. What fills my eyes first is pure rage, and then memories of two summers ago, followed by a falling sensation low in my belly as Ronny's arms flex with every dive his shovel makes into the dirt. I know just how strong those arms are since he held me, standing upright and suspended in mid-air as he plunged—

"Ronny, do you know where Wyatt is? I thought he was with you?" Avery asks, completely oblivious to the thoughts just racing through my head.

I adjust the mat under my arm and grind my teeth like I want another scolding from my dentist as Ronny—Wyatt's farmhand and annoying neighbor—stops flinging shit everywhere and meets my eyes. They're so damn...pretty—dark brown at the edges of his irises that lightens as it closes in on his pupil. But he'll never hear that from me. At least I won't tell him again. I've sworn off all things Ronny, and if it weren't for my best friend—who is marrying his best friend—I would have sworn off farms, too. But I can't do that since Avery insists I visit her at least every couple months. So, I'll just have to suck it up for another whole week and keep the past where it belongs: in a meat grinder.

He spears the shovel into the ground and rests his hands on top. "Haven't seen him in at least an hour. Try the horse barn."

He tips his chin behind us toward the big, red barn that will serve as the backdrop for the outdoor wedding in exactly eight days.

Avery nods, then looks at me. "I'll catch up with you later. I'm going to go see what day Wyatt's family is coming to settle into the cabins."

I open my mouth to say something, but her back is already to me, the word *BRIDE* spelled out across her shoulder blades. This is her second day wearing that shirt, and I don't see her taking it off anytime soon.

My gaze slowly swivels back to Ronny, and I make a fist at my side. "Ronny."

He uses his tongue to shift his toothpick to the other corner of his mouth with a sly smile. "Tilly."

I want to snap that toothpick in half, throw it in his face, and then kiss that full mouth of his. Instead, I hike the yoga mat higher under my other arm and glare at him.

He leans further into his shovel and tips his cowboy hat back, revealing more of his dark-toned skin that feels as soft as it looks. At least it did two years ago. "You did something new with your hair."

I resist the urge to touch my newly cropped hair. The first time we met, my wavy locks reached my mid-back, and I'm sure he remembers that since he held a fistful of it in...never mind. It's a shade darker than my usual basic brown, but I treat my hair as an accessory and change it often to mix things up. I'm a hairdresser; it's what we do.

I wave a hand in front of him. "I see you're still the...same."

My voice catches on the last word. His wide shoulders, narrow waist, and scruffy jawline are all as I remember from a few months ago when I visited Avery, but it's what he's packing beneath his T-shirt that looks new. How has he developed *more* muscle tone? It makes me hate him more. I'm a mixed bag of wanting to rip the buttons on his shirt and hitting him over the head with the shovel he's leaning on.

He studies me through a squint. "I like consistency."

I give a pinched laugh and take that as a diss. Everything Ronny says to me might as well be. "Yeah, okay."

He stands straighter, wrists still stacked, one on top of the other, holding that damn shovel. "Is there a reason that's funny to you?"

Two years is a long time to hold a grudge. But no one ever blamed me for being mild-mannered. I'm as batshit stubborn as they come. I will die on this molehill before I let this man best me. Once upon a time, for two blissful months, we were great together. Electric and wild, fun and spicy. It only took one conversation to change my mind, and now, I can't stand him.

"Hilarious, actually." I push out a hip. "Don't you have work to do?"

"Don't you have goats to annoy?"

I scoff. "Don't you have shit to fling?"

He lifts the shovel and drives it into the ground at his side. "Don't you have wedding things to stress about?"

I take a step closer, and so does he. "Don't you have chickens to lasso?"

His smirk drops into a frown. "You don't lasso chickens."

"Whatever." Another step, and I'll be in his personal space so hard, he'll hate it. But my brain is struggling to think of a good retort when we're this close. My eyes have never left his except for now when they dip to admire his new muscles up close. "Don't you have tractors to bench press?"

He steps closer until our noses are almost touching. "Are you offering to spot me?"

I go mute. Thoughts are hard, words are harder, and Ronny's biceps are the hardest. I open my mouth to say something, but nothing comes out.

He pulls out his toothpick and sticks it in the front pocket of his flannel, grazing my shoulder since both of us refuse to leave these tight quarters first.

It's at this moment Vincent Van Goat decides to take his shot and head-butt the back of my knee with his empty skull, shoving me forward into the brick wall of Ronny's chest.

Arms circle around my waist, gripping me tightly and threatening not to let go. And for a split second, I believe those arms will be everything they once promised they would be. Protective, loving, safe, *home*.

I peer up at him as he looks down at me. Those lips were as familiar as my own once. The havoc they created on every inch of my skin is felt now like it happened yesterday.

But it didn't.

This doesn't work; we don't last. He told me that two years ago.

I shove myself out of his arms, looking more like a bird who accidentally flew inside and is trying to get out.

I spin around and point at Vincent Van Goat. "You."

He could give zero fucks right now as he makes one of his many irritating sounds while the goatee on his smug little chinny-chin-chin moves, too. I'll be searching the internet for goat-roasting recipes later.

Ronny snickers from behind me, and I whirl around and point at him.

He holds up one hand in surrender, then walks to the side of the small outbuilding Avery called the Hooves Hotel, where he leans the shovel against it. Sliding his hands in his jeans pockets, he stares back at me.

"It's good to see you again, Till."

The fumes coming from my ears at the usage of my nickname on his lips could start a forest fire. My brain barely registers the *it's good to see you* part since I know those words are lies before he even says them.

He turns, opens the gate, and exits the pen, strutting—yes, strutting—off to go plow something. Or someone. I loosen my grip on the yoga mat. The possibility of Ronny finding someone else is there. It's been a reality for me, too. I just never found anyone. I've dated, as I'm sure he has—you don't look like Ronny and possess as much swagger as he does and stay home on a Friday night. But nothing has stuck. Love doesn't work for me like it works for other people. I've tried.

I rub my forehead and pull my hand away with dirt smeared there. Just great. The first time I've seen Ronny since my last visit and the longest we've spoken to each other since *that day*, and I've got dirt on my forehead.

Vincent's throat vibrates with another sound.

"Shove it, goat!" I yell loudly, scaring a flock of birds that take flight from a nearby tree.

I need a shower. Cold first, then piping hot.

About the author

Christina is a lover of love who has been writing stories in her head since middle school. She also holds the titles of 'mom' and 'babe' and lives in Montana with her four children, husband, and two cats.

When Christina isn't reading or writing, she is wrangling her kiddos, homeschooling, taking baths, baking, or watching PBS.

For more information or to sign up for my newsletter, visit authorc hristinahill.com.